I0760924

Hateful Prince

K. Loraine
USA Today BESTSELLING AUTHORS
Meg Anne

This book is a work of fiction. The names, characters, places, and incidents are products of the author's imagination or have been used fictitiously and are not to be construed as real. Any resemblance to persons, living or dead, actual events, locales, or organizations is entirely coincidental.

ISBN:

978-1-961742-33-8 (Paperback Edition)

978-1-961742-34-5 (Hardback Edition)

No artificial intelligence was used in the creation of this work of fiction.

Edited by Mo Sytsma of Comma Sutra Editorial

Cover Design by CReya-tive Book Design

Photographer: Wander Aguiar

Model: Diogo S.

For the anxiety-ridden, smut-loving, booktroverts. We see you. We're proud of you.

“Come not between the dragon, and his wrath.”

— WILLIAM SHAKESPEARE, KING LEAR

Hateful Prince

AUTHORS' NOTE

Hunted Beast contains mature and graphic content that is not suitable for all audiences. Such content includes scenes of CNC, drugging and drug use, ritual sacrifice, mentions of mental illness and more. **Reader discretion is advised.**

As always, a detailed list of content and trigger warnings is available on our website.

SESSION TRANSCRIPT: DECEMBER 9TH

Dr. Temperance: This is Dr. Nathaniel Temperance. The date is December 9th. I am recording my observations from the past week's events at Blackwood. Subject—

<<door opens and closes>>>

<<footsteps>>>

Dr. Temperance: Lizzie. I wasn't expecting you.

Dr. Masterson: Getting comfortable behind my desk? You knew this was only temporary, Nate.

Dr. Temperance: Just doing a bit of housekeeping per the extensive set of instructions you left for me.

Dr. Masterson: *flirtatious chuckle* You always have been very good at following directions.

<<squeak of a chair>>

<<rustling of clothes>>

Dr. Temperance: Yes, well. Motivation goes a long way.

Dr. Masterson: Continue. I was interested in what you had to say. Subject . . .

<<pocket watch opens and closes repetitively>>

Dr. Temperance: Right, where was I?

<<papers rustling>>

Dr. Temperance: Subject N001 has continued to display staggering control in the days since his release. All previous studies indicate that it should be impossible, but perhaps his newly forged mate bond overrides all other biological imperatives.

Dr. Masterson: *hum of approval* Interesting.

Dr. Temperance: We will continue to observe him in the days to come, especially with regard to how he responds to threats against his mate. Subject U002 remains without access to his memories. Power spikes have been recorded, and it appears he has a strong connection to Subject M120. Masterson's indications that he could be another potential mate seem likely.

Dr. Masterson: Smart woman.

Dr. Temperance: Despite all efforts, subject's canine companion continues to attend all sessions and refuses to take orders from anyone but his master. Familiar status seems likely. The search to identify his actual magical classification continues. My current best guess is mage, but with the most recent data around his power spikes, we could be looking at something much stronger.

Dr. Masterson: Ah, very good. You're better at this than I gave you credit for.

<<clothes rustling>>

Dr. Temperance: Subject D174 has managed to maintain separation from his dragon, even after claiming M120 as his mate. Surprisingly—as dragons are historically selfish creatures—he has successfully co-existed with the other males in their unit. As requested, I have paid specific attention to any additional appearance of dragon-like abilities. So far, there have been none of note. It remains unclear whether the mated status will have any impact on the subject's relationship with his creature.

Dr. Masterson: I find it interesting you didn't put him in solitary as soon as you realized she had more than one mate. He could have lost it and burned this place to the ground.

<<pocket watch opens and closes repetitively>>

Dr. Temperance: *clears throat* Finally, Subject F523. His madness grows with every passing day. His delusions are nearly constant, and it has become clear he no longer has a solid grasp on reality. Nothing he says can be taken as fact. Staff has been instructed to wear warded amulets in order to keep them immune to his glamour, which has grown stronger than his medications can control.

Dr. Masterson: My, my, Nate. Has the pirate gotten under your skin? You seem tense.

<<chair being pushed back>>

<<clothes rustling>>

Dr. Temperance: Lizzie, what are you doing?

Dr. Masterson: *murmurs* If I have to explain, then I must not be doing a very good job.

Dr. Temperance: I thought you wanted me to finish my dictation.

Dr. Masterson: There's only one subject left. Tell me, how is Dahlia progressing?

<<belt buckle and zipper>>

Dr. Temperance: She's, um . . . oh God, I can't think when you're doing that.

Dr. Masterson: Sorry, shall I stop?

Dr. Temperance: God, no. *heavy breath* Dahlia remains evasive. *pleasured groan* I haven't . . . gotten through to her.

Dr. Masterson: No matter. You just leave her to me. Was there anything else you needed to dick-tate?

Dr. Temperance: *panting* Just the . . . Donoghue . . . visit and, fuck me, gala.

Dr. Masterson: What an excellent suggestion, Doctor. I've missed you. We'll talk about the trustees' yule gala later.

Dr. Temperance: Hang on . . . let me switch this thing off.

<<fumbling slaps on desk>>

Dr. Masterson: Leave it. You know I love a record of my work.

Dr. Temperance: Christ. Straddle me. I want to touch you.

Dr. Masterson: *giggles*

<<rustle of clothes>>

Dr. Temperance: *grunt of pain*

Dr. Masterson: Is something wrong?

Dr. Temperance: *voice tense* No. Don’t stop.

<<static>>

End of transcript.

CHAPTER ONE

HADES

October 25th
Los Angeles

She was here. My Persephone. After centuries of not knowing, of endless searching, I'd finally felt the brush of her power. Her soul called to mine. No, it screamed for me to find her. But *here* was the last place I wanted to be.

A hospital.

Dread curled in my belly, the sensation making me grit my teeth against intrusive thoughts that wanted to take hold. Was she hurt? Had someone dared harm her? Was I too late . . . again?

It had taken some time after the initial burst of power to track her here. All I had to go on was a location and then, with a little reconnaissance, a name. Well, two names. One of which was an alias.

Ruby Spector and Dahlia Moore.

My wife. My eternal love.

The name didn't matter; it was the soul I was after.

We would not be parted again.

She was mine in every lifetime.

I made polite conversation with the chronically ill man sitting next to me, but I barely paid attention. I couldn't with that pull in my chest. Not that he was wise to the divide in my focus. You couldn't rule the underworld without the ability to multitask.

Her name whispered across the room from the lips of a gossiping nurse, soft enough no one should've heard it, but I wasn't an ordinary man. It took a considerable amount of restraint not to leap from my seat and rush the nurse so I could demand more information.

"If you'll excuse me, I need to go pay someone a visit." I stood, prepared to find my woman and take her home, but the pleading note in the man's voice kept me rooted, as did the hand he placed on my arm.

"You never finished what you were saying. About miracles."

It took me a second to remember what we'd been talking about. Oh, right.

"Your soul."

"Excuse me?"

"It's the one thing you possess that's more valuable than money. The only true currency. You want to buy yourself more time, sell it."

His disbelieving chuckle died at my hard expression. "You're serious."

"Why wouldn't I be?"

"H-how would I even do that?"

I never did this. Never encouraged humans to entangle themselves with demons or soul collectors. That was Lucifer's territory. But today I was feeling . . . generous.

"Make a deal."

"With who, God? Pretty sure he's not listening."

I laughed. "That's because he's not the one interested in collecting souls. You want the other guy. One of his contractors, actually."

"A demon."

"Sure."

"You're telling me to sell my soul to a demon."

My patience was officially waning. "I'm not telling you to do anything. I'm just saying you have options. Listen, I really have to go. Good luck with your situation. And if you do decide to go through with it and they give you any trouble, tell them Cain sent you."

Later, I would wonder why I had given him my name. Names held weight. They were a currency in their own right when used in the correct circles. But I had more important things to worry about now. Like why my wife was being kept in the psychiatric ward.

What the fuck happened tonight?

She didn't need to be here. And she certainly shouldn't be pumped full of antipsychotic drugs. As soon as I found her, we'd leave this place and return to the underworld, where I could properly care for her. Give her exactly what she needed. She was my goddess, and the only thing making her mad was the separation from her true mate. Anything they were treating her with was surely doing more harm than good. She wasn't a human.

Storming through the corridor, I took the elevator up to the floor the helpful woman at the counter indicated and then paused. It was quieter up here. There was no waiting room. No patients moving about. Just a single woman behind a desk, her attention locked on the computer in front of her.

"Excuse me," I called, hoping she could tell me what room my wife was in.

"You're not supposed to be up here without clearance," she grumbled. "Visiting hours are posted right there." She pointed to a sign on the wall.

"I'm Dr. Alexander. Here to see my patient Dahlia Moore."

She narrowed her eyes and checked something on the computer screen. "I don't see your name in the log."

Calling on my shadows, I created the illusion of identification for her to check. "I assure you, I am supposed to be here. I'm part of her regular care team. Ms. Moore needs constant supervision."

"I'm sorry, Dr. Alexander. You're not the doctor on record. That's Dr. Temperance. You'll have to take it up with him. I can't let you see her without his permission."

I swallowed a growl. "Then get him up here."

"No. I don't know how things are done where you work, Dr. Alexander, but here we follow protocol." She was not intimidated by my display of temper. I might be impressed with her backbone if I wasn't so fucking frustrated. My Persephone was just beyond those locked doors. Within reach. But this woman stood between us.

I had half a mind to burn this place to the fucking ground and see what the woman had to say about protocol then, but until I knew for certain where my wife was, I couldn't ensure her safety.

My fingers sparked with the threat of my fire, but I snuffed it out.

"Call him," I snarled, more insistent than before.

She must've seen something in my eyes this time, because she jumped backward and grabbed the phone.

"Dr. Temperance to psych reception. Dr. Temperance to psych reception."

She held my gaze with a haughty glare I itched to remove. No one dared look at or speak to me the way she did. Pride demanded I put her in her place, but instinct warned me to tread carefully. These humans had the one thing I craved above all else. I would play by their rules. For now.

Instead of a lab coat-wearing doctor, two beefy security guards came through the doors, gazes trained on me, one with cuffs already in his hands. The cunning woman must've hit a panic button while I'd been busy plotting arson.

"If you think those buffoons will protect you," I started, icy menace coating every word.

To her credit, the only sign I'd gotten to her was the way her throat worked. Otherwise, she didn't even flinch. Ballsy wench—though I guessed, given where she was employed, she'd probably seen her fair share of violence.

But the damage was done. I'd threatened her in front of those brutes. They rushed me, one wrapping his arms around me from behind, the other shackling my wrists. It was a real shame I was going to have to kill them. They were only doing their jobs. Well, I might add. Not that it was about to do them a bit of good.

They might be trained to handle unpredictable mortals, but I was *far* from mortal.

Nothing in any training manual they'd ever studied would prepare these men for me.

Drawing the heat of my flames into my hands, I let it build until my skin practically glowed from the power. Then, with a single lift of my brow, I placed my palm on the shackle of my other wrist, the heat I'd gathered melting the metal and rendering the cuffs useless.

"Wh-what?" one of the guards stupidly asked.

"Whoopsie daisy. Looks like these are broken." I reached out with both hands and pressed them to each guard's chest before sending my shadow fire into them and burning their souls to dust.

They fell to the floor, smoke curling from every orifice and nothing but charred holes for eyes.

"Sorry, fellas. Nothing personal." Then I turned back to the little nurse who'd started all this. "Now, tell me where my wife is before you meet the same fate as those two."

She gaped at me, little squeaks of fright coming from her as she shook her head.

I sighed. I didn't want to send her to the underworld too, but she'd seen too much, and honestly, I may have broken her mind already.

"You should have just let me see her," I said, quite reasonably, if I do say so myself.

"What's all this?"

I turned my head to the left, where a blond man in a white coat had just arrived.

"Dr. Temperance, I presume."

He took in the slaughter at my feet and the shadow flames licking up my fingers.

Before the doctor could answer me, pressure and a stinging sensation radiated from my neck. Cold spread through my veins, and I turned a shocked gaze to the nurse, who was now standing, an empty syringe in her shaking hand.

There was no room for emotion other than shock. Had this mortal truly bested me? How?

My knees gave way, my limbs going numb.

Fuck. They would pay for this. I'd see them all burn and then be there to greet their souls when they washed up in my realm. Trust me when I tell you no one wanted Hades's personal attention.

As the world around me dimmed, Temperance's voice filtered into my ears. "Call Masterson. I've got another one for her."

CHAPTER TWO

DAHLIA

"I found you. Persephone."

Cain was still inside me, his cock pulsing his release as he called me another woman's name.

"I'm sorry, I must be sex deaf. What did you just call me?"

If I thought his eyes had held burning intensity before, they were searing now.

"I can't believe it's you. You were right here the whole time?" The awe in his voice, pure reverence, brought me up short. "When I sensed you in LA, I thought . . . fuck, I don't know what I thought. That I'd take you back with me and we could pick up right where we left off. Only this time, things would be different. I would be different. I've had lifetimes to reflect on the error of my ways."

"Cain, what the hell are you talking about?"

He blinked and cradled my face, dipping down to steal a kiss before breathing that goddamn name against my lips again.

"Persephone . . ."

I shoved him off me. "That is not my name."

Pure disbelief washed away the adoration in his eyes. "Yes, it is. It's you. My goddess. My wife."

"Wife? Hold on just a second. I'm no one's wife. This is crazy."

"You are. You're mine. I've been searching for you since you left me."

Sitting up, I pulled the sheets to my chin, hiding my body for the first time in a long while. I was entirely too vulnerable sprawled out with his skin pressed against mine and his cum dripping down my thighs. This felt like a conversation that required . . . protection. Even if it was an illusion.

"No."

Blazing azure irises met mine before his lips twisted in a smirk. "There she is. Always fighting me."

"Cain, I don't know what you're talking about. I just met you here at Blackwood. I'm not . . . Persephone."

The smile slowly faded from his lips, his body recoiling as he pulled away and really looked at me. It was like my words had finally penetrated whatever fog he'd been stuck in. "You really don't remember? It didn't come back to you . . ." His gaze grew distant, telling me he'd retreated into his mind palace.

Shifting until he was seated on the side of the bed, he dropped his head in his hands and took a few long breaths. The man was so painfully beautiful, naked and posed the way he was, but there was an agony in his presence I hadn't ever sensed from him. No, that wasn't true. Cain wore grief like a sweater on a chilly fall day. The difference was now he seemed to know what he'd been grieving.

"I thought it came back. That I had you back with me, but . . . fuck, the Fates wouldn't be so kind, would they? Of course you don't remember a godsdamned thing. Of fucking course you belong to someone else, and I was too late to claim you. Your memories weren't taken. You don't even have them—and you never will. That's not how reincarnation works. Everything we went through, the way you finally loved me . . . it never happened for you. Now I have to walk through this life and watch you love someone else, and I can't do a damn thing about it because if I kill him, it'll take you too."

The words fell out of him in a rush, like water bursting through a dam. He was talking to himself more than me. It was hard to know if he even remembered I was still here.

A soft cry left him as he tugged at his hair, his body still bowed and facing away from me.

"You were supposed to be mine. Mine for all eternity. Instead you were torn away from me after little more than a season."

The torture in his voice reminded me of a condemned soul begging for mercy. I didn't know how to help him. I wasn't this woman he claimed me to be. Was I?

"Cain." I reached out to touch his shoulder, but he turned on me, catching my wrist and staring into my eyes.

He whispered a kiss over the palm of my hand, breathing a word into the center as though for safekeeping. "Hades."

I had to blink, my mind not fully tracking yet another sudden turn in the conversation.

"What?"

"My name. It's Hades."

And the penny finally dropped. The air left me like wind from a ship's sails.

"And you think I'm Persephone." Where his words were impassioned, mine were wooden.

"No, goddess. I *know* you are. We are destined. Your soul has been bound to mine for lifetimes. I've scoured the earth searching for you since I lost you, and I've loved you to the depths of my being every moment."

His declaration was beautiful and poignant, but it wasn't all-encompassing love I felt in its wake. It was sorrow. Sorrow, because it wasn't meant for me, Dahlia. It was for some other woman. His Persephone.

The woman he loved, chased through lifetimes, wasn't me.

He was in love with someone else.

A little laugh bubbled up. Hadn't he warned me of this very thing? So why did it hurt so badly?

Because he was just inside you.

Well, this is awkward.

I pulled my hand away, scooting back as far as I could. "I'm not her."

"You are. Do you think I would mistake you? I've known your soul for countless years."

"I'm. Not. Her. Cain."

"Hades."

I shook my head, trying to wrap my brain around the new moniker. "When did you remember who you were?"

"When we came together. It all rushed back. Me. Us. Our past. I thought it would have for you too." He sighed, his eyes dimming again. "But then I realized the truth. My memories were stolen or blocked while your soul was reincarnated."

"And these are different because . . ."

"Your slate was wiped clean. Nothing will bring our past back to you because there's nothing there that has been hidden. But that doesn't change the love between us."

Love?

"You don't love me."

"I do."

"No. You love her. Persephone."

He turned his body so he was fully facing me, one leg bent on the mattress, the other over the side of the bed. He didn't give a single damn that he was still naked.

"You don't believe me. Fine, I'll prove it to you. You may not remember our life together, but your soul recognizes mine. It's why you feel that pull to me. How you know the second I enter a room or exactly where I'm standing. Same as I do for you." He let out a humorless laugh. "Gods, I was such a fool. Here I thought I should hate how you made me feel when it was your soul calling to mine the whole time."

I stared at him mutely, shaking my head. I should be throwing my arms in the air and shouting out my victory. I finally got the broody man I'd been lusting after since I saw him arrive in his straightjacket. Yes, I am aware how messed up that sounds. But I just felt hollow. Like something had been taken from me.

Then I realized what it was.

Hope.

All this time I'd been holding out hope that Cain would wake up one morning and stop fighting his feelings for me. And wouldn't you know it, he did, but those fucking feelings weren't *for* me. They were never for me. They were for the ghost of his Persephone.

Fucking ghosts.

He must have sensed the war raging in my mind because he reached for me. I flinched. I didn't mean to do it, and I regretted the unconscious act the second I saw the shattered look in his eyes. Though it was quickly replaced by mounting frustration.

"I would never hurt you, Dahlia. If I wanted to, I could take you back to my realm here and now, lock you up, and throw away the key until you come back to your senses. But even then, I would never harm a single hair upon your head. Don't you know you are precious to me?"

I must have been an absolute masochist because I could not help but poke the bear. "So why don't you? That's supposed to be your shtick, right? Hades takes what he wants."

He bared his teeth at me in a silent snarl. "Because I've learned my lesson. I went against the Fates once and lost everything. I will not risk our life together again. This time, I will play by their rules. It's obvious they brought us to this place for a reason."

Putting that terrifying revelation aside for now, I focused on the problem I could actually tackle. "I can't be her for you. You know that, right?"

"You're mine, baby doll. Whether you remember us or not. I don't want you to be her. But I need you to be mine."

He was saying all the right things, but words didn't mean much when the truth had already been spoken as another woman's name. I believed that I had her soul, that my magical vagina brought back his past, that he'd loved and lost her. But this man's feelings weren't for Dahlia, the woman I was. The roots of his love were deeply bound to the soul of his Persephone, someone I would never be. Which made all this something else entirely.

"Cain . . ."

His eyes flared, but he didn't correct me.

Still, I felt the reprimand and couldn't help but acknowledge it. "Am I really supposed to call you Hades now?"

His lips quirked up in a sexy smirk. "I'd rather you call me Daddy."

Me too.

Before I had a chance to respond, his smile dimmed, and he blew out a breath. "But no. For now, it's probably best you keep referring to me as Cain. At least when we aren't alone."

Unease was a twisted lump in my belly. "You don't want them to know you've gotten your memories back?"

"Not yet."

"I thought you were going along with fate's plan."

"The Fates, baby. There are three of them. And yes, I'm following their plan, but someone saw fit to steal my memories and lock us both in here. I intend to find out who and then . . ."

"And then?"

This time, his smile was a malicious twist of his lips.

"Then I intend to make them pay."

CHAPTER THREE

DAHLIA

"How are you feeling this morning, Dahlia?"

I couldn't help the smirk that twisted my lips at the rather stereotypical opening. How did I answer this question? If we were talking about my body, I'd say so well loved my joints were still loose and I was walking like I'd just gotten off a horse. Something told me she didn't want to know that.

"Fine."

Dr. Masterson raised a brow. "We've been working together long enough now that you know I'm not going to let that slide. Elaborate, please."

"Oh well, if you're going to say please . . ."

"Dahlia."

I sighed, feeling a bit bullied by my therapist, but in the way of a sibling or friend rather than someone who actually had malicious intent.

"I'm . . . lost and found all at the same time. God, that doesn't even make sense."

She made a note on her pad of paper along with a soft murmur of understanding. "It makes sense to you, so it's a good place to start. Let's begin with the easier of the two. Why lost?"

"Because I'm not who he thinks I am, but I really wish I could be."

"Tor?"

I shook my head.

"Kai?"

Feeling my cheeks flush with embarrassment, I shook my head again. Masterson and I had discussed the men in my life before, but we hadn't had an opportunity for me to get her up to speed on the new developments within these relationships.

"Cain," I muttered.

Her brows lifted, not with judgment, but interest. "Really? Hmm. I thought he'd hold out longer." Then she laughed. "And here I thought Caspian would be the first to give in." Shaking her head, she made a couple more notes on her pad before lifting her eyes back to mine.

"Not for Cas's lack of trying. He's . . . problematic."

Brows furrowing, she silently bade me to continue.

"Oh God, I don't even know how to tackle that mountain. Cas is a relentless flirt, but it seems harmless. Like he just wants to get laid, or at least that's what I thought in the beginning, but then he hits me with these one-liners that make me feel like it's the verbal equivalent of standing before me naked, and then I think maybe he's interested in way more than just getting in my pants—"

"Breathe, Dahlia."

I followed her instructions and took a few long breaths. "I . . . I'm confused and torn, and I don't know what to do. Tor claimed me. So did Kai. Now, Cain says I'm the one he's been searching for, and Cas is . . . a lost boy."

Dr. Masterson smiled softly but didn't comment.

"And maybe none of that is much of a revelation, but the part that has me twisting myself into knots is that Cain thinks I'm the reincarnation of his one true love, and I can't help but think he's using me as some sort of sexual scapegoat or replacement for the woman he really wants."

Masterson sat up in her chair and leveled her gaze on me. "What makes you think you aren't?"

Ouch, Lizzie.

I glanced down at my sweater, mindlessly reading the cheeky text: *My book boyfriend is better than yours.* Today the words didn't make me smile.

"A replacement?"

Her expression softened. "His one true love."

"You actually believe in that stuff?"

This time her expression didn't change, and I knew that meant she was about to lob one of her truth bombs at me. "Why wouldn't I? Is it any less plausible than the other things you've come to learn are true since your arrival here? You've met a number of spirits. Seen for yourself that souls very much exist on this plane. Why is it such a stretch that one can be reborn in a new body?"

Scoffing, I rolled my eyes. "There has to be a limit to reality, right? Next you'll be telling me the Loch Ness monster is real."

She raised one eyebrow.

Jesus.

"Sasquatch?"

Still nothing.

"The boogie man?"

"Ah yes, Hank. He's quite a laugh after a few pints."

"Are you fucking kidding me?"

"Yes. The boogie man is a construct. There is a local drunk named Hank, though."

I laughed, thankful she'd lightened the mood.

"So tell me why you think you're lost? Do you feel like there's something wrong with having more than one mate? You write books about this very thing."

She had me there, and honestly, I didn't have an answer. I just was.

"Maybe if there'd been time for us to talk about any of this before leaping off the cliff and flinging ourselves headlong into it, but there hasn't been time for anything other than reacting. Tor basically wifed me up the day he met me. Kai's dragon went feral the second *that* happened and decided that meant it was time to assert his claim. And then Cain slid in and Persephonied all over me." Fuck, I wasn't supposed to tell her that. Hoping she'd let it slip, I kept talking. "Not to mention Cas, with his delusions, calling me Wendy-bird and sneaking into my room and dickmatizing me. And me? I'm just holding on for dear life, wondering when they're going to realize I'm not worth any of it."

Masterson simply smiled. "This is the way of things when fated mates are involved, Dahlia. Ask yourself one question. Do I feel the same way about them? Go on, close your eyes and ask the question."

So I did. I closed my eyes and pictured each of them. All the doubts I had disappeared. My chest swelled with a feeling I couldn't quite understand yet when I let myself see them.

"Yes. I mean, our individual relationships are all over the place, and some feel more . . . settled than others, but I can't subtract any of them from the equation." And that's been true since I met them. Even before Cain had his little epiphany and finally gave in to what we'd both been feeling, I had never let myself discount him.

It had always been the four of them calling to me.

"That makes sense. Your bonds are solidifying at different speeds, but they're all there. Time and proximity will strengthen all of them."

"So, you're saying . . . go forth and polyamory?"

She set her pen down, clasping her hands and leaning forward. "I'm saying listen to your heart."

I gaped at her. "That was not what I expected you to say."

"Why not?"

"It's so . . . frou frou. You're a doctor. That's like, the opposite of the stuff you white coats are supposed to endorse."

She pursed her lips. "I disagree. I'm supposed to endorse things that are healthy for you. Being without your mates is the opposite of healthy."

Well, let's address the elephant in the room, shall we?

"So why keep Tor and I separated?"

She sat back in her chair. "That was never my intention, you know. I actually was planning on helping the two of you move into new accommodations that would allow you to foster your new bond, but then . . ." The doctor paled, her focus going a bit distant before she blinked and refocused. "Anyway, by the time I was in any position to do anything about it, the damage was done. And I can't fault Nate for doing what he believed was safest for our residents. Perhaps he did not go about it in the right way, and we could argue endlessly about what he should have done differently, but the facts are the facts. Because of you, Tor has learned how to control his beast, at least enough to be reintroduced to the others."

"Is that your version of 'the ends justify the means' speech?"

"Don't they?"

"Touché."

That smug grin twisted her lips again.

"So how do we do this, then? Are we all moving into some new house? Is there a love nest on the grounds? A sex shack?"

"Not one big enough for you and four mates."

"Technically there's only two."

Or was it three now? Did what happened with Cain—shit, Hades—last night mean we were officially mated? Ugh, there was still so much about my new life I didn't understand.

Masterson gave me the drollest stare. "For now. It's only a matter of time."

"I wish I had your certainty."

"You do, Dahlia. You just refuse to believe what your heart has been shouting at you since the beginning. But if you can't trust your heart, trust this: it's going to happen whether you believe it or not. That's what fate means."

"I've never been very good at trusting my instincts."

She reached out and took my hand. "Then trust mine. It's not something you can resist. The writing is on the wall, and those men will claim you. They've already started, and you're just prolonging the strain between you by not listening to the call of fate."

"The Fates," I corrected. "Cain said there are three of them."

"Interesting."

I couldn't help but blink at her. "That's the thing out of all of this that you find interesting?"

"Not exclusively."

I shook my head. "This place is such a mind fuck. A month ago, I didn't even know supernatural creatures were real—or that I'm one of them—and then *wham,* here I am. Right in the fucking middle of Disneyland for the supernaturally insane."

"Keep your arms and legs inside the ride at all times," she murmured.

"Did you just make a joke?"

"Aye. Speaking of you being a creature, let's move away from the topic of your mates and on to your new identity, shall we? How are you feeling about your gift?"

How was I feeling? I hadn't given it much thought lately, what with the mating and the Cain fucking and massive orgy that broke out yesterday.

"Um . . . fine?"

Masterson laughed.

"I don't know, doc. If I'm being honest, it's all starting to feel like some kind of cosmic joke. I can see and talk to ghosts, but like . . . why? For what purpose? Am I supposed to help them? Because if so, why is one tormenting me?"

"You're being tormented?"

"Haunted. Yeah. And I don't know how to make it stop. Cain banished her once, but I don't think she's gone for good."

"Why haven't you mentioned this to me before?"

I squirmed uncomfortably in my chair. "I forgot?"

"Dahlia . . ."

"Okay, fine, I didn't want you to think I was nuts."

The disapproving scowl on her face had me sinking into my chair. "Right, well, we need to address this. You need a line of defense. Cain won't always be with you."

That made a little pang of heartache stab me in the chest. "Are you gonna give me a potion or something? Joffrey took my necklace."

"You don't need an amulet of protection. That's what your powers are for. I think it's time you learn how to use them."

"You keep saying I have powers, but all I can do is see some ghosts."

"How do you know that's all you can do? Have you tested the theory? When you arrived here, you could only see them, but not even a minute ago, you said you can speak with them now. If you've never properly explored the limits of your ability, how can you say with any certainty what they are?"

"Well, if you're going to get logical about it."

She stood and strode to the wall of carnivorous plants, standing in front of them for a moment before sweeping her palm in an arc through the air. As I watched, the plants turned to a mist and revealed shelves filled with all manner of witchy odds and ends.

"Wait, you're a witch?"

Masterson stared at me, then turned back to her shelves. "Obviously."

How the hell had I missed that?

As she perused the contents, she continued our conversation with a vaguely distracted tone. "So, aside from your ghosties, have you been able to do anything else?"

"Besides my exceptional ability to craft the written word?"

"Is this a joke to you, Dahlia?"

"No," I grumbled. "Sorry."

"It's just the ghosts speaking to you. That's surprising. Usually mediums have more psychic abilities. Telepathy, telekinesis, compulsion . . ."

I chewed on my bottom lip for a second. "Well, I guess there's the scream, but that's not really—"

"The scream?"

"You know, from the premiere, and the night my dad tried to sacrifice me. Oh, and with Tor."

She went still. "You've used it since the premiere?" The way she turned and stared at me had me squirming in my chair.

"Yeah. On accident. I didn't hurt him. I swear. Just knocked him out a little."

Her shoulders drooped, her arms falling to her sides as unmistakable emotion washed across her face. The disappointment was so sharp it made my stomach cramp. "Dahlia, when are you going to trust me enough to share these developments with me?"

All I wanted to do was get back in her good graces. "I just did. And I mean, to be fair, I didn't know they were developments, so you can't really hold it against me."

She rolled her eyes and returned to her desk, an object concealed in her hands. The guilt ate at me, so I racked my brain, searching for anything else that might be of interest. "Oh! Cain called me a banshee."

The laugh that burst from her was so sharp it startled me. "You're not a banshee. Honestly, men think they know so much."

"So I just have a mind-melting scream. Cool."

"Telepathy can be fatal. If you don't know how to control it."

I sighed. "How do I learn?"

She placed a small jar filled with swirling black mist on the desk. It was sealed with a cork, and a soft blue glow emanated from within the vapor. "With this."

"Smoke?"

"So you can see what's inside?" she asked, her lips curling into a triumphant smile.

"Yeah, can't you? There's a bunch of glowy smoke swirling around."

"No, Dahlia. I'm not a medium. I can't see what's inside the spirit jar."

"Spirit jar? You mean there's an actual ghost in there?" I poked it, half expecting a face to manifest, complete with fangs ready to snap the digit from my hand.

Masterson nodded. "Yes, this is Katarina. A mischievous little spirit who came to my coven for safekeeping after one of her practical jokes almost got an entire orphanage burnt down."

"Your ghost has a name."

"Don't they all?"

Swallowing hard, I nodded. "I guess they do. What am I supposed to do with her? Have a whole chat?"

"We already know you can speak with them. I want to test something else."

A sense of dread swirled through me, my very own mini anxiety tornado, as Masterson twisted the cork off the jar. The smoke immediately escaped, but she couldn't see it. She wasn't even looking in that direction since her eyes were locked on mine.

"I want you to put her back."

What.

The.

Fuck.

An evil cackle filled the room, accompanying the heavy buzz that prickled across my skin. I was sure my hair was standing on end like I'd been shocked.

"Finally. Stupid fool. I've been locked away for too long in that prison. I'm ready to play." The ghost's voice echoed as though she was speaking in a cavern, but there was a youthfulness to it I couldn't deny.

"She's a kid," I whispered.

"She was old enough to know what she was doing when she died. Now, catch her before she escapes and finds an open flame. She'll burn this place to the ground if you don't."

"That's a lot of pressure to put on me for my first go-round, don't you think?" I snapped, my voice squeaky and high-pitched.

"It's not a true test if there are no stakes."

"You and I need to have a chat about your teaching methods, woman."

"Focus, Dahlia."

Huffing out a breath, I watched the spirit whip around the room. Not that I needed to be able to see her to track her path. Everywhere she went, objects fell to the ground. She wasn't just a firebug; she was an absolute chaos gremlin.

"I don't know what I'm doing!"

"Yes you do. Focus on her essence. Use your mind to wrap her in your power. You can contain her."

"You say that like I know what that means."

"Instinct will guide you. You were born for this."

"How can you be so sure? We don't know what my limits are, remember? What if I'm a dud?"

"Just try, Dahlia. Now!"

It was the sharpest her voice had ever been with me, and like any good pupil, I obeyed.

Katarina's childlike laughter filled the room as she rushed in circles, sending wind blowing my hair in my face, and fear gripped my heart. Until I saw it—the faint glow in the specter's chest. The center of her essence, what we might call her soul.

Gathering all of my will, I sent it outward. Tendrils, not unlike Cain's shadows, wrapped around the ghost, binding her.

She fought, her voice a scream of protest so shrill I was sure my ears were going to bleed, but I used every bit of strength I had to hold her.

"Give me the bottle," I gritted out.

Masterson held the jar out to me, but as I attempted to take it, the glass slipped and shattered on the floor.

"Fuck!"

"We need another vessel," Masterson muttered, eyes sweeping

around the room frantically.

"Don't you have another jar?"

"No? Why would I? But I know where one might be. Hold her there. I'll be right back." Masterson rushed from the room, leaving me holding an angry, petulant ghost child.

Her laughter swelled, joining the tickle of energy along my skin. Shit.

I wasn't sure how long I could hold on to her. It was already too much. Like the build of a lightning strike. Or the threat of a sneeze.

Wait.

Oh no. Not now.

Pressure built behind my eyes, the tip of my nose tingling.

It *was* a fucking sneeze.

The ghost laughed.

I couldn't hold back. I sneezed, eyes closing, body jerking, focus vanishing.

When I opened my eyes again, Katarina was nowhere to be found.

Oh fuck.

Masterson's office was eerily quiet. I didn't trust it.

"Hello?" I called, my voice betraying my nerves.

Silence.

Masterson rushed back into the room, hair a frizzy mess around her flushed face. "Where is she?"

"I, uh, don't know."

"What do you mean, you don't know?"

"She got away."

"This isn't good. We have to find her."

A tinkling laugh came from somewhere in the room, and Masterson's face paled. I followed her gaze to the creepy as fuck doll sitting on the shelf, her dead eyes staring off at nothing. Then she turned her fucking head and stared straight at me. "Come on, Dahlia. Don't you want to play with me?"

Oh fuck no.

CHAPTER FOUR

TOR

Thanks to Dr. Masterson's extended session last night, I'd been away from Dahlia for far too long, and now my beast demanded I let my primal side out to play. Ideally, that would be something I could take care of with my mate, but now it was her turn to see the good doctor, so blood sports it was. Anything to release the mounting tension.

The scents of dirt and clean morning air were welcome distractions from my urge to be with my mate, reminders of the world around me outside of the perfection being with Dahlia provided. I would have to learn how to function without her. If I never left her side, how could I ensure she had her needs met?

Besides, Dahlia would likely stab me if I didn't force myself to give her space. She was like my mother in that regard. A Berserker's mate had to be. Timid, docile creatures would never appeal to our baser urges. We needed strong women. Ones that would stand up to us and put us in our place regardless of our size or temper. That's what made winning them over so appealing.

She'd hand me my arse, and I'd spank hers.

A tiny growl caught my attention as I bounded through the

forest, the sound stalling me as I searched for possible prey. A gift for my beauty?

No.

The last thing she wanted was a dead animal at her door. Perhaps a pet, though? She seemed to genuinely love Asshole. Maybe she needed a furry creature of her own. I broke through the trees to find a little nest and the source of the growls.

I'd never had reason to come across the creature known as an owlbear, but there was no mistaking the cub for anything else. It was about the size of a large puppy, its chubby body feathered, its sharp beak tipped toward the sky.

"Well, hello there, little one. Aren't you fearsome?" Yes, I spoke to the cub in a baby voice. How else does one talk to an infant?

The cub ceased its hungry growls, looking at me with wide golden eyes. It was too young to fear me, not having yet learned about the danger of other predators. I didn't want to be the one to teach it that lesson. Some things should be protected at all costs, innocence chief among them.

A high-pitched whine left the cub as it took a few shaky steps toward me. This baby was hungry; there was no doubt in my mind. Unfortunately, I wasn't the only predator out here in the Black Forest, and a chubby morsel like this would be easy pickings.

"No, no, little one. Stay put. Stay quiet. You'll draw unwanted attention."

A rustle in the brush proved me right. It was far too low to the ground to be the cub's mother, which meant whatever was sniffing around could only be a threat.

I spun around, my protective instincts surging to the surface. My beast was never far these days, so it wasn't like it took much to pull me to the killing edge.

I'd come out here looking for a fight, and it seemed like I was about to get it.

The baby at my feet let out a little squeak, attempting to follow me as I took a step forward.

"Shh. Try not to get underfoot, little one. Nothing will harm you."

The wolf's snout came into view first as it crept forward out of the protection of the bushes. Jaws snapping, spittle flying, the feral creature proved itself to be a shifter based on size alone. Easily three times the bulk of a natural wolf, this one also had eyes that glowed a threatening red and teeth longer and sharper than a switchblade. Its focus wasn't on me but on the fat little snack at my feet.

That was its first mistake.

It was about to be its last.

The feral dog finally spared me a glance, spittle dripping from its snout as it bared its fangs at me. It let out a low growl, staking its claim. I couldn't help but laugh. "Am I supposed to be scared?"

It continued to growl.

"I can do that too," I said before releasing a roar of my own.

The wolf's ears flattened, but it didn't back down. Instead, its scruff stood on end, and its whole body tensed as though ready to pounce on me. That was fine. I'd ruin him here and now and return victorious with a new pelt for my mate's bed. Surely she'd appreciate that. She was always reaching for a blanket.

The hunter leapt, intent on taking me down so it could claim its prize. It had to be starving; there was no way it could think to best me. But I was the first to admit that oftentimes instinct overrode reason.

"You're a fool. But that won't stop me from killing you." I caught the beast in midair, hand clamping around its thick throat as I slammed the large body into the ground.

Unfortunately, he still hit me with the razor-sharp claws on his hind legs, slashing across my belly. The pain didn't register. In fact, it only fueled my rage, and within moments, the shifter beneath me was nothing more than a pulpy mass of fur and guts. So much for the pelt.

I was still kneeling over my kill when the cub came to inspect it.

"Not so fast," I murmured, using my body to shield the savage scene beside me. Bits of bone were poking up from the slaughter. I didn't want it to hurt itself.

And that was how its mother found us. Me bloody, with an arm outstretched toward the cub. Her growl was much more menacing than any the cub had to offer, and she was . . . not cute. In fact, she was terrifying in her viciousness. It was a thing of beauty.

"Easy now, mama. You have nothing to fear from me." I kept my voice low and soothing, moving slowly and keeping my hands in plain sight. I had no way of knowing if she'd see the move as a threat, but I could only hope she sensed my sincerity.

The cub made a series of growling chirps and bounded off to its mother. When I didn't move to follow, she seemed to relax, though I'd have to be stupider than the wolf if I thought that made her any less dangerous. She was all power and muscle, faster than she looked, I was sure.

"I'm going now. I have no quarrel with you. Enjoy your meal."

She kept her golden eyes locked on me as I backed out of the clearing. My little friend tried to follow me, but she stopped him with a large paw, pinning her cub in place.

"Until we meet again," I said, eyes still on hers.

The way her head tilted to one side said she was listening. Then she dipped her beak before turning and walking away with her cub still between her legs.

I heaved a sigh and stared at the remnants of the wolf in the clearing. A kill a day keeps the Berserker away. That was what my father always used to say, and until now, I hadn't truly understood. Hopefully these woods were well stocked, because I had a feeling there were many more of these morning hunts in my future.

It was all part of finding the balance between the beast and the man.

Feeling far more in control after the bloodletting, I made my way back to Blackwood. I paused only long enough at the edge of the forest to ensure I wouldn't return to my mate empty-handed. She mentioned flowers. Hopefully these would do.

Folks gave me a wide berth as I stalked through the grounds back to Dahlia's room. I glanced down at my bloody hands and shirt, not finding any issue with either. I was a man on a mission. If they were jealous of my prowess, perhaps they should find their inner monsters in order to win their own mates.

Heart thudding as I reached Dahlia's door, I glanced hopefully at the bouquet of purple flowers in my fist and forced myself to relax my grip just enough to keep from strangling the blooms. Clods of dirt fell to the floor at my feet from the roots, and I had a brief thought that Joffrey was going to complain about having to clean up after me.

I knocked once, but there was no answer, so I tested the knob, pleased when it opened without issue. That meant she was back. My relief at the knowledge was instantly soured by protective ire. We would be having a conversation about the dangers of leaving her door unlocked.

The sound of the shower explained her lack of answer. Yes, a conversation about safety would most definitely be happening. My mate couldn't take risks like this when I wasn't around to protect her. Anyone could've come in. For fuck's sake, there was a killer on the loose.

My breaths came in long, growled drags as I laid the bundle of flowers on her desk. So much for my therapeutic hunt in the woods. I was already keyed up again. I needed to take the edge off, see her and prove to my Berserker that our mate was safe.

Stripping out of my ruined clothes, I left them on the floor before stepping inside the steam-filled bathroom.

I could just make out her shadow on the other side of the curtain.

"Kærasta—"

"What the fuck do you think you're doing?" Cain cut me off, his fully naked form catching me by surprise.

"What the fuck do *you* think you're doing?"

"Showering. Do you mind?"

"Where's Dahlia?" I snarled.

"She was gone when I woke up."

It was the worst thing he could have said.

"If you're just going to stand there, can you hand me the soap?"

Correction. *That* was the worst thing he could have said.

My bloodied hand was around his throat before I registered what was happening. I had the man suspended in the air, eyes wide as I choked the breath out of him.

"She. Is. Mine."

Instead of panicked, Cain's expression twisted into one of murderous intent. He reached up, wrapping his hand around my wrist. But he didn't try to break my hold. Instead he squeezed, his fingers digging in so hard they turned the skin beneath them white.

The pain was as unimaginable as it was unexpected. Generally, I couldn't feel my injuries if I was raging, but this wasn't a normal injury. The pain wasn't in my body, but in the very depths of my soul. It felt like I was burning from the inside out.

I cried out in agony, releasing my hold on him and collapsing to the floor.

Cain stood over me, chest heaving, eyes a startling blue as he stared down. "You think you're a match for me, demigod? You'd be wrong. Don't try me again."

Before I could respond, Dahlia skidded into the doorway. "Guys, what is going on?"

CHAPTER FIVE

DAHLIA

"So you think they'll bite?" I asked Kiki as I made my way up the stairs.

She'd sent my drafted synopsis and outline in for approval last night, and we were both nervous they'd reject it because instead of a sequel to Rebel, I'd come up with something completely different.

"I mean, if they know what's good for them, they'll be all over it, but you never know with those guys."

"You're not making me feel very confident."

She frowned on the screen, her perfectly manicured brows pulling in. "Listen, if they turn it down, then you indie publish that bitch, and I'll ride shotgun as your freelance editor."

I grinned. "Well, at least I know you liked it."

"Babes, you wrote it. Of course I love it."

Sighing, I adjusted the height of my phone—what? My arm was hurting from holding it out for so long to avoid all the double chins.

"You're the best."

She beamed. "I know." Her expression turned serious as I

continued down the hall. Leaning close to the phone, she whispered, "Did you know you have a stalker? A hot one, but still."

I blew out a long breath and rolled my eyes. "Yes. He thinks he's doing something. I'm just trying to let him have his win."

I hadn't bothered to drop my voice, so I wasn't completely surprised when Cas called out, "If I hadn't wanted you to know I was here, love, you wouldn't."

Kiki gave a little shuddering sigh. "Love. Gawd. Does he just love you all over the place like that?"

"I would if she'd let me. A little exhibitionism never hurt anyone."

I stopped and glared at him over my shoulder. The fucker was leaning against the wall, partially obscured by a tall potted plant. "That's not what she said."

"It's exactly what she said. Hang up, and I can love you right here."

"Oh my God." Kiki's whisper was almost reverent.

"I think you mean my captain."

If the sexy pirate didn't stop, I was going to elbow him right in the gut.

I huffed in annoyance while Kiki swooned.

"Seriously, tell me you've fucked him."

"Kiki, he can hear you." I bit out each word, my cheeks on fire with embarrassment.

"I know. I was hoping he would tell me the truth even if you wouldn't."

"I haven't had that exact pleasure, but it's only a matter of time. I'm a patient man." He pushed off the wall and swaggered his way toward me. "By the way, darling, what are you doing later?"

My gaze flitted from Cas to Kiki.

"The answer is *him,* Dee. Him," Kiki said with a saucy wink.

"I always knew I liked you," Cas replied with a panty-melting grin. Or maybe since he was British, it was knicker-destroying.

I should have hung up on her.

"I'm doing what I always do."

"Riding dragons?" Kiki teased.

"No, you asshole. Hiding in my room. Fending off ghosts."

"Well, you know where to find me if you need company," Cas offered. "I may not be a dragon, but I know how to rock a boat."

"Do you want some macaroni with that cheese?"

I snorted, Kiki's unimpressed voice taking some of the wind from Caspian's sails.

"There's my bestie," I said, smiling as I took the last few steps to my room, pushing open the door and readying myself to fall onto the bed so Keeks and I could keep talking.

"What's that noise?" Kiki asked at the same time the sound of running water registered in my ears.

"Fucking ghost."

"A ghost? Ohmigod. I'm going to have a real-life encounter. Don't you dare hang up. In fact, flip the camera. I need to see this with my own eyes."

"You do know I'm the only one who can see ghosts, right?"

"Don't ruin this for me."

I'd have laughed if I wasn't worried about what I was going to find waiting for me. There was no oppressive weight or frenetic buzz beneath my skin, so I was fairly sure this was Non-Moaning Myrtle. But still, you never knew in this place, and after the little shit in Dr. Masterson's office, I was officially over all ghost-related nonsense today.

Flipping the camera, I held it out like a weapon as I entered the bathroom. Instantly I realized what a huge mistake it had been to listen to Kiki. She screeched, I gasped, and both Tor and Cain looked right at me. Did I mention they were stark naked?

"Guys, what is going on?"

"Ohmigod, they do have donkey dicks."

"Kiki, I'll call you back," I said without taking my eyes off the spectacular sight in front of me. I've heard of nightmare fuel, but this right here? Fantasy fodder. I didn't care what they were actually doing. In my head, one of them was about to get his dick sucked. Probably Cain, since Tor was on his knees.

Or, even better, they were readying themselves for me. I'd already been the filling in a Tor/Kai sandwich. Cain pulling my hair while I sucked Tor down didn't sound bad in the slightest.

"This isn't what it looks like," Cain said, pushing the dripping strands of his hair off his forehead. "He snuck up on me taking a shower."

A little growl escaped Tor. "I thought I was joining you."

I wasn't sure if that was an accusation or a complaint.

"I brought you flowers," he added, getting to his feet.

That's when I clocked the dirt and blood streaked across him. "Please tell me these flowers weren't attached to a wood nymph."

Cain snorted, reaching for a towel and tossing it at Tor. "Those are weeds."

A low rumble was Tor's only response before I stepped forward and placed a palm on his firm chest. "Thank you for the flowers."

"You haven't even seen them yet," Cain muttered.

"Doesn't matter. It's the thought that counts," I said without taking my eyes off my beast. "Now, why are you covered in blood? It's barely ten thirty in the morning."

"I was hunting," he said, wrapping the towel around his hips while Cain did the same.

I immediately mourned the loss of all that eye candy. *Note to self: do less laundry.*

"And you?" I asked, nodding to Cain, whose chest still glistened with the remnants of his shower.

"I needed a shower. I didn't want you coming back to find me in any state other than ready for you."

That rumble built in Tor's chest again.

How to handle this . . .

I glanced between them, not sure how to explain what had transpired between Cain and me last night. He'd asked me not to tell the others about his returned memories. I was pretty sure that included that he thought I was the reincarnation of Persephone. But how else did I explain how we ended up in bed together?

"Um. There was an orgy."

"Excuse me?" Tor growled.

Shit. Probably not the best opening.

"Merri, you know, the new succubus? She sort of set everyone off. Cain and I narrowly escaped."

Cain's arms were crossed over his chest, his lips quirked up in amusement as I dug myself a deeper hole.

"Blame that little succubus all you want. She just opened a door the two of us were keeping locked. You're mine now, baby doll. After last night, there's no way for either of us to deny it."

Lightning flashed in Tor's rapidly darkening eyes. Cain was about to get his head ripped clean off his body if I didn't get this under control fast.

"I'm his soulmate," I blurted. "Same as with you. It's like I told you, I'm connected to all four of you."

Cas and I hadn't technically crossed that bridge, but after his twin flames proclamation the other day, it was just a matter of time. It seemed I was destined for a four-layer footlong. Or would it be five? I wasn't sure if I counted in that combination.

"Glad to see your time with Masterson has helped you accept the truth," Cain drawled.

Tor was still frightfully quiet. I'd never hidden my attachment to the others from him, but that didn't mean it was easy for him or his beast to accept. He'd done remarkably well with Kai. I was just hoping the trend continued.

"Tor?" I whispered, looking up at him and trying desperately not to take it personally when he looked away. He was sucking in breaths, his hands opening and closing into tight fists at his sides. He was fighting to remain in control.

"It's all right, my beauty. I just . . . I need a moment. I didn't expect to have to share you with *him*. Especially not after the way he's treated you all this time."

"Me either," I said with a little laugh.

"That's all over now. I know who and what she is to me. I'm done fighting it."

My eyes snapped to Cain's blazing blues. The intense longing in his gaze had my belly twisting, my arms aching to wrap around him and hold him close.

God, it was hard to keep any distance between us when he was looking at me like that. No matter how many times I told myself his feelings weren't real, that they were for someone else, when he was standing right next to me, looking at me like I was his reason for breathing, it was a whole lot harder to believe it.

"Your soulmate?" Tor bit out.

"Yes. She's been mine since before you were an itch in your daddy's pants, Viking, and I'm not letting her go."

"Cain!" I snapped, watching Tor's muscles swell at the mention of his father. "Knock it off. Stop trying to provoke him. You know you wouldn't take the news of me belonging to someone else any better, so stop being an asshole. Hey, speaking of, where is my sweet boy?"

The puppy popped up from behind the tub, his cute little face making me smile and instantly cutting the tension. I crouched and held my arms out, waiting for him to bound into them.

"Where the hell were you?" Cain grumbled. There was a beat of silence before he added. "And you didn't think to intervene? You could have at least bitten an ankle."

Asshole whined, then licked my face.

"Fine, hide behind the pretty girl. But we're talking about this when we get back to my room."

Tor glanced between Cain and the puppy, then at me. "He speaks to animals now?"

"I talk to *you* just fine, big boy."

"Cain."

The god of the underworld smirked at me. "What?"

My cheeks burned at the look in his eyes. Hades. Not Cain. I could see it now. The mantle of power that came along with his true name and title. This man, this god, wouldn't cower before anybody. He was a force to be reckoned with. A god with a big swinging dick that he knew exactly how to use.

Tor ran a hand through his hair before sighing and making his way out of the bathroom. He was struggling, but I knew he'd come back to me. His beast hated sharing, but his human side knew this was what I needed. And that, more than anything, would bring him around.

Twisting away from the gloriously bare-chested man still standing next to me, I moved to follow my demigod, but Cain's warm palm encircled my elbow and he tugged me into him.

"Not so fast, baby doll."

My fucking traitor nipples were hard enough they hurt. "What?"

"Give your man some sugar before you leave."

I opened and closed my mouth, worried I might swallow my tongue. Dear lord, I'd thought the man was potent when he was barely tolerating me, but now that he was actively pursuing me? I wasn't sure I'd survive the experience. I guess that was fitting, given who he was.

I'd finally managed to pucker up when a knock sounded on the door. I twisted my head on reflex, preparing to answer it, but Cain held me tightly, whispering, "Leave it to the beast."

Before I could even agree, a scream of terror came from my bedroom.

Cain sighed. "Oh, hell. What now?"

CHAPTER SIX

KAI

It was the scream of abject terror from upstairs that dragged me from my sketchpad and set me on instant alert. It didn't matter whose it was; there'd been enough terrible things happening recently that I couldn't be sure my mate was safe. Not without laying eyes on her.

As I ran up the stairs, Caspian came tearing down the hall, heading toward Dahlia's room. Usually the pirate wore an unaffected expression at all times. Not now. He was just as worried about our girl as I was. Good. The little prick had plenty to make up for, and seeing him genuinely concerned made me feel a lot better about having him near her.

He spotted me but didn't say a word as we sprinted the last few yards to her room. A small crowd was blocking the door, but I could tell from here that it was wide open.

"Move!" I bellowed, sending folks scattering.

Whatever curiosity they were trying to sate wasn't worth the wrath of a dragon. Hook shoved one straggler out of the way but stopped before I could get through the door. His shoulders shook with silent laughter that quickly turned to heaving guffaws. My gaze followed his, and I found Tor cowering behind Dahlia while both of them stared down at an innocent porcelain doll.

"Don't tell me the big bad beast is afraid of a wittle dolly?" Hook wheezed, saying the last in a baby voice.

"Get that thing out of here," Tor bellowed, fear evident in his tone.

"What did this child's toy ever do to you?" Hook asked, reaching down and picking it up by the hair.

"Watch it, you Captain Jack knockoff. I'm delicate," the fucking doll said.

Tor flinched, sending Caspian into another bout of laughter. "Gods, this is priceless."

Dahlia rolled her lips together, trying hard to fight laughter of her own. "This is my fault."

"What do you mean?" I asked.

"I sort of possessed it by accident. Well, I'm not personally possessing it, but I'm the reason it's possessed. You know, with the ghost powers and the Jennifer Love Hewitt of it all."

The doll giggled. "Your tits are way better. Give yourself some credit."

Dahlia shot the doll a scathing look. "I thought you were a kid. You shouldn't be looking at anyone's tits."

"How can I help it? Also, I'm older than you, Tits McGee. I've been around for three hundred years, most of it trapped in that damn jar. All I had was whatever trash TV my captor was watching to keep me company."

The high-pitched child's voice only added to the hilarity of the moment. Well, at least for us. It seemed to send Tor spiraling deeper.

"Someone make it stop talking."

Dahlia turned around and cupped Tor's cheek. "It's okay, baby. Kat won't hurt you."

Cain chimed in from further inside Dahlia's room. "How are we supposed to shut her up? Her mouth don't even open and close."

Since he was still holding the doll, Hook slid one of his hands over her painted mouth.

"Nice try, stuffing-for-brains." The doll's reply was crystal clear and perfectly enunciated, Hook's hand doing nothing to muffle her speech.

The pirate shrugged. "Well, I tried. You can't say I'm not being supportive."

"Let's take this inside," I muttered, grabbing Hook by the elbow.

"No! Don't bring it in here!" Tor shouted, stumbling over himself as he hastened away.

Cain gave him a withering look. "How is it you are terrified of a harmless fucking doll?"

"Who you calling harmless, Foghorn Leghorn? I've burned entire houses to the ground."

The lights in the room flickered as Cain scowled.

There was no hiding my dragon's amusement. "Child's play. Speak to me when you've razed entire villages to little more than embers."

The doll's head slowly twisted until those glass eyes stared unblinkingly at me. "Noted."

"Lucky for you, I don't hurt children."

Cain's words only seemed to amuse her, if the ghostly laughter floating through the room was any indication. Tor flinched as she returned her attention to the others. "Lucky for you, I'm already dead."

"You think death would stop me? That's when I'm at my best, little girl."

Dahlia's eyes went wide, and more than one eyebrow was raised in Cain's direction. He seemed different today. More self-aware, perhaps.

"Release yer fire, rid us all of this ridiculous wee pest. She's a distraction we can ill afford."

If I did that, who knew where the spirit would end up? Also, I'd kill Hook. Hmm, the idea had merit.

"Lock it up, I beg of you," Tor said, skin leached of all color. He wasn't quite trembling, but it was close. He looked seconds away from losing his breakfast.

Caspian leaned against Dahlia's wardrobe and let out a low chuckle. "Oh, this is so entertaining. Like an elephant and a bleeding mouse."

"Tor, I thought you weren't afraid of ghosts?" Dahlia asked, taking the doll from Cas's hands.

"I'm not. Dolls are another matter. There was an incident when I was younger," he replied as she opened the chest at the foot of her bed and placed the doll under a pile of heavy blankets. Tor visibly shuddered as Dahlia dropped the lid.

"Hey! It's dark in here!" The muffled sound of her little voice was creepy, I had to give Tor that, but I suspected that even if she wasn't possessed, the Beast of Novasgard would still be afraid of her.

He looked the worse for wear. Especially since all he was wearing was a towel wrapped around his waist and he was covered in dried blood and dirt.

Hook howled with laughter at his obvious embarrassment. "I'm sorry. It's just . . . too good. I can't . . ."

"Someone shut him up before I do it with my fist," Tor warned.

The pirate wiped away the tears streaming from his eyes. "I can't take you seriously. You've lost all credibility." He held his hands up daintily, prancing in place as he mocked, "Oh help me, there's a scary dolly after me. I'm a big Viking monster, but I need my girlfriend to rescue me from the *child's plaything*."

"She's my mate," Tor growled. "Say another word and I'll end you."

Cas crossed his arms over his chest. "Sure you will. Until I grab that doll and hold it up between us. I know your weakness, tough guy. My days of fearing you are long past—if they ever existed at all."

Tor snarled, Hook laughed, and Dahlia got between them.

"Tor, go get cleaned up. Cas, do us all a favor and shut up before my room gets destroyed."

"Finally, someone says something useful," Cain muttered.

"Don't let her out," Tor whispered as he shot a glance at Dahlia, then the chest.

Our mate, to her credit, didn't make him feel bad about his fear. Instead, she sat atop the chest. "Promise."

Tor collected his discarded clothes on his way to the bathroom. I turned my focus back to my gem. Now that the doll had been dealt with, it was time to get to the bottom of this debacle. "Explain again how ye placed the spirit in the doll."

"I don't fucking know."

"How can ye not know?"

"I sneezed."

"Bless you?" Caspian offered.

"Did it come shooting out of your nose and into the damn porcelain?" Cain asked, scooping up Asshole and running his fingertips between the pup's ears.

"No. I . . . ugh, Masterson released her from a spirit jar so I could work on my control. I had her, but the jar broke, and while I was waiting for a replacement, I sneezed and lost her. Or . . . maybe I threw her into the doll? I don't know. And I don't really see why she has to be here with me. Is this a punishment? It's unfair to force me to take care of a creepy possessed doll when it wasn't my idea in the first place."

"Breathe, baby doll."

"Are you intentionally attacking me right now?" she asked, eyes narrowed.

Cain lifted a brow. "I always call you that."

She chewed on that for a second. "I guess you do. Fine. As you were."

"Glad we've established who wears the pants in *your* relationship," Cas tossed out.

Cain shot his gaze to the pirate, shadowy tendrils of power creeping out from his hands.

"What was that?" he asked, voice low.

The way Hook visibly recoiled sent a reminder of the time I had to rescue him from Cain's wrath once before.

"Easy now, Cain." I held out a hand to the towel-clad man in a gesture meant to calm him.

"W-w-we all do, obviously," Cas said through fits of nervous laughter. "I mean, you don't at the moment, but once you change, you will. And I . . . erm . . . Dahlia, what do you say we take a walk, love? See the mermaids? Or those pixies you like so much? I heard the shimmers were born."

"Shimmers?"

"You know. The wee ones. Babies."

"Already?"

"Can we please return to the topic at hand?" I asked, not bothering to conceal my annoyance. "You've never been able to do anything like this before, gem. What changed?"

"Nothing."

Cain cleared his throat, eyes hot on hers. Dahlia's cheeks went pink, and I understood.

"He fucked her," Tor offered as he strode back into the room.

"What? No! I thought for sure I'd be the next lucky bastard," Cas whined before pointing a finger at Cain. "You don't even like her."

"She's mine," Cain simply stated.

My dragon didn't fucking like that at all. Nor did I, truth be told, but I'd already come to the conclusion she had more than two mates destined for her. The Shadow Queen had four, and I was pretty sure my treasure did as well.

"She's ours," I emphasized. "That includes you, Cain."

"And Caspian," Dahlia added. We all looked at her. She'd never declared him as one of her men before. "It's all of you. I can feel it. I'm stronger when you're with me. Even right now, standing here, I can feel the power inside me buzzing."

My brain snagged on a detail even though she hadn't spelled it out. "Wait. Does the power grow each time you accept a new mate?"

She sat down on her bed, and her brows drew together as we all watched her consider my question. "I don't know. I think so? I mean, I could see the ghosts, and that was it, but after Tor, I tapped into my scream again. Then when we were together, Kai . . ." Her cheeks turned a tempting shade of pink.

"Go on," I urged.

"I never told you this, but I did something in the greenhouse."

"Kinky fuckery, eh, darling?" Cas teased.

She snorted and rolled her eyes. "No. Not unless you think killing and then reviving all the plants in one go is kinky."

"Oh, I don't know. With the right circumstances, watching you doing just about anything is kinky."

"Zip it," Cain said, eyes flashing. "Don't speak unless you're called on."

"You're not my daddy. I'll do what I like."

Dahlia's gaze flicked to Cain, then back to the floor. "I've never controlled a ghost before. Not until after Cain and I found each other again."

"Again? There was a time before this one? Oh, you wound me, love." Hook made a show of clasping his chest.

"She was mine in another life. And she's mine now."

"Reincarnation," I mused. "Interesting."

"So he says," Dahlia muttered, dimming a bit at his declaration.

"Be that as it may, it sounds like you're right. Every time you join with a new mate, your power grows."

"I know a surefire way to test the theory," Caspian offered, hands dropping to his fly.

"Back up, Casanova," Cain said, tying him up in strands of shadow.

"Oi, you villain. I'm only trying to help our girl realize her full potential. Let me go." Cas struggled, but the wispy shadow tendrils were stronger than they appeared.

"Let me get a handle on the latest developments first, okay?" Dahlia said, with the hint of a smile.

Hook lifted his hands. "All right, it's not a no, which means it's an eventual yes. I can work with that."

"Your logic is flawed," Tor grumbled. "It's not a yes until it's undeniable consent."

"Oh, it'll be undeniable once we get there. It'll be a resounding, '*Oh yes, Caspian.*' Everyone will know."

"That's enough from you," Cain said, muzzling Caspian with a gag made of shadows.

"Hmm, he's practically tolerable this way," Tor said, sitting on Dahlia's desk.

Dahlia's shoulders slumped, and she heaved a weary sigh. "It's great that your magic dicks are helping me get more powerful, but what's the fucking point of it all?"

"Fate?" Tor said.

"Destiny?" I tossed out.

"Isn't that the same thing?" she asked.

"True love."

We all went silent at Cain's softly spoken statement. There was no question in his words, and they sat heavy between us.

Dahlia was the first to break the silence, her laugh stilted and awkward. "Love and ghosts, huh? Sounds like a recipe for a great time. Just my kind of happily ever after. Not."

Cain's grunt of displeasure pulled my focus to the towel-clad man. He looked down at the puppy in his arms and muttered, "Just because she can't admit it doesn't mean it's not true."

Wanting to spare my mate from another uncomfortable moment, I spoke before she could. "You're not the only one gaining power, gem."

"He's right. I've never had more control over my beast. You gave me that."

"The same goes for my dragon. And if the way Cain has been talking is any indication, you've brought things out in him too."

Dahlia stood and began pacing in the small space left in the room. We really needed a bigger place if all four of us were going to be spending time with her together with any regularity.

"That's great, but *why* do I even have power? What is my purpose?"

"Purpose?" I asked, flabbergasted. I'd never questioned why I had a dragon. I simply did. It was irrefutable.

"Yeah, my purpose. You know, my hero's journey. My raison d'etre. True love is great and all, but my reason for existing cannot just be to fuck the four of you. Especially not with power like this. It has to serve a greater purpose. So what is it? I'm not exactly saving lives over here. If anything, it seems more likely I do the opposite."

"You saved me, beauty." Tor's voice was soft, and if her little gasp was any indication, she hadn't expected that.

"Perhaps it's not lives you need to save, darling." When the fuck had Hook gotten free of Cain's shadows?

Dahlia blinked and turned her attention to the pirate. "What are you talking about?"

"You speak to the dead. Lost souls. You've been given a connection most people don't ever have."

"So . . . I should help them? They come to me for help," she said, understanding dawning. "I *need* to talk to them." She smacked her palm on her forehead. "Duh, of course I do. That's literally the premise of every medium show ever. It's the damn ending of my book."

"Spoilers!" I blurted. I was still working my way through her backlist.

"Sorry, handsome. It's unavoidable at this point. But I understand what I have to do now."

Hook smirked. "And what's that?"

"I'm going to catch the Ripper."

Protest bubbled up inside me; I didn't want her anywhere near that serial killer. But someone else beat me to the punch.

"And how exactly do you think you're going to do that?" Cain drawled.

"Well, first I need to interview some of his victims."

CHAPTER SEVEN

HOOK

"Are ye sure that's wise, gem? The last time . . ." Kai took her hand, and the earnestness in his eyes would have been pathetic if I didn't understand exactly how he felt.

Dahlia crossed her arms. "The last time?"

Oh, she was going to make him say it. That she'd fled in terror. That she hadn't been able to handle it on her own. Not a choice I would have made when attempting to win her over, but then few were as clever as me. I simply sat back and watched the disaster unfold. Where was the popcorn when I needed it?

When he didn't speak, she poked him in the chest. "The last time worked out really well for you, dragon, so I'd watch it."

"Kai's right. It's not safe to let you wander around hunting ghosts without one of us—namely me—with you."

Ah, yes, the shadow magician needed to throw himself on the bomb too. Of course he did. His little assistant yipped as though agreeing with him. I had to smother a smile at the image of Cain wearing a top hat and tails. Instead of a bunny, he could pull his little dog out of his hat. Dahlia would make a lovely diversion, her curves on display in one of those little red fringe dresses.

Fuck me, I was going to have to excuse myself to the loo if I kept up this fantasy.

"We just discussed how her powers have grown," Tor pointed out. "Who's to say she can't handle it?"

"Thank you," Dahlia said with an emphatic wave of her hand. Then she blew Tor a kiss. "Good beast. I'll make sure to show you my appreciation later."

The hulking arsehole purred. Yes, like a cat.

"Okay, this has been fun. I've got work to do, so you all need to go." Dahlia moved toward her desk, but no one moved. Not even Tor, who was still seated on top of it. She gave us all a heated glare. "Did I stutter? Make like a tree and leave. Or maybe since there's a group of you, it would be a forest?"

Tor reached for her, grabbing her around the waist and hauling her into his chest. "Are you sure you want me to leave you, beauty?"

I saw the moment she faltered. A soft shudder worked its way down her body as she nearly melted into him. But she shook her head and pressed a light kiss to his lips. "Yes. I won't get any work done if you're here."

"Or will you end up inspired to write your next bestseller because of it?"

"Oh, he's abandoned the crazed beast and has latched on to the swoony prince now, has he?" Cain muttered to his dog.

"Come on, you guys. I'm serious. I'm not planning on running out and doing any ghost hunting this second. I have to get Keeks some chapters, or she might come out here and do the Ripper's job for him. I'll call you if I need you. I promise."

Kai's pupils lengthened into slits as an unhappy growl left him at her words.

"Too soon?" she asked. "Haven't you learned that humor is one of my favorite defense mechanisms? It's right up there with avoidance, denial, and manic anxiety spirals."

I pushed off the wall where I'd been posed in my best sexy lean.

"Fine, we'll leave you. None of us will like it, but we'll do it if that makes you happy, darling."

I wasn't sure who in the group was more stunned by my easy acceptance. Dahlia or the rest of her men.

My lips curled up as I snickered. *Look who just realized I know how to play the game? That's right, lads. Captain Hook is in the building. They're called boundaries, boys. Look it up—I did.*

Cain strode to the bed and rustled around in the sheets, snagging a pair of boxer briefs before dropping his towel and slipping into them. He left first, not giving a damn that he was clad only in his skintight underpants. I wondered what the appeal was to those infernal garments. I never wore anything under my trousers. Easier access. Less of a delay.

See? Clever.

Kai was next, making a point of grabbing Dahlia by the back of her neck and spinning her around for a kiss before he exited the room. She was still swooning when a scowling Tor removed any hint of Kai's kiss with a lingering one of his own.

I rolled my eyes and cleared my throat when hands started wandering. "Still here, fucker."

By the time he released her, she was panting. Her lips were swollen and pink, eyes glazed.

"It's fucking weird having you all in my room like this. Taking turns and passing me around like a bottle of beer on the wall."

"You say weird, I say enticing," I murmured. "I've read your book. Chapter seventeen starts very much like this."

She laughed softly. "I'm pretty sure they were coming, not going."

I wasn't going to touch that one with a ten-foot pole. Not when I was actively playing the role of her respectful hero.

"Come on, big guy, let's leave our darling to write her cliterature."

Tor grumbled, his disappointment etched into every line of his body. Furrowed brow down to slumped shoulders and stomping steps. If you ever wanted to see a grown man throwing a silent temper tantrum, Tor was your guy.

But he did as she bade, and I? Well, I lingered until the very last, needing to keep her in my sights as long as possible. I finally headed for the door as she pulled out her chair and opened her laptop.

"Not you, pirate. I need to talk to you."

Ding dong. Had my plan worked even better than I expected?

"Yes, love?" It was all knight in shining armor instead of my usual ruinous rake. Hey, I had a part to play, and I was committed to my character.

"I had a couple of questions for you about the night of your attack."

A chill raced down my spine, and those bloody whispers echoed in my memory. I hated the whispers.

"Go on," I said, as cavalier as possible while on the inside, I was a knotted mess of unease.

"Did you see his face?"

"No. He was wearing a mask. A plague mask."

"And you're sure it was a man?"

"Of that, I have no doubt. He was too strong, his voice clearly male although modified by some sort of device."

She nodded, jotting down notes as I spoke. "You mentioned he'd gone underground. Do you remember specifically whereabouts that was?"

My mind became a mess of images, all jumbling together, visions of the forest superimposed with endless stretches of blue sea. "No."

"How did you escape?"

I swallowed. "I didn't. He left me there because of you."

"Me?"

"Yes, love. Did you think I was just roaming the woods for fun?"

She set her pen down. "I don't understand why I, of all people, would have scared the Ripper off."

"It wasn't you specifically, so much as the idea of him being caught. The three of you were quite loud. It's easy to mistake roars of passion for those of an enraged predator on the prowl."

She blushed. "So he just chased you through the woods, pushed you up against a tree so he could take care of business, and then vanished into the night."

It sounded rather pleasant when she put it like that. "That sounds like a scene from one of your books."

"I haven't . . . uh, CNC isn't something I've written yet."

"Why not? You've clearly given it a lot of thought."

As have I, ever since the seed had been planted.

She blew out a breath. "I wondered if you were going to bring this up again."

I cocked my head. "Why? I told you I wanted to have a discussion with you before we explored together."

She didn't want to meet my eyes; instead she focused on her fingers and twiddled the pen. "Because you changed your mind? I dunno."

"I am a man of my word, darling. Besides, anything that makes you that horny is something I want to do over and over. But we have to set some ground rules. You have to trust me before I can make certain every dark fantasy you've ever had comes true."

"You already know the big one," she murmured, finally risking a glance.

"Taking you in your sleep?"

She nodded.

"And what else?"

"Kidnapping. Captivity. But I don't want to be bound. I need my hands and feet free."

My throat was fucking dry. "What about sensory deprivation? Blindfolds specifically."

"As long as I can hear your voice."

My voice. Not anyone else's. Fuck, this woman was made for me.

Her gaze lingered on my mouth before she asked, "Is that something you're interested in?"

"I'll kidnap you better than anyone ever could, love. But I won't be physically violent. I can't."

"You're a pirate," she teased. "Isn't that part of the job?"

"I'm your lover first. Pirate second. I won't hurt you. Nothing outside the realm of a good rough fuck. Fingerprints, bite marks, sure. But hitting you? Purposely drawing your blood? No. It's a hard limit for me."

Her breath hitched, and my gaze dipped down to her chest, a groan catching in my throat at the sight of her hard nipples pebbling under the fabric of her shirt.

"Sounds good to me," she managed.

I had to force myself to drag my eyes back to hers. This was important; I needed to stay focused. "And the element of surprise, that's crucial for you, right? You don't want any indication that it's coming?"

She bit down on her bottom lip and nodded.

"How will I know if I'm not welcome?"

Her brow furrowed as she considered my question. "I don't know."

Glancing around the room, I looked for some sort of identifier for us to use. Hair ties littered her small dresser, but those were too common. I stopped, holding out my right arm, which sported three different bracelets. Perfect.

Removing my favorite, a whiskey-brown braided leather, I secured it on her wrist. "As long as you're wearing this, the door is open. If you're ever not willing, leave it off, and I'll know."

As I stared at the piece of jewelry adorning her skin, a loud, persistent *ticktock* infiltrated my joy.

Ticktock

Ticktock

Tick . . .

"What is that?" I shook my head at the incessant and painfully loud sound.

"What are you talking about?"

"Ticking. It's a clock. Where is it? How can you stand it? The damned thing is so loud."

She reached out and cupped my stubbled jaw. "Cas, there's not a clock in here."

"Yes there bloody well is. Fuck." I was desperate to get the noise under control. "Turn it off."

"I can't."

The hairs on the back of my neck stood on end as the whispers rushed through my mind.

"Time is up."

"Get out while you can."

"Before it's too late."

"I have to go," I said, frantic.

"Cas, what's happening?"

I couldn't answer her. I pressed my hands to my ears as the ticking clock continued so loud I thought my ears would bleed. Shaking my head at her, I stumbled out of her room and down the hall to my own, desperate to find something that would drown out this infernal torture.

With each pulse of my heart, I grew closer to the truth. It wasn't a clock in her room tormenting me. It was all in my mind. It was my madness.

The whispers were right. I was running out of time.

SESSION TRANSCRIPT: DECEMBER 11TH

Dr. Masterson: This is Dr. Elizabeth Masterson. It is December 11th, and the time is 1:00 p.m. This is a recorded session with Cain Alexander. Cain, it's been a while since our last session. Why don't you tell me how you feel your progress has been?

<<dead air>>

Dr. Masterson: Cain?

Cain: What? Oh, sorry.

Dr. Masterson: You seem preoccupied. Is something wrong?

Cain: I just thought the other guy would be here.

<<scratching on door>>

<<dog whining>>

Cain: He's going to do that the entire session. If you'd just let him in here—

Dr. Masterson: I told you, no distractions. I made special allowances for him as you adjusted.

<<clothes rustling>>

Dr. Masterson: Would you prefer Dr. Temperance?

Cain: Not particularly. I just had a bone to pick with him.

Dr. Masterson: About?

Cain: Nothing that concerns you, Doc.

Dr. Masterson: Oh, I don't know about that. Everything that upsets you concerns me.

Cain: I'm not upset.

Dr. Masterson: No? Then why is my favorite pillow currently smoldering?

<<frantic thumping on fabric>>

Cain: Shit. Sorry about that.

Dr. Masterson: You're clearly not doing well. Tell me why you're so out of sorts.

<<scratching on door>>

<<dog whining>>

Cain: *heavy sigh* Can you please let him in here? He's my emotional support Asshole.

Dr. Masterson: *choked laugh* You have become very attached to him. But no. He chewed the leg of my antique table the last time he was here.

Cain: I'd say he was better behaved these days, but it'd be a lie. He does and says whatever the fuck he wants.

Dr. Masterson: Says? He speaks to you?

Cain: How much trouble am I in if I say yes?

Dr. Masterson: Trouble? Why would you be in trouble?

Cain: Only crazy people talk to dogs.

Dr. Masterson: *snorted laugh* If that's the case, most of my family would be categorized that way, then. Talking to animals isn't unheard of in our world, Cain. He's your familiar. Of course it stands to reason he'd be able to communicate with you. Has he told you anything that helped you recall your past?

Cain: Did you miss the part when I told you he says whatever he wants? Usually he just insults me. Pretty sure he doesn't know the meaning of the word useful.

<<series of furious dog barks>>

Cain: Oh, can it. You know I'm right.

Dr. Masterson: So he's more a nuisance than anything?

<<dog growls>>

Cain: I named him Asshole for a reason, Doc.

Dr. Masterson: Fair enough. Well, it would seem you've been making all sorts of progress then. Your powers are growing, your relationship with your familiar is deepening. What other changes have there been recently?

Cain: What do you mean?

Dr. Masterson: Well, to what do you attribute these changes? A certain writer, perhaps?

Cain: What does Dahlia have to do with anything?

<<rustling clothes>>

Dr. Masterson: You tell me. Last we spoke, you were doing your damnedest to avoid her, but by all accounts, you've been spending a lot of time in her room these past few days. I'm honestly surprised Tor allows it.

Cain: *snarls* He has no say in what I do.

Dr. Masterson: *patronizing laugh* Don't let him hear you say that. Mated Berserkers are notoriously unhinged when it comes to their mates. Dragons too, for that matter. I can't imagine Kai or Tor will make it easy for you, possessive and territorial as their beasts are.

Cain: I claimed her first. There's nothing that could eclipse our bond.

<<chair squeaks>>

<<rustling clothes>>

Dr. Masterson: Tell me more about that.

Cain: She. Is. Mine. Has always been. Will always be. 'Nuff said.

Dr. Masterson: C'mon, Cain. I need more than that. You're singing a completely different tune. In order to help you, I need to know what changed.

Cain: *heavy sigh* A gentleman doesn't kiss and tell. You should know that, and if you don't, you need to be looking for a different man.

Dr. Masterson: How much of your memory has returned?

Cain: Why does it matter so much to you?

Dr. Masterson: Helping you get back on your feet and proving that you have control has always been the goal here, Cain. You don't have to be so antagonistic. I'm not the enemy.

Cain: Hmph.

<<chair squeaks>>

Dr. Masterson: *sigh* Cain, if you're not going to be honest with me, then I can't help you.

Cain: Glad we're finally on the same page, Doc. Guess that means our session is over.

<<clothes rustling>>

Dr. Masterson: Cain . . .

<<footsteps on hardwood>>

<<door opening>>

<<series of dog barks>>

Cain: See you around, Doc.

<<door closing>>

Dr. Masterson: Session terminated at 1:27 p.m. Subject's refusal to admit that he has recovered some, if not all, of his memories is concerning. If he's returned to full strength, the Ripper may not be Blackwood's biggest threat. Recommendation going forward: additional surveillance when possible and reservation of maximum security holding cell in No Man's Land should he become a danger to himself or others.

<<static>>

End of transcript.

CHAPTER EIGHT

HADES

"Took you long enough." Asshole pawed at my leg until I stooped down and picked him up.

"You heard me asking her to let you in."

His laughter floated through my mind. *"Never thought I'd live to see the day big bad Hades asked permission for anything."*

"Yeah, well, I never thought I'd live to see the day Cerberus started slumming it as a Bichon, but here we are."

"Excuse me, pal. The ladies love a Bichon. The number of belly rubs I've gotten from Dahlia alone should make you jealous."

I rolled my eyes. "That's not the part of me she likes to rub."

"Word on the street is that she's not interested in rubbing much of anything now that she knows your secret."

Shoulders stiffening, I gripped him a little too hard around the ribs, and he squirmed as I continued striding away from Masterson's office. Where I was going, I had no damn idea, but I needed some distance from that infernal woman.

"Hey! Watch the hands, man! I still gotta breathe!"

I loosened my hold until he settled.

"Jesus. Dahlia might be into asphyxiation, but it's a hard no from me. I only have one throat in this form. I'm used to having two backups."

I ground my teeth so hard I could practically hear them cracking. The last thing I wanted right now was a reminder of what my woman did and didn't like. Mostly because the top of the didn't like list was me. Which made no fucking sense. She was my soulmate. She should already be desperately in love with me.

Against my better judgment, I'd given her some space like she asked for, hoping she'd come to her senses and seek me out. But she hadn't. It'd been radio silence since I left her room the other morning. Did she not want me?

"Maybe it's 'cause she already has two others. You're less potent or whatever the fuck."

"How many times do I have to tell you to stay outta my damn head?"

But was the cute little prick right?

"Yes. I'm right. And you know the rules, boss. I go where you go. I'm the one watching your back, keeping you safe, etc., etc. I need to stay in the know at all times."

I grumbled audibly as I passed by the demon Kit, who was walking in the other direction with his nose in a book—his own book of plays. Of fucking course he was. Narcissistic fuck.

"Your curvy confection is in the music room."

"Alone?" I asked the demon, refusing to make eye contact.

He let out a sardonic laugh as he swanned past us. "Is she ever alone?"

Asshole yipped and jumped out of my hold as flames worked their way up my arms.

"Not all of us are fireproof, you grumpy motherfucker."

"Sorry," I muttered, sparing him a quick glance and finding him busy licking himself between the legs.

"You almost neutered me. Again."

"You say that like I was responsible for the first time. You're the one who signed up for it."

"It was the responsible thing to do. Can you imagine a whole underworld of me *running around? I'm too busy to be there for my children. I will* not *be a deadbeat dad."*

Something about his response seemed canned, like he'd rehearsed it a hundred times to get it *just* right. But the last thing I wanted to do was interrogate him about his doggy vasectomy. I had other questions in need of answers.

"By the way, who did you leave guarding the gate? Maybe you should go back to the underworld for a while to check in and recover. I'll be fine."

As if he expected that from me, he turned and huffed, tail up, chin high, like a damn show dog. *"Is that even a question? This ain't my first rodeo. Dieter is keeping watch till we get back."*

"Dieter? Are you serious? He wouldn't know his ass from a hole in the ground. He's a fucking mouth breather. He once asked me why they call my realm Hades."

"If you're really that worried about it, we can leave right now. Grab your girl and let's go."

The temptation to do exactly that had been so strong I'd nearly given in more than once. But the problem was, someone set me up, and if I took her now, I may lose her all over again. I had to deal with the threat first, then we'd see about going home.

"No."

"All right, then. You're just going to have to put up with me. And trust that I know how to do my godsdamned job. You know, the same one I've been doing for millennia."

I heaved a sigh. "I asked you one fucking question, and we've been here arguing for the last ten minutes."

"Six. But who's counting? Now, come on. I have some belly rubs to collect."

He trotted down the hall, his little nails click-clacking on the hardwood.

I followed him belatedly. Not because I didn't want to see Dahlia, but because I did. And I didn't think I could take another of her rejections. I poured my heart out to her, and she'd shut down. Accused me of using her as a stand-in for someone else.

As if I wouldn't recognize my own soulmate. Fuck, even when I didn't know my damn name, my soul still cried out for her.

"Asshole, sit," I hissed as he reached the partially open music room door. The last thing I needed was for her to see me spying on her.

Thank fuck, the pup did as I commanded. That was the thing about him. When I really meant it, he listened.

The heavily ornamented strains of the piano rang out, and I couldn't help myself as I peered into the room. Hook sat at the piano, rocking on the bench, eyes closed as he played while Dahlia sat near him and scribbled in her notebook.

"Of course he'd choose the Sarabande from Bach's fifth French suite," I muttered under my breath.

Maybe I should shove him out of his seat and show her how well my fingers worked those keys. A little Chopin. Maybe some Rachmaninoff. I had the hands for it.

"You sound jealous."

"If I want your opinion, I'll ask for it."

"Hey, everyone needs someone to hold up the mirror and call them on their shit. I'm just being a good friend. One might say, your best *friend."*

I rolled my eyes but couldn't find it in my heart to disagree. Instead I squatted down beside him so I could give him a few conciliatory ear scritches. "Good boy," I grumbled.

"Aren't you gonna go in there?"

I wanted to, but a big part of me also wanted her to come to me first. Something in me needed to know I was chosen. The devil take it, she was ruining me.

My palm was on the door, the urge to go get her like he asked burning through me. I could go inside, snag her by the wrist, drag her down to the underworld, and make her my queen all over again. But would she ever love me if I did that?

Asshole whined and turned big dark eyes on me. *"You took away her choice once before. We saw how well that turned out. Maybe don't make that mistake again."*

The scent of burning wood hit my nose, and I released the doorframe with a muttered curse, grimacing a little at the seared handprint.

"She'll come to me. She will."

Asshole pawed at my leg, asking me to pick him up. I scooped him into my arms, and immediately, the pup licked my chin. *"That's right. That's some big dog energy."*

I'd never admit it out loud, but his reassurance eased some of the ache in my heart as I forced myself to walk away from the only thing I'd ever truly wanted.

CHAPTER NINE

DAHLIA

"Why does your face look like that?" Kiki's assault hit me as soon as our video call connected.

I wrenched away from the screen, then immediately flicked my gaze to the little version of myself in the corner to make sure I didn't have ink staining my cheeks or something. "What do you mean? It's just my fucking face, Keeks. Not all of us can look like you, no matter what the situation." I took in her dewy, glowing skin, the intricate Dutch braid keeping her hair off her face, and the hot pink sports bra she wore. "I bet you just ran a marathon or something, didn't you? Not even a drop of sweat, you asshole."

"Power pilates, actually. And I don't sweat. I sparkle."

She waggled her eyebrows, and before I could say anything in response, she waved her hands in front of her like they were windshield wipers and chanted, "I sparkle, I bubble, I get in a whole lot of trouble." She giggled at the end, and I couldn't help but do the same.

"Do you need me to get you pom-poms for Christmas this year? Maybe a cheerleading costume?"

"They're called uniforms, babes."

"Fuck off. You knew what I meant."

"You're in a mood this morning. Now the face makes sense. What's going on?"

My gut twisted. "How late do I have to be before I start worrying?"

"Late for what? A therapy session?"

I stopped dead and stared through the camera. "Late, Kiki. The only late a woman cares about."

"But . . . I mean, the dragon gave you a"—she leaned in close to the camera and whispered—"magical vagina tattoo."

"He did. It should've worked, but I'm not sure. I've been pretty regular for the last few months, and if the schedule is still solid, I'd be on day two."

"You're not regular. Even when you're regular, you aren't regular."

"Yeah, but—"

"Magical. Vajayjay. Tattoo."

I heaved a sigh. "I know. But what if the magic didn't work and I've got a Viking baby in there—or a dragon? Oh God, what if it's an egg? I can't give birth to an egg."

"Pretty sure eggs are supposed to be in there."

"No, Keeks. A dragon egg."

Her expression was comical, or it would have been if I were in a laughing mood. Her eyebrows were in her hairline, and her jaw was hanging open. She blinked at me several times before sputtering, "Is that even possible? Oh my God, do you have to lay an egg and then sit on it like a chicken until it hatches? Can you even get warm enough as a human mama and not a dragon mama? Or is Kai the one who has to keep it warm? Girl, I have so many questions."

"So do I. I'm not ready to be a mother. I can barely feed myself most days. This is going to be a disaster."

"Hang on, we don't know you're knocked up. Give it a few days. The more stressed you are, the worse it is. Remember that time you were on deadline and didn't have a period for two months?"

That made me feel a little better. She was right. There'd been no possible way I'd been pregnant then. "But that time, there weren't any active swimmers up there. The wall hadn't been breached."

There was no hiding Kiki's laughter. "Babes . . ."

"I'm serious, Kiki. What do I do?"

She schooled her expression. "What I already said. You wait it out. You did what I can only assume was a responsible thing and trusted Kai when he said the tattoo would protect you. If for some reason he was wrong, or it didn't take, then you figure out what you want to do and talk to your men. Neither one of them seemed like they'd run screaming from their responsibilities. It's your body, babes. The choice is yours."

I swallowed past the lump in my throat. "I'm just freaking out. I know it worked. It had to. Magic. Magic is like . . . infallible. Right?"

Her eyes widened, and she looked at me like I was wearing a weiner dog as a hat. "Yeah, sure . . . I guess." The way she said it, drawing the words out as though working through a plot hole with me, made my gut sink.

"Way to instill confidence in me, Keeks."

She threw up her hands. "Well, I don't know! Until you got there, I didn't even think magical tattoos and dragon dicks existed. Now these guys are all 'let me put my baby in you' with you every night, and I don't know what to do with it." She blinked at me, a smile creeping across her face. "Well, I mean, I know what to do with it, but I'm no expert on magic."

"So do I need to take a test? Or just—" I stopped midsentence when I spotted Sorcha Blackthorne standing at the end of the hall, a devilish grin on her lips. Fuck.

"Or just . . ." Kiki said, waiting for me to continue.

"Don't stop on my account," she purred, leaning against the wall and crossing her feet at the ankle like she was getting comfortable. "Incidentally, your friend is right. Neither of those boys would leave you if they got you up the duff."

My cheeks burned, and the thought of Kai or Tor as daddy material had me feeling some kind of way.

"What you'd really need to worry about is whether Masterson would even let you keep the baby."

The vampire's words sent my heart straight into my ass. "Wh-what?"

"Do you see any nurseries around here? A playground? Frolicking children? Blackwood isn't intended for the young and meek. We can't be trusted, remember? Who would dare leave an innocent child in any of our care?"

"Wow, Sorcha. Doom and gloom this early?" Oz said, sauntering up to her. "It's not even dinnertime."

"Just having a little tête-à-tête with our precious writer."

Kiki piped up. "Technically it's not a tête-à-tête. I'm here. A tête-à-tête is between two persons, not more."

Sorcha's smile froze on her face, and ice ran through my veins. Kiki was a ballsy bitch, but I wasn't sure she'd have been as brazen if faced with Sorcha in the flesh.

"Okay, fun chat. Don't say a word, Sorcha. There's nothing to worry about."

Sorcha took a long, deep inhale and smirked again. "We'll see, won't we?"

Remembering that she'd given me a heads-up last time, I couldn't ignore the glaringly obvious fact that she didn't bother to do so now. Was she fucking with me? Punishing me for Kiki's snark? Or was she . . . could she . . .? Fuck my life.

"I'm leaving this conversation now," I muttered. "Creepy fucking vampire nose."

"I heard that," Sorcha called after my retreating form.

"I figured!"

Kiki's laughter filtered through the phone and pulled my attention back to her. "Okay, I'm sure you didn't call me unannounced just to tell me I look weird. What's up?"

Sitting up a little straighter, she put her serious face on. "We need a Rebel sequel. I'm sorry, I tried to pitch your new idea, but they turned it down. The studio wants to option it too. We need that first, then you can do the passion project."

I groaned as I began trudging up the stairs to my room. "But I don't want to write a sequel. I already gave Rebel and her guys an HEA. A sequel means I have to blow it all up so there's a reason for people to be reinvested. No one is interested in happy people fucking like bunnies."

Kiki made a considering face. "Have you never heard of the multi-billion dollar industry called porn?"

"I can't make a whole storyline out of happy sex scenes."

"Well, I don't know, throw in a ghost hunter, or maybe they Scooby-Doo it and have to solve other murders?" She blew a raspberry. "An apocalypse! Or a surprise ghost baby . . . Yikes, too soon?"

I glared at her through the tiny phone screen. "Way too fucking soon. You're skirting the line of musty scrotum territory, Keeks. We're talking a demotion from cool godmother to the weird mothball-ridden aunt everyone avoids at family reunions because she has grabby hands."

"That was frighteningly specific."

"I know things."

"That's a weird thing to know. Especially since you don't have any aunts."

"Semantics." I heaved a sigh as I circled my brain back to the real issue. I didn't have a plot for Rebel. I didn't want to write it. Some writers could just pull an idea out of a hat and run with it, but that wasn't how my brain worked. I needed inspiration. The muse had to speak to me. If I forced it, everyone would be able to tell. "I don't know if I can—"

"Dahlia, you have so little faith in me. We will figure this out, even if it takes late-night brainstorming sessions when you're a little punchy and weird. We'll play our favorite 'what if' game. We always come up with our best stuff that way."

"I love how you say *our* when I'm the one doing all the work."

"Rude. I help."

I felt a little bad for diminishing her role, but when she was telling my brain what to do and expecting me to execute it, I struggled with sharing the credit. "Fine, we'll figure it out."

"Good. You have forty-eight hours to prepare. Then, it's on. Tell your boys you're out of commission because Kiki needs your brain."

"I'm sure they'll love that. They barely agreed to give me a few hours a day to myself for writing."

"But they did agree."

I nodded. "Begrudgingly. If they had it their way, one or all of them would be breathing down my neck every minute of the day."

"Some women would be into that."

Honestly, I didn't hate the idea of them being around all the time. Surprisingly, I felt as comfortable with them as I did on my own. It was just more about needing time to reset with no one else's emotions filling my space. "I am not some women. I am a barely reformed—or dare I say recovering—hermit. I need my me time. Space to be weird and talk to myself and dance in my underwear."

"When have you ever danced in your underwear?"

"Semantics, Keeks. God."

"You keep using that word. I don't think it means what you think it means."

"Don't you dare quote *The Princess Bride* to me."

"I—Helloooo, handsome," Kiki said, her retort cut off before it had legs as Taylor came into the frame behind me. "There's another one?"

"He's not mine."

"Can I have him?"

Taylor arched a brow before reaching out and ending our call. "No phones in the hallway, Miss Moore."

"Since when has that been a rule, T. Swift?" I asked, tucking the phone into my pocket.

He rolled his eyes, although I couldn't tell if it was because of my question or his nickname. "Since you nearly walked into three people while you were talking and didn't even register it."

I glanced around the empty corridor. "I did?"

He pointed at some priceless heirloom. "You almost took out that bust too."

I grimaced. He wasn't wrong. Two more steps, and it would have been bye-bye, Mr. Darcy. Or whoever the fuck it was.

"Where are you off to?"

Why did he care? "My room."

"Everyone's in the rec room. That's where you should be too."

I laughed. "Are you sure that's wise? Do you remember yesterday? The full-on, actual orgy. I doubt they've even finished cleaning it all up." I shuddered thinking of the amount of fluids something like that left behind.

"That's exactly why you should be there." He took hold of my shoulders and turned me around. I hated that he was touching me. So would Tor. And Kai. And Cain. Oh fuck, Caspian wouldn't like it either. Any moment, I expected Tor to show up and give Swiftie a stern, 'I'll thank you to get your hands off my wife.' Or maybe just an animalistic tackle.

He was really taking his life into his hands with this casual maneuvering. Did he have no sense of self-preservation?

Just to be safe—I didn't want to find pieces of him in a box tomorrow—I took a small step to the side, forcing him to drop his hands.

"Your logic is flawed."

"How so?"

"You say the orgy is the reason I need to go back to the scene of the crime. I say otherwise. One of us is right. The other is you."

"Right or wrong, your presence is required. Didn't you get the summons?"

Oh, I hated him and his confident smile. "I've been busy. No summons."

"Come on, I'll escort you." With no room for argument in his tone, he headed toward the rec room. "Trust me, you'd much rather I bring you there than Joffrey."

"Oh, I dunno. There's something special about that little spring loaded Troll doll."

Swiftie raised a brow. "I wouldn't let him hear you call him that."

"But you risk life and limb by touching me? Your priorities are seriously out of whack, buddy."

"What are you talking about?"

I had to blink at him. How could he not know about Tor? Everyone knew about Tor.

"You ever heard about the Beast of Novasgard?"

He nodded, his palm resting on my shoulder once more.

"He's my man."

Taylor blanched and dropped his hand.

"Maybe there's hope for you after all," I muttered. "Lead the way, Swiftie. Just a word of warning: I won't need a cat-eye sharp enough to kill you if Tor sees you touching me. Save yourself."

We walked the entire way to the rec room with Taylor holding his hands up like I had a gun pressed between his shoulders. And I laughed to myself the entire time. Tor would be so proud.

CHAPTER TEN

DAHLIA

"I've never been summoned to the rec room before. Are we having a party?"

"Something like that," Swiftie murmured, pushing the door open for me.

I expected to find the usual suspects, Sorcha scowling at someone and Oz reading a book or poking fun at her. Maybe the shifters would be doing their woodland landscape puzzles or Caspian and Cain would be playing cards. No. It was a whole ass assembly with chairs and an aisle and everything.

"What the fuck is this? An intervention?" I squeaked, suddenly afraid he was going to pull me up on the makeshift stage beside Joffrey, who was currently standing on top of a stool. "Please tell me this is a talent show or there's a comedian? Maybe a magician. Oh, I know, it's like when Johnny Cash used to visit the prison. Are we getting a performance from The Apocalyptic Unicorns?"

"Sit down, Miss Moore. Do stop your rambling," Joffrey snapped.

Before I could slink to the back of the crowd, where I found all four of my men standing, Sorcha's cool fingers wrapped around my wrist, and she tugged me hard. I sat in the plastic chair between her and Oz.

"Saved you a seat," the vampire murmured.

"Uh, thanks?"

She smirked, and I swore I heard three different sets of growls behind me.

"Now that we're all here," Joffrey intoned, his voice as bored and put upon as ever, "let's get down to business."

Did I hum the song from Mulan in my head? Yes, of course I did. But I quickly pushed that earworm out of my mind and leaned close to Sorcha, murmuring, "What exactly is the business?"

"Sex, darling. He wants to talk about the sex."

"But I didn't have the sex." She leveled me with a look, and my cheeks burned. Well, not in the rec room, anyway.

"Didn't you?"

Oz laughed as Joffrey shot Sorcha and me a glare.

As usual, Sorcha lost her patience with me immediately. "The orgy, you dingus. He wants to talk about Merri's accidental orgy."

"I figured. I just don't know why I have to be here."

"Are the two of you quite finished whispering to each other?" Joffrey droned, looking impressively buff as he crossed his arms over his barrel chest. With the exception of his red hair, he looked like a tiny Popeye. All bulging biceps and forearms. All he needed was a corncob pipe and maybe an anchor tattoo.

"Yes, troll daddy," Sorcha said sweetly.

"I am not a troll. I am a—you know what, never mind." Joffrey rolled his eyes.

"Such a tease."

He glared again. He was really a champion glare-er. "Whilst Merri is here, it is of the highest import that you all keep your wits about you. She has broken no rules and cannot, therefore, remain locked in No Man's Land."

"Broken no rules? She used her power on us without our consent," an angry wolf shifter snarled.

"That may be the case, but she's not fully in control. It wasn't done intentionally. She will do the work on her end, but you all need to take precautions. We're lucky no one was killed."

"What were we going to do? Fuck to the death?" Cas called out, a smirk in his voice.

Joffrey's face went stonier than it usually was. "Yes, Caspian. That's exactly what could have happened. Why do you think she's here?"

I wondered what she did. Did she fuck someone's soul out of their body? She was drop-dead gorgeous; maybe that was something I needed to take literally?

"Did, uh, everyone make it out okay yesterday?" I asked, realizing I didn't really know what happened after Cain and I left.

As if he knew I was thinking about him, Cain's shadow touch trailed along my ankle, then up my calf, making me squirm. Surely he'd stop there, right? Nope. That phantom caress continued all the way up my leggings until he was touching my inner thigh. I sucked in a gasp, and Sorcha turned her attention to me.

"What the blazes are you doing over there?"

"Nothing," I squeaked. Instead of a growl, this time I was certain I heard a snicker.

"No one was harmed," Joffrey said, oblivious to my plight. "But a few lines were crossed, and two alpha wolves were sent into rut. They've been isolated until it . . . works itself out."

"Knotty," Oz said under his breath, laughing at his terrible pun. "Get it? Cause alphas have knots?"

"So do dragons," I muttered.

"Oh really? We're going to talk about that later."

"No we aren't."

A bone-deep shiver worked its way through me as Joffrey continued his lecture. I couldn't make sense of what he was saying as Cain's touch crept closer to the apex of my thighs. God, this was really hot. So why was I shivering?

"In conclusion," Joffrey said, his breath visible in the freezing room, "we won't be allowing anyone within—"

The lights flickered out, casting us in complete and utter darkness. In that moment, I knew exactly what was happening. The oppressive hum of furious energy, the weight of malevolence coating me like a deadly shroud. She was here.

Several shrill screams filled the air, followed by a couple of angry growls. Almost on cue, familiar hands shackled my shoulders.

"Tor," I breathed, recognizing him by touch alone.

"Nobody move!" Joffrey shouted, shocking me with his rare display of emotion. Even he was frightened.

The darkness was unnatural. Not even my own hand was visible when I waved it in front of my face. The only senses I had to help me were touch and hearing. It was disorienting, to say the least, and I wasn't the only one struggling. Noises from around the room ranged from hushed conversations to people clearly not listening to Joffrey as they stumbled into each other and ran into chairs.

"I've got you, Kærasta." Tor held me in place.

"I can't see shit," Oz said, panic lacing his voice.

"Neither can I, and I'm a vampire," Sorcha said. "This must be some kind of spell."

"So this isn't part of the presentation, then?" I asked.

"What gave it away?" Sorcha deadpanned.

Tor snarled at her. "Keep talking to my mate like that, and I'll rip out your tongue."

"Yeah, yeah. Blah, blah, bloody blah. Scarier men than you have threatened me with death and dismemberment. Take a freaking number, beast-boy."

Having Tor's hands on me helped with the uneasy feeling prickling across my skin.

"It's your ghost, baby doll," Cain whispered, his lips brushing my ear from behind.

"Yeah, I got that."

"We need to get everyone out. She's spitting mad."

"And how do you suggest we do that in the dark?"

"Carefully."

"Look who went and got a sense of humor along with those memories," I snapped.

The shadow on my leg tightened as though in warning. Right. We weren't supposed to talk about that. Oopsie daisy.

My head throbbed as the pressure from the spirit increased, her anger and the knowledge she could be anywhere in the room making my heart race. Cain and I were the only ones who could see her either way, but I had a sneaking suspicion she could hurt more than just me.

"I need to know where she is," I said.

Without another word, Cain snapped his fingers, and a blue flame illuminated the space around us. I wish he hadn't. A scream tore from my throat as a ghostly face appeared a hairsbreadth in front of my eyes. The details were muddied, but she was more human-looking than she'd ever been with sunken eyes—two burning black pits filled with hatred—a gaping maw of a mouth, and the suggestion of a nose.

I didn't think so much as react. I didn't want this thing anywhere near me, and I sure as shit didn't want it to touch me. Just like before, I had the inescapable sense that if she got her hands on me, I wouldn't make it out alive. On instinct, I lifted my hand to shield myself, but this time it was she who backed away. Except she didn't get very far. I had her in my metaphorical hold, her energy running down my arm, the sensation like needles under my skin.

"Good girl, baby doll. Keep her there," Cain crooned in my ear.

"I can't. It hurts."

"If you can hold her still for us, we can try to get the others out," Tor said.

"I . . . there's no way," I said, shaking my head. Every second I held the malevolent soul in place felt like an eternity. Her energy battered me, zinging through my body like a thousand volts of electricity.

"Hold on a little longer. I'll banish her like last time, but I'll have to extinguish the light."

If I couldn't see her, there was no way I'd be able to keep hold of her. The ghost screamed, her rage flooding me and bringing tears to my eyes as agony rippled across my arm.

"No!" I shouted, flinching and losing my hold. It was the sneeze all over again, but worse because the stakes were so much higher. I had no business playing around with power I didn't understand. Masterson's lesson was finally sinking in. I needed to practice so the next time something like this happened, I wouldn't accidentally possess another inanimate object.

Instantly, the lights came on, and the temperature in the room returned to normal. I could breathe again.

"She's gone," I said through harsh pants.

"Are you sure?" Tor asked.

"I can't sense her," Cain agreed. "You did good, baby doll."

Kai and Cas rushed over to our little group.

"Dahlia," Kai breathed, ashen. "Are you all right?"

"Yes?"

Cas hip-checked the others out of the way—a bold move if ever I saw one—but all I felt was relief as he slung his arms around my neck. "Don't scare me like that, darling."

I patted his back, unsure what else to do, but when he pulled away and looked into my eyes, I saw real fear there. "I'm okay."

"Good. That's good," he grumbled, clearing his throat and straightening as he put on his dashing captain facade.

"I'd feel a lot better if we got her out of here," Kai said, taking my hand.

"Agreed," Tor said, his hands reaching for my hips. Before he could grasp me and bodily remove me from the room, which I was sure was what he was intending to do, Cas's face twitched in confusion.

"What the bleeding hell is wrong with him?" he asked, looking at someone over my shoulder.

There was barely time for more than a glance as screams erupted throughout the room again, and a vacant-eyed man lurched toward me.

CHAPTER ELEVEN

KAI

I didn't sign up for fucking zombies.

I could deal with nearly anything thrown at me. Vampires? I'd turn them to dust. Berserkers? We'd fight to the death. Shifters? Don't threaten me with a good time. But zombies? That was my hard line in the sand.

Why? Because they were impervious to basically everything but fire, and I couldn't afford to play with my fire. Not here in a room filled with creatures, with my mate so near. If my dragon got control, he'd burn this place to the ground, and we'd be lucky to get Dahlia out in one piece.

He was oddly silent in my mind, but I could feel him hovering. He wasn't taunting me with his presence so much as waiting. It was an odd shift between us. I was so used to him forcing the issue. Maybe Dahlia had cracked the code when she suggested we work as a team.

"Get behind me, beauty." Tor's booming voice ricocheted off the walls as he shoved her behind him.

Together we created a wall between our mate and the shambling creature. The problem with zombies wasn't that they were mindless ghouls intent on eating brains. No, they were rage-filled mindless ghouls, stronger than they should be, *and* they were intent on eating brains, not to mention any other part of you they could get to.

"Wait, this is my fault. Get out of my way. I need to pull the spirit out."

"Never gonna happen, love. Let those two be your meat shields," Caspian said from behind us.

It might be the first sane thing I'd ever heard him say.

"We are born protectors, lass. It's our privilege as your mates to keep you safe."

"You are not fighting my battles for me," Dahlia argued.

"The hell we're not," Tor grunted.

When I glanced his way, he was fucking grinning. A little shudder of self-preservation rolled down my spine. I dinnae fear the Berserker, but I recognized a threat when I saw one.

"Please, you have to let me try. Don't kill him. This isn't his fault," Dahlia protested, her hands shoving at me because she likely knew moving Tor would be akin to attempting to move a marble statue.

"It's no use, baby doll. He's already gone." Cain said, and I wondered how he knew.

My eyes shifted to my mate, her expression ravaged by guilt. She was focusing hard on the creature making his way toward us, her teeth gnawing on her bottom lip. I caught the second she realized Cain's words were true. It was like the guttering of a candle.

"I killed him," she whispered.

"It's not your fault," Cain said, shifting so he could place a hand on her shoulder.

"What's the plan here, folks?" I asked, my attention bouncing between the monster and the conversation taking place behind me.

"Kill him," Tor said.

"Technically, he's already dead," Caspian pointed out.

"How is that helpful?" I snapped.

"I was just proving that I was listening to my sweet girl."

Cain and I both glared at him.

"Neutralize the ghost." Dahlia's voice was a soft wobble.

The snapping, snarling zombie was closing in, and no one was doing a damned thing about it. At Joffrey and Swift's urging, the rest of the residents had already fled. It wasn't the nature of most supernaturals to be selfless, so they did so without hesitation. Only Sorcha and Oz had shown any hesitation when they realized the zombie was coming for Dahlia, but even their friendship with her hadn't been enough to keep them here.

Not that they were needed. Tor and I were more than capable enough to handle a single creature on our own.

I quickly thought through possible moves. Anything that would help me slow him down so Tor could rip his head from his body. Short of fire, it was the only way to ensure he was well and truly neutralized.

I could bash his brains in with a chair leg. Perhaps break apart the coffee table in the corner and shove the wood through his eye until I destroyed his brain stem? But if he bit any of us, we'd become infected.

"So, we kill him then?" I asked. "Lass?"

Dahlia took a few steps back, along with Tor, as the creature continued toward us. My urgency mounted until I could no longer keep it from my voice.

"Gem? I'd much rather ye tell me it's okay, but I willnae hesitate to kill him if he tries to harm you."

The walking corpse was now close enough I could see the pinprick of its pupils through milky white eyes.

"Freya's tits, this is ridiculous," Tor snarled, shoving past me and making a beeline for the zombie.

It happened so fast that Dahlia's protest hadn't finished echoing off the walls before the man's head was nothing more than bloody pulp between Tor's hands.

"Well, that's one way to do it," Caspian drawled.

"I suppose you think you could have done better?" Tor asked, entirely unfazed as he let the pulpy mass drop to the floor with a distinctive splatter. He didn't bother to wipe his hands clean as he leveled the pirate with the full force of his battle-crazed stare.

"Uh . . . um . . . n-no, I wasn't implying that at all, mate. Brilliant work. Stellar. Never seen better."

Tor smirked before closing the distance between himself and the pirate. The smaller man backed up until he hit a table and couldn't go farther. Then Tor took his time as he wiped both his hands clean on Hook's billowy shirt.

"Good."

Even my dragon was impressed with the sheer size of the Berserker's balls.

Point made, he turned to Dahlia. "I'm not going to apologize for putting your safety and life above all others. If it comes to saving you or anyone else, it's you. Every time."

Dahlia was about to reply when her eyes widened to the size of saucers. "Shit. It's loose."

"What?" I asked, my gaze whipping around the room. I saw nothing out of the ordinary. Until she took a sharp breath. Cain had stepped up next to her, his fingers linked with hers as they both stared at an empty space in front of them.

While the rest of us watched, the air seemed to shimmer before darkening into something ominous and sinister. Nothing in my life prepared me for the malevolence of the spirit that was now visible to all of us. I'd seen evil many times, usually in the eyes of desperate men or women, but this was something else. Something perverted and twisted. A complete lack of anything good or pure. Without knowing why, the word rotten floated through my mind.

"I've never seen one that looked like this before," Caspian murmured.

Dahlia's head snapped in his direction. "You can see her?"

"Dahlia, ah damn it," Cain growled as the spirit surged forward, claws outstretched and aimed right at my mate's throat.

Fear unlike anything I'd known slammed into me. I could protect my woman from damn near anything, but a vengeful spirit? What good were claws and brawn against an intangible foe?

"Those aren't yer only weapons. Let me free."

I hesitated, my dragon's voice burning through me. *"Release me!"*

In the time I spent considering the roared plea, Cain took matters into his own hands. Blue flames burst to life, the unearthly fire licking halfway up his arms. And they didn't stop there. This time the same flames danced in his hair, not burning so much as enveloping and sending strands flying out in every direction.

"Get back," he shouted, sparing us a brief glance that lasted only long enough for me to note his eyes burned with the same blue fire.

The spirit screamed, the sound so loud my ears rang, but compared to Dahlia's banshee wail, it was but a whimper. In the blink of an eye, she was gone, leaving nothing more than a cold spot in her wake. The resulting silence was so loud it was damn near painful.

Dahlia slumped forward, her skin covered in goosebumps as she shivered violently.

With the threat neutralized for now, the only thing left to do was comfort my mate.

Caspian was of a similar mind, and I couldn't help but smirk when I was faster, my arms snaking around Dahlia's hips and pulling her back into my heat. I hated knowing she was in discomfort. If there was anything I could do to ease her, I'd do it. Fuck, I'd give her the very heart from my chest if she required it of me.

"Are you okay, gem?" I murmured into her hair.

"I . . . don't even know what just happened. I'm pretty sure I fucked up. Again."

If anyone else was listening to our conversation, they didn't give any indication of it. Instead, Tor's low, rumbled question had all of us turning to look at him.

"How did you break free?"

Dahlia stiffened in my arms. "Wh-what?"

"Not you, Kærasta. Him." He pointed a bloodstained finger at Cain. "When did you escape the underworld, Hades?"

There was no change in his expression as Cain's eyes met each of ours. "Well, guess the cat's out of the bag."

CHAPTER TWELVE

TOR

The god of the underworld, well-known mischief maker and soul stealer, Hades, had been here all along, plotting. Was he responsible for the spirits tormenting my mate? Was he going to steal her soul next?

Hades held my stare for several heartbeats, and it didn't take a genius to figure out he was stalling.

"The truth, Hades."

Hades rolled his eyes. "You really think you did something there, don't you?"

I crossed my arms, not about to let him off the hook. "Was it all a lie? Have you been pulling the wool over our eyes all this time?"

The cocky bastard laughed. "I'm not that good an actor."

"You're a god. Of course you're a skilled liar. It's basically the number one requirement when gods play in the mortal world."

He spread his hands out on either side of his body. "What do you want me to say, boy?"

There was no hiding the fury that ripped through me at his disrespect. I may only be a demigod, but I was still a Berserker. "I am no boy, and you will not address me that way again, or you will never say another word at all."

Hook shifted from foot to foot in my periphery, muttering something that sounded like, "Careful, mate, he'll burn your soul to cinders."

Kai remained silent, but his eyes were watchful as Dahlia broke free of his hold. She moved until she was sandwiched between Hades and me and then placed one hand on each of our chests. Her concerned expression faltered and turned to something resembling wonder. Tentatively she dug her fingers into my pec, murmuring to herself, "I wrote a scene that started this way once."

"Quite a few, if memory serves," Kai finally said.

She blushed but ignored him, seeming to remember what she'd been intending to say when she came between us. "You two need to stop this. We're a team, like it or not. All five of us. Something brought us together—"

"The Fates, baby doll. They're fucking with me."

"Is that how you ended up here?" Caspian asked. "The Fates?"

Some of Hades's bravado faded. "I'm not sure. Something . . . someone, stole my memories and sent me here."

"But you remember who you are now, obviously," Hook pressed.

Hades's lips curled up in a smug smile I was desperate to knock off his face. "Dahlia brought them back. Didn't you, baby doll?"

"Can you please stop rubbing it in? We all get it. She fucked your memories back into your thick skull. Congratulations."

"Well, you asked for it, pirate. Don't ask the question if you don't want the answer."

Hook frowned. "It wasn't technically a question. More like an observation, really."

"If your memories are returned, shouldn't you know who was behind stealing them?" Kai asked.

It was the same question I'd intended to ask, so I simply lifted a brow, waiting for the god's answer.

"Wouldn't that be nice? But no. I must've been unconscious when they were stolen."

"Well, what's the last thing you remember?" Dahlia asked.

I guess sharing what he remembered hadn't been part of their pillow talk. A little growl built up in my chest at the thought of them sharing intimate moments until I remembered that I fucked my mate so good she could never stay awake long enough to get to the pillow talk.

"All right, this seems like a very important sharing moment. Shall we get some chairs and make this into a real group session?" Cas tossed a glance at the remains on the floor. "Or can we at least get away from *that?"* He flinched, and his gaze darted to the corners of the room. Apparently the ghost had frightened him more than he was willing to admit.

At first no one seemed inclined to move, but then Dahlia gave one of the folding chairs a longing glance. Almost as one, the four of us burst into motion, Kai taking a chair in each hand, the rest of us selecting one for ourselves and setting them in a loose circle. I realized exactly what the sneaky bastard was up to when he sat down in one and patted the seat for Dahlia to sit beside him.

With a low growl, I kicked out, knocking the chair over.

"Tor!"

Ignoring her protest, I snatched her up and sat in my chair, plonking her down in my lap. "Your seat's right here, Kærasta."

"Fucking smooth bastard," Cas said, his voice holding admiration as he straddled the back of his selected chair.

Hades rolled his eyes as he sank into his own seat.

"Now let's discuss how we're going to make this work for all of us," Cas began, gaze searching the four of us.

"No. I want to get to the bottom of Cain's missing memories." Dahlia squirmed in my hold, but I tightened my arms around her rather than letting her leave me.

"There's not much to tell. I was trying to get to you at the hospital in LA. A pissy little nurse called security on me, and she stuck me with a sedative while they distracted me. Oh, and Temperance was involved, though he didn't exactly get his hands dirty."

"Temperance? As in *Doctor* Temperance?" Dahlia squeaked.

"Do you know of another one?"

"Well, no, but why are you just mentioning this now? That seems like a pretty big detail."

Hades shrugged. "I don't know what his involvement in all of this is outside of the fact that he was your doctor and is likely the reason I got sent here when I lashed out with my powers."

"And you don't think that's significant?" Kai questioned.

"I think everything is significant, but I don't know what any of it means."

Gods, this was frustrating. "Why were you stalking Dahlia, Hades? Maybe Temperance was trying to get her away from you?"

"Then why would he send me here too? That doesn't track, Viking."

No. I don't suppose it did.

Caspian saved me from answering. "So are you really Hades? As in *the* god of the underworld."

"One of," I snapped.

Cas frowned at me. "What do you mean 'one of'? He's the only one you hear about. Well, him and that other one . . . Lucifer."

"Ignorant cur," I snarled. "Hel is every bit as powerful as her counterparts."

The pirate held his hands up. "Fine. Fine. No need to get all snippy. I was just wondering where the southern accent came from."

Hades sighed and ran a hand through his hair as though he got this question all the time. "The South got the accent from me, Captain."

"I beg your pardon? Aren't you Greek?"

He chuckled. "I've been around for eons. Immortalized in stone by the Greeks. That doesn't make me Greek."

Caspian shot us wary looks and whispered, "They're literally called *The Greek gods.*"

Hades leveled him with an exasperated glare. "And you're Captain Fucking Hook. What's your point?"

Cas glanced between me and Kai. "I thought it quite obvious, but fine, I'll spell it out for you. You sound like Foghorn Leghorn."

Realizing this was going to carry on until one of them killed the other, or more likely until I killed one of them, I heaved a sigh. "The gods have always existed, Caspian. Civilizations claimed the ones they interacted with as their own, some giving different names to the same deities. It doesn't make the gods an exclusive part of that civilization."

"It's like rocket and arugula," Dahlia offered.

"Beg pardon?" Caspian asked.

"You know. Eggplants and aubergines. Different names for the same thing."

"Yes, but Lucifer and Hades are two separate individuals."

"Because they claim different realms but contain similar powers. Just like Dahlia and Cain," I pointed out.

Now everyone's attention was on me.

"What do you mean, like Dahlia and Cain?" Dahlia asked, using a parody of my voice.

I pinched her thigh. "Behave, brat."

"We are two sides of the same coin, baby doll. Your power compliments mine. Because you were made for me." Hades said the words with such confidence even I had to believe him.

"We're still working on the banshee theory?" Kai asked.

Hades shook his head. "Dahlia's powers far surpass that of a simple banshee. She doesn't follow any of the rules of their kind. Yes, she has their scream, but that's in addition to her ability to see, touch, and manifest actual souls."

"Masterson said the side effects of my scream were caused by my telepathy. Just call me Dark Phoenix," she added in a grumpy mutter. When it became obvious none of us understood the reference, she rolled her eyes and changed the subject. "Manifest, is that what we did earlier?"

He nodded. "Your ability to interact with souls is far more in line with my ability to control and punish them."

Caspian squirmed in his seat.

Dahlia focused her attention on Hades. "So what am I, then, Mr. Know It All?"

"Mine," all of us answered as one.

Her round arse wiggled in my lap, and I had to bite back a groan at the friction. "Careful, Kærasta. I'm not ashamed to take you right here in front of all of them."

"Don't threaten me with a good time."

Caspian stood so fast his chair fell over. "I've been preparing my whole life for this moment. Tor, you stay there. Dahlia, get naked. Cain, wait, Hades. Fuck, what are we supposed to call you now?"

"Cain," the god of the underworld said as he got to his feet and began unbuttoning his shirt. "Until we know who's behind this and why, I'd rather keep the rest between us. And if you think you're directing this, you couldn't be more wrong. Go stand in the corner and take notes. Something tells me you need to learn a thing or two."

"Oh, get fucked, mate," Caspian said, throwing his fingers up in a reverse peace sign to emphasize the message. "The hell I'm sitting this one out. Team building, that's what it's called, right? I can't think of a better way for the five of us to bond. What do you say, darling, would you like to see the Eiffel Tower?"

"What the hell is he going on about?" Kai asked.

"It's a sex position," Dahlia murmured. "The girl is bent between two guys, and they, uh, high five, and it resembles—"

"Say no more, gem. This time I'm taking you from behind. Tor, you can fuck her face."

"There is no realm in existence where I will be high-fiving anyone during sex. Least of all one of you miserable clingers-on."

"Not even me?" Dahlia asked, smirking. "What if I do a *really* good job?"

I tried and failed to fight my smile. "I'll make every exception for you, beauty."

Dipping my head, I kissed her neck, loving the way she melted into me. Her sigh of pleasure went straight to my cock. So we were doing this, then.

"This has been a very strange day," she whispered on a moan as the other three approached.

"But you like strange, love. Admit it," Cas said.

"I—God, I—" she began, but the godsdamned door opened, and that infernal troll Joffrey cleared his throat.

"Oh, so you're not dead. Very good. Congratulations. Now leave. This room needs to be sanitized and saged. Recreational time is over."

"Motherfucking son of a whore," Caspian groaned. "Will my dreams never come true?"

"Yours and mine both," Dahlia laughed softly. "Better luck next time, Cas."

"Oh, my girl is a cruel mistress."

"Did you lot not hear me? Get out. Rec room is closed for . . . ugh . . . cleaning." Joffrey stalked across the room and began slamming chair after chair atop one another.

"To be continued?" Dahlia asked us.

"Yes, beauty. Absolutely."

CHAPTER THIRTEEN

HOOK

Ticktock Ticktock Ticktock

"Find the bloody clock," I whispered as I stumbled down the hallway, opening door after door in search of the source of that never-ending noise.

Spotting a bookcase, I tore into the room and began flinging books off the shelves, tossing them behind me in my hunt for that infernal ticking. It had to be here. They'd hidden the fucking clock in the books. Of course they had. Tricky, tricky doctors and their tests.

"No, no, no," I muttered, desperation making me clumsy as I came to the final shelf.

"The key is lost."

"You will never return home."

"You failed."

Ticktock

Ticktock

Ticktock

I pounded my forehead against the wood shelf in time with the incessant ticking. The dull ache between my eyes distracted me, but only just. Heaving a sigh, I returned to ripping books from the final shelf and desperately rummaging like a feral raccoon. Reaching the final book, I let out a savage cry before chucking it behind me with the others.

"Oi, pirate!" A booming voice pulled me from my crouched position.

I stood, straightening my shirt sleeves in an attempt to hide my rapidly advancing madness. "Kit, I don't recall inviting you on my little scavenger hunt."

"Is that what this is?" he asked, lifting a brow as he scanned me from head to toe. "You look bloody awful, Hook. Been on a week-long bender?"

I waved a hand at him. "Come on then, we're searching for the tickety-tock. Tickety-tock, tickety-tock, let us find the missing clock."

Kit blinked at me, his amusement obvious. "Have you been hiding the good drugs, Caspian? Naughty, naughty. Sharing is caring. Especially amongst friends."

"No drugs. No. Not for me. Not since the tick, tick, ticking started. And the voices. They're everywhere. Can't you hear it all? They keep pushing, pushing, pushing. Trying to drive me mad, they are. Bloody pixies. So fast I can't even see 'em." My eyes darted around the room, checking to make sure they were still invisible to me.

"Trying? Mate, I'd say they've succeeded. You're madder than a hatter."

"Tell me where you hid the clock, demon!" I snarled, rushing him and grabbing the man by his collar.

He shoved me back until I slammed into the now empty bookcase. My head bashed against the edge of the wood, bringing with it a small starburst of pain and a sweet flicker of clarity.

"Dahlia."

"She's the cure."

"Go to her."

Kit smoothed down his shirt, his voice thick with anger. "Never lay hands on me again. I won't give you another warning."

But I wasn't paying any attention. I was already consumed by my need to get to my Wendy-bird. Since my attack in the woods, there was no true reprieve from the voices, but at least the ticking seemed to be muted when I was in her presence.

Shaking my head in a vain attempt to keep my wits about me, I lurched out of the room and through the halls of Blackwood, every step harder than the last as my focus waned. Fuck, I was losing my grip on reality so bloody quickly these days. Even now, as I glanced out a window I knew didn't exist, my brain struggled to accept that the view beyond the glass wasn't real. Had there been an actual window, I would be seeing misty treetops and endless expanses of green and gray. Instead I saw gulls flying across the horizon and the never-ending roll of the sea.

Ticktock

Ticktock

Ticktock

The staccato sound echoed in my skull, this time loud enough to send spikes through my brain. A sweat broke out across my forehead, nausea curled in my gut, and I thought I might be sick before I made it to her.

Gritting my teeth, I focused hard on my goal, muttering a panicked and nearly unintelligible chant under my breath. "Have to . . . must keep . . . Dahlia . . ."

Hand shaking as I reached her room, I went for the doorknob, praying my girl had left me easy access to her. Usually that wouldn't matter; I have yet to meet a lock I couldn't master, but given the state I was in, I couldn't be certain of my skills.

My eyes swam as neon lights bloomed before me. I would have sworn they were accompanied by childlike laughter.

"Away, you buggers," I cried, swatting at the Neverflies as I pushed open the door and tumbled inside.

I was quick to shut it behind me, pressing my trembling form against the wood as if I'd been on the wrong end of a wild pursuit.

Dahlia rolled over in her sleep, a soft moan escaping her, which I took as her welcoming me. Approaching the bed, I let out a little hiss of disappointment to see that she was not alone. Kai had apparently drawn the lucky straw tonight. His bulky form curled possessively around her, cradling her against him.

A better man would have left them to it, but I had never been a good man—though I was fast becoming a desperate one.

"Let me in, Wendy-bird. Please?" I whispered, stripping until I didn't have a stitch of clothing on.

Her body was barely covered by the sheet, all that glorious flesh calling out to me as she curled herself around her dragon. It didn't make me jealous, knowing Kai'd obviously been inside her tonight. All I wanted now was her skin touching mine. She was my safe harbor, a place I could finally know peace. Already my proximity to her had eased the chaos of my mind. The whispers were gone, along with the tick, tick, ticking. At least for now.

I must have been standing there for a while just staring at her, because I hadn't noticed Kai open his eyes.

"Well? Are you just going to stand there, or are you getting in?"

His eyes were luminous in the darkness, lit from within by some inner fire.

For a second, I wondered if that meant his dragon was close to the surface.

When I didn't move or speak, an annoyed growl slipped from him.

"Ticktock, pirate. Get in the bed, or get the fuck out."

A shudder racked my frame, his casual echo of the sound that tormented me so sending me diving under the covers. The instant my skin made contact with Dahlia's, it was as if a blanket of soothing warmth wrapped itself around my soul. Blessed silence replaced the wild, frenetic energy in my mind.

Something more akin to a whimper than a sigh escaped me as my eyes fluttered closed.

Safe.

I was safe.

For now.

CHAPTER

FOURTEEN

DAHLIA

I was warm. Deliciously so, in fact, and the scents of woodsmoke and the sea curled around me, cocooning me in the blanket of sleep. My eyelids were heavy, limbs languid. I didn't want to leave this peaceful in-between place.

Caspian's roughened voice filtered into my awareness, a soft melody that tickled my ears. "Way ay, blow the man down," he sang, his lips feathering over the spot on my neck he knew instantly got me wet.

My lips twitched with laughter, but still, my eyes remained closed.

"Well, aren't you a pretty sight to wake up to, gem?"

Kai's sleep-roughened brogue sent a jolt of awareness through me. As did the hand lazily moving over my belly. I couldn't tell if he was heading up toward my breast or down between my legs, and that, more than anything, woke me the rest of the way up.

Blinking a few times to clear my eyes, I attempted to shift my position, but Caspian, who was wrapped around me like an octopus, clung to me more tightly, locking me in place.

"Where do you think you're going, love?" His palm found my breast as he nuzzled into my neck. "It's early yet, and I was having the best dream."

"Did it involve a ship, by chance?"

He lifted his head a little to peer down at me, his eyes the endless blue of a summer's ocean. "How'd you know?"

"You sing in your sleep, Captain."

Rocking his hips forward, he offered me a low hum of approval. "Mmm, call me that again."

Kai was apparently done being ignored, because he reached for my chin and tipped my face in the other direction, where his lips were waiting for me. Without a word, he plundered my mouth with a thoroughness that would surely make my pirate proud. Or, more likely, jealous.

God, I could live here like this. Kai's mouth on mine, Cas's hands roaming my bare skin. If only my other two men were here. My little bathtub fantasy didn't seem as out of reach as it once did. With the way things had progressed in the last couple of weeks, who knew? Maybe I would wake up in a sexy cuddle puddle. And, I mean, technically I was. It was just smaller by two people.

"She's doing that thing again, with her eyebrows," Cas said, lips trailing down my body until he reached a nipple.

"What thing?" Kai asked.

"That furrow. She's thinking." He bit my nipple and made me arch my back up into him. "She needs to be feeling."

"Good luck turning this bad boy off," I muttered, tapping my forehead to indicate my brain. "Once it gets going, it doesn't stop."

"Oh, I do love a challenge," Cas murmured, a smile evident in his voice. "Shall we see which one of us gets her brain to melt first?"

I'd rather we ruin the sheets than melt my brain. I needed my brain for the writing. But apparently, I didn't have a say because Kai's fingers slipped between my thighs, and he was playing with my clit before I could so much as make a peep.

"Seems like we're off to a good start," Kai teased as he played me like a fiddle, drawing out little mewls of pleasure. "Mmm, gem, the sounds you make drive me wild."

"Aye," Cas growled in my ear, his lips and tongue traversing across my chest as he teased and nipped my breasts.

The contrast of his warm mouth and Kai's nimble fingers had me squirming in earnest. I went from zero to the brink of an orgasm in less than sixty seconds.

"Come on, darling. Fill the room with your cries. I've been desperate for you since the last time." Cas traveled farther down my body, his teeth grazing my hip even as Kai worked my pussy. Apparently, the two of them had no reservations about teamwork, because Cas looked up at him and said, "Fuck her with your fingers. I want to taste her clit."

Usually this is where Kai would get all growly, but my dragon seemed on board. Neither of them appeared to shy away from accidental touches either. Don't get me wrong, the focus was all on me, but they didn't seem at all distracted or put off by the presence of the other. And was it my imagination, or did Cas's tongue just brush against Kai's fingers?

"Fuck, gem, you're gushing."

"Spread her lips open for me, dragon," Cas murmured before Kai did as he was asked.

My God, the way Cas sucked my clit had me nearly bucking off the bed. I moaned and writhed, but Kai held me in place with his free hand as his fingers curled up inside me, hitting that spot—you know the one.

"Oh God," I moaned, fighting against the need to let my eyes close. The picture these two men painted as they worked together to get me off was too good to miss. I might have written well over a dozen of these kinds of scenes, but the reality was so much better than the fantasy. The ragged breaths. The moans of approval. The heat of their bodies pressing against me.

Fuck, I could feel Kai's hard cock pressed along my leg as he rocked his hips ever so slightly. I bet he didn't even know he was doing it. Somehow, that unconscious search for friction was the hottest thing he could've done.

Cas was no less affected. He was positioned a bit off to the side, his chest resting against the top of my thigh as he lavished my clit with attention. He had one hand braced on my other thigh, supporting his weight, while the other was between his legs, slowly working up and down his swollen length. Ever the diligent researcher, I took mental notes about the way he touched himself. How he used a far firmer grip than I'd have attempted, the slight twist he added on the downstroke, and how every now and then, he'd reach back and tug on his balls. A soft grunt accompanied the movement, sending little vibrations skittering over my sensitive skin.

If he wasn't so far away, I'd have taken over, but a big part of me loved being able to witness this firsthand. The sting of his teeth on my clit brought my focus back to what he was doing to me, what *they* were doing. I cried out again, and Kai grunted.

"She liked that. Fuck, she's soaking my fingers." He slipped them out, then sank deep again, the sound of my arousal so loud I would've been embarrassed had it not been so erotic.

Cas suckled my clit until I was trembling and clenching around Kai's digits, but when my dragon told him I was close, the prick stopped. He sat back, his lips twisted in a wicked grin, and looked directly at Kai.

"Jesus, Cas. I'm all for edging, but this is ridiculous," I whined.

Kai stopped too, pulling his fingers from my fluttering cunt and smirking as he brought them to his lips. Cas stopped him in a bold move, shackling his wrist and tugging my dragon's hand toward himself.

"Give me a taste."

I watched in rapt attention as the pirate sucked my arousal off

Kai's fingers. The little hitch in Kai's breath didn't go unnoticed by me either. Was I mistaken, or was there a flare of discovery in his eyes?

"Mmm, you taste like fucking ambrosia, love."

"Couldn't you taste me earlier?"

"Not like this." His gaze snapped to Kai, and he said, "Switch with me. I need to bury my face between these thick thighs right bloody now."

It took a second for my brain to catch up with his words. Kai didn't have nearly as much trouble. His fingers slid over my clit, pinching and teasing me while Cas got into position, spreading my legs as far apart on the bed as they'd go so he could comfortably settle himself between them.

Unwilling to go any longer without touching at least one of them, I wrapped my palm around Kai's jutting length, loving the hiss of pleasure that escaped him at the contact. It was surprising how both familiar and foreign his dick felt. I was intimately familiar with all the delicious ridges by now, but that swollen knot was still unexplored territory. Was it sensitive? Would it feel hard, like a muscle, or more pliable?

The moment I touched it, I had my answer.

"Good fucking goddess, lass. Careful with that," he gritted out.

Cas hummed a laugh as he filled me with his tongue.

I repeated my caress, wrapping my fingers around the base of his knot and giving it the same gentle tug I might give his balls.

Kai's pleasured groan was everything. If I could have, I would've giggled, but the way these two men were touching me allowed for only one option. A ragged moan.

Fuck, I was on the precipice of my orgasm, but never given the opportunity to fall over the cliff. They were going to edge me to the end times, weren't they?

Eh, worth it. Definitely the best way to go.

Start with a bang, go out with a bang, am I right?

But then my damn phone rang from where I'd left it charging on my desk.

"Leave it," Kai growled into my neck, rocking himself into my grip.

Cas pulled away, drawing a protesting moan from my lips. "No, don't."

"Wh-what?" I asked, my head foggy with lust.

"Answer it, love. Let's see if you can get through the chat without the caller picking up on what you're up to."

"I won't."

"You can. And I'll do you one better. If you make it through, I'll give you everything you've been dying for. If you don't . . . well, then I guess we'll just have to revisit this another time."

"Cas," I whined.

"Dahlia," he countered.

Meanwhile, my phone continued to ring.

"What do you say, darling? Are you up for a little game?"

I nodded, frantic eyes flicking to the phone. "Answer."

Kai reached for the device, his muscles flexing beautifully as he easily picked up the call and put it on speaker as he held it near my face.

"Took you long enough," Kiki sniped. "And why didn't you answer the video call?"

"I'm naked."

She giggled. "Ooh, kinky. Is anyone there with you?"

Cas smirked between my legs, lifting one glistening finger to his lips in a shushing motion before he dove back down and got to work. I bit down so hard on the inside of my cheek I damn near drew blood.

"No," I managed. Barely.

The slight hesitation before Kiki's soft, "Hmm," told me she wasn't buying what I was selling.

Kai's fingers drew slow circles around my swollen clit as he watched me, the mischief in his eyes setting me on fire. He liked this as much as Cas did. Cas, who curled his fingers just right and sent a flood of wetness rushing from me in response.

My little gasp was, unfortunately, not soft enough to escape Kiki's notice. "What the fuck are you doing over there, Dee?"

"Nothing, I just stubbed my toe."

"That was not an 'I just stubbed my toe' cry. That was a 'my world is being rocked' cry."

It took everything in me to keep my voice steady. "You're projecting, Keeks. You've convinced yourself I live in a never-ending orgy."

"Don't you? But seriously, though, The Neverending Orgy has a ring to it. Could be your next bestseller. Yeah, I can see it now, Falcor the Dick Dragon. Tor the Clit Biter. Cain can be that wolf thing. And your pirate . . . he's probably that weird turtle."

It was impossible not to laugh, but all that did was rock my whole body deeper into Cas's face.

This was up there with the wildest moments in my recovering hermit life. Mid-threesome, on the brink of climax, while brainstorming a Neverending Story erotic fanfic with my bestie. Who even was I? Was this real life?

"Come on, love," Cas whispered against my pussy. "Give me what I want."

"Dahlia Elizabeth, who the fuck was that? He sounded deliciously male and, if I'm not mistaken, very piratey."

"Someone in the hall."

"You lying little slutbag."

"What was that Keeks? The connection is terrible. I think I'm losing you." I proceeded to make a series of what were supposed to be static noises, much to Kai and Cas's amusement. The former laughed against my neck while Cas's laughter turned into mind-melting vibrations that had my toes curling into the sheets.

Kiki's tinny protests continued until Kai snatched the phone and threw it so hard it shattered on impact with the wall.

"Kai!" I protested, but then he and Cas went to town on my pussy, and I was beyond lucid speech.

The two of them joined forces like a couple of fucking Captain Planet extras, and they sure as hell became my heroes when they finally sent me over the edge. I think I blacked out; I wasn't sure, but whatever happened next, I knew I was going to have some explaining to do on my next call with Kiki.

Worth it.

CHAPTER FIFTEEN

HADES

Asshole's insistent panting had me gritting my teeth as I buttoned my cuffs. "For the love of me, will you please shut up."

"For the love of you? Wow, someone is feeling pretty big in his britches today. You don't have to wait for your person to let you out so you can take a shit."

When he put it that way . . .

"Don't you dare shit in my shoes," I warned, already knowing the threat was imminent when he started walking in circles.

"I'd be a lot more diligent about checking them for the foreseeable future. Also, I left a puddle on your bathroom floor since you were too busy jerking it to bother letting me outside."

"What the fuck, man? You couldn't use your words? You sure as hell don't seem to have a problem speaking up any other time."

Asshole let out an indignant huff. *"You're my human. You should pay more attention to my needs like I do yours."*

Well, shit. He was right, wasn't he? I'd been so focused on finding myself and my soulmate I hadn't taken the time to appreciate him.

"I'm sorry."

"What was that?" Asshole cocked his little head to the side and stared at me.

"You heard me. I'm sorry. I've been taking you for granted. You are a good dog, Asshole."

He was silent for a beat, and then his tail started to wag. *"Damn straight. And don't you forget it."*

Cerberus and I had been a team for longer than I could remember. I may not be able to call him anything other than Asshole now, because no matter the form, it was fitting as fuck, but he'd always looked out for me. I owed him the same level of loyalty.

"You want to help me sniff out a rat?"

"Can I take a shit first?"

I chuckled softly. "Sure, unless you want to find a pair of his slippers and use them instead."

"Oh man, you are feeling guilty, aren't you?"

"We're a team. We always have been. Now, let's go find some shoes for you to leave a present in."

He pranced in a circle, panting happily. *"Which one of the guys are we targeting? Please tell me it's the pirate."*

This time I let out a full-on belly laugh. "Not today. Though I wouldn't stop you if you wanted to seek him out on your own. Zeus knows he could serve to be taken down a peg or two."

"Who are we hunting then?" he asked, beating me to the door.

"Temperance," I answered, opening the door and finding a dark-haired Berserker with his fist in the air.

"Tor," Tor said, his expression confused.

Asshole cocked his ears. *"It's a good thing he's pretty."*

I had to bite back my laugh. "Not you."

"I'm confused."

"Obviously, beefcake." Asshole pawed at my leg, pulling my attention down to him. *"He must be dynamite in the sack. That's the only thing saving him."*

I shook my head, not particularly wanting to entertain that line of thought. "What are you doing here, Tor?"

"I came to finish the conversation we started the other day."

"I have lots of conversations. You'll have to be more specific."

A low snarl left the big Viking before he stared into my eyes. "I know who you are, what you're capable of, and plenty about your history. I don't trust you as far as your puppy could throw me."

"Huh, maybe he isn't as dumb as he looks. Still, if you want, I can lift my leg right here. He's basically built like a tree trunk anyway."

"Leave it," I bit out, causing Asshole to whimper.

"Fine, you're on your own, then. I don't want to hear you complaining about it later though," he called out as he zoomed past the two of us and down the hall.

"What's wrong with him?" Tor asked, tracking Asshole's speedy retreat.

"Small bladder."

"Ah. This is why we only have large dogs where I come from. They're far more useful and deadly when need be."

A dark chuckle escaped me at the thought of Cerberus not being deadly. "Don't let the fluffball fool you. He could tear your throat out before you even woke up."

"I'd like to see him try. Dahlia deserves an adorable fur muff. I just won't tell her where I got the fur."

Rage flooded my veins, sending blue sparks from my fingertips. "Say that again, beast. I dare you."

"You're the one picking fights. I was born to finish them."

"You're the one darkening my doorstep. I don't recall offering an invite, so perhaps you should kindly fuck off."

"I told you, I came to talk."

"Yeah, well, I have a prior engagement. So you can take your talk and shove it. I have nothing to say to you."

I pushed past him, which was fucking hard to do since he was the size of a semi-truck. Unfortunately for me, the demigod fell into step beside me.

"That's fine. I am perfectly capable of walking and talking simultaneously."

"I'll alert the media."

"What?"

"Never mind," I said with a beleaguered sigh. Asshole would have appreciated the joke.

"So, explain to me why the god Hades would be skulking around in search of Temperance? It seems odd and out of character for you."

"What do you mean?"

We continued down the hall until we reached the staircase. I'd genuinely been hoping he'd lose interest, maybe be waylaid by a shiny object of some kind, but no. He was still fucking here.

"I mean, you have a reputation for taking what you want, regardless of the consequences. Why wouldn't you have already absconded with her? What are you plotting?"

I spared him a quick glance, my brow raised in mocking tribute. "Are you really complaining that I didn't run off with your mate? I'll make sure to let Dahlia know."

He slammed a meaty palm against my chest, fisting my shirt and lifting me up on my toes. The indignity of it all had sparks flying from my fingers.

"I want to know what you're up to. I don't trust you. And if you threaten my mate again, I will do everything in my power to make your life a living hell."

"Is that the best threat you can come up with? I rule hell, you manchild. I have nothing to fear from the likes of it or you. Especially since you can't kill me."

Tor stiffened, lightning flickering in the obsidian depths of his eyes. "Perhaps not, but I can fucking try. And I don't have to kill you to make it hurt."

"It'll be so fun to let my *wife* nurse me back to health. Go ahead, pummel me. She'll fall so far in love with me she'll forget all about the rest of you and *choose* to come with me to the underworld."

This time Tor didn't take the bait. He laughed in my face. "First of all, she is not your wife. No vows have been exchanged between you in this life. Second, she is the other half of my soul. She could no more forget about me than she could stop breathing by choice. Fuck off with your threats, Hades."

"It's called holding your breath, Tor. Clearly you haven't made her come so hard she forgot to breathe, have you? Good to know."

Tor swelled in size, his breaths labored as his beast took hold of him.

I eyed the sharp ends of his horns and the pointed tips of his claws with a slight grimace. The demigod may not be able to kill me outright, but that didn't mean I wanted to be toyed with like a mouse either. He was still twice my size and strong as hell. I wasn't really in the mood to be in pain today. Even if my goddess would be there to care for me.

"Calm down, pal. Neither one of us is going to get anywhere with her if we're out here drawing blood."

"Speak for yourself," he snarled. "Violence is my love language."

"What the fuck do you know about love languages?"

Something in his face changed. "I . . . did a lot of reading last year. When I was working on myself."

"An introspective monster. How nice. Put me down, would you? You're wrinkling my shirt."

Tor released me without another word, and I fell to my feet with a teeth-clattering thud. It took everything in me not to crumple. Fucker was tall.

Realizing he was only going to continue to follow me until he got his answers, I sighed. "Listen, the reason I didn't abscond, as you say, with Dahlia is the same reason you haven't. There's more at play here. Why else would all of us end up in this exact place at this exact moment in time? It's not easy to get one over on a demigod, let alone a full god. And there's no way Dahlia isn't at the heart of this. And I cannot in good conscience allow a threat against her to remain. So in short, there's a puzzle to solve. I don't know about you, but I like a good puzzle."

He considered my words and released a breath of his own,

returning to that in-between state he'd existed in since the last petal fell. Not quite a man, but not a beast either.

"Fine, I'm coming with you."

"Why would you do that?"

"If there's one thing I learned growing up a twin, it's that two heads are better than one. And I still don't trust you."

"That's fine. I can't stand you either."

He growled at me. I couldn't help but roll my eyes.

"Oh, please. You know that posturing shit doesn't work on me. If you're going to insist on tagging along, just stay out of my way."

Tor cracked his knuckles and grinned. "Excellent. Where do we start?"

"Temperance's room."

"You really think he's behind this?"

"I think he was there when I got captured, and that means he's as good a place as any to start."

"Works for me. Lead the way."

CHAPTER SIXTEEN

TOR

Where had my little mate run off to this time? I'd hoped to find her naked and waiting for me when I returned from my unscheduled adventure with Hades last night. But she'd begged off, asking for time to finish up her latest chapter. It went against every instinct to agree, but I comforted myself with the promise that I would find her first thing this morning and that I'd wake her up with my face buried between her legs. Instead her room was empty, the bed neatly made, and she was nowhere to be found.

Had she gone to breakfast without me? No matter. I could wait. Her laptop sat on her desk, the broken pieces of what looked like her phone sitting next to it. She wouldn't be gone long, not without those. At least I hoped not.

Unable to sit still without making myself useful to my mate, I picked up the pieces of her phone and held them between my palms, tapping into the rarely used power my mother had passed down to all of her children. As usual, there was no discernible moment of knowing the magic had taken hold. One second the phone was broken, and the next it was the same as the last time I'd seen it.

Complete with a couple of chips in the paint and a small crack in the screen. I could have easily made it shiny and new, but Dahlia seemed to have a soft spot for familiar things.

I understood.

Having small creature comforts after being separated from the people I loved was the only way I held on to my humanity. A ring my father had given me, the knife Alek and I both received for our first hunt, and the thin black elastic band Dahlia'd been wearing around her wrist the first time I saw her.

Touchstones, all of them. They kept me grounded, and if I could bring back something important to her, I would. Seeing to her needs, both spoken and unspoken, was my privilege as her mate. In this, I would not fail.

That matter handled, I sat back down on the edge of her mattress, my fingers drumming a rapid tattoo against my thighs. Without an obvious task to focus on, my mind was left to wander back to what Cain and I had discovered the night before. He'd been on to something with his suspicions of Temperance.

We'd gone to his room intent on confronting the man, but he hadn't been there. Not wanting to waste the opportunity, we performed a quick investigation, not that he'd tried very hard to hide anything. There was an entire folder of notes on all of us, but none thicker than the one about Cain. More alarming to me, however, was that Dahlia's was nearly as thick and contained a series of Polaroids from her time before Blackwood. Almost like he'd been keeping tabs on her.

Which didn't make sense if he hadn't known of her existence prior to her ending up in that hospital. What was he playing at?

A rattling from the chest at the foot of the bed startled me out of my thoughts, sending my already tense muscles coiling tighter. That fucking doll. Someone needed to get rid of it, and it wouldn't be me.

I knew my twin would be rolling around in fits of laughter if he could see me right now. Ever since he played that prank on me when we were younger, I hadn't been able to look at a doll the same way.

Lucky for me, I hadn't come across any until now. The arse had promised one of the village girls a kiss if she'd give voice to my little sister's dolly. When I thought the toy had come alive, I'd been so scared I'd pissed myself and had yet to live the humiliation of it down. But I still maintained that being stalked by a creepy porcelain doll was the most terrifying experience I'd yet to have.

The rattling came again, this time more insistent, and I positioned myself in a defensive pose as I stared down at the chest.

I'd burn this whole castle to the ground before opening that damned chest. Perhaps I could dispose of it without anyone knowing? Chains wrapped around the wood, some hefty weight attached to them, and a solid throw into the nearby lake should do the trick. As faðir always said, the best kind of kill is overkill.

For good measure, I could set it ablaze as well. Hades could assist.

"Tor? Why are you staring daggers at my chest?"

Dahlia's amused question pulled my focus to where she stood in the doorway, arms crossed, a smile on her lips.

Her unintended double entendre made me laugh. "As a rule, I try to only stare at your chest in adoration. Or perhaps supplication."

She giggled. "What are you doing here?"

"I've been missing you. The last few times I've come to see you, you've been busy with someone else. Both fictional and real."

Her expression softened with tender understanding. "I'm sorry. Are you feeling left out?"

"A little," I admitted, feeling equal parts embarrassed and vulnerable. "I'm not built to share, and we aren't going about this in any way I'm familiar with."

"What do you mean by that?" She reached out, placing a gentle hand on my cheek, and gods help me, I leaned in and soaked up every ounce of her affection.

"I mean, the only relationship like this I know is one where all parties are welcome at all times. I know Sunday makes time for each of her mates individually, but generally speaking, they've always seemed to work as a unit. It's hard to understand my place in a group when instinct demands I keep you all to myself."

"I see what you're saying. It's a lot to juggle, honestly. My writing schedule and your competing needs. Not to mention the four of you don't really get along that well on a good day."

I let out a little grumble of agreement. "Alpha males don't share well. Not our women or anything else. We prefer to establish a clear pecking order."

She snickered. "You don't say. And here I thought you were all the picture of rational, securely attached men."

I smiled at her words, though it morphed into a frown when she whimpered.

"What's wrong?"

Her hand clutched her lower belly. "Excuse me for a second. I'll be right back."

Senses on high alert, I watched her dash into the bathroom. Was my mate sick? Had someone poisoned her coffee this morning? I'd tear the perpetrator's guts out through their arsehole.

"Thank fucking God and all the saints!" she shouted from behind the closed door.

My eyebrows flew into my hairline. I couldn't recall a time I'd ever rejoiced while in the toilets.

She emerged a few minutes later with a mixture of relief and pain etched into her features.

"Are you all right, Kærasta?"

"You'll be happy to know you did not plant your giant Viking baby in my womb." Her smile was wide, but her eyes were still pinched with pain.

"Why would that make me happy?"

Her jaw dropped. "Were you *trying* to knock me up with your big-headed babies?"

I shrugged. "Not specifically, but if Odin sees fit to bless our union, why would that bring me anything other than joy?"

She shook her head, at a loss for words. "I . . . You . . . We." Then she took a long breath, eyes closed, face tilted up to the heavens. "We have known each other for ten minutes. You can't possibly want to have babies with me, you fucking weirdo."

Warmth filled my chest at the thought of creating our own little brood of Vikings and Valkyries. "We've known each other much longer than that, and the idea of making a family with you is more than satisfying."

"Oh my God. This is like that series I read about the women who crash landed on a frozen planet and then each found their big blue be-spurred alien mates. All they wanted was to fuck and breed them too. But I guess they ended up happy in the long run, and the orgasms were nice. Although the pelts and furs and fucking snow seemed like a lot to take."

I couldn't stop my smirk as she rambled on and on about something I didn't even want to try to understand. "Do you have an aversion to snow, Kærasta? Novasgard is quite cold."

She threw her hands up in the air. "Way to miss the entire fucking point, Viking."

"Was there a point somewhere in there?"

Dahlia blew out a heavy breath. "Probably not. You flung me into a spiral."

"I'm . . . sorry?" I ventured. It seemed like the safest response.

"And another thing. You might make Viking *beast* babies. What if they come out with horns and claws too? My vagina is too pretty to deal with horns, Tor. She can take a pounding, but at her core, she's a delicate flower. Not to mention Kai is a dragon. A *dragon*. I'm pretty sure they make big, huge eggs. I'm not built to push an egg out of my—"

I stopped her with my palm across her mouth. "Shh, beauty. None of us has impregnated you. You're getting very spun up over something that hasn't happened."

She glared up at me and licked the inside of my palm. If she thought that would be a deterrent to keeping my hand in place, she was mistaken, but I released her anyway.

"That's what anxiety *is*, Tor. Worrying about things that haven't happened yet. But they *could*."

"Well, for what it's worth, I doubt you'll have to worry about horns and claws. I was cursed. My kind are not genetically predisposed to this form. As for the big heads, well, all the males in my family are large. There's nothing I can do about that."

"I guess we'll have to pray for girls."

"I'd be very happy to father a great many girls with you."

She deflated a bit, a smile playing on her lips. "What about the dragon eggs?"

I shrugged, knowing nothing about dragon reproduction. "Maybe you can convince Kai to sit on it and keep it warm for you."

"I don't want to lay an egg, Tor."

"Then I suppose you'll have to let me be the first to give you a child. What Kai doesn't know won't hurt him."

"And you think Cain and Cas will just stand aside and let you?"

My beast raged a bit at that. "If they know what's good for them."

She shook her head, laughter shining in her eyes. "How did this go from me starting my period to you convincing me to let you father our unborn children?"

I smirked. "I am irresistible. It's a fact of life." Pulling her into my chest, I dropped a kiss to the top of her head. "Are you in pain, beauty?"

"Yes. I should've realized what was going on so I could prepare a little more, but Sorcha was cagey about it, and I was late. I kept telling myself there was no way I could be pregnant because of the tattoo Kai gave me, but then . . . accidents happen."

Stiffening as her words sank in, I pulled back and stared into her gray eyes. "This whole time, you thought you might be pregnant and didn't think to tell me?"

She winced. "Oops."

I could feel the apology rolling off her. She hadn't kept anything from me intentionally. It truly hadn't occurred to her to mention anything until she knew for sure.

Sighing, I pulled her with me to the bed, where I tugged her down onto my lap so I could hold her. "I am your mate, Kærasta. You can tell me anything. Your burdens are mine to share."

With a happy little noise, she nuzzled against me. "Then I'm going to tell you I need to do something to make these cramps go away before I start crying."

"That bad, my beauty?"

She nodded. "I've had worse, but I know from experience these aren't going to go away on their own. I need medicine, or . . ."

"Or?"

"Maybe a couple of orgasms."

At the soft request, my cock hardened so quickly it sent an ache straight to my balls. "That can be arranged." I stared her down. "Get on the bed. I'll get a towel."

"Wait, I need to remove my, er . . ."

"I'll take care of it. I'll take care of everything. You just lay back and relax."

She blushed and then giggled. "I thought you were going to say think of England."

I winked at her over my shoulder as I walked away. "Never, my love, I only want you thinking of me."

CHAPTER SEVENTEEN

DAHLIA

Tor told me to relax, like that was something I've ever been able to do. I wanted to prop myself up on my elbows, look him in the eye, and say, "I have anxiety. I don't know how to relax."

Not to mention the fact that I'd just asked him to fuck me while clearly on my period. I knew it was a thing; some of the best solo orgasms I'd ever had occurred during Aunt Flo's visits, but part of me still worried he was going to get grossed out when push came to thrust.

Then again, I worried about everything, so this was not new. And my mate had a hard-on for blood and gore in general. So if ever there was someone to ask . . .

When Tor returned, he was shirtless, those joggers I loved hanging low on his hips and doing nothing to disguise his insistent erection. He held a towel in his hands and had pulled his long hair back into a bun atop his head. The man was ready to make a mess, and I was here. For. It.

"Lift your hips, Kærasta," he instructed as he climbed onto the bed.

I followed his instructions, waiting as he positioned the towel under me, and only when he pressed on my belly did I lower myself. In one quick movement, my Viking pulled off my leggings and panties, not wasting any time.

"Every time you touch me, it feels . . . better. How do you do that?" I asked, marveling at the waves of soothing comfort that seemed to be washing away the cramps I was so used to.

"Perks of our bond," he said with a roguish grin. "It's the same reason I was able to find control over my beast when you were near." His palms skated across my inner thighs. "Tell me where it hurts most. Allow me to see to your needs, my beautiful mate."

God, where did I start? "Aside from my contracting uterus? My hips, down my thighs, my lower back. Fuck, where doesn't it hurt might be a better question."

He chuckled, his hands slowly caressing the various parts of my body as I listed them. "What about here?" he asked softly, fingers gliding over my labia.

I expected to be embarrassed when he gave the little string between my legs a tug and took care of the potential barrier. But he did it so matter-of-factly, barely sparing it a glance as he chucked it in the bin before those midnight eyes returned to mine. I couldn't focus on anything other than him and what he was doing to me.

"Are you sure?" I asked, a little breathy and a whole lot turned on.

"Serving you while you're in need of me is one of the greatest honors of my life. I am beyond certain." His lips trailed heated kisses over the sensitive skin of my inner thigh, and when he looked up at me from the frame of my shaking legs, an answering wetness flooded my core. "Is there anything off the table, Dahlia? Anything you don't want me to do?"

"You're the one doing the heavy lifting and getting all . . . dirty. Shouldn't you get to decide?"

He grinned up at me, and I swear if I'd still been wearing panties, they'd have incinerated. "If it were up to me, I'd take you so fully you wouldn't be able to walk tomorrow. But this is new to you. We'll take it slow."

"Slow sounds nice," I murmured when he started kissing a lazy path up my belly. I was still wearing my *I have no shelf control* shirt, so the soft fabric slid up as he did.

The play of his lips on my skin was maddening, and it wasn't long before I was squirming beneath him, tugging up on his shoulders to move his body into the position mine craved.

"What happened to slow?" he teased.

"I changed my mind. It's my prerogative as a woman."

"I see." He notched his swollen head at my entrance, pressing forward just the tiniest bit. It was perfect torture. Especially when he released a low, growled sigh. "Mmm. Hot and slick. Exactly how I like it."

"I'm always wet for you, Tor."

"I know. It's one of my greatest achievements."

I couldn't help but laugh at the arrogance of his answer. It was so patently him.

"Shut up and kiss me," I ordered, the breathlessness of my demand removing any sting from the words.

"My pleasure." Bringing his lips to mine, he rocked his hips forward at the same time and sank into me. It was slow, just as he promised. A delicious fullness I'd never experienced while in this state.

Any lingering discomfort was replaced by glorious pleasure. That pinch in my back was now languid warmth. The knotting in my lower belly sensual pressure.

"Oh God, I think your dick might be magic."

A rumbled laugh vibrated over my mouth as he claimed my lips again. "It is. Mate magic. Now let me make you feel good."

"Already succeeding," I panted.

He stopped moving, his body perfectly poised above mine. "Should I stop, then? Consider this a job well done?"

I grabbed his ass, my fingers holding him so tightly I was certain there'd be a ring of bruises there later. "Don't you fucking dare."

"Tell me how you want it, beauty. I only desire to draw out your pleasure."

For once, I didn't have a ready answer. Everything sounded good; all I knew was that I wanted *more*. More of this. More of him. More of us.

"Just don't stop," I whispered, my lips feathering over his due to our proximity. "Go as slow or as fast as you want, but please don't stop."

He rocked forward, proving that he'd been holding back as he sheathed himself fully within me. I damn near arched off the bed as his length proved to be almost more than I could handle.

"Shh, my love. Relax and open for me."

Strong fingers found my clit, and he began to trace slow circles around the sensitive flesh as his thrusts continued. Like the cliché she was, my pussy opened for him, blooming like a goddamn flower.

I'd known this was what I needed, but it was even better than I'd expected. Usually my cramps were too painful to entertain the idea of anything but painkillers and a nap. But in the rare instances they weren't, an orgasm or two almost always got the job done, the release and resulting flood of dopamine helping my muscles to relax. Tor's prowess, combined with our mystical mate bond, worked better than freaking morphine. I was absolutely blissed out, riding high on the waves of euphoria his touch sent cascading through me.

"Why is this so good?" I panted when another roll of his hips sent my eyes fluttering closed.

"It will always be good between us, Kærasta. We were made for each other. Our union is a gift from the gods."

"Remind me to thank them later. I'll light some incense or get on my knees or name our future giant-headed babies after them."

The self-satisfied growl that left him as he thrust deeper into me made me clench around him. Oh, he liked that. A whole fucking lot.

"Faster, Tor. I'm ready for you to go feral on me now. I need it."

"Are you sure? I don't want to hurt you."

"You're my mate. You won't hurt me. I was made to take everything you can give me, remember?"

His pupils were nearly blown in response to that. His beast was close to the surface. Well, it was always close to the surface now that the curse had run its course, but his hold was stronger than usual. If I had to guess, I'd say he might even be in the driver's seat.

Remembering something from our time in the forest, I reached up and ran my fingers along one of his horns, caressing it the same way I would his dick.

A garbled groan escaped him as he shuddered in ecstasy above me. I was so close to my release, riding the waves of pleasure as they built with each of his thrusts and every brush of my clit against his pelvis.

"Tor, I'm going to come."

"Yes, fuck, Kærasta. Take it. Gods, you're squeezing me so tight." His words were labored, punctuated by groans and heavy breaths, and I loved every single one.

Hearing him lose control was enough to change those teasing waves of orgasm into a powerful tsunami that hit me hard and fast. I came with a scream that left my throat raw, and he followed right along, his own roar making the window rattle. The window *and* the little chest at the foot of my bed.

Best not to mention that. No need to send my Viking fleeing for the hills.

After a few moments of shared silence, Tor finally pulled out of me, making the both of us groan. A rush of wetness escaped from between my thighs in an unbidden reminder of his absence. I missed him instantly.

"Good thing you put down that towel," I murmured, my gaze trailing down his bare chest to his blood-streaked cock. Fuck, it was everywhere, his thighs, my thighs, the towel. How was this hot? This wasn't supposed to be hot, right?

Don't yuck my yum, Dahlia. We don't kink shame, remember?

Of all the times for Kiki's voice to float through my mind. I had to swallow back a laugh. She would love to know that she haunted even my most intimate moments.

"You have your choice for clean up," Tor said, his fingers drawing small circles on my knees. "You stay right where you are and I take care of you. Or I draw you a hot bath, and I—"

"Take care of me?"

He grinned. "Precisely."

"Who's going to take care of you?"

A look of adorable confusion washed over his face. The unexpected expression combined with his monstrous countenance was more than a little endearing. It had me sitting up and wrapping my arms around his waist in an impromptu hug.

"I . . . what?"

"You're just as in need of cleaning up as I am."

"Easily remedied, I can—"

"Join me in the bath. We'll take turns caring for each other."

He held my gaze, emotion filling the space between us. "I'd really like that," he rasped, his voice gruffer than usual. Leaning down, he pressed a lingering kiss to my lips. "I love you, Kærasta."

My heart swelled, and as he scooped me into his arms and carried me to the bathroom, I looked up at the monster who'd become my mate. "I love you too, Tor."

CHAPTER EIGHTEEN

HADES

"You're the god of the underworld. Put me out of my misery, why don't you? Just kill me now and end it."

I knew the words were in jest, but they sliced through me regardless. Dahlia had been curled up in the middle of her bed when I'd stopped by this morning. Tor had left not long before to go for his morning romp in the forest and do whatever beastly things he did out there. I'd been surprised he left her in such a state, but since it gave me an opportunity to care for her, I can't say I minded it.

At least, not until she started begging me to kill her.

"Never say that, baby doll. Losing you once was more than enough."

She opened one eye and glared at me. "Do not start comparing me to some other woman. I will throw something at you. A shoe. Or . . . fuck, I can't even move to grab one. So maybe a pillow." She closed her eyes with a little mewl of pain, muttering pathetically about storing weapons under her pillows. "A pillow is hardly an appropriate threat."

I growled my frustration before settling on her bed so we were facing one another. "Throw whatever you want, but it won't change the facts. I am not comparing you. I'm simply recalling the life our souls shared."

"It's not fair."

"What isn't fair?"

"That you have a whole history with me I can't access. It's like you watched an entire season of a show, and I have to jump in without all the backstory."

I stared at her, her eyes pinched with pain, skin pale and clammy. I hated that she was suffering, that my touch didn't seem to have the same healing effect as Tor's. Why would it? I hadn't been created to care for the living. I was born to rule the dead.

Swallowing my frustration, I tucked some sweat-dampened hair behind her ear and offered the one thing that might bring her a measure of comfort. "I could bring you up to speed. Share the highlights. If you really want to know."

Fuck, all I wanted was to tell her everything and help her understand how powerful this connection was between us. Although . . . there were some more unsavory parts of our story. Things she wouldn't be too happy to hear about directly from my lips.

"And have you try to rewrite the facts? Everybody knows the gist of the Hades and Persephone story. You stole her away to the underworld and fell deeply in love, and she got Stockholm syndrome."

"It was *not* Stockholm syndrome."

"Oh, please. This story is the original Stockholm syndrome tale. Dark romance at its finest."

"Are you trying to offend me?" I asked, cupping her cheek and staring down at her until she returned my gaze.

"Nope. Just trying to keep you honest. You do have a bit of a reputation, you know."

I did, and I loved that she wasn't afraid to call me out. My temper was almost as notorious as my love for her. But she hadn't been afraid. Not back then, and not now.

"I've never claimed to be a hero."

"Can I tell you a secret?" she whispered conspiratorially.

"I want all your secrets, goddess."

Her soft intake of breath sent a rush through me. "I've always been a sucker for the hot villain."

"Given the stable of men the Fates have selected for you, that's hardly a secret."

Rolling her eyes, she let out a laugh and reached up to run her fingers through the hair at my temple. "So spill the tea, my lord Hades. Are you really as bad as all the stories say? Mythology paints you as the biggest baddie in Greek legend."

I was too hung up on the way my cock jerked to attention at her referring to me as 'my lord' to register the rest of her question. "What was that?"

"Are you stalling, or did you actually not understand what was honestly a softball of a question?"

"I was distracted. I like the way my . . . name sounds on your lips."

"Oh, do you, my lord Hades?"

She added a bit more verve to it this time, her voice pitched low and dripping with sex.

I used a bit of shadow to tug her hand down until it was resting against my straining length. "You tell me, Dahlia."

"Stop trying to distract me with your dick, Hades. We can play with your shadows later. You said you wanted all my secrets. It's only fair for you to give me yours in exchange."

She didn't know how on the nose her statement was. But I guess that led us right down the path of one of my worst deeds. "Careful, little flower. You bargain with the god of the underworld, and you will lose. I always win."

Dahlia rolled her eyes again. "Of course you do. Death *always* wins in the end."

I don't think she realized just how poignant that sentence was. I might be the ruler of the dead, but even I had been taken down a couple of pegs by death. It's what took her from me the first time. I, better than anyone, understood the sheer futility of attempting to stand in death's way.

"So aside from stealing women from their beds and keeping them as your own, you make deals only you can win? You're like a mob boss."

"It's not like that. I can lose, I just never do. Temptation is the root of all evil, and it's ruined many a person."

"Stop stalling. You're dancing around this subject like Gene Kelly in *Singin' in the Rain*. I can see it in your eyes. You want to tell me a story. What are you afraid of?"

"Maybe I don't want the way you look at me to change."

She shoved at my chest. "I *just* told you villains get me hot and bothered. Hell, I write them as the love interests in my stories. Why do you think it would make me see you differently?"

"They always have a redemption arc. I don't."

"You might be a god, but not even you know the future, Hades. Just because you haven't had your redemption arc doesn't mean one isn't available to you."

"Spoken like a true romantic."

"Isn't love the greatest motivator of all?"

This was it. I had to rip off the Band-Aid and show her how wrong she was. "Exactly. And it's the greatest weakness. Do you know the story of Orpheus and Eurydice?"

"She died. He begged you to let him have her back . . . ."

"Yes. I made a bargain with him that I knew he would break. There isn't a man in existence strong enough to withstand the urge to look back for his true love. I knew as soon as I saw him that his faith would never be greater than his need to see with his own eyes that she was following him. All he had to do was walk, and he could have had her, but he couldn't manage something even that simple. He couldn't let go and *believe* in her."

"It wasn't her he had trouble believing. It was you."

"Whose side are you on, goddess?"

"Love's. Always love's. The rest of it is inconsequential."

"If that's the case, then you stand on the side of history with some rather unsavory characters."

"How do you figure?"

"Well, if you're love's champion, then you're there cheering on the Hades of the world. Those of us who would break every rule and moral code to ensure we end up with the one we love."

"Would you turn around and look back for me?" she asked, and goddammit, my heart broke.

"No. No matter how much I wanted to, I'd stay the course. I won't lose you."

Tears swam in her eyes, the emotion behind them making me want nothing more than to kiss each one away.

"You will lose me one day. I'll be a ghost wandering the halls, haunting your grumpy ass."

"You're forgetting that I am uniquely equipped to interact with ghosts. They're basically my bread and butter."

She sighed and rolled over onto her back, gaze trained on the ceiling as she winced through what must've been a cramp. "And I'm uniquely equipped too, but I can't even do what I was made for because of my stupid period. This is so frustrating. How am I supposed to go investigate when I can barely stand upright?"

I gently rested a hand on her lower belly, wishing I could take her pain into myself. "This will pass, and then you can do all the investigating you desire."

She made a face at me. "Spoken like a man. Just suffer through it and *then* do the important thing. Do you have any idea how often there is no 'then' in that equation? Usually we have to suffer *and*. Being a woman sucks. If men were the ones getting cramps that took them out once a month, they'd get paid sick leave. It is so unjust. You know what? I'm going to invest in one of those period simulators, and then we can talk about enduring and 'this too shall pass.' No one gets to weigh in on suffering if they haven't lived through it."

It took everything in me not to chuckle at her rant. "It is a woman's cross to bear. I'm just here to hold your hand through it."

"Grumble."

"Why don't you roll over, and I'll massage your lower back for you? Would that help?"

"You just want to touch my ass."

"Of course I do. It's a fantastic rear end. Best I've ever had the pleasure of grabbing on to."

Giving me a little smile, she did as I instructed, but before I could get into position, I felt the shift in the room's energy, an awareness of a presence manifesting. This fucking ghost wasn't getting her hands on my wife. Dahlia was in enough pain as it was, and the last thing I'd allow was the addition of a spiteful, rage-filled spirit.

One palm pressing on Dahlia's back to keep her still, I turned my head and stared down the intruder. Writhing smoky energy at the foot of the bed greeted me.

"Not this time," I murmured, calling my power and sending a burst of it into the soul. "Stay back." One final pulse of my fire and the specter vanished.

Dahlia let out an inquisitive mumble. "Hmm?"

I stared at the now empty spot on the bed, ensuring the specter was well and truly gone before returning my attention to the beautiful woman beneath my hand. This morning hadn't gone exactly the way I'd expected, but as she'd reminded me, my time with her was precious. I wouldn't squander a second of it.

"Never you mind. Just lay there and try to relax, all right? Let me make you feel better."

CHAPTER NINETEEN

KAI

"I thought I'd be freezing my tits off out here, but having a dragon boyfriend really does have its perks." Dahlia snuggled in closer to me as we walked along the water's edge. The loch was too deep to fully freeze, but the edges were iced over, and all the nearby foliage was covered in thick frost.

"Careful now, watch yer step. The last thing I want to do is go diving in after you if ye fall in."

She giggled softly. "My heroic dragon. Are you afraid of a little cold water?"

"Nae. But I can still freeze if the temperature is low enough. Something tells me my warmth isn't the only part of me you like. Wouldn't want any of my dangly bits falling off, now would we?"

She paused, tapping a finger against her chin as she thought. "Hmm, I dunno. I feel like I could make good use out of a detachable dragon dick. There's a whole ass market for that, you know. You get a Kai, and you get a Kai." She laughed at her joke, although I dinnae share her amusement, or quite understand it, if I was being honest. "I'm pretty sure there's a company that will send me all the stuff I need to make a replica. How do you feel about me starting an Etsy shop called Dragon Dicks R Us?"

I reeled her into me, her chest pressed up against mine, my lips hovering over hers. "The only one who gets to make use of my dick, wee little mate, is you."

Then I spanked her soundly on the arse.

"And no more jokes about it falling off."

"You started it."

"Aye, and then I finished it."

"Grumpy dragon."

I frowned and growled at her, although inside, my dragon was highly amused. He loved playing with her like this. Where it was just the two of us trading banter back and forth.

"Are ye feeling any better after getting a wee bit of exercise, gem?" I asked, shifting the subject away from my cock.

"Yeah. It's doing wonders for the tightness in my lower back. This was a good idea. You all have been so great about trying to help me through it in your own ways."

"We're yer mates. That's what we're supposed tae do."

It was funny how easy it was these days to admit that we all played an important role in her life. Somewhere along the way, we'd turned into a team. Or at least had the makings of one.

"Yeah, but when you read about it in books, it's all orgies and sex parties. Not period care. Reality never quite lives up to the fantasy, does it?" We walked another couple of steps before she contradicted herself. "Actually, strike that. I'd take the period care over the orgies any day. That's true, selfless love."

"Oh, I dunno, gem. The orgies sound pretty fun too. No reason both can't be part of your reality."

She guffawed. "Oh ho ho, a dragon gets a couple of threesomes under his belt, and suddenly he's begging for orgies. I've created a monster."

I nipped her neck, my teeth elongating just a titch as my dragon rose to the surface. "I've always been a monster, love."

"And now you're mine."

"Aye, lass. I am."

Gripping her by the chin, I stopped our progress forward and made her look at me. "I am yours, and I always will be." Then I dipped my head so I could taste her lips again. It'd been too long, and I craved her in a way that should be illegal.

"Found you! You two are horrible at this game," Hook said as he popped out from behind a bush.

Dahlia stiffened and then collapsed against me in peels of laughter. "Did someone forget to tell me we were playing hide and seek? Also, how long have you been waiting there?"

I had to check to make sure literal smoke wasn't coming out of my nose. So much for alone time with my mate.

"Good job, Caspian. Now you go hide, and we'll come find you."

In, say, six or seven years.

"Nah, I don't want to play anymore. I found what I was looking for."

The pirate sidled up next to Dahlia and slipped his arm into hers. I couldn't stop myself from releasing a snarl.

"Take your hands off her." It was a warning he didn't deserve. "You should know better. Dragons don't like anyone touching their treasure."

Hook met my heated stare head-on, his expression uncharacteristically violent. "Dragons aren't the only ones interested in treasure, Kai. There's not much a pirate wouldn't do in his quest for a rare jewel or trinket, let alone an entire trove."

"Are you two actually fighting over me like two dogs with a bone?"

"Yes," Cas said.

"Nae," I countered.

"Maybe you should tattoo a big X on me, you know, to mark the spot."

"I don't need any help finding your spot, darling."

I couldn't help myself; I reached over and bodily shoved Caspian away. I couldn't stand the way he was leering at her.

"And here I thought you were all getting along so well," Dahlia said with a long sigh. "So much for the orgies."

Hook was nearly comical in his reaction. He went from murderously glaring at me to abruptly stopping, snapping his head to look at Dahlia and blinking twice. "I'm sorry. What about orgies?"

Dahlia fought hard to hide her smile. "Nothing, apparently, since you two don't know how to play nice."

Caspian sauntered to my side and slung his arm around my neck. "Sure we do. We're best mates, aren't we, dragon?"

If he wasn't careful, I was likely to take his head off. "Unhand me."

"So formal. I sucked your fingers just the other day. Remember that? We've seen each other's pricks. We're beyond niceties."

Dahlia moaned, her face turning a lovely shade of pink. "God, Cas. You can't just lob things like you sucking me off Kai's fingers like sexy little grenades and not do anything about them."

"My favorite kind of bombs are love bombs. And who said I wasn't going to do anything about it? Lie back on that rock, and I'll take care of you right here for anyone to see."

"A rock, really? At least use the tree and spare Dahlia's poor arse."

Dahlia pointed at me. "Man has a point. Rocks hurt."

"The mermaids never seemed to mind it," Cas said with a shrug, "but who am I to judge? A rock, a tree, the ground . . . wherever, whenever, darling."

"And then there were three," Dahlia murmured, sending a confused look skittering across Cas's face, but I saw exactly who she was talking about.

Tor emerged from the trees, bits of dirt streaking his face, but an air of calm coming from him. He'd been hunting again.

"I'm doomed to never have ye to myself, aren't I?" I whispered into her hair.

"It looks like it."

"Oh, and there's the full house," I grumbled, Cain coming into view a little ways down the path.

"Where one goes, the others follow," Dahlia said.

"Nae, love. Where *you* go, the rest of us follow."

Tor strode straight for her, gripped her by the nape, and tugged her hard into his body. He claimed her lips without a word, and the way she melted into him would've made me jealous if she didn't do the same for me.

"Well, fancy seeing you misfits all in one place," Cain said, closing the distance between us, Asshole yipping and jumping up on Dahlia's calves.

"Is this just going to be my life now? All of us wandering the grounds and trying to find quiet places for the orgies where Joffrey can't find us?" Dahlia teased.

"No, Kærasta. When we get out of here, I'm going to create a home we can all share so we're not all on top of one another all the time."

"Can my room have a ship theme?" Hook asked.

"Very funny." Dahlia rolled her eyes at him.

"Why is that funny? Portholes are excellent windows."

"No, not that. Decorate your room however you want. I meant because we're not leaving."

I frowned at her. "We cannae build a life here, gem."

"We have to. This place is the Scottish Hotel California."

When we all stared at her like she had grown an extra head, she elaborated.

"You know, you can check out any time you like, but you can never leave?" Then she played a little air guitar.

"I don't know what you're on about."

"Really? Oh God. You really don't know." Her entire countenance dropped. "I hate to be the bearer of terrible fucking news, but we're never getting out of here. Like ever. This is a prison only with a spell instead of bars."

"Who told you this, beauty?"

"Sorcha. She said no one ever leaves." Dahlia stared solemnly back at the estate. "Apparently there's a hidden cemetery with thousands of bodies buried there, I mean here. They kill the ones they can't control. Well, I guess technically, all of us."

"That cannae be true. I've seen people leave."

"Did you? Or did you see what the higher-ups wanted you to see? Do we really know where they go once they 'leave'?"

"She's right," Cain said, his eyes bouncing between Dahlia and Tor. "Temperance has files on all of us. Tor and I found them in his room."

"He's one of our doctors. What's so strange about that?" I asked.

"These files predate our arrival at Blackwood. They're more like what you'd expect to get from a private investigator rather than simple medical records," Cain clarified.

"There's something about Temperance I don't like," Tor added.

"But Masterson is legit, right? I mean, why else would she try so hard to help us?" Dahlia asked.

"Masterson may not be in on it, but something smells rotten. And with what you learned from Sorcha, there's definitely more at play here. Blackwood is not what it seems."

"This doesn't make sense. Why would they want to keep us here? Also, I've left plenty of times. Tor too." Hook looked as unbothered as I'd seen him. "This is a bunch of poppycock."

"And yet you came right back. We're all under a spell. Compelled to return no matter what," Dahlia pointed out.

Dread sat in the pit of my stomach like a stone. I couldn't stay here forever. Not even with the promise of Dahlia in my bed. "They willnae keep me here. My dragon would never allow it. Hell, the Shadow Court would never allow it. They have plans for me to take over for my father in Faerie. They'll take me when my time comes."

"Wait. You're leaving?"

"Eventually."

"And what about me? Will you take me with you?"

Cain and Tor both visibly reacted to the thought of Dahlia being taken from them.

Sadness punched me in the gut. "Nae, gem. You cannae come to Faerie. You won't survive."

Hurt swam in her eyes. "And you didn't think to mention any of this to me? I thought we were mates, Kai."

"We are."

"Then you can't leave me."

Agony ripped through me as I leveled my gaze on her. "I'm sorry, lass. When the time comes, I'll have no choice."

SESSION TRANSCRIPT: DECEMBER 16TH

Dr. Masterson: This is Dr. Elizabeth Masterson. It is December 16th, and the time is 10:00 a.m. This is a recorded session with Caspian Hook.

Hook: *annoyed huff* Yes, yes. You're worse than a bleeding parrot with all your repetitive yammering. Some of us have other places to be, you know. It's quite rude to hold us hostage simply so you can read the same blasted script ad nauseam.

<<clothes rustling>>

Dr. Masterson: There's something to be said for order and procedure. Why don't you try going to university for four years in the human world and then another four at Ravenscroft, then you can set the procedure. How's that?

Hook: Or, how about I don't and we just say I did. It's not like I had to go to school to be a captain. I just stepped into the role, and it's worked out brilliantly.

Dr. Masterson: Well, since you brought it up, let's chat a bit more about that.

<<pen scratching on paper>>

Hook: Doctor, why are you taking notes? You usually just record our sessions.

Dr. Masterson: Because with you, I've learned I need as many references as I can get when typing up my reports.

Hook: *dubious humming* We've been over my rise to fame before.

Dr. Masterson: Not really. All you ever say on the matter is that the role was vacated, and you filled it. How exactly was it vacated? Why are you the one who stepped in? Was it a matter of necessity? Convenience? Destiny? There's more to this story, Caspian. And something tells me it's at the heart of your issues.

Hook: There's always more to every story. Mine's been told before, but no one gets it right.

<<pen scratching on paper>>

Dr. Masterson: Well, you have a captive audience in me, Caspian. So set the record straight, once and for all.

Hook: Fine. Once upon a time, there was a fae prince. Handsome, dashing, a real ladies' man. Honestly, he was an equal opportunity lover, and everyone loved him back.

<<pen scratching on paper>>

Dr. Masterson: Delusions of grandeur.

Hook: Oh fuck off, you asked for the story. Are you going to listen or sit there and headshrink everything that comes out of my mouth?

Dr. Masterson: Continue.

Hook: So there I was, poised to take my place as the next ruler of the Sea Court, when the generational tithes came due. There's no set time frame, so it wasn't like we knew they were coming. But it wasn't exactly as though we could avoid paying the price either. I say we, but I guess it was really me that had to pay, wasn't it?

Dr. Masterson: You're referring to the fae courts sending one child per court to Ravenndel?

Hook: *sucks teeth* Do you know of any other generational tithes?

Dr. Masterson: Yes, actually.

Hook: Well, la-di-fucking-da.

<<chair creaks>>

Hook: Anyway, I was minding my own bloody business when suddenly I'm summoned to the throne room. There she stood, The White Lady, Faerie's most powerful mage. She took one look at me, and I knew my parents had chosen to get rid of me.

Dr. Masterson: That's an interesting way to describe it.

Hook: What else would you call it when parents select one child to throw away while keeping all the rest? It's not like they sat there and played rock paper scissors to make their choice. They hardly blinked before chucking me out like yesterday's bath water.

Dr. Masterson: *hums in approval* And how did that make you feel?

Hook: *scoffs* Oh, brilliant. Fucking wonderful. Best day of my whole life. Of course it made me feel like a piece of shit on the bottom of my father's shoe. Jesus, I thought you were insightful, Doctor. Seriously, I don't think all those years of schooling did you any good. You should ask for a refund.

Dr. Masterson: I think you're misplacing your anger, Caspian.

Hook: No, I'm quite certain it's aimed directly where it belongs, Doctor.

Dr. Masterson: *musing hum* Please continue, Caspian.

<<pen scratching on paper>>

Hook: Well, it's a tale as old as time, innit? By the ripe old age of seventeen, I was the abandoned child, the unwanted prince, the not-so-lost boy. A boy king, really, bred to rule, only it didn't end up being the Sea Court I was leading. It was a bunch of other lonely kids whose parents couldn't be bothered to fight for them.

Dr. Masterson: And did you?

Hook: Did I what?

Dr. Masterson: Fight for them?

Hook: Of course I bloody did. You really need to work on your active listening skills, Doc. I fought for them every moment of every day. I still fight for them. They're my crew. My family. The only one that ever truly mattered.

<<pen dropped on notepad>>

Dr. Masterson: *awed gasp* I understand now. You were Peter Pan, the leader of the lost boys, and you fought to protect them from the pirates.

Hook: Maybe there's hope for you after all, Lizzie darling.

Dr. Masterson: A fight must have ensued that led to their captain's death, and Ravenndel doesn't allow vacancies.

Hook: You have done your homework. Go on, then. Might as well finish since you're on a roll.

Dr. Masterson: When you killed him, you became him?

Hook: Ding dong, Doctor. Well met. And the lost boys, they're men now. My men. My crew. And I'm no longer their boy king. I'm their captain.

Dr. Masterson: An ever-evolving, self-sustaining realm. That explains the madness. Your time away from your realm is seen as a vacancy, only you aren't actually dead, so there's no one to take your place, and Ravenndel is desperate to fill the void. It's tearing at you. Trying to pull you back and restore the balance. *dramatic pause* Caspian, what happens if you don't return to Ravenndel?

<<chair squeaking>>

Hook: My, my, you are a clever girl, aren't you? Finally put it all together? The big reveal. Yes, I can tell by the horrified look on your face that you have. But here, I'll spell it out for you anyway. What happens if Captain Hook doesn't return to Neverland? Well, both he and it cease to exist, don't they? Right along with every other fairy tale tied to the realm. *resigned sigh* In short, doctor, it's the bloody end of the world for all of us.

<<static>>

End of transcript.

CHAPTER TWENTY

HOOK

An itching persisted under my skin, all over, annoying and frustrating because I couldn't quite pinpoint the source. All I knew was discomfort. I felt unwelcome in my own body, like I was wearing a suit that didn't fit. And no matter what I did, nothing eased the pervasive sensation.

Pair that with the motherfucking tick, tick, ticking in my head and the bloody whispers that felt more like roars, and I was going to be stark raving mad before long.

If I was being honest, I was nearly there already.

Dahlia's form came into view, and an instant flood of relief hit me. The itching died down, and the chaos of my mind settled into a sweet summer storm versus the maelstrom it had been working up to.

"Oh, dear. Caspian, you're a junkie, and she's your drug of choice," I murmured to myself. Though I suppose given the alternatives, she was at least a healthy addiction. If there was such a thing.

An electric current of anticipation raced down my spine as I watched her move through the crowd of people gathering for lunch.

She was wearing my bracelet, displaying the leather proudly and with abandon. A not-so-secret message just for me. This was it. The solution to my problem. Captain Hook was always at his best when he had a mission to execute or, more specifically, a treasure to claim. And Dahlia was nothing if not the ultimate treasure. The plume in my rather extraordinary hat.

Where the bloody hell was my hat, by the by?

The sliding of my thoughts was all the warning I needed that Dahlia was on the move. She was a bit of a divining rod these days, her presence holding the madness at bay, keeping me whole—or as whole as I was capable of in this realm. My ability to retain my sanity on my own was greatly diminished. I was barely able to make it a few seconds without her in my sights anymore before the tick, tick, bloody ticking returned.

She wanted me. That was enough for me to use as a touchstone. Something to hold on to and look forward to. But first, a few provisions were required. My girl wanted me to do bad things to her.

And who better to do the very best bad things than Captain Fucking Hook?

~

Tick

Tick

Tick

My eye twitched in time with the incessant ticking, and it took biting down so hard on the inside of my cheek that I drew blood to keep me from using my dagger to stab myself in the ear. It had taken longer than expected to gather my supplies and hunt down my quarry. The resulting distance from Dahlia had led to a full-out battle with the madness.

I was sane only in the sense that I knew my name and my

purpose. But even that was getting fuzzy at the edges. I needed her. Even just a glance would help. Hell, her scent on the breeze would get the job done.

She was my anchor.

And I was a ship amidst the very worst of storms.

I needed her if I had any hope of surviving.

A little brown spider skittered across my hand as I lay in wait in the dank secret passage I'd come to know and love. My time spent studying the blueprints of Blackwood had paid off in spades. How else would I have known about this escape route? These old castles were filled with them. Ways for the old kings and queens to make a hasty retreat in times of war or siege. All one needed to know was what to look for. Or a map.

Pirates loved a good map.

Was my hiding spot glamorous? No. The corridor smelled like wet earth and mold. I was fairly certain I'd seen a rat or two as well, but if I didn't bother them, they wouldn't bother me.

While not really romantic, my hidey-hole did lend itself to an air of mystery befitting a sexy pirate. I'd snatch my fair maiden, abscond with her into the castle walls like the Phantom of the bleeding Opera, and then make her mine until she sang my name to the heavens.

All that was missing was her.

This was her preferred route back from her afternoon sessions with the doctor. Unless I'd made a serious miscalculation, she'd be coming around that corner any second.

One. Two.

Tick

Tick

Tick

This time I punched myself on the leg to try and beat the sanity back into me.

Like clockwork—see what I did there?—she came round the

bend. All smiles and relief, Dahlia looked like she'd just set down something heavy and was finally able to rest.

I barely remembered to breathe as she sauntered past the wall hiding me from view. I waited exactly one heartbeat before I hit the lever that sent the door soundlessly sliding open.

She only made it a few steps further before I was on her. The rag with the sedative snug against her nose and mouth, my other arm banded about her hips, and my hard cock pressing against the base of her spine.

Her wriggles of protest sent a shockwave of lust careening through me, so I brought my lips to her ear.

"I told you I'd make it special, darling. Now be a good girl and stop struggling. It only makes me harder."

There wasn't time for her to respond, even had she been able to speak behind the rag. She went boneless in my arms, and I made quick work of hefting her over my shoulder and sneaking back into the yawning darkness. Following the route I'd long ago memorized, I made my way to the abandoned cabin in the heart of the woods and the freshly made bed awaiting the two of us.

Not long later, I sat near the warm fire in the hearth and waited for her eyes to flutter open so we could really begin our play. She looked so beautiful like this, bathed in nothing but firelight, bared to me. I'd removed her clothing and mine and placed each piece in a neat stack—after sniffing her knickers, of course.

And stashing them away to enjoy again later.

What? The dragon didn't deserve to be the only one collecting souvenirs.

This was the most at peace I'd felt since waking up in my darling's arms. Watching her sleep. Timing my breaths with hers. It was heaven, and I could happily spend the rest of whatever time I had left on this plane right here, so long as I was with her doing exactly this.

"Mmm," she moaned, shifting her body and making her full tits sway enticingly.

My little captive was coming to. I couldn't wait to use her the way she wanted.

Now that she was lucid, I left my perch in the corner and moved to the bed, needing to give in to the urge to touch her. Taking a seat beside her, I reached out and traced the circle of her areola, delighting in the tight beading of her nipple at my barely there touch.

“More, please,” she whispered, arching into my hand.

“Yes, love. You'll have everything you want.”

Part of me had wanted her to wake up with me already buried to the hilt inside her tight cunt. But this was our first time, and I found myself feeling a mite sentimental about it. We'd waited this long; what was a bit longer to ensure that it was a transcendental experience for us both?

You didn't know I was a romantic, did you?

Me either.

Surprise.

My mouth watered as I stared at her rigid nipple. All I wanted was to suck it between my lips and make her cry out. So that's exactly what I did. Dipping my head low, I latched on and reveled in the sounds she made in response. My fingers slipped between her thighs, and I groaned when I found her already slick with need.

Now that the time was upon us, I was in this weird tug-of-war with myself. I wanted to rush ahead, but also stretch every second out. It was messing with my confidence, making me question every choice to ensure whether it was the right one.

Did I taste her first? Or should I sink into her and leave us both panting?

“Cas, you're so beautiful.” Her words were soft, thick with desire as her eyes trailed over my body.

“No, love. I'm not. Not when I'm standing in the same light as you are.”

Who was this man she'd turned me into? More prince than pirate at the moment. It wasn't the first time either. I had an entire collection of moments now where she brought this long-forgotten piece of my soul out of hiding. I'd have thought her a witch if I hadn't known better.

"I think you might be part siren," I confessed. "Either that or a descendant of one of those ancient sea nymphs. You have me utterly enraptured."

"I need you to stop talking and kiss me, Caspian. Please?"

The look in her eyes was a plea for intimacy, for a deep connection I hadn't ever given anyone before. She was trusting me with her heart, and I wanted to be good enough to take it from her.

Perhaps it was lucky that there were three others to ensure I wouldn't bungle it.

Instead of jealousy, the reminder that she had other men to protect and care for her provided intense relief. They wouldn't let me hurt her. She would be safe. I could let go and see this through to whatever end existed for us.

Holding tight to that thought, I leaned down and met her lips with my own. It was nothing like the sensual acts I was used to. Those were for show. Smoke and mirrors to cultivate the distinct mood I required for the performance I was putting on. This was real. It was terrifying. Because while I could hurt her, it was more apparent than ever before that she could also hurt me.

The last people who'd had that power over me had thrown me away. I wasn't given the option of anything but survival last time, but something deep within warned me I would not enjoy the same fate were she to do the same. If I lost her, I'd never recover.

Fuck. How had she done this to me?

I broke the kiss and fitted myself between her thighs, on my knees so I could see every curve of her gorgeous body. With featherlight touches, she trailed her fingers down my back and over the rise of my arse, the contact sending sparks dancing across my skin. I craved her attention, needed it like a flame needs oxygen.

"I need you inside me, Cas. We've waited long enough."

Who was I to argue with flawless logic such as that?

Taking myself in hand, I slid my weeping tip through her swollen folds, both of us groaning at the intimate contact. Her eyes were half-lidded and filled with need when I notched myself at her entrance.

"We do this, darling, you'll never be rid of me."

Her grin hit me square in the chest. Then her focus faltered, attention no longer on my face but at the place where our bodies connected. "Cas, what are these? Tattoos?"

Her fingers traced crescent-shaped patterns on my hips, and I nearly came undone as immense pleasure bloomed where she touched me.

It couldn't be.

My eyes darted to the path she traced along my skin.

Bloody hell, it was.

Mating marks.

The iridescent scales only appeared for sea fae when they found their true mate and accepted their destiny. I'd nearly forgotten my past and replaced it with my life in Ravenndel. But here it was, clear and bright, reminding me who I was supposed to be all along. Hers.

"I . . . uh . . ." I wasn't sure how to explain what was happening. I'd never expected to have this moment. I had to clear my throat and try again. "They're our marks. Our mating marks, I mean."

Her eyes filled with joy. "Will I get them too?"

"No. You're not sea fae." She was wondering if she'd get marks? But the most important part of this seemed to have passed her by. I'd essentially just married her. "Did you hear what I said, though? They're not just marks. We are mates."

She snorted. "Yeah. I got that a few weeks ago, Caspian. I was just waiting for you to catch up."

I blinked at her, equal parts stunned and amused. "Of fucking course you did, darling. You're brilliant and perfect and every happy thought I've ever had in one delicious package."

All the feelings and cravings I'd been having since meeting her made so much more sense. This wasn't obsession. It wasn't addiction. It was fate. Love. True love.

And it was mine.

She was mine.

So it was about damn time I did something about it.

With a groan, I pushed inside her to the hilt. Goddess, she was hot and slick and gripped me like a fucking glove. Fuck, I couldn't come already. But I was damn close.

"Don't move. Just stay there like that, darling. Please."

She giggled, which moved her, so I growled and pressed down on her hips to keep her still.

"I said don't move," I gritted out.

She rolled her hips, which sent my eyes back in my head.

"I never was very good at following instructions."

"Of course my mate would be a brat."

"Takes one to know one, pirate."

The devilish woman clenched her inner muscles, milking me as she stared me down.

There was no arguing with her, not when she was giving me everything I'd ever wanted. "This is going to be over before it starts if you keep that up."

She did it again. "I bet you've got more than one in you."

My fingers slid over her clit as I pulled out to the tip and slammed home again. If I was going to come like this was my first time, I'd make sure she joined me. Pirate or not, I was a generous lover—it was the prince in me.

It wasn't long before she was moaning my name and seeking out more of my touch. A flare of heat across my collarbones and my throat sent a wave of certainty through me. The last of the marks. We were fully mated. I could let go.

"You are so beautiful," she breathed, her fingers dancing over the glowing scales along my collarbone.

Just that ghost of a touch was enough to snap the last thread of my control and send me hurtling toward release.

"Dahlia, oh fuck."

I poured everything I had into my mate, my hips jerking as euphoria took hold, and her walls clenched around me as her own pleasure crested. The ripple of her inner muscles sent a second orgasm crashing into me. I didn't even know that was possible, but I wasn't complaining. I'd take everything she wanted to give me, and then I'd beg for seconds.

"Uh, Cas?" she breathed, a little fear in her voice.

"Yes, love?"

"Are we floating?"

I looked down to find we were indeed hovering over the bed a few inches. Smirking, I locked eyes with her. "Looks like I found my happy thought."

"I thought it was Peter and the lost boys who had the happy thoughts."

I just held her gaze. "We might take on new roles, but some things are eternal, Dahlia-darling."

"Does that mean you'll wear the tights for me? Maybe that cute little hat?"

A frown tugged at my lips, and we fell to the soft mattress. "You know, I seem to have lost every one of my hats. Can't remember where I left a single one."

"Is that a no to the tights, then?"

"Everything is a yes for you, love."

She smiled at me with such love in her eyes that I couldn't help but lean down and kiss her. Then, even though I was spent and soft, I stayed inside her as I rolled us over so she was astride my hips.

"Rock your hips for me, mate. I just want to watch you move on top of me."

As her body swayed, I got exactly what I wanted. I thickened all over again, filling her to the hilt and making her moan.

"That'll teach me to question your stamina." She giggled.

I smacked her arse. “Are you laughing while I’m inside you?”

“Not at you, promise.”

“What’s so funny, then?”

Her smile was blinding in its beauty. “My collection’s complete.”

“So it is.”

CHAPTER TWENTY-ONE

TOR

The longer I was separated from my mate, the harder my beast raged. It was a burden I hadn't yet conquered, this urge to see her safe and in my arms at all times. I was her protector, and I couldn't do my job if I wasn't able to lay eyes upon her. Our bond, while powerful, still had its limits. Limits that had consequences because of my beast's unhinged nature.

The connection my parents shared was unique in many aspects, not the least of which was the fact that it was a true soul bond. Not long after they found each other and recognized that they were fated, they'd participated in an ancient ritual that merged their souls together, the results of which were cataclysmic—to say the least. I wasn't interested in the shared manifestation of their powers so much as the ever-present ability to feel and sense their mate. Such a gift would help soothe me now, because even if I couldn't see Dahlia with my own eyes, at least I would be able to sense whether she was safe and use the connection to locate her.

A small smile hit my lips as I thought of Dahlia's reaction to learning of such a thing. She'd probably compare it to a mate GPS.

I was certain I could track down the spell needed, that I could even perform it, but that would mean Dahlia would have to share this curse with me. I wouldn't do that to her.

Glancing out the window, I scowled at the darkened sky, frustration getting the better of me. Where was she? I hadn't seen her since yesterday. She'd spent the night in Hades's bed, and I'd gotten up early this morning to hunt. I'd hoped to find her at lunch and claim her this afternoon, but she'd had a session with Masterson she couldn't miss, and then she never showed up for dinner. Thus my growing restlessness.

I paced her room, pervasive growls escaping my throat with each passing moment. Her scent was barely there when it should've been all I could smell. Stopping near the foot of the bed, I took stock of the destruction I'd wrought. Embarrassment crept up the back of my neck, hot and stinging.

Gods, I was ridiculous. A child having a tantrum over his favorite lovey. I hated feeling this way, like I was always one step away from losing control. We'd fought so hard to get me here, to a place where I could coexist as both man and beast in an uneasy alliance. I wasn't fully one or the other, but a blend of the two. Thanks to my Kærasta.

It wouldn't take much at all to tip the balance, though, and there was doubt who would win if that happened.

Me, the beast snarled in my head.

Fucking hell, I was on the edge. I needed aid because if I lost it and ended up back in No Man's Land, I'd never come back to myself. One strike, and I'd be out.

I heaved a sigh. It was time for reinforcements. The dragon would know what to do. Better yet, if he had the same reaction to her disappearance as me, then no one could fault me for overreacting.

Tearing out of the room and not bothering to shut her door behind me, I stalked down the hallway toward Kai's door. A burly shifter named Logan stood in my way as he leaned over a tiny female.

"Move," I snarled.

He cut me a glance, then returned his attention to her. "Make me."

Rage turned my vision red. This arse was asking for it. "My pleasure."

Taking hold of him by the back of the neck, I hurled him to the ground, all but throwing him down the hall. I heard his collision with the floor but didn't spare him a glance. Not even when he started shouting at me.

"Motherfucking cocksucker! You won't be smiling when my pack and I come for you in your sleep."

I stared hard at the female he'd been flirting with. "Muzzle your dog before he ends up with a mouth full of blood instead of teeth."

She blinked a few times but scurried over to where Logan was pulling himself together and rising to his feet. "You don't know what you've started. This isn't over, Novasgardian."

"For your sake, you better hope it is. I let you live. That's something I rarely do."

And with those parting words, I made haste to Kai's room. It was a good thing he answered the door after the first knock. With the unsated bloodlust thumping through my veins, I was liable to tear the fucking door from its hinges.

"What the hell, Tor?" Kai growled, one hand gripping the towel around his waist. "Ye nearly broke the wood pounding on it like that."

"Is she with you?" I asked, panting for breath.

"Dahlia?"

"Yes, Dahlia, you fucking prat. Who else?"

His eyes flashed with anger, but he didn't bite back. "She's not in here. You haven't seen her?"

I didn't bother answering the question. Why the fuck would I be here looking for her if I'd seen her?

Genuine worry careened through me. I turned on my heels and stormed away, my next destination not far.

"Where are you going?" Kai demanded from his doorway.

"Cain!"

"Right behind you," he called after me, shutting the door to presumably get dressed.

My heart was racing, and my legs ate up the distance between Kai's room and Cain's. Once again I pounded hard enough to rattle the wood.

A furious wave of barking preceded the door opening.

"Can I help you?"

Kai reached me just as I opened my mouth to respond. "Is she with you?" I asked, peering over Cain's shoulder. Part of me relaxed simply because he was still here and hadn't fled with her to the underworld. No matter what Sorcha said about Blackwood preventing its residents from leaving, something told me Hades couldn't be kept from his kingdom.

"Dahlia?"

I blinked at his stupidity. Was everyone lacking for brains here? What other woman would I possibly have any interest in?

"Aye," Kai said, the urgency in his tone matching my own.

"No, I haven't seen her since this morning."

"No one has seen her."

Sparks ignited from the tips of Cain's fingers while Asshole's low growl joined mine.

Rage bubbled close to the surface again. If she wasn't with any of us, that left one option. "The pirate."

The sparks turned to a full flame, turning Asshole's white fur a soft blue and casting his shadow onto the wall behind me. As I turned, I had to blink, questioning what I saw. For it was not a tiny dog's shadow filling the wall, but an enormous three-headed beast. Cerberus. Of bloody course.

"Holy hell," Kai muttered.

"Indeed."

"Asshole. Find her," Cain ordered.

I was quick to step out of the Bischon's way, showing the fluffball a level of deference I probably wouldn't have had I not learned his true identity. He shot past the three of us, running as though his tiny tail was on fire. We were hot on his heels, all three of us jockeying for position as we gave chase.

Instead of turning right toward Hook's room, Asshole went left, leading us back to Blackwood's central foyer. As we passed Joffrey, he called out, "No running in the halls!"

As usual, we ignored him, our only goal finding Dahlia.

"What the hell is this?" Sorcha asked with a cackle as we raced past her. "Did the clowns lose their car?"

"Maybe the pup stole the last condom," Oz offered.

"You're an even bigger idiot than I thought if you believe they use condoms."

"All right, fine. The lube, then."

I didn't give them another thought as we continued following Asshole out the door. My heart sank as soon as we tumbled out into the night and caught sight of the swagger-soaked idiot himself. He was sauntering up the main walkway, a sated, dazed expression on his face.

"Where is she?" I snarled, my beast front and center as I caught him by the throat and held him up until we were at eye level. I could smell her on him, which only made me squeeze harder.

"I . . . don't . . . know," Hook choked out.

Cain laughed, low and bitter. "Fuck her and chuck her, huh? I don't know why I'm surprised."

Asshole yipped twice, sharp and insistent, as he jumped up on Cain's legs, begging for attention.

"Where?" Cain asked the dog. "Which way?"

The puppy took off again, heading not for the forest from which Hook had come, but in the direction of the lake.

I let go of the pirate, letting him drop to the ground with an audible *oof*. I was already in pursuit of Cain and his dog but could easily hear Kai and Hook's rushed conversation taking place behind me.

"What the fuck is going on?" the pirate asked, pain threading through the question.

"Dahlia's missing. C'mon. No time to sit around on your arse."

"She was with me all afternoon and into the evening."

I stopped in my tracks and rounded on him. "And you lost her?"

"She must've gone while I was sleeping."

"If she gets hurt because of your negligence—"

Kai placed a hand on my shoulder. "It could've happened to any of us. She has her own mind, and you know that. Now we have to find her and make sure she's all right."

A furious growl was my only response.

Asshole's insistent bark drew my attention back to him. He'd come to a stop a few yards away from the edge of the lake.

"There she is," Cain said, pointing to our woman as she stood at the shore.

"What's she doing?" Kai asked.

As we watched, Dahlia fell to her knees, hands pressed into the loamy earth, head bowed, blonde hair luminous in the moonlight.

"What the devil is in the water?" Hook asked, voice low and filled with tension.

I spared him half a glance, only to find him pointing at the horizon. Mist floated along the top of the lake's surface, but just there in the direction Hook indicated, it was shifting. Almost like it was parting to allow something or someone passage.

And it was headed right for my Kærasta.

"Dahlia!"

CHAPTER TWENTY-TWO

DAHLIA

Twenty minutes earlier

"You could be snuggled up with a sexy pirate right now, maybe having round three of epic sex. But nooooo, you had to be an overachiever and do your assignment," I scolded myself as I approached the cold, dark lake, the heavy mist hanging over the still water adding to the eerie visage. "Next time Masterson gives you homework, you wait until the sun is up or you have adult supervision. You are a bad adult, Dahlia. The worst adulter who ever adulted. Wait, I think that means something else."

I stared at the gravestone the mermaids had placed at the lake's edge, taking in the beautiful statue of Nautica that had been carved into the marble. As was fitting, she was tits out for the lake. Nautica and the rest of them were always tits out. Maybe it was a mermaid thing. They spared no detail in honoring her, ensuring down to the starfish and pearl headdress that it was a perfect replica of the fallen lady fish.

"I'd pour one out for you, but alas, we were not homies. You will have to settle for a bit of spirit summoning and some light interrogation."

Fuck, how did I even do this? In theory, it should be easy for me. Close your eyes, visualize the spirit you need to talk to, and summon a bitch. But there were so many spirits here, and the buzzing of their energy, especially at night, was distracting. Was there a special incantation? A code word? Did I need a password to gain access to her, like in a speakeasy?

I was spiraling, I knew I was. This sort of unknown shit always set me off. I'd survived for years because I controlled every aspect of my life. It made me feel safe. This was pure chaos. Nothing was in my control anymore. Even when it was supposed to be. Case in point, the ghost in the doll currently imprisoned in my hope chest.

"Pull yourself to-fucking-gether, Dahlia." I shook out my shoulders and kicked off my shoes, letting my toes sink into the chilly soil. Scotland in December was not what one would call balmy. I was taking my toes' lives into my hands here, risking frostbite and possible amputation for this stupid assignment. Best to get it over with as quickly as possible.

Closing my eyes, I let the bone-deep cold radiate through me, and I pictured Nautica. Perfect. Beautiful. Horny for my man. The words came to me on instinct. I didn't know if they were right, but it felt like they were.

"Nautica, I call you back from your eternal slumber. Come to me and answer my questions."

I stayed there with my eyes closed for one heartbeat. Two. Three. When not even a ripple of water greeted my summons, I risked opening one eye, casting it from side to side. But nope. Nothing.

My shoulders slumped. Well, shit. I really thought I was onto something.

"Next time, Lizzie, you better write this shit down for me. I want a numbered list. Step one: locate spirit. Step two: incantation. Step three: put it back where it belongs. Side note: that does not include children's toys."

Gaze trailing back to the headstone, I tried to find anything I could use to connect with her. Aside from her fucking perfect tits, I found myself at odds with who she was to me. Until I read the inscription on her grave.

Beloved one true mate of Captain Caspian Hook

That fucking bitch.

"Nautica, you horny cunt, crawl out of whatever hole they dropped you in and get your slippery, bescaled, fishy ass over here right now!" I hollered, meaning the angry words with every fiber of my being.

I fell to my knees as I felt the power rush out of me. This was unlike anything I'd done before. It left me lightheaded and a little queasy.

As I caught my breath and got my bearings, I stared down at where my palms were pressed into the ground. The quiet lapping of water against the shore should've been soothing. Instead it seemed to grow louder and more insistent.

"Dahlia!" Tor's shout of my name on the wind had me snapping my head up and turning to find all four of my men standing in the distance, shock on their faces.

In any other circumstance, I might have cheered a little to see the four of them joining forces like this, but their expressions were anything but happy. It was Hook's shaking finger in the end that filled me in. Looking in the direction he was pointing, I saw what had them so frightened.

"Oh fuck no," I gasped, shooting back and crab-walking away from the water.

Well, good news, Nautica heard me this time. Bad news, she was doing her girl from *The Ring* impersonation as she crawled out of the lake.

She'd once been a true beauty. Not anymore. Her eyes were a milky white, her skin a ghastly gray, and the hair, which had once been vibrant, now hung in stringy clumps with bits of scalp exposed. An entire chunk of her face had been ripped away, revealing a section of her yellowed teeth. One of her full breasts was completely gone, exposing her ribs, and I was pretty sure there was an eel or something squirming around in there. Gag.

The creepiest part of it all was the mermaid tail that began at her hips. The scales were dull and lifeless, fins tattered and riddled with holes, like something had been eating her.

She dragged herself out of the water quicker than I expected, her gaze trained on me with such hatred. As her teeth snapped, she snarled, and water slipped from her mouth.

"No. Bad mermaid. Stay."

Asshole barked in the distance, distracting her momentarily. Long enough I could get to my feet at least. And if my knees were shaking so hard they knocked together, so what? I was still upright.

"Listen to me, Nautica," I said with a shaky voice. I'd summoned this creature; I should be able to control it, right?

She hissed, more water bubbling up through her lips.

"You don't have to like me, but you do have to listen to me."

She opened her mouth as though to respond, only instead of words the eel that had been playing peekaboo in her ribcage shot out of her mouth.

"Jesus fucking Christ, you really let yourself go."

Cain's voice was at my ear. "I appreciate your vim and vigor, baby doll, but now is not the time to taunt the zombie."

"Oh, I'm sorry, not all of us are the lord of the fucking underworld. Do you have any suggestions for how to handle this, or are you just going to offer critiques?"

His palm settled at the base of my spine, and a strange rush of strength pulsed through me. "Ask her what you want to know."

"Tried that."

Though come to think of it, maybe I hadn't. It was hard to keep track of everything going on right now. It wasn't every day a girl came face to face with a dead mermaid.

"Try again. I've got her. She won't hurt you."

His calm strength went a long way to soothe my frazzled nerves. Giving him a slight nod to indicate I heard and understood him, I took a deep, calming breath and then focused hard on the creature before me.

"Nautica, how did you die?"

The mermaid's head twitched, her teeth snapping in an irritable gesture. "Cold. Alone. Painfully." Her voice wasn't the usual lyrical melody I'd known when she was alive. Now it was a sibilant rasp, like air blown between pieces of paper.

Well, that was about as helpful as a bologna sandwich. As in, not remotely.

"You've got, at best, a couple minutes with her before she deteriorates beyond saving. The soul cannot withstand being trapped in a dead vessel. She will wither and become something vile."

"Because she's not already?"

"Focus, Dahlia. You can do this."

"Who killed you, Nautica?"

Her head tilted back, and she let out an agonized wail. "He did."

"He who? What did he look like? What was his name?"

Cain gripped my arm hard. "Too many questions at once. She needs one at a time, or you'll lose her."

"He who, Nautica?"

"Don't know. Don't know. Don't know," she wailed, each refrain more unhinged than the last.

"What color was his hair?"

"Blond."

"Did he speak to you?"

"Yessss."

This was going much better. Short and sweet it was.

"Did he have an accent?"

"American."

"Her description matches the man I fought in the forest," Cas whispered at my right.

Which meant I hadn't really uncovered anything new. We already knew it had been the Ripper. Fuck. I was messing this all up.

"Hurry, baby doll. You don't have much longer."

"Do you remember what he said to you?"

A full-body shudder tore through the dead girl's body, water gurgling down her chin. Another pulse of Hades's power rippled through me, and I knew Nautica felt it too, because her milky eyes turned the exact shade of blue as his flame.

"I am death's most humble and loyal servant. Your sacrifice is a great honor."

Before I could continue this line of questioning, she gasped and fell forward, her body seizing and a terrible gurgle coming from her. Then she went completely still. I couldn't feel her any longer. Her soul was gone.

"Crap, we lost her," I said.

"Well, that was . . . exciting," Cas offered after a beat.

"Is it over? She's gone?" Tor took my hand and squeezed.

But it wasn't. Nautica's rotting body twitched, and a screech of rage escaped her as she lurched toward us. Cain pulled me back as quickly as possible to keep me from her reach.

"The soul we knew as Nautica is gone, but her body is still animated."

"Like the zombie from the other day?" Kai asked.

"No. That was out-and-out possession."

"Meaning?" Tor asked.

"There was still a viable spirit in a live vessel," Cain explained. "This time, the dead body corrupted the soul, eating away at it until nothing remained except the magic. This isn't Nautica anymore. She's nothing more than a soul-sucking ghoul."

The ghoul crawled up the shore, reaching for any of us she could get. She moved inhumanly fast, her skeletal body slithering up the bank with ease.

"How do we put her back?" I asked, stumbling away from her.

"It's too late for that, baby doll. That's why I warned you not to push her too hard. The only thing that creature is concerned with now is replacing the soul it lost by any means necessary. Namely, eating ours."

Fuck. I'd done this to her? Once again, my ignorance put all of us at risk. Why did Masterson keep asking me to do things so clearly out of my league?

"Okay, so how do we stop her?" I asked, my voice trembling with my guilt.

"This is beyond the scope of our powers. We deal in souls, not the soulless."

We couldn't just let a ghoul run around Blackwood. I needed a weapon, some way to stop her. But before I could even scan our surroundings, a blast of dragon fire engulfed the ghoul, leaving her screaming until she was nothing but a pile of dust.

All of us stopped, turning to look at Kai, who stood to the side, heaving, his eyes glowing purple with reptilian slits for pupils. Black scales decorated his cheekbones and temples, and a coronet of small horns sat at his hairline. He was more dragon than I'd ever seen him.

"Kai," I whispered, awestruck.

"I'm done waiting for permission, gem. I willnae risk yer soul." Kai's voice was all gravel and rasp, and I knew it was the dragon speaking to me. "It belongs to me."

"That's a lot more fun to watch when you aren't aiming it at me," Tor said, giving Kai an approving slap on the shoulder.

"Are we all going to ignore what just happened?" Caspian asked.

"That I can apparently raise the dead?"

"No. That was a neat trick, but I mean what she said about the Ripper."

"She didn't say anything we didn't already know."

"Yes she did, love." We all waited for Cas to illuminate us. "Blond, American, male. There's only one of them on Blackwood's grounds."

"Oh my God," I whispered. "Taylor Swift is the Ripper."

CHAPTER
TWENTY-THREE
HADES

I've never been so excited to tear a soul from a body as I was right fucking now.

"I should've known it was him. He was the problem. Never trust a man whose name is the same as a pop icon. Never." Asshole pranced alongside me, head held high. *"Let's go show him exactly what it's like to come up against the antihero."*

"I'm not an antihero. I'm the motherfuckin' villain."

"Someone is feeling himself right now," Dahlia muttered, giving me a healthy dose of side-eye.

"You said so yourself, baby doll."

"Yeah, but usually you don't look quite so murdery when you say it."

"Does it scare you? The truth about who I am and what I do?"

She squirmed, cheeks going pink. "Nope."

"It turns her on, boss man. Read the fuckin' room."

I was going to put this dog in a kennel at the other end of the estate if he kept it up.

"I cannot be contained. Try me."

I raised a brow but refrained from comment. We had bigger fish to fry.

"Where's he at right now?" I asked, looking to Tor and Kai.

"Why not ask me?" Hook protested. "I know everyone's whereabouts."

"All right, small fry. Since you're so eager to help. Where's Swift?"

"Wait," Dahlia said, placing her palm to my chest. "Shouldn't we make sure we have the right guy first?"

"You're the one who named him," Kai pointed out.

"Well yeah, but . . . innocent until proven guilty, right?"

"Not in my world," Tor offered. "Murder first. Apologize later."

"And it's not like Nautica was completely cognizant of the world around her. What if she wasn't giving us everything? All we have to go on is that he's a blond American male. That could be Ryan Gosling, for all we know."

"Ken would never," Asshole grumbled.

"What the fuck are you talking about?" I asked him.

"Watch a movie once in a while, man. Sheesh."

Everyone stared at me, and I realized I needed to let them in on Asshole's secret. "He can talk. The dog. In my head."

"And we're sure he's not a figment of your imagination?" Hook drawled.

"It's Cerberus," Tor said, surprising me with his insight. Then again, the demigod did seem the most in the know about me and my kind, so maybe it wasn't that much of a stretch.

"Exactly."

Asshole stood a little taller. *"That's right, big boy. And don't you fuckin' forget it."*

I would have sworn the little fucker winked at me.

"Big dog energy. Just like you said, super chief."

"You're never gonna let me live that down, are you?"

"Nope. Your morning pep talks were the highlight of my day. Don't think I'm letting you give those up once we go home. I need my ups."

"Does anyone else wish we knew the other side of this conversation?" Dahlia asked.

"Trust me, you don't. He's a lot to handle."

Asshole lifted his leg and pissed on my shoe.

"Case in point," I grumbled.

"Seems like maybe he doesn't appreciate the way you talk to him," she said mildly, stooping down to pick him up.

He held my stare while he nuzzled into her breasts. I was five seconds away from murdering him. He knew it too. There was no missing the smirk in his beady black eyes as his tongue lolled out of his mouth.

"So what are we going to do about Taylor? Since y'all won't let me obliterate him here and now, I need to know."

"It's not like we can trust a word out of his mouth. He'll lie outright if he is the Ripper," Kai said.

"We can torture the truth out of him. Nothing a few broken bones can't fix." Tor's voice held such delight even my stomach turned.

Dahlia paled. "Maybe there's a less bloody way to do this."

"What are you thinking, baby doll?"

"Oz can read minds. He could let us know if Taylor is being honest."

"Sure, we could do that if you want to take all the fun out of it," Tor grumbled.

Dahlia rested her palm on his chest, staring up into his eyes. "Are you feeling okay? You seem a lot more *beastly* than usual."

"We were apart for too long."

Her brows lifted. "It's only been—"

"Too long," he repeated.

"Oookay. Noted."

"So where are we holding this little inquisition?" I asked, glancing back at the estate.

"My tower. No one will hear the screams if we need to utilize Plan Beast."

Hook gave Kai an approving once-over. "You're funnier than I remember."

"I have my moments. Now, we need to draw Taylor out, get him to come to us of his own free will."

"You leave that to me. I know exactly how to get him." Hook took off, heading up the hill toward Blackwood.

"I guess I'll go get Oz?" Dahlia said.

"I'll go with you," I offered.

Tor growled like he was going to protest, but Kai intervened. "You and I should get the tower ready. Make sure you have everything you need prepped for his arrival."

Tor cracked his knuckles and then his neck. "I don't need props."

"I was thinking more about chains and a chair."

"Oh. Right, that would be useful."

If we had to torture him, it wouldn't be too pretty. For Dahlia's sake, I hoped Oz did what she wanted.

~

Hook

I DID LOVE a good plot to catch someone in their own game. But I especially loved being able to take part in said plot. As I stood outside Swiftie's door, I was positively giddy with anticipation. A few grains of pixie dust danced on my fingers, ready for release.

Tick

Tick

Tick

Hoping the others were ready for us in the tower, I knocked on the door, eager to get on with the show. I needed to get back to Dahlia before the whispers joined in with the near-constant ticking.

As soon as his smug face appeared, a frisson of anger swept

through me. Was I staring into the eyes of my attacker? He was certainly the right height and build. I tried to envision a plague mask on his stupid head.

"You're not supposed to be in this wing. This is for staff only," he said, instantly puffing up his chest and looking down his nose at me.

I leaned on the doorframe, one arm above my head so I could sprinkle the granules of dust over his. "Not even if I've got a special message from the object of your desire?"

The suspicion on his face swiftly transformed into lustful intrigue. Bless pixie dust. It truly was the greatest discovery of all time. And so versatile.

"Merri?"

"Yes, that's right. Merri is waiting for you. She's spread out like a . . . Thanksgiving feast." It was Americans who did the whole turkey and pie thing, right? I thought so.

"Where is she?"

Bingo.

"Follow me. I'll take you to her. She paid me handsomely to find the two of you somewhere private. We can't risk anyone overhearing and attempting to ruin your fun, can we?"

The wanker didn't even bother grabbing a shirt. He just followed me like I was an avatar of the Pied Piper. More the fool. We know how well that turned out, don't we?

In a few short moments, we were climbing the stairs of Kai's tower, Swiftie breathing harder with each step. For someone who appeared fit, he was actually pretty out of shape. A niggling worm of suspicion burrowed in my brain at that observation. Was a diabolical killer such as the Ripper really unable to ascend a staircase without becoming winded?

That didn't bode well for the revenge plot brewing in the tower. Cain and the others were going to be seriously disappointed. But that was their problem. I'd played my part rather gloriously, if I do say so myself.

Tick

Tick

Tick

I shook my head fiercely to rid myself of the unwanted sound. I was nearly there. Nearly with my darling. She'd banish the madness. She'd ground me.

"You should go first," I said as we reached the last curve of the staircase. "Best you don't keep her waiting."

He nearly shoved me down in his haste to obey. My lip curled in anger. We needed him alive, but he didn't have to be unharmed. Maybe just a little slip of my dagger to help him remember his manners?

Tick

Tick

Tick

"Merri? Wait, what is this?" he asked, walking backward once he reached the top and discovered that it was not a sexy succubus awaiting him, but a very different sort of welcoming committee.

I braced myself on the wall of the stairwell, not willing to let this sod get the better of me. "Oh, no you don't." Catching hold of him as he tried to flee, I forcefully shoved him up the remaining few steps and into the room.

"I don't understand. You said she was here. What are they all doing?"

"Looks like it's time for us all to come clean, Swiftie. Merri's not here. She never was. But you? You have some explaining to do."

"M-me?" he stuttered, his sense of self-preservation kicking in. Though it still wasn't enough to counteract the pixie dust.

"We have a seat for you and everything. Think of it as a party, and you're tonight's entertainment." I gave him another little shove, and this time Tor was there, grabbing Swiftie by the arm and yanking him down into the chair he and Kai procured.

As soon as they took over, I considered my part concluded and immediately sought out Dahlia. She'd been standing the furthest away from the door, sandwiched between Cain and Kai, Oz hovering in front of her.

"How do you want him, Oz?" Tor asked. "Does he have to be conscious?"

Swiftie's eyes widened. "Oz? No. He'll melt my brain. Don't let him touch me."

Oz stepped forward, a strange sort of excitement in his eyes. "I haven't done this in a long time. He's right. I might do just that."

"Try not to. We need answers, not another body," Cain said.

"Bodies are not a problem," Kai answered, his eyes flashing with a hint of his dragon.

Swiftie gulped audibly.

"Do it," Tor ordered, staring at Oz.

One touch of his palm to Swiftie's bare skin had Oz's eyes rolling into the back of his head. An almost euphoric look crossed the mind reader's face. Swiftie grunted and twitched, his skin breaking out into a sweat.

Almost instantly, the expression on Oz's face changed, and he dropped his hold.

"You little shit. Your name's not even Taylor. It's fucking Brian."

"What?" Kai asked.

Oz shot him a look. "He's Brian Swift. His claim to fame is that he can vaguely control water particles."

"But he could still be the Ripper," Tor observed, his expression murderous.

The indignation Oz was throwing off was now replaced with apology. "I'm not going to be able to help you with that. Despite his complete lack of meaningful talent, he does have an extraordinary ability to shield his mind. I can't get past the surface-level bullshit. Not without liquefying his brain until it leaks from his nose."

"Is that really what happens?" Dahlia asked, horror in her voice.

"Yeah. It's not pretty."

Kai cracked his knuckles and rolled his big shoulders. "Then I guess it's time for Plan Beast after all. Oz, you can go. Dahlia, you too. It's best you're not here to see this next part."

Oz scampered out of the tower like his arse was on fire, but Dahlia held her ground.

"I'm not leaving," Dahlia protested. "I need answers as much as the rest of you. Maybe even more so."

"Oh, you're leaving, baby doll. Seeing your mate tear into someone without remorse will haunt you the rest of your days."

She tossed him a scathing look. "Why would that haunt me? I might be named after a flower, but I'm not delicate. I've seen Tor decimate creatures right in front of me, and it didn't change a damn thing."

"I was defending you, Kærasta. This is different. What we're about to do to him is criminal." Tor closed the distance between my darling and himself. "I don't want you to see me torture him. This is a far cry from fighting to the death."

"But—"

"No, Dahlia. My soul will bear these sins so that yours never has to. That's the trade-off. It's what I was born for. Leave me so I can do it without fear of judgment or disgust. You need to see me as a protector, but right now, I need to be the beast."

Poor Brian was so out of it he didn't even register the threats of imminent torture.

"Fine. But even if he is the Ripper, please don't kill him unless you have to. Other people need justice. His death is not ours to claim."

"Speak for yourself," Cain muttered, but there was a little twitch around his mouth that told me he was joking. Kind of.

Dahlia took Cain's hand and cast us each a meaningful look before leaving the room.

"Anyone have a shower curtain or plastic tarp?" I asked, poking around the space. "We'll need something to catch all the blood. No use having it drip through the floorboards or stain anything."

"B-blood?" Brian spluttered.

I smirked as Tor manifested a big blue tarp beneath the chair.

Stepping forward, I pulled my trusty dagger from my boot and twirled it a few times. "Oh yes. Buckle up, Swiftie. Unless you start singing for us, it's going to be a long night."

CHAPTER TWENTY-FOUR

KAI

"Where should we make the first cut, lads?" Hook asked, flipping his dagger and catching it expertly by the blade.

"Start with his sweaty scrotum. It won't kill him, but it'll hurt like nothing else," Tor snarled, stepping up behind Swiftie and grabbing him by the hair. "Hold still. If he nicks your femoral artery, there will be nothing for it. You'll bleed out right here and now."

"Works for me," Hook said, stalking forward.

"N-no. Please, God, no," he whimpered, his fear blooming in the room, filling the space with the rank stench of old sweat mingled with piss.

A tingling sense of uncertainty prickled the back of my mind. Something wasn't quite right. "Wait," I said.

"Wait? Are you serious? I'm in my element. This is where Captain Hook shines, boys. Don't stop me now."

I ignored him and focused on the innate sense of knowing tugging low in my belly. I'd interrogated my share of prisoners. My father had wanted to ensure I was prepared for every facet of my future position. This man was not reacting like a hardened criminal.

If anything, he was acting . . . innocent. His fear was too genuine. His surprise unfabricated. This was not a show; the man was truly terrified. He wasn't a ruthless serial killer.

We couldn't torture an innocent man. We needed to be sure before we met out any version of justice.

"I need my kit."

"I beg your pardon? Your kit?" Hook glared at me.

"We won't get the truth from him this way. He'll lose his mind first."

"Welcome to the club." Cas twirled his blade a few times before slamming it into the wood between Swiftie's spread legs, narrowly missing his crotch. "Once you get used to the voices, it's not so bad. Except for the constant tick, tick, ticking. That's the one that will have you reaching for your blade and attempting to puncture your own eardrums."

Tor and I exchanged looks before refocusing on Caspian. Just how far gone was Dahlia's pirate? There was no missing the feverish gleam in his eyes now that we were looking for it.

I moved slowly, not wanting to startle him. "Why don't you just give me this for now," I said gently as I removed the dagger from the chair.

Caspian sulked, but didn't fight me. Thank the goddess.

"So what do you suggest?" Tor asked, his fingers more claws than digits now.

"I can give him a tattoo. A rune that acts as a truth spell. He will never be able to utter a lie again without experiencing debilitating pain."

"Wh-what?"

"Can it, Brian. We aren't talking to you right now." The sliver of growl in Caspian's words had my dragon nodding in appreciation.

"Why not mention this before?" Tor asked, his eyes bottomless black pits.

"Dahlia seemed sure of Oz's ability, not to mention her own certainty. It seemed redundant to offer."

"And now?" he pressed.

"He smells like . . ." I was struggling to find the words to explain to them what I was sensing.

"Prey?" Tor offered.

But he didn't. It was more like the opposite. Almost like this Brian was decidedly *not* prey. Prey were supposed to be hunted and devoured. My gut was telling me he was not.

"No," I replied, sounding only just this side of sure.

The other two men looked at me with raised brows, waiting for me to elaborate. But I didn't know how to.

When in doubt, blame the dragon, right? That always seemed to work in the past.

The beast in question huffed in response to that.

"My dragon thinks we have the wrong person. Dahlia wanted us to be sure before we did anything."

That took the wind out of Tor's sails. "She'd never forgive herself if we were wrong."

"It wouldn't be her fault. That's why we sent her away." Cas leaned against the table where my treasures were piled, and it took everything in me not to shove him bodily aside.

"She wouldn't see it that way, and you know it, pirate."

"Oh, fine. Have at your arts and crafts, but then I call dibs at filleting the flesh off that dangly little worm betwixt his legs."

Tor gave Caspian an appreciative look. "I didn't know you had it in you." At the same time, Brian sputtered. "It's perfectly average."

Cas shot him a look of pure chastisement. "Not the time, Brian."

Kit in hand, I laid out everything I needed and locked gazes with Tor. "Hold him still. Cas, I need you to roll down his lower lip and keep it in place. If he moves, I could kill him."

"If you're trying to dissuade me, that was probably not your best argument, mate. I'm in a killing mood tonight, or have you not noticed?"

"I'll let you taste Dahlia first next time," I offered.

"We have an accord!" he crowed, slapping his thigh before jumping up and moving into position.

Tor held Brian down by pressing on the top of his head. "Don't move. All I have to do is apply pressure, and your spine will compress until it shoots out your arsehole and through the chair's bottom. Do you understand? Whimper if you do."

Brian whimpered, and the distinct scent of hot piss filled the room. Sure enough, the man's pants were soaked all the way down his legs.

"I'll take that as a yes," Tor muttered.

Giving Cas a nod, I readied my gun and started tattooing the sigil. It didn't take long. It was a simple rune and had to be fairly small due to the area I was working with. In less than ten minutes, it was done, and Brian was a blubbering mess.

Spit and snot covered his face, and he'd sweated through his pants.

"There now, all done. Let's start with a test run, shall we? Brian, why did you tell everyone your name was Taylor?"

Brian stared at us, his swollen lower lip trembling. "B-because it made people pay attention to me."

"My turn!" Caspian said, hip checking me out of the way. "Is it really average, or are you just overcompensating?"

"F-four inches is average."

"Not where I come from, mate."

"I'm pretty sure you need at least five inches to be considered average," I said.

"Is your spell defective, then?" Tor asked.

I shrugged. "He believed what he was saying, so technically it wasn't a lie. At least as far as he knew."

"Hard or soft?" Hook asked.

"Why does that matter?"

"Because a hard one is bigger. Maybe he's four inches when he's flaccid. You never know. He could be a grower. Shall we all whip ours out and see? We've got a good range here, it would help us settle the matter."

Tor shook his head. "No, that'll just make him feel worse. He's already pissed himself."

As entertaining as a devolving Caspian was, I needed to get us back on track so we could return to our mate. "Brian, are ye the Ripper?"

"Wh-what? No! Of course not."

Caspian crossed his arms. "Hmm. I'm not convinced. How do we know he's telling the truth?"

I stared at him. "Because of the tattoo."

"But he technically lied about the penis thing. You said it only hurt when he lied, not that he *couldn't* lie. We need to see what that looks like to be sure."

"I never pegged you for a sadist," Tor said.

"You've never pegged me at all," Caspian said with a saucy wink.

"Don't get your hopes up."

"Brian, what's the worst thing you've ever done?" I asked, training my focus on the wretch sitting in front of me.

"I lied about my qualifications so I could get this job." The moment the last word was out, Brian began seizing. Foamy spittle trailed out of his mouth as he convulsed on the spot.

"That's what it looks like when he lies."

When he came back to himself, he was panting, exhausted, and trembling.

Cas snatched his dagger from where I'd placed it and approached our suspect. "Take two. The truth this time, if you please."

Sweat and what looked like a hint of blood dotted Brian's brow. He was debating lying again but was still in such pain that he couldn't quite bring himself to try. "I . . . I've been spying on Merri."

Tor's fingers gripped Brian's head harder, dragging another whimper from the man. "Spying how?"

"W-watching her. In her room, while she showers . . . you know."

"Ah, you're a Peeping Tom," Caspian said.

Tor glared at me from over his head. "You said he was innocent."

"I said I thought he was innocent of the crime we were accusing him of. Not that he was innocent in general."

"Can we kill him now?"

"For spying on Merri? While reprehensible, I'm not sure it's a killing offense."

Tor growled. "What if he did it to Dahlia?"

"I didn't! I-I swear!"

Now Caspain was glowering. "Why not? Our mate is fucking gorgeous. You would be so lucky to lay eyes on her."

"He's not the Ripper. He's a perverted bastard, but not a serial killer." I stared Tor down. "We cannae kill him."

"I could take his eyes. It would be a just punishment, and Dahlia doesn't have a set in her collection yet."

"What's she gonna do with a pair of dried-up eyeballs, you daft twit?" Cas slid his finger over the blade in his hand and winced when he cut himself. "Ouch, that's sharp."

"No eyes. Yet. We send him away, and if we ever see him again, you can string them up and use them to decorate for Christmas if you want."

My dragon had been surprisingly quiet during this entire exchange, and I wondered what he was plotting. He usually had plenty to say about my choices. And if anything, usually he was the one opting for violence over more sane courses of action. It was a little off-putting to find myself the voice of reason in the crowd. Either I was growing, or the company I kept was questionable. Either way, it definitely said something about the lot of us; I just wasn't sure it was anything good.

"Our mate's wishes were clear," my dragon said, answering my unvoiced question.

Who knew a wee mate was all I'd needed to keep him in check all these years?

"Me."

"All right, you scallywag. On your piss-covered feet." Hook

pointed the dagger at Brian and waited for Tor to release his hold on the man's skull.

As soon as Brian got to his wobbly legs, Cas notched the blade against his throat. "You're gonna come with me, you'll stay silent, and when I leave you, there won't be a moment you consider returning. Understand?"

Brian whimpered and gave the barest of nods.

"Careful, my blade is sharp enough to kill a man, Swiftie." He snickered at his own joke, the two of them exiting the room.

Tor stared after them for a beat before that obsidian gaze returned to me. "What now?"

I crossed my arms, shaking my head as I answered. "I'm not sure. He's the only one on paper who matched the mermaid's description. So I guess we're back at square one."

"Well, if it's not him, then who is it?"

"Someone who isn't at all what they seem."

CHAPTER TWENTY-FIVE

DAHLIA

"I can't believe you all wouldn't let me be there. I mean, he's after me. He's trying to kill me. The ghosts said so. And you think I would look at you differently if I saw what you could do to him? What if that turns me on, huh? What if I'm a dark, twisty creature who thrives in the shadows, but you think I'm a sweet sunshine girl? Do you even know me? I guess not."

Hades watched me with the same amused expression he'd worn since we got up to his room. Somehow he'd maneuvered me into the big armchair by the fireplace, where Asshole had immediately jumped up onto my lap and started licking my face.

But not even the sweet puppy had been enough to distract me from my snowballing thoughts.

"You done, baby doll?"

"Ha! You'd like that, wouldn't you? This is what you get for hauling me away from the action. Now you have to listen to me rant."

"I love your rants. I love your quiet moans even more, though."

I spluttered. "I . . . you . . . stop trying to distract me."

"Go on. Rant away. It gives me more of an opportunity to watch your fuckable mouth move."

Said fuckable mouth was still hanging open when my brain finally registered that he'd managed to shut me up. "You . . ."

"Me what?"

"Are something."

He smirked. "I sure am."

"Why are you enjoying my misery so much?"

"Because it gets you so fired up. One of my favorite things about you is your temper. It translates into passion. Makes me think about ways of working it out of you."

"Fucking it out of me, you mean."

"Same difference, really."

Hades jerked his head to the side, and Asshole sprang from my arms and jaunted over to the door.

"When did you get a doggy door?" I asked when Asshole let himself out.

"Tor offered to make me one the other day. Decided to take him up on it so the pup could come and go as he pleased."

"That was . . . thoughtful of him. Even if he's keeping me from the possibility of vengeance," I grumbled.

Hades stood in front of me, his body positioned between my thighs, and all I could do was look at either his crotch or gaze up until I found his face. I chose his face—until he began unbuckling his belt. The sound pulled my eyes back to where I knew he was already hard and straining.

"What are you doing?" I whispered.

"I thought we might play a little show and tell."

"What?" I asked, my eyes darting to his eyes, certain I'd misheard him.

"I'm gonna show you my dick and then tell you what to do with it."

Oh fuck me, that was a great line.

"I'm stealing that line," I said after swallowing and fighting to find my voice.

"As long as you suck me until I come down your throat, I don't care what you do with my words."

"What makes you think I want to suck your dick, huh?"

"Well, mainly the way you keep licking your lips like I'm about to offer you a lollipop."

He had me there. It was hard to maintain the high ground when just the sight of his erection had me grinding my hips against the chair in search of friction.

"Just think of it like a sexy pacifier. Something to help your mouth and brain shut up for a while."

"Pacifiers aren't sex—" I began, but before I could finish, his cock was there, pushing into my mouth and stopping any words.

I was sure the feminist part of me should be offended by the manhandling, but she wasn't. The dude had a point. I needed a distraction, and his dick was the best one I could think of. And I couldn't exactly have an anxiety rant while choking on it, so . . . game point to him, I guess.

Salty precum hit my tastebuds as he gripped my hair and pushed inside as far as I could take him. My mouth watered, and I reminded myself to breathe through my nose as he used me. Fuck, I was wet. I could feel the moisture collecting in my panties.

Using the hold he had on my hair, he worked me up and down his length. He wasn't so much fucking my face as using my face to fuck him. If that made sense. I felt deliciously used, in the absolute best possible way. Right now, in this exact moment, nothing else mattered except him and me and getting him off.

I was a tool of his pleasure. An extension of himself. His in every way that mattered.

"Yes, baby. Take it all down your throat like the good fucking girl you are. Fuck."

A happy groan escaped me at the praise.

Using his free hand, he caressed the side of my face and down my neck, his groan joining mine when his fingers brushed along the front of it. "Fuck, baby doll, I can feel myself sliding down your throat."

Somehow he was touching me everywhere—featherlight brushes across my tits, my hips, up my inner thighs. His shadows. They were busy even as he was in the throes of what had to have been the best blow job he'd ever had, if the way he was panting and groaning was any indication.

His enjoyment was ratcheting up my own, and it wasn't long at all before the rocking of my hips matched his. The shadows wrapped around my legs and parted my thighs wide. I was still dressed, but that meant nothing to the wispy tendrils composed of magic and darkness. One of them slid under my waistband as Hades gripped my hair with both hands now, fucking my face and bringing tears to my eyes.

Oh God, he was going to get me off with his shadows.

I thought he might tease me with it, rubbing it along my clit the same way he did with his fingers, but he surprised me by going straight for my aching core, filling me up in one smooth and perfect thrust. I let out a garbled moan, which in turn made him grunt. His thighs were trembling from the effort he was using to hold back his climax.

I wanted to tell him it was okay. That I was right there with him. But it was pretty hard to say anything with my mouth full of him. I was close, so close. I swallowed around his length, and he barked out a harsh cry.

"Together, or not at all, baby."

I didn't have a chance to wonder what he meant by that because soon, a second shadow joined the first. Except instead of my core, it was teasing that forbidden pucker. None of my men had taken me there yet, though I knew it was only a matter of time. I'd written these scenes before. I knew what was required when one woman had multiple men to satisfy.

I was pretty eager to experience it if I was being honest.

"One of these nights, I'm going to fill your tight little ass with my cum, baby doll. You'll beg me to do it, and it's going to feel so fucking good."

If the way I was clenching around the shadow fucking my cunt was any indication, he was right. Just the gentle circling and prodding at my back door had me seeing sparks in my periphery.

I hummed enthusiastically around him, hoping he knew how good he was making me feel.

"Ready for more, baby?"

I nodded, my cheeks and eyes wet with tears, though I wasn't in any pain. For all his roughness, he wasn't actually hurting me. I was loving every second of his undivided attention.

"Hold on to me," he said with a hot grin, his hips picking up speed as the second shadow pressed inside me, all three appendages thrusting in sync.

I was immediately overwhelmed, my brain incapable of handling this much simultaneous pleasure.

"Come, Dahlia. Come right the fuck now."

I detonated around him, awash in sensation from every point where he was inside me. His cock swelled and pulsed as he cried out and pumped his release down my throat.

He slid out of my mouth, his expression as blissed out as I was sure mine was. One hand was still twisted up in my hair, the other gentle as it brushed sweaty strands of hair out of my eyes.

"You look beautiful like this, goddess."

"Sweaty and well fucked?"

"I was going to say well loved, but that works too."

I smiled at him as his thumb brushed against the side of my mouth, wiping away a bit of drool.

"Feel better, baby doll?"

"I'm not sure. We might need to try again, you know, to make sure I'm really distracted, Cain."

His eyes flashed with blue fire, and he tightened his hold on my hair. "It's Hades when we're alone."

"Oh, right. I'm sorry. Can you distract me some more, my lord Hades?"

He smirked. "I abso-fucking-lutely can."

CHAPTER TWENTY-SIX

TOR

Rustling woke me from a heavy slumber filled with dreams of Dahlia and me returning to my homeland. A terrifying sight greeted me, making me snap out of bed with a scream.

"Loki's minuscule testes, what are you doing in my room?" I shouted at the doll.

"Silly Daddy. You freed me. I was watching you sleep. I love to watch you sleep."

A shudder worked its way down my spine.

"I can make sure you sleep forever and ever. Like me."

Stark terror drove me from my bed. There was no time for rational thought. The only thing that mattered was getting as far away from this fucking demon as quickly as possible. I threw my sheet over the doll on my way out the door as though simply covering it would keep the possessed toy away.

"Daddy. Daddy, wait for me!"

"Stay the fuck away from me, you creepy crawly menace," I roared as I bolted down the hallway in search of my mate.

Someone needed to get this horrifying plaything out of Blackwood, and it certainly wasn't going to be me. On instinct I turned to go to her room, but remembered at the last second that she'd gone with Hades last night.

Spinning on my heel, I tore off the other way. The change in direction took me past a rumpled Kit and notably unrumpled Sorcha.

Sorcha eyed me from head to toe, a shit-eating grin stretching her crimson lips. "Well done, Dahlia. I'd heard rumors about Vikings and their . . . assets. It's nice to know the stories were true."

"I'm standing right here, my little viper." Kit's annoyed chastisement had her clucking her tongue at him, but I didn't have time to bother with the rest of their conversation. I was certain that doll was hot on my heels.

I came to a skidding halt at Hades's door. "Cain!" I bellowed, slamming my fist repeatedly against the door. "Dahlia! Let me in!"

The door swung open, Dahlia blessedly standing in front of me now with wide eyes and concern etched on her face. She was wearing one of Hades's black button-down shirts and nothing else. In another time, I may have stalked in, torn his clothes from her body, and marked her with my scent right in front of him. But right now, all I could do was rush into the room and slam the door shut behind me.

I fell against it with a relieved sound that might have been a whimper.

My heart was racing, sweat dripping down my face. I had to look like I'd just run for miles instead of simply escaped from my bed.

"What the hell happened?" she asked. "Why are you naked?"

I glanced down at my completely nude form and then back up at her. "There was no time."

"What? Why?"

"The doll. She's after me."

Hades chuckled, shaking his head from where he was still lounging between the sheets. Asshole yipped and nibbled at my toes.

"She's locked up in my chest in my bedroom. How could she be after you?" Dahlia asked.

"I can assure you she is not."

"But how?"

Now that the threat had passed, embarrassment crept up my neck, blazing a path to my cheeks. "I might have accidentally released her."

Dahlia's eyes narrowed. "Whhyyy?"

"I threw a fit when I couldn't find you yesterday."

"And by fit, you mean tantrum?" she asked, hands on her hips. I probably shouldn't have noticed the way the move pulled the fabric of the shirt taut over her ripe breasts.

"I was worried."

Her lips quirked into a small smile, and fuck, they were tempting.

"Hell, man, cover that thing up. I didn't consent to this," Hades grumbled, throwing a blanket at me.

I caught it one-handed, then glanced down at my rising erection with a smirk before I wrapped the blanket around my hips and adjusted myself.

"I guess I should, erm, go and clean up the mess I made of your room," I offered, knowing that my magic would repair the worst of it. Hopefully before she ever had to see it.

"Wait," she murmured, coming over and placing her hand on my arm. "Before you go, tell us what happened with *Brian* last night."

"He's not the Ripper. He's a prat and a Peeping Tom, but he's not a murderer."

"Wait, what? He was spying on us?" Her lip curled back in disgust.

"Just Merri, evidently."

"So what did you do with him?" Her eyes narrowed as she waited for my response.

"They dropped him off at the train station, baby doll. Isn't that right, Viking?" Hades leaned back against the headboard, arms crossed behind his head.

"I'm not sure where Caspian took him, truth be told. But he and Kai made it clear that the creep wasn't welcome back here. Ever."

"Is he dead?"

I shook my head. "We made you a promise. And despite his crimes, he didn't deserve death."

Her eyes went unfocused, and she blew out a heavy breath. "So we're no closer to finding the Ripper than we were *before* I accidentally created a zombie mermaid. Cool."

"We really should talk about that too," Hades offered.

"No, we shouldn't."

"Why not?"

Dahlia rolled her eyes. "I don't have any way to answer the questions you're going to ask. I was trying to talk to a spirit. Instead I turned her into a zombie and then a ghoul. I am categorically bad at being whatever I am."

The defeated slump of her shoulders had me tugging her into my arms. Resting my chin on the top of her head, I cuddled her close. "You are perfect exactly as you are, Kærasta."

She laughed, but it was hollow. "You're biased. And wrong. But thank you."

Hades surprised me by joining us and positioning himself at her back as he pressed a kiss to her shoulder. "He's not wrong. You're incredibly powerful, and that's something anyone would struggle with if it was just foisted upon them without warning."

"Not to mention that your power is evolving nearly daily. You haven't had a chance to get used to it before the rules change on you again."

She let out a bitter scoff. "So what you're saying is I'm a ticking time bomb with no actual timer. I'm actually a land mine. Unpredictable and dangerous."

"You could just as easily be describing me," I murmured.

"Or me," Hades added. "Or Kai, and Cas is . . ."

"A wild card," Dahlia finished. "He's getting worse," she added in a softer voice. "Did you notice?"

"We noticed, baby doll."

"I can't be with all of you twenty-four seven." Her words were so quiet I almost didn't hear them. "I'm going to let one or all of you down."

"Don't worry about managing us. We're grown-ass men. We can take care of our damn selves," Hades said.

"What about Cas?" she whispered. "He's really struggling."

"We'll keep an eye on him," Hades promised. "Right now the only thing you need to worry about is trying to get a handle on your powers. The last thing you want is to be in a position where it surprises you. Knowing what you're capable of, and your limits, is the most responsible thing you can do."

"Even if I raise an accidental zombie army in the process?"

"Even so. At least then we'll know what we're working with. And I'll be there to help you put them back where they belong."

I backed away from her and forced her gaze up to meet mine with a finger under her chin. "Our bonds aren't one-sided, Kærasta. You need us as much as we need you. We're all in your corner. The first thing you should do is discuss what happened with Masterson. She can likely tell you where you went wrong."

"And the Ripper? We're back to square one. What do we do now?"

"Technically, *we* don't have to do anything. The Ripper is not actually our problem," Hades pointed out.

"He's murdering people left and right."

"I'm just sayin', you can be selfish. Understanding your power comes first. Once you've got that figured out, you can worry about what comes next."

"And if you want to practice," I offered, "maybe you can start with that fucking doll."

Her eyes lit up. "You're right. I can summon her spirit out of the doll. Maybe put it somewhere safer?"

"Like the bottom of the lake?"

She giggled. "I'll think of something. You don't need to worry, Tor. I'll protect you from the mean ol' dolly."

"Thank you, Kærasta." I dropped a kiss on her lips and moved to the door.

"Where are you going?"

"To take care of the mess I made of your room." Reaching for the knob, I opened the door, and my heart stopped.

Sitting there, grinning creepily up at me, was that porcelain-faced, ringlet-haired menace.

"I found you. I'll always find you, Daddy."

CHAPTER

TWENTY-SEVEN

DAHLIA

"What are we going to do with you?" I asked, staring at the doll I'd rescued Tor from.

"Play with me?" Katarina—or Kat, as I'd started to call her—offered, blinking those creepy fucking eyes at me. I didn't know if it was Tor rubbing off on me, but I definitely understood why she freaked him out so much.

"This is a prime opportunity to practice your skills, baby doll. I'm right here to help."

I turned to Hades, the beautiful fucker, and shrugged. "Sure, but I don't know what to do. I've already trapped her in a doll. What more is there?"

"What has Masterson been trying to teach you?"

"Control, I guess. How to summon and hold a spirit."

His handsome face turned thoughtful. "Seems like she thinks you're some kind of necromancer."

"Is that what *you* are?"

"I'm a god. My power can do all sorts of things, but ultimately it's tied to souls and death magic."

"Is there an old, musty library in this place? One with books about necromancy I can study? I do a lot better when I have information."

"There's a library, but I can't speak to its contents. Easy enough to check, though."

"Okay, and in the meantime, what are we supposed to do about her?" I asked, tipping my head back to the doll.

"Play with me," Kat said again. As if repetition might get her what she wanted. "I like fire."

"No," Hades and I said at the same time.

"Give me back to Daddy. He's fun." The way her face didn't move as she spoke sent chills racing down my spine.

"He's not your daddy," I snapped.

Her head swiveled ever so slightly, keeping those glass eyes on me. "Is he *your* daddy?"

"No," Hades said.

I bit the inside of my cheek. Shadow daddy was feeling possessive.

"Does he let you watch him sleep? He lets me watch him sleep. He freed me. Daddy loves me best."

And now *I* was feeling possessive.

"Shut it. You've done enough to Tor." I sat her on the bed and stood there, hands on my hips, as I tried to figure out what my next step was. Did I pull her out of the vessel and . . . I didn't know what came next.

Hades was there, his warm hands resting on my shoulders. "One step at a time, all right? Start with seeing the soul. You've interacted with enough spirits to know how to isolate their energy. It feels different. Has a different weight, sort of like oil floating on water, right?"

As he spoke, I closed my eyes, realizing he was correct. If I sent my awareness out, I could feel exactly where the spirit was placed. I could even sense the one wandering down the hallway. They were less intrusive, less aggressive. Or maybe I was just better at managing.

"Yeah. I can definitely feel her. I can almost see her in there." If I focused hard enough, I thought perhaps I could see a haze of blue in the glass of the doll's eyes. "Are souls blue?"

"Yes. They're the same color as my fire. Some are more vibrant than others. The weaker they get, the less color they have."

"Makes sense."

And it did, in a weird way. I didn't feel like I was learning something new so much as reclaiming something I'd learned a long time ago. I couldn't help but wonder if this was something my father and The Scythe Society knew about. Had they been necromancers? Had *he*? Was that where this power came from? So many unanswered questions.

"I see your brain going a million miles an hour, goddess." Hades wrapped his palm around the back of my neck and gave it a squeeze. "One thing at a time."

Taking a steadying breath, I did my best to listen to him. "Okay. First thing, locate her spirit."

"Very good."

"But where will I put her if I am able to control her?"

"Hmmm." He rolled his lips together, eyes squinting as he looked around the room, searching for an appropriate container. "There we go," he said, beelining for his dresser.

"Uh, I don't think a drawer is going to cut it."

"Not the drawer," he corrected, lifting the crystal decanter of Brimstone whiskey. It was just over a third of the way full. Before I could utter another word, he took the little stopper out of the top and necked the entire thing.

"Jesus," I whispered, watching the way his throat worked and feeling some kind of way about it.

He pulled the crystal from his lips with a loud, appreciative smack. "Hot damn."

I went temporarily mute as he thumbed a bead of the amber liquid off his full lower lip.

"Stop looking at me like that, baby girl."

I blinked, refocusing on the task at hand and pulling my inner snark around me like a protective blanket. "Just what I need, a drunk god helping me."

"I'll help you with whatever you want, baby. But first let's get this spirit put somewhere she's less of a hassle."

"I'm right here, you know," Kat said.

"Yes. We're aware."

Hades placed the crystal on the floor in the center of the room, then looked to me expectantly.

"What?" I asked.

"Take her out of the doll and put her inside the bottle."

"You say that like it's easy."

"It is."

"Then you do it."

"This isn't about me. Now focus, Dahlia, and do it. Or I won't let you come tonight."

"Where's she going?" the doll asked.

My cheeks burned. I was *not* going to explain innuendo to the ghost of a psychotic child. "Okay, just like last time. Only no sneezing."

Closing my eyes, I did the same thing I had when Hades had been speaking. It was a lot easier to visualize the spirit this time. Basically the mental equivalent of flicking a light switch on. Once I saw her, I pictured myself reaching out and plucking her spirit the same way I might a flower. Delicately, between two fingers.

"Hey! Hey, what are you doing?"

"Shh, I'm focusing. Do you want to end up in a toothpaste tube this time?"

"No, please. Don't put me back in that jar. I don't want to be in the dark again. I hate the dark."

Goddammit, I was a sucker. Guilt flashed through me like a back draft from an opened window in a house fire.

"Hades, is there anything we can do? She's just a kid."

"That kid is a couple centuries old."

"Please."

He sighed, arms crossing over his chest. Asshole must have said something because his attention shifted to the little fluffball curled up on the armchair.

"You want to risk it?" he asked.

My gaze bounced between them. "Want to share with the class, or should I just play Mad Libs and start filling in the blanks myself?"

"He's offering to take her to the underworld."

"What'll happen to her there?" I asked.

"She'll be judged. But she won't be imprisoned in a vessel ever again."

"Does this little aptitude test count if I don't actually get her in the bottle?"

"Are you still holding onto her without issue?" he countered.

"Well, yeah."

"Then I think you proved that you've mastered the basics of control. Helping her spirit pass on doesn't change that." He stared at me. "Why are you frowning? That should be good news."

"I guess I'm just surprised it was so easy this time. Last time it felt like holding onto a live wire."

"Last time I wasn't there to help you, and I think you've failed to realize how your powers have grown."

My grip didn't falter as I pulled Kat completely from the doll. "Do I just give her to Asshole?"

The puppy yipped and sat in front of me, waiting patiently, tail wagging.

"This is what he was made for," Hades said encouragingly. "Just offer it to him like you would a bone. He'll do the rest."

"Uh, here you go, boy," I said, holding out the hand that contained the spirit. If I closed my eyes and pictured it, it looked a bit like a glow stick, the bright neon blue light pulsing with energy.

Asshole gently took the spirit in his mouth, his shadow changing from the little puppy shape I was used to into an enormous three-headed dog.

"Oh, wow. Okay. So it's a costume."

"It's a persona."

"Like you having a southern accent?"

Hades sighed. "Sure."

I watched in awe as my big, strong god of a man knelt down in front of his dog and patted him on the head.

"You're a good boy," he murmured. "I'll see you when I see you. If you come back, it's steak dinners for a week."

Asshole couldn't yip with his mouth full, but his little tail wagged enthusiastically, and then he trotted forward. Between one doggy step and the next, he vanished.

"Wow, that was pretty impressive. Although I sort of expected a door to form in the wall, you know, like it did in Beetlejuice when the minister guy appeared for the wedding." I was full ramble when Hades's words finally caught up to me. "Wait. What do you mean 'if'?"

"What do you mean, what do I mean?"

"You said 'if' Asshole returns. Why wouldn't he return?"

Hades turned serious eyes on me. "He was sent here the first time. His purpose was to protect me and help me find out who I was. He's done that. We may never see him again. Not until we return to the underworld."

My jaw fell open, and I punched his arm. "And you just let him leave without allowing me to say goodbye? Rude!"

"Hit me again, and you'll see exactly who your daddy is, baby girl."

Heat curled low in my belly. Should I give him a little pat? Poke the Shadow Daddy?

"Don't look at me like that, Dahlia. I know you have an appointment with Masterson shortly. If I get you under me, you most definitely won't make it."

"Ugh, all right, fine, you thief of joy. But we should probably do something with that," I said, gesturing to the now inanimate doll.

"Burn it with fire?" he offered, fingertips bright with blue flame.

"Fire is always good. But maybe this time we try tossing it in the lake?"

He nodded, then handed me my clothes since I was still only wearing his shirt. "Get dressed, and we'll go send her to live with the lake monsters."

"Tor will love that. A fitting end for his own personal monster."

SESSION TRANSCRIPT: DECEMBER 19TH

Dr. Masterson: This is Dr. Elizabeth Masterson. It is December 19th, and the time is 11:30 a.m. This is a recorded session with Tor Nordson.

Tor: *growling*

<<chair squeak>>

Tor: Why did you summon me here? I am not scheduled for a session.

Dr. Masterson: I had something I needed to speak with you about, but we'll get to that in a second. You look a little worse for wear this morning. Anything you'd like to share?

Tor: *annoyed grunt*

Dr. Masterson: All right, let me rephrase. What's eating you, Tor?

Tor: There's this haunted doll.

Dr. Masterson: *laugh* I am aware. Though she has been quite elusive. We've been trying to locate her since Dahlia relocated the spirit now inhabiting the doll.

Tor: Elusive for you, perhaps. She won't leave me alone.

Dr. Masterson: *soft hum* I see. Well, perhaps after we wrap up today, I can be of some assistance with your doll problem.

Tor: *low growl* Dahlia's handling it.

Dr. Masterson: Is she now? Brilliant. Glad to hear she's practicing.

<<paper rustling>>

Dr. Masterson: Now, tell me, aside from your issues with the doll, how do you feel your control is coming along? We haven't had any issues since the last time you were in No Man's Land. Anything I should be aware of?

<<beat of silence>>

Tor: No.

Dr. Masterson: Are you lying, Tor? I can only help you if you let me.

Tor: *heavy sigh* I might have trashed Dahlia's room a little when I couldn't find her. But I wasn't out of control. Just worried. My daily trips to the woods have been going a long way to slake any lingering bloodlust.

Dr. Masterson: Good. That's very good. Do you still find yourself more at ease when she's nearby?

Tor: Of course I bloody do. She's mine. *agitated huff*

<<scribbling on paper>>

Dr. Masterson: That tracks with what we know of Berserkers and mate bonds in general, truth be told. Especially such a new bond. How is that working, sharing your mate with others?

Tor: *series of growls*

Dr. Masterson: I'll take that to mean it's a work in progress. Well, I suppose that is to be expected. Anyway, back to why I was asking. Blackwood is about to have some guests. A few you may recognize, actually.

Tor: What?

Dr. Masterson: Yes. For the gala. This year the Donoghue Trust will be represented by the Duke of Canterbury and his mate, and if the guest list is accurate, at least one of the Mercer brothers will be in attendance. I believe you have a history with them both.

Tor: *explosive growls*

Dr. Masterson: Tor? Tor!

<<door opens>>

Bruno: Everything all right in here?

Dr. Masterson: We're fine. Thank you, Bruno.

Bruno: I'll be right outside if you need me.

<<door closes>>

Tor: *growling continues*

Dr. Masterson: Calm yourself. If this is how you react to the name alone, then you will be banned from attending at your mate's side. Do you want that? To be locked away again, or worse?

Tor: *softer growls*

Dr. Masterson: I didn't think so.

Tor: I nearly killed Bentley Mercer.

Dr. Masterson: I am aware.

Tor: How? You shouldn't be able to speak of . . .

Dr. Masterson: The fights? The staff at Blackwood aren't beholden to the same muzzling spells as those who deal in the fight ring. The Council requires us to have all information available at all times. Consider it an extension of doctor-patient privilege. How else can I best help you if I don't have all the facts?

<<paper rustles>>

Dr. Masterson: Do you think you'll be able to control your rage at the gala if Bentley chooses to retaliate?

Tor: It's hard to say. I don't have a problem with him, but if he threatens me or my mate, I will have no choice but to protect her.

Dr. Masterson: I was worried you might say that. But I can't say I expected anything different. *resigned sigh* All right, well, we will play it by ear, I guess. I'll tell Bru to stay close for the entirety of their visit. I expect you to be on your best behavior, Tor. I mean it. Unless it is clear that you are provoked and acting only in defense of yourself or your mate, you will end up back in No Man's Land. And this time, I'm not sure even Dahlia will be enough to get you out.

<<static>>

End of transcript

CHAPTER TWENTY-EIGHT

DAHLIA

What was it about therapy sessions that made me so hungry? Maybe it was the fact that I hadn't eaten since last night, and I'd been *very* active between the sheets with Hades more than once before we finally fell asleep. Tor hadn't given me much of a chance to do anything before he'd shown up starkers and running from the doll.

And by the time Hades and I—do you have any idea how weird it is to say that unironically?—got finished ditching the doll in the loch, I barely made it to my appointment with Masterson. So maybe it was therapy that made me hungry as much as, you know, not eating.

Go figure.

At least I'd had time to put real clothes on. Something told me Masterson wouldn't have appreciated seeing me in nothing but Hades's rumpled shirt.

Or maybe she would. I did have some epic curves. Who didn't appreciate a bodacious bod?

My stomach gave a grumble as I approached the lunch buffet. I had to admit, the offerings were impressive and inclusive. Vegan, gluten-free, veggie, and kosher options were readily available alongside stuff for us carnivores and the—gulp—blood bar. But we didn't talk about the blood bar.

I loaded up my plate with a mountain of mashed potatoes (without garlic, because fuck garlic. It made my tummy hurt), mac and cheese, a couple pieces of fried chicken, and exactly two pieces of broccoli. Did I plan to stick them into Mount Mash so they looked like trees? Yes, yes, I did. And if they had offered dino nugs, I would've strategically placed them around the mountain and recreated the volcano scene from that one Jurassic Park movie. If you're not playing with your food, you're not living, friends.

"So, which one of your menagerie of men gets the privilege of being on your arm at the gala?" Sorcha asked as she filled a wine goblet with blood.

I had to chew and swallow the bite of mac and cheese I'd gobbled because I literally couldn't wait to sit down to start eating. "What gala?"

She gave me one of those long, 'How are you still alive? You're too stupid to live' stares. "The fundraiser? In like two days? The one they've been decorating for all week?"

My cheeks went warm, and I knew it the moment my flush registered because the vampire's pupils dilated. Shudder. "I've been busy."

"Busy getting railed," she muttered under her breath, but not so quiet I hadn't heard. "By the way, how'd your last cycle go? It was only, what, four days this time?" The smirk on her lips told me everything I needed to know. She'd been toying with me after witnessing my crisis in the corridor.

"Yeah, about that. You could've saved me a lot of stress if you'd just put me out of my misery."

"Where's the fun in that? I'm a Blackthorne, darling. Causing misery is what I live for. Besides, we don't get much other entertainment here."

"I'm so glad I could be of assistance," I said drily.

"Me too."

One of us was being sarcastic. The other was Sorcha Blackthorne.

"There's really a gala?"

"Oh yes," she said with a nod as she took a sip of her cocktail. The only way I could stand here and watch her drink the tomato-red liquid was to tell myself it was a cocktail.

"Like ball gowns and black ties?"

"And dates and dancing," she confirmed with relish.

"I don't have a ball gown. Did you come here with a ball gown? No one said there would be fucking ball gowns."

I was panicked. Fully freaked. Not about who would be on my arm, I'd deal with that later, but if you said to me, we're gonna send you to rehab for what happened at your last black-tie event and need you to have a designer dress option in your suitcase, I would've laughed in your face. Talk about absurd. Not to mention a fucking trigger. Like, what the actual fuck, Lizzie? You couldn't give a bitch a heads-up? I was *just* with you.

"You should probably breathe, Dahlia. You're turning purple."

"Why is it every time you talk to me you deliver bad news?"

Sorcha chuckled. "You're such a charmer. I love the way you compliment me."

She swanned off with her hips swaying, and all I could do was watch her go. I didn't have a gown; I didn't have anything close. Was there even time for me to send off for one? I'd have to call Kiki. She'd know what to do.

Which I guess left the question of which guy was supposed to be my date. Apparently later meant in ten minutes. Everyone was just starting to get along. How the hell was I supposed to navigate this? Cas was two crumpets short of a tea party, Hades had a literal god complex, Tor could barely stand to see anyone touching me without wanting to break them in half, and Kai . . . I guess he'd tolerate it, but how much more was my poor dragon going to have to tolerate for my sake? He deserved better. They all did.

Fuck. I was the worst. Why did they like me? I wouldn't if I were them.

Kiki's voice echoed in my mind, *Don't talk like that about my friend.*

I stared down at my still completely full plate with a sad sigh. What a waste of a good potato mountain.

"What's gone and positioned that storm cloud over your head, lass?" Kai's voice smoothed over me like a warm blanket, and I instantly felt a little better.

"Did you know there is a fucking black-tie gala happening in a few days?" Did my voice have a hysterical edge? Shut up. Stop telling me how to live. "And that I need a dress? And to pick someone to accompany me? And . . . oh fuck, there's probably dancing. I can't dance." I blinked up at him with tear-filled eyes. "I've never been to a dance, Kai. I grew up in a cult. Then I went to foster care and tested out of school as soon as I was legally able. I can't do this. Everyone will laugh at me. I don't want to be the joke of the party anymore."

Kai's big hand rested on my forearm. "Shh, my sweet treasure. I'll accompany you. It would be my honor. And as far as a dress, you'd look beautiful in a flour sack."

"Liar. I wouldn't fit in a flour sack."

"Not my point."

I dropped my head into my hands and let out a hearty harrumph. "You don't get it. You look perfect in anything. And even if you didn't, no one would dare to laugh at you because you can flambé them."

"I could. You're right."

Staring at my plate of food, I gave a little sniffle. "And I was so hungry. But now I don't have an appetite because I'm too stressed to eat."

Kai's eyes traveled over to my plate. "Is that a little mountain, complete with broccoli trees?"

"Yes."

"I'm impressed."

"Thank you."

"It would be a shame for it to go to waste."

"I know."

He smirked and grabbed a broccoli before scooping up some potatoes with the crown and offering it to me.

"Are you really feeding me?"

"Aye, lass. Eat your veg."

I opened my mouth because how could I not? The gesture was sweet as all hell.

I still wasn't hungry, but I knew I needed the food. So when he did the same thing with the second little tree, I allowed it. Although I laughed out loud when he came at me with the piece of fried chicken. I heard Sorcha gag from somewhere to my right as I took the offered bite. I blindly flipped her off. I'd take deep-fried Foghorn Leghorn over her DNA juice any day.

"There, good girl. Do you feel better?" Kai asked, brushing a tendril of hair behind my ear.

"No."

His expression was tender, but I could see the worry line between his brows deepen. He was trying so hard, and I felt like such an ass.

"I'll be fine. I just need to let the anxiety run its course. It's like this sometimes."

He nodded. "Is it just the idea of the gala in general, or did something else bring it on?"

"You've been spending too much time with Dr. Masterson."

He chuckled. "I have been here a while."

"To answer your question, I'm not sure. But I think it might have something to do with what happened the last time I was at a big event. Namely, killing everyone and then magically bringing them back. Or did I hallucinate the whole thing? I never did figure out what happened that night."

"Take a breath, okay? You're spinning yourself in circles. I'm here, holding your hand. I'm not leaving. You're not going to kill anyone."

God, I wished I could believe him.

"Come on. Let's get you upstairs. A nice bath and a massage will do wonders for you. And if not, then I'll be there with you, and we can weather the storm together."

Tears filled my eyes and I nodded. "That sounds really nice."

He took my hand and led me away from the pile of food I hadn't eaten and the dining room filled with people who could never understand my trauma. I let him. And honestly, I loved him for it.

CHAPTER TWENTY-NINE

KAI

Hands laden with a tray filled with food, I came through Dahlia's door and found her awake and sitting up on her bed. She'd fallen asleep shortly after her bath, giving me a window to run out and ensure she didn't miss another meal. But now her laptop was in front of her, and she was typing away.

She peeked over at me in surprise. "I'd thought I'd run you off."

"Never, gem. I come bearing gifts."

"I see that."

The glimmer in her eyes sent a shot of pride through me. I'd done that. I'd made her happy.

"What are you working on now?" I asked.

"It's an epic grovel. One of the heroes really fucked up. He's begging for forgiveness."

I quirked a brow, intrigued. I had nae intention of ever needing to grovel, but having access to her idea of a proper one seemed like something I should take advantage of. Just in case the need ever arose.

"And how does he do that?"

Her laughter was infectious and made me chuckle in response. "Taking notes?"

"Maybe. Though if I ever need to beg your forgiveness, I would hope as your fated mate, I'd know how without question."

She eyed the tray in my hands. "Something tells me you're probably going to be just fine, dragon boy."

"I brought you dinner."

"You speak my love language."

"Aye, lass. I do." Setting the tray on her desk, I crossed the room and joined her on the bed. "Do ye need me to leave so you can finish your scene without distraction?"

She shut her computer and shook her head, swinging her legs over the side of her bed. "Just the fact that you offered means a lot."

Her lips brushed over mine, soft as a butterfly's wings, and then she stood and padded over to my offering of food.

"Mmm, all my favorites. And you even made a mashed potato mountain."

"Well, you did such a fine job with the last one. It was a shame you dinnae get to enjoy it."

"Some people would think it was silly to create a landscape out of your food."

"Some people are stupid and have no sense of adventure." I winked at her and watched my woman take a bite. The way her eyes rolled back in her head as she moaned in pleasure made me eager to pull that sound from her for a totally different reason.

After she finished her meal, of course.

She sidled up to me, bringing her plate with her. "Eat with me? I don't like to eat when someone else is with me unless they're enjoying the meal too."

"Of course, whatever you desire, gem. There's only the one set of silverware, though, so we'll have to share."

"Oh shucks, I guess you'll just have to feed me. However will I endure the misery of it all?"

Little did she know, the act of feeding her by hand was a fucking turn-on. Dragons were possessive, we knew this, but they were also devoted caregivers when their mates were concerned.

I fed her from the plate, letting her do the same for me until it was empty, and we set it aside. Then I let myself take something else I'd been hungering for. Her mouth.

"Mmm, dessert might be my favorite part." She snuggled against me, her arms wound around my neck as she came in for another kiss.

With the strength of a saint, I pulled away. "Hang on, gem. If we get started, we won't get to do what I came here for."

"You mean you didn't come here to rail me into next week?"

Shaking my head with a gentle laugh, I said, "No. I came here to feed you and teach you to dance so you're prepared for the gala."

"I . . . you . . ." She blinked at me a couple of times, emotion making her eyes stormy. "Kai," she finally managed, her voice a tender whisper.

"You mentioned it was something that you were worried about. I may not be able to do anything about the other things that make you anxious, but with this one, I definitely can. Care to dance with me, my treasure?"

I stood and held out a hand, waiting for her to take it. After a brief hesitation, she fitted her palm into mine and allowed me to pull her up until she was against me.

"What if I'm bad at it?"

"Impossible."

"It is not," she protested with a laugh.

Smug male pride filled my voice as I leaned in close, my lips at her ear. "Nae, gem. It is, because I've seen the way you move when you're riding me. You have all the grace and rhythm you need."

The way her cheeks filled with an embarrassed flush had me tipping her chin up so I could kiss her. "Never be embarrassed about how beautiful you are."

"What kind of dance are you going to teach me?"

"I thought we'd start with something slow and basic."

"Sounds good." Then she surprised me by stepping out of my arms and over to the bed.

"Where are you going?"

"We need music, don't we? I don't think teaching me to dance without a beat is going to be very helpful."

I held out my hand for her phone. "Let me choose the song. I know exactly which one."

As soon as the first chords filled the room, I took her in my hold and began teaching her the steps. A slow waltz that allowed us to look into each other's eyes while she learned to let me lead.

"Thank you, Kai," she breathed after one dance turned into many. Her head was resting on my shoulder, her body pressed close to mine.

I placed a gentle kiss on her forehead, loving the way we fit together. "No need for thanks, gem. It is my pleasure to dance with you. I don't care what we're doing so long as we're together."

She hummed happily and stayed right there in my arms. It was almost too good to be true, the knowledge that it was all falling into place. We were together, joined forever. And while there were still many obstacles we'd yet to face, not the least of which was my inevitable return to Faerie, I'd do everything in my power to keep it that way.

Dahlia

"You knew there was a fucking royal ball and didn't tell me?" I screeched at the little version of Kiki on my phone screen. It was the next afternoon, and with Kai gone, all my intrusive thoughts had found their way back to the forefront. Needless to say, I was a giant ball of anxiety. A video call with my bestie was supposed to help, not make me more stressed.

"It's not a royal ball. Those require royalty."

"The guy's a duke, Keeks."

She ignored me and kept talking. "And yes, I did know. That's why you have some dresses out for delivery as we speak. Also, before you get all snippy with me, some of them even have pockets. See, I listen."

I rolled my eyes, thankful for her foresight but frustrated that she left me in the dark. "Why did you think it was a good idea not to mention any of this before now?"

"Because I know you. You latch on to any reason you can find to poo-poo all over large social gatherings. I just took care of one reason, so what others do you want to lob at me?"

Heaving a sigh, I flopped down onto my bed and stared up at the cracked ceiling. "There's the issue of who I'm going with."

"How did that even make the list? All of them, obviously. Next."

"Um . . . there's a whole fucking serial killer running amok."

Under her breath, like clockwork, Kiki whispered, "Amok, amok, amok."

"Seriously, Keeks. There's a crazy psychopath who likes to steal body parts out there, and Masterson thinks it's a good idea to bring strangers on the premises so we can all pretend everything's fine?"

"Maybe Masterson didn't get a say. It's run by the donors, right? The Donoghue Trust or whatever? Maybe they steamrolled her. Rich people think they're invincible. Besides, all the residents are supernaturals like you, right? So who's to say the donors aren't as well. Pretty sure a bunch of hot-shot vampires can take care of themselves. Next," she called again, like she was ushering in the next in line for an audition.

"No, Kiki, seriously. This guy is picking people off left and right. He's a serious threat."

"Well, use your scream thing on him. It seemed to work with Tor."

"And take out everyone else at the gala? God, it will be the premiere all over again."

"But you brought everyone back," she pointed out unhelpfully. "Just do that again. But more selectively this time."

"You say that like I know how the hell to control it. I don't just decide when to scream and who to knock out, Keeks. It just happens. And I have no freaking idea how I brought those people back, or if the whole thing was some sort of fluke. What if I attempted it and accidentally raised an entire army of the dead? Then where would we be? In the middle of a damn horror movie, that's where!"

"Why not ask your shadow daddy about it? He seems to have a pretty good idea about how your powers work."

A rush of answering heat made me flustered and took the argument out of me. "God, you're frustrating when you have answers for everything."

"You're welcome."

"I don't remember saying thank you."

"It was implied. I'm a master at reading subtext."

"Is that so?" I asked, staring deadpan into the camera. "Well, what's my face saying now?"

"That's not how subtext works, Dee."

A sharp rap on my door had my stupid heart leaping into my throat. Kai hadn't been gone that long, but already I wanted to see him, or Tor, or Hades, or Cas. Hell, I missed them all. I was an oversexed mess, and I didn't care one bit.

"Hold that thought," I said, propping my phone on the desk before rushing to the door.

Instead of one of my handsome men, I found Oz's handsome Bruno. He gave me a dashing smile and held out a large package.

"It's not a werewolf torso or something, is it? I told Tor no more bloody souvenirs. And I mean that literally, not in the British sense."

Bru laughed. "Well, it's not dripping, so that's a good sign. Also, it was delivered by a courier, so I think you're probably safe."

"It's the dresses!" Kiki shouted from my phone. "Fashion show! Right now!"

Bruno raised a brow. "I should probably leave you to it."

"Or you could stay!" Kiki offered on my behalf. "Provide the male perspective."

"I prefer to keep my dick where it is, but thanks for the offer. There's no way Tor would be okay with me being near his mate while she was in any state of undress."

I peered around Bruno and into the hall, searching for my Viking.

"He's not here." Bruno's voice was gentle as he handed me the box. "He's freshening up before he comes to you."

I gave him a self-deprecating smile. "Am I that easy to read?"

"Only when it comes to them."

"Thanks for this," I said, hefting the box in my arms. "Since when do you make house calls, anyway?"

"Since Joffrey got stuck with preparations for the gala."

"I bet he just loves that."

"You should have seen his face. Positively murderous."

"So just another Tuesday, then?"

"Exactly," Bru said with a chuckle.

Fuck, this box was heavy. I shifted my grip and gave him a smile that held a hint of desperation. "Okay, well, this isn't getting any lighter sooo . . ."

"Right. Good luck with the fashion show." He shut the door as he left, and I promptly dropped the box in the middle of my room.

"God, I hope you like the green one. It'll make you look like you stepped out of the Emerald City."

"Did you send me a pair of ruby slippers to go with it?"

"Listen, Dorothy. You act like I'm new here. Have a little faith in your fairy godmother, please."

I paused to picture Kiki in a sparkling pink ball gown, grinning as the image built in my mind. "You totally are Glinda. Quick, sing Popular for me."

"Does that mean I get to ride around in a giant bubble? Don't tempt me. I've always wanted my own iridescent transportation device."

"As long as I don't have to paint my body green, you can do whatever you want."

"Deal. Just some bronzer or maybe body shimmer. Now get naked, bitch. I want to see you in these dresses, even though I already know which one you're going to choose."

"How can you possibly know that?"

"Because. I. Know. You."

I huffed and made quick work of opening the box before pulling out dress after dress. Rich fabrics, sequins, beading, layers, ruffles, and . . . crinoline greeted me.

"Six? You said a few."

"It's more than a couple and less than a dozen."

I swallowed down my protest, knowing it would only fall on deaf ears. "A corset, Keeks? How the hell am I supposed to strap myself into this one?"

"That's a you problem. Save it for last. Do the blue velvet one first."

"You are really fucking bossy for someone I can hang up on."

"And you're whiny for someone who knows I'm never wrong."

I muttered under my breath while wriggling myself out of my leggings and *Booktrovert* sweatshirt—in case you were wondering, a booktrovert is a person who prefers the company of fictional characters to real people. Relatable, right?

A soft buzzing began under my skin, and I turned my focus to the ghost standing in my bathroom door. Even Myrtle was interested in the fashion show. "If you laugh, I will exorcise the shit out of you," I threatened.

"I want to see the sparkly one on you. It's been ages since I wore anything that sparkled."

"Who are you talking to?" Kiki asked. "Oh, wait. It's a ghost, isn't it? That's going to take me a while to get used to."

I laughed and pulled out the blue velvet number. "I've kind of forgotten no one else can see them. Well, except for Cain, I guess," I mused, pulling up the body-hugging gown. It was made for a woman with curves, accentuating the dip at my waist and the flare of my hips. It had a sweetheart neckline and two delicate little sleeves that slipped off my shoulders to fall prettily on my arms.

"Good to know when I die you'll still be able to talk to me like this, then."

"Bite your tongue." Turning around to face the camera, I struck a pose. "What do you think?"

Kiki was prepared with a notebook and a permanent marker. "It's a solid eight."

I ran my hand along the soft fabric. "Really? Just an eight? I liked this one."

"I'm holding out for a sleeper hit. Do the green one next."

"No, sparkles," Myrtle argued. Though it was a bit of a one-sided argument, seeing as Kiki couldn't hear her.

Still, I felt torn. Reaching for the sparkly silver gown, I waved it around. "What about this one?"

"Ugh, fine. But be quick about it."

"You're the one who picked six dresses."

"Just hurry up. I have a hot date."

"Seriously?"

"With my yoga instructor. But it's hot yoga, so you know, it counts."

I laughed, and we chatted away as I tried on dress after dress. The velvet and, surprisingly, the soft pink cupcake-like ballgown with the corset were the two top contenders. Until I reached the final option.

I pulled the emerald green silk situation out of the box. There was beautiful hand-beaded detailing along the waist, and I could already tell there were cutouts of some description, probably around the sides, based on their placement.

Kiki squeed and clapped her hands. "This is the one I've been waiting for."

"Really? I never would have guessed."

As I shimmied into the gown, I understood why she was so

excited. With its high neck and cap sleeves, it was unlike any of the others. The skirt fell to the floor in a graceful pool of green, and the skin from my shoulder blades down to the small of my back was exposed. There was also a smaller, diamond-shaped cut-out between my breasts and the top of my belly. It was flattering as hell, taking my curves and making them look ripe and inviting.

"That's the one," Myrtle said.

"Yes, this is the one," I agreed. Although Kiki thought I was agreeing with her, and I wasn't going to change that.

Keeks leaned back in her chair and sighed. "God, I'm good. I should moonlight as a stylist."

"With all your spare time?"

"Exactly. Spare time and monopoly money, two of a girl's best friends."

"In other words, made-up things that let us pretend we can do and buy things we cannot in fact afford or have time for."

"That's what I said."

I sat on the bed, happy the dress was easy to move in, and looked at the mess of fabric strewn about my room. "I need to get this cleaned up."

"And I need to get the chapter you sent me cleaned up so we can keep making epic things happen for you." Kiki stretched and took another sip of her coffee. "Just package the rest of those back up and send them off with the return label. If you don't send me a photo of you in that dress with all of those beefcakes looking dapper as fuck, I might never forgive you."

"Seems like a fair trade."

"Damn straight. All right, babes, it's time for me to get bendy and stick my ass in the air. Who knows, maybe today's the day someone will take me up on all my advertising."

"You are absurd."

"Love you too! Byeee," she sang as she hung up.

I laughed and shook my head, reaching back to unhook the back of the dress. Only the little hooks didn't want to play along.

"Dammit," I growled, sweat building beneath my arms and down my spine as I struggled to get myself free without destroying the delicate fabric in the process.

"How the fuck did I put this on if I can't get it off?" I glanced behind me at the ghost. "A little help here?"

She shrugged. "I can't touch anything. Sorry." Then she fucked off and left.

"Great." This was my nightmare. Fear of being trapped in my clothes might seem like something irrational, but tell me that when you were in a fitting room with a shirt stuck halfway over your head.

"And this is how you die, Dahlia. Congratulations. At least you'll look pretty when they find your body."

I was in a full-blown panic now, my shaking hands not faring any better at working the little hooks. One must be crooked or something, which explained why I could get it in, but not easily get it out.

A decisive knock on my door had me equal parts elated and mortified. But the truth was, I didn't care who was at my door as long as they could unhook the fastenings on my dress so I could get back to my regularly scheduled leggings and sweatshirt.

Pulling open the door, I gasped at the sight before me. Four handsome men, all looking like my fantasy come to life and all staring at me like they wanted to eat me for dessert.

Caspian's approving gaze was the first to return to mine. "Well, well, well, looks like we're just in time for the party. What do you say we get you out of that dress and into bed, darling?"

A relieved sigh left me. He had no idea how perfect his response had been. "Yes, please."

CHAPTER THIRTY
HOOK

If I said Dahlia had a hot body, would she hold it against me? But seriously, her in that fucking dress with those big eyes and flushed cheeks? Fuck me. I was a goner, and I hadn't even walked through the door yet.

When Kai had come door-to-door collecting us like a holiday caroling team, I have to admit I was dubious. But hearing his story about how Dahlia was struggling and needed a good distraction, well, that was my bread and butter.

Far be it from me to let her down. I'd done that once before. Never again. And now, I intended to prove just how reliable I was. Pulling on my most piratey persona, I gave her a solid leer.

"Well, well, well, looks like we're just in time for the party. What do you say we get you out of that dress and into bed, darling?"

"Yes, please."

There was no mistaking the relief bleeding through her reply. Either she was that needy, or I was missing something.

"I'm stuck," she explained after a beat, arms reaching behind her to demonstrate the point. "I thought I was going to die in this thing."

"I'd sooner rip it from your body," Tor growled, stealing my thunder like he always bloody did.

"That would be a crime," Kai countered, pushing past me to move to Dahlia. "Our mate is a fucking vision in this gown."

"I think it'd look better on the floor," Hades offered.

I stepped closer, taking her hand and pressing a kiss between her knuckles. "Any chance there are stockings and garters under that silk, little rabbit?"

She bit her lower lip, the lust she was trying to conceal swimming in her eyes. "No. Not this time."

"Pity," I murmured, continuing my trail of kisses up her arm.

"We doing this in the hallway, or are we taking this inside?" Hades asked, hands working the buttons of his shirt.

"In a hurry?" Dahlia teased.

"For you? Always."

She backed up a few paces, the faintest furrow visible between her brows.

"What is it, darling?"

"Y-you're all here."

"Aye, we are," Kai confirmed.

"We're here for you, Kærasta."

"Isn't that what you want, baby doll?"

"Well, yeah, I guess. But shouldn't we talk about it or something?"

"Is talking really what you want to do right now?" Hades teased.

"No?"

We all laughed at her obvious confusion.

"Am I dreaming? It feels like I'm dreaming. You four showing up at my door ready to ravish me. It's like the start of a porno."

I couldn't help myself. I pulled off my shirt and let it fall to the floor. "Oops. I dropped my shirt." Then I winked at her. "Now it's like a porno."

"D-don't get me wrong," she babbled, her eyes huge as she tried to look at all of us at once, watching as we all continued to undress in her doorway, "I'm not complaining. I'm just wondering what brought this on. The last time there was an orgy, it was because of succubus pheromones."

"Kai said you needed distracting," Hades offered, as if that explained everything. Which it must have because Dahlia let out a long, "Ohhh."

"So naturally, we figured you'd be best distracted by our dicks," I finished. Listen, I know she got it, but I needed to say it because the line was far too good to waste.

"Any more questions, beauty?" Tor asked, herding her back toward the bed.

"Nope. Consider me up to speed."

"Excellent," he murmured, grabbing her around the hips and lifting her up over his shoulder.

She let out a little squeak as he smacked his palm on the round globe of her arse hard enough to leave a handprint on the silk.

"Careful of the dress!"

Tor grumbled something unintelligible while I leaned against her desk, watching with more restraint than I'd given myself credit for. Honestly, I wanted her under me right now, but anticipation and all that.

Standing her on her feet again, Tor spun her around and made quick work of the delicate hook-and-eye closures on the back of the gown. The fabric fell to her ankles in a soft whoosh as it puddled on the floor, leaving her in nothing but a pair of knickers with the word Wednesday written across the back.

I snickered, loving that she had days of the week knickers but couldn't be bothered to wear them on the accurate day. My little rebel.

The scrape of a chair across the floor pulled my attention from the luscious curves I craved. Hades had positioned himself with a perfect view, his trousers already open, eyes hot on her.

"So, how are we going to do this? Her on top? Me on top? My face in her cunt? Your dick in her mouth?" I asked Tor.

The Viking snarled at me, his possessiveness getting the better of him.

"Now, now, we're sharing. We talked about this."

"Talking and doing are nae the same," Kai said to me while Dahlia moved to Tor.

"Are you okay with this, big guy? It's okay if you aren't. You don't have to do anything you don't want to do."

"I want to please you."

"You do please me."

"I need to be part of this. I'm your mate. I need to serve you in every way. You want this, so I want this."

Gag.

But also, it was a good line. I might save it for another time.

"Are you sure?"

"I'm sure."

"Would it help if you were restrained?" Hades asked.

"Restrained how?" Tor asked.

"No chains. You have my word. But my shadows are strong enough to hold you back if your beast tries to break free. Think of it like a safety net if your instincts get the better of you."

Dahlia gave a little shiver none of us missed.

"You like the idea of that?" Tor asked.

She was blushing as she nodded. "I had a dream about you that went sort of like that. You were at my mercy while I rode you. And then . . ."

"Well don't stop now, love. You're just getting to the good part," I encouraged.

"There might have been other participants. Mouth stuff."

She waved a hand like it was no big deal. But from the way she was looking at me, I knew exactly what she was referring to. This was the dream I'd interrupted with my dick in her mouth. Oh yes, we were absolutely going to reenact this scene.

"Well I, for one, vote we make this dream a reality," I said. "You in, beast?"

Tor didn't spare me a glance; he was too busy hungrily eyeing Dahlia. "I'm in."

Dahlia squeezed her thighs together and let out an almost inaudible whimper.

I knew it went without saying. Her body language was speaking volumes. But I also knew all of us wanted to hear her ask for it.

"And you, darling? Are you ready to take care of your beast while I and the others take care of you?"

"Y-yes."

"Then get on the bed," I ordered.

"Who put him in charge?" Hades grumbled while Dahlia and Tor moved into position—him naked on his back and her kneeling between his spread thighs.

"Hush. Do you see how turned on she is?" Kai whispered back. "Sometimes the best thing we can do is sit back and wait for our turn."

"Is that what we're doing?" Hades asked.

"Aye. It doesn't mean it won't be enjoyable," Kai answered.

Dahlia looked back at them over her shoulder, her hair swinging temptingly across her skin as she did. "I like knowing that you'll be watching."

"Put on a good show for us, gem. Maybe if we feel inspired enough, we'll reward you."

I was close enough to her that I heard her breath hitch and saw her pupils flare with excitement. "Hades, I'm going to need you ready with those shadows. As soon as I touch her, he's going to lose it."

He gave a terse nod, then I turned my focus back to my girl. She brushed her hair away from her face, taking hold of Tor's straining—and bloody enormous —erection before licking the tip like it was her favorite treat. The big Viking grunted, his hands fisting the sheets as she continued toying with him.

"That's it, love. Show him how much you like what he's got for you."

It was impressive watching the way she swallowed him down,

taking his considerable length deep into her throat. I wasn't the only one who thought so. All four of us let out appreciative grunts and moans as she did.

"Goddamn, Dahlia, you look like a fucking goddess." Hades's voice was tight, and with a quick glance, I caught sight of his fist shuttling up and down his own length.

"She does, doesn't she? Her round arse looks like a juicy peach I can't wait to sink my teeth into." I climbed on the bed behind Dahlia, unable to keep my hands off her any longer. "Hades?" I called, hopeful the man wouldn't be too distracted by her to keep Tor contained.

"I've got it under control," Tor bit out, but his snarls and grunts said something very different.

"Just think about how much our mate enjoys the thought of you at her mercy," Kai said. "It's not for you, it's for her. Everything is for her."

"Yes," Tor agreed, sounding nearly hypnotized. Not that I blamed him. With the way Dahlia was bobbing up and down on his cock, I would be too.

Palms skating across her soft skin, I leaned down and nipped one cheek hard enough she flinched. Goosebumps broke out across her flesh, and fuck if I didn't groan. I could smell how much she loved this, her sweet scent flooding my nose in a tantalizing rush. It would be so easy to bury my face in her cunt and drink her down right here, but I had plans. I needed this to last longer than a few minutes.

Righting myself, I slid my hand up her back until I could wrap my fist in her hair in a firm grip. Was it dangerous to take control of Tor's blow job? Probably. But I had a god on my side, and Dahlia loved it when someone else took the reins.

She hummed in approval when I gave her hair a firm tug.

"Easy, love. We only want to bring him to the edge. When he comes, I want to see it dripping out of that pretty cunt."

Dahlia moaned her agreement.

"I'm going to set the pace, make sure we all stay honest."

Oh, the beast did not like that. He growled at me, but I only smirked in response.

"Do you really think it's a good idea to threaten the man in control of your orgasm?"

"Careful, pirate," Hades warned as his shadows slithered across the bed. In moments, Tor's wrists were restrained above his head, one tied to each bedpost as he fought half-heartedly.

"Fuck, that's so hot," Dahlia whispered after popping off of Tor's dick.

"Be a good girl and swallow him down. Make him beg you for it, darling."

My fingers went to her sopping pussy, sinking inside easily as she did what I told her.

"I've never wanted tae be restrained before, but it's looking more appealing by the second," Kai admitted. "Goddess, gem. You're beautiful."

Wanting to maintain control of the scene but also desperate to get my hands dirty—well, my face dirty, if we're being honest—I laid down a new order. "He only gets your mouth until you come, sweet girl. So take as long as you'd like, but don't let him finish."

Tor's thighs were trembling with the effort it took not to buck his hips. I recognized that need. I'd felt it more than once.

Releasing her hair, I sat back on my heels so I could replace my fingers with what I really wanted. "Arch that beautiful arse back for me. Give me access to you like I need."

As soon as she did, I buried my face in her dripping center, sucking and licking her like I was working to win a medal. She may want to edge Tor, but I was going to make her finish come hell or high water.

At first she rocked into me, chasing the pleasure I was offering, but as her climax crested, she attempted to squirm away.

"Ah, ah, ah," I tutted, the vibrations of my voice rolling over her slick flesh. "You're not going anywhere, love. We're just getting started."

Then I shifted my position so that my hands were banded around her thighs, locking her into place. There was no squirming away now. Not on my watch.

She whimpered around Tor's dick, and he bit out a string of curses.

"Finish him off or let him go, darling. Your choice."

Her walls fluttered as I drew the orgasm on and on until she released Tor's length and begged me to stop. It was the perfect torture for all of us. I, myself, was painfully aroused, dying to be inside her.

"Stop, oh God, stop, Cas. You're killing me."

"But what a way to go, right, sweet girl?"

Tor growled and thrashed under his restraints. "Enough of this. I need you, Kærasta."

I smirked as the thought of what we could do next flickered to life in my mind. "Go on, love. Ride your Viking to the finish line. I want to see you take his cock."

"And what are you going to do?" she asked, looking back at me.

"Me? I think you mean *we*, darling. What are we going to do?" Then I winked. "Guess you'll just have to mount up and find out."

Her eyes widened.

"Do you trust your captain, Dahlia?" I asked.

"Yes."

"That's my good girl."

CHAPTER THIRTY-ONE

TOR

Freya's heaving bosom, I had no idea how I'd managed to last through that without giving in to my beast or at least finding release. Dahlia's mouth was the sweetest torture, its wet heat a near perfect imitation of her silky cunt. Except, of course, for the teeth. That was something else entirely. The occasional scrape of her teeth along my shaft sent a thrill through me. It was the ultimate tease for a man who thrived on danger. Knowing she could either bring me immense pleasure or indescribable pain with one snap decision. Fuck, my balls throbbed at the thought.

I pulled on the shadows restraining me and flicked my stare to Hades, who was watching with rapt attention. He simply shook his head. I wouldn't be released until our mate said so. I eyed the smoky tendrils with interest. They looked immaterial but were stronger than any metal I'd ever come across, with the added benefit of causing no discomfort. At least it was no true hardship, being at my mate's mercy.

Dahlia's palm pressed to my sternum, right over my tattoo, bringing my focus back to her.

"Tor?" she whispered.

"Take me, beauty."

In mere moments, she straddled my hips, the heat of her slick core gliding over my pulsing length and making a feral growl rip from my throat. Then she notched me at her entrance, the tip pressing inside but just barely.

"Fuck, Dahlia. You're so bad," Hook murmured approvingly, reminding me he was there.

A snarl slipped free at the reminder. It was easier for me when I could pretend it was just the two of us. I didn't resent them for helping me bring her pleasure, but my beast had a near-constant need to assert his dominance. Probably for the best I was tied down, so I didn't accidentally slip up and knock one of them out. Or worse.

Without warning, a smoky tendril wrapped around her waist and forced her down until I was fully sheathed inside her. She cried out, a wail of pleasure that matched my own, then turned her head to look over her shoulder at Hades.

"Not fair."

"Who said anything about playing fair?"

She huffed, opening her mouth like she was going to argue the point, but a tendril filled her mouth instead.

"We'll talk about it when it's my turn, baby doll. Now be our good girl and take him for a ride."

Kai approached the bed, dick in his hand, as Dahlia began to move on me. He brushed her hair away from her face, and when the tendril of shadow disappeared, he slipped his thumb between her lips. "Suck, lass."

She moaned, rocking her hips slowly and making me wish my hands were free in the worst way. The lack of control was as exciting as it was infuriating.

I thrashed my head against the pillow, growling out my frustration.

"You doing okay, big guy?" she asked, voice breathy with exertion.

"Yes," I gritted out, but apparently that wasn't much reassurance, because she huffed out a laugh.

"You sure?"

"Fuck, Kærasta, you feel so good."

"Just wait until I get what I want," Hook said, coming up behind her. "Lean over him a little more, darling."

He spit on her arse, his thumb following in the wake of the saliva, and he must've pushed the digit inside her because she tensed around me.

"Oh God. What's that?" she gasped.

"That's my thumb. If you're good for me, I'll give you more."

"Yes. Oh please, yes."

For my part, I wasn't sure I could stand more. The added pressure just his thumb caused had me seeing stars. And the way she clamped down around my cock every time he thrust it in and out only made it harder for me to hold on.

"Lube," she cried in a frantic whisper. "Kai, get it, please?"

"My pleasure, gem." Kai opened her nightstand drawer and grabbed a bottle of clear liquid, tossing it to Hook, who caught it easily.

"Look at that. We're a crew already."

The flick of the cap opening was all the warning I had before she tensed and her walls became unbearably tight around me as Hook pushed his way inside her.

"Odin, fuck," I bit out. I could feel the slide of him through the thin barrier separating us. It was unexpected and forbidden, and such a foreign sensation that I was about to come here and now.

"You can come if you need to, Tor. It's okay, baby," she said, her lips grazing my nipple as she rocked slowly over me. "God, I'm close too."

"Then let's see about sending you over the edge," Kai murmured, his hand wrapping around her throat as he lifted her up enough that he could slide the tip of his dick along her lips. "Suck me off, gem."

She took him into her mouth eagerly, her cheeks flushed and her eyes heavy-lidded.

I would not find my release until she did. There wasn't a chance in hell that would happen.

"Give me my hands, Hades. I need to touch her."

"No."

I snarled. I think I liked him better when he didn't know who he was. "You'll regret this."

"I don't think I will. Tell me where you want to touch her, and I'll do it."

"How does that help me?" I snapped.

"It's not about you, remember?"

I had to bite down on the inside of my cheek to keep from swearing at him. I hated that he was right. That I was riding the razor's edge of my control, not just against release, but also against the monster within.

"Her clit. She needs to find her climax again—fuuck." My words were cut off by a desperate groan as she squeezed me tighter and a garbled sound left her.

Glancing down her body, I saw the smoky tendril doing exactly what I'd planned on, moving over her clit in slow drags.

"Pinch it," I growled.

Dahlia whimpered as Hades's shadows did just that.

"Oh fuck, she loves that," Caspian moaned, his hands moving around her body to play with her heavy breasts.

"She wants more," I said, knowing by the way she writhed on me that we were nearly there.

A sharp crack echoed through the room, Caspian's hand connecting with her arse. "Then give it to her, someone, please. I'm dying."

Kai shifted, sliding his hand between Dahlia's legs to join Hades's shadows. The added attention must have been the secret ingredient because she detonated like a bomb, her inner walls milking me for all I was worth.

I pulled my hips back, then drove home hard as my own orgasm barreled through me, pulse after pulse of my cum filling her. My vision went white from the pleasure, and I heard a distinct scraping noise as my fingers turned to claws and dug into the wooden headboard.

Cas's grunt joined mine as he too fell over the edge.

I was floating in a euphoric fog, too blissed out to manage actual words. Even my beast was caught in the afterglow. His overwhelming presence in my mind blunted for the first time since the curse took hold.

"Fucking hell, that's the tightest booty I've ever plundered," Caspian said, a note of teasing in his voice.

Hades groaned. "Good gods, why do we keep you around?"

"Because someone needs to lighten the mood around all you sorry sods. It's like living in a telenovela with all the moping and brooding you three do."

I felt it the moment Cas pulled out of her, and her answering sigh only confirmed my suspicion.

"Enough waiting," Kai said, his voice all dragon now. "She's mine."

Dahlia gasped as he lifted her off me, her legs wrapping around his waist like this was a dance they'd rehearsed countless times.

I couldn't even be jealous. Not as I watched my cum drip from her.

"Ours," Hades corrected.

"Aye. But right now, it's my turn."

CHAPTER THIRTY-TWO

KAI

The others were talking, but I couldn't make out a word of what they were saying as I slid Dahlia down on my dick. Fuck, holding her up and letting gravity join us was pure heaven. Why hadn't I had her like this before? Her little intake of breath, the way her eyes flashed in a combination of panic and pleasure, and the brush of her full tits against my chest almost had my knees weak.

Dahlia's mewl of pleasure had my dragon surging to the surface. I could feel my nails elongating, my teeth sharpening into the making of his fangs, and I knew if I could take my eyes off Dahlia's flushed face, I'd find a peppering of black and purple scales along my body.

"Holy fuck," Hades murmured from his place in the chair.

"That's not something you see every day, now is it?" Hook offered as he strode toward the bathroom. "I wonder if his dick transforms too?"

"It does," Dahlia panted as my cock swelled inside her. "Oh God, it does, and . . . fuck, it just did."

"I know exactly how tae please my mate. I was built for it," my dragon said, addressing the room at large.

"Ribbed for my pleasure," Dahlia quipped, but I rolled my hips, turning her words into a garbled moan.

Tor snarled and struggled in his bindings on the bed. "Release me, Hades. I need to go to her."

"Are you gonna rip off his arms and beat him to death with them? Because if the answer is yes, my answer is no."

"He willnae hurt me," I said, knowing it was true. The Beast of Novasgard and I had an accord. We'd learned how to partner in this dance with our mate and were well acquainted with the steps. "Release him."

The power in the room shifted, leaving a sort of chill as the shadowy tendrils receded. Tor was there almost instantly, his large frame behind Dahlia, palms skating over her ribs and up until he cupped both breasts.

"Remember that I let you have yer turn. I dinnae interfere," I warned as he started kissing along the side of her neck.

"I remember. I'm only here to help."

"You're very helpful. The most helpful helper," Dahlia babbled, completely swept up in the moment.

"Lie back on me, Kærasta." Tor guided her until she was draped against his chest and I held her by the hips.

I couldn't lie; it was the perfect adjustment. I could see my cock moving under the skin of her lower belly. Filling her so full she could barely take me. The change in position also freed me to lift her up and down my length. She was completely helpless in this position. Not bound, but unable to do anything except take what I and the others chose to give her.

"Oh, that's . . . wonderful," she breathed, eyes falling closed as I slowly pumped in and out of her.

"What a pretty picture you make, sweet girl."

It was funny how only a few weeks ago that pirate swanning in here and stealing her attention would've made all of us jealous.

Now? The way she fluttered around me at the sound of his voice only added to the moment.

Caspian also seemed content to take on a supporting role as he drew a lazy squiggle down her torso, his fingertips ghosting down between her legs, teasing her clit and then drifting back up until he was tweaking her nipple.

"So. Many. Hands," Dahlia breathed. "But I need more. Please, my lord Hades."

The grunt that left the man in the corner was one I was all too familiar with. He'd been hanging on by a thread since the moment I told them all we needed to take care of her. What I couldn't understand was why he refused to join in and physically touch her. But to each their own.

Dahlia cried out, arching up as someone did something to her, but as far as I could see, nothing had changed. Her pussy gushed around my dick, and an unmistakable climax rocketed through her.

"Ask and you shall receive, baby doll."

Cas tossed him a healthy side-eye. "Not all of us have to resort to tricks to get the job done, you know."

"It's not a trick. It's a skill."

"It is. It *really* is," Dahlia breathed.

No one could really refute a point made in a voice like that. She was the definition of well-pleasured.

Glancing over my shoulder, I caught sight of Hades, jaw clenched, hand fisting his cock, eyes narrowed in intense focus.

"Hold her still," I gritted out as I gripped her hips harder, the pointed tips of my nails leaving little divots in her skin.

Tor nodded and held on tighter. Cas continued to play with her body, alternating between using his fingers and his lips as he plucked at her nipples and rubbed her clit.

"Oh my God, Kai." Dahlia's panted exclamation had me following her gaze until I saw what she was staring at. My tattoo had worked its way across my torso, the dragon's head resting just below my navel so his face was eye level with her pussy.

I guess he wanted front row seats to the show. I didn't blame him. She really did have a beautiful cunt.

Closing my eyes, I let my dragon have more of the control he'd been craving. He'd been so patient, sitting in the shadows and waiting for me to let him have our wee mate again. This was the safest place I could give him room to stretch his wings. Here with her other three men. Men who'd die for her.

I'm trusting you.

"When it comes to her, you never need to fear me."

With that promise echoing in my mind, my dragon's wings—or their fae equivalent—burst out of my back. I rolled my shoulders, welcoming the unfamiliar weight. It was my first time fully in this in-between form. Both fae male and dragon. It felt . . . right.

Dahlia gasped, her eyes wide—and not from pleasure.

"Fuck me," Hades murmured in awe.

"No fair. You already have a dragon dick." Caspian's fingers reached out and played with the membranous flesh of one of the leathery black wings.

Oh fuck. That was sensitive.

"Stop touching me," my dragon growled before turning his attention back to Dahlia. "You, however, can touch me as much as you'd like."

"Your wings," she whispered, "Kai, they're so beautiful. And big. I think if you extended them, they'd fill the entire room. Oh my God, can you fly? Will you take me with you?"

I rocked into her so deeply she whimpered. "Focus, my wee mate. We'll discuss the finer points of flying after I've filled you so full of my spend ye cannae walk without me spilling from ye."

Tor growled low in his throat, not appreciating the reference to my cum filling her. I could see it in his eyes; he was already plotting how he could replace it with his own. Poor Dahlia, surrounded by territorial males with a primal need to mark her every which way.

"Are ye ready to be filled, my treasure?"

"Yes."

Hades must have used his shadows again because Dahlia writhed, grinding down as much as she could on my cock.

"Just lending a helping hand," the smug bastard drawled from his chair.

"Fuck, I'm ready to go again as well. Maybe someone can lend me a helping hand?" Caspian asked, looking to Tor, who simply snarled, then to me.

"Mine are full, pirate. Use yours."

Dahlia gave a half moan, half giggle, then reached out for Cas, slipping her palm over his chest and down until she reached his straining length.

"That's my sweet girl. Always thinking of others, even when she should be focused on herself."

"Who can focus with all four of you—oh," she moaned.

"Less talking, more fucking," my dragon growled.

I gripped her so tightly my nails broke the skin, sending little rivulets of blood running down her hips. For a moment I worried Tor would lose it and raze us all to the ground, but Cas leaned in and licked the blood clean before anyone could do a thing.

Then I drove into her, hard, fast, punishing, as I chased my release.

"Make her come, Caspian," I ordered. "Make her come all over my cock."

Cas leaned in, spreading her open farther with his fingers before sucking on her clit, his lips almost touching the base of my dick in the process.

"Come for us, beauty. You look so beautiful when you fall apart."

Her cries of pleasure were closer together now, her orgasm just out of reach.

"That's it, baby doll. You're taking his dick so well. Come for them so you can come for me next."

That did it. She fell off the edge and shattered around me, dragging my own climax along with her. I released a pained groan, my knees buckling for the briefest moment before I was able to put myself right again. Never had I been more thankful for Tor. I may have dropped her were it not for him and my newly acquired wings. They were doing some of the work as well.

My dragon began to recede, content now that he'd laid claim to his mate. My body returned to its normal status, well, minus the wings. Those remained.

Fuck, were they permanent? How was I supposed to get dressed?

My dragon huffed in amusement. *"You can put them away whenever ye like, but our wee treasure fancies them. Ye might want to keep them around for a while so she can play."*

I pulled out of her carefully, and Tor helped me shift her until I held Dahlia in my arms, not trusting her legs to hold her upright just yet.

"All right, fellas. Put her on the bed and get the fuck out. You had your fun. It's my turn."

CHAPTER THIRTY-THREE

HADES

I stood from my chair and stared them down, wondering how angry my goddess would be if I used my shadows to toss the other three out into the hall.

"Oi, we let you stick around and watch. Not our fault you wanted to keep your hands to yourself," Caspian grumbled.

"Technically he participated," Dahlia said, her voice dreamy after the powerful orgasms she'd had.

I definitely fucking participated.

"They aren't mutually exclusive. He still kept his hands to himself," Cas said, pointing to my open fly and rock-hard erection.

"Are we going to debate the finer points of how we fuck her? I really don't have any patience left for you to take up more of my time."

Dahlia turned soft eyes on me. "Don't make them leave, my lord Hades. I want them to stay. I like knowing that they're here, even if they're only allowed to watch."

There was no way I could deny her anything, especially not when she begged so prettily.

"You heard her. Sit down and shut up, or if you can't, then get out."

"That's how you can tell he hasn't really participated," Cas whispered to the others. "He's grumpy when he should be smiling."

I'd show him exactly how much I could participate. "Get on the bed, baby doll. Part those thighs for me so I can see what I've waited for."

Tor's gaze flicked from me to her. He was clearly at war with himself.

"I can restrain you again if you need it, Tor. But I'm taking what's mine. I don't need your permission."

A soft snarl left him, but he shook his head no and claimed my seat in the corner. Kai helped Dahlia to the bed, his hands lingering over the marks he'd left on her hips.

"I'm sorry if I hurt ye, gem."

"Only in the good ways," she promised, reaching out to brush her fingers over his wings.

His fucking wings. I'd say he was overcompensating, but I'd seen what the dragon was working with. Now he was just showing off.

I bet my shadows could make wings.

The three men had taken up positions around the room, Kai standing in the corner, Cas perched on the desk, Tor in the chair where I'd been testing the limits of my self-control. How fitting. I was ready with my shadows if Tor lost himself while I took Dahlia. It had been one thing for him to be part of her time with Kai; it was another to watch her in the throes of passion with me alone.

Shoving my pants down my legs, I crawled up the bed with my eyes trained on hers. I needed her in the worst way.

"How do you want me?" she asked with a wicked grin.

"Any way I can get you."

She sat up, reaching for me, but I used a wisp of shadow around her throat to stop her, forcing my sweet flower back down on the bed. This position would do just fine for what I wanted. The way she writhed as I applied a little pressure presented her breasts like an offering to me. Her nipples straining, tempting me like ripe berries ready to be plucked.

I slid my shadows over her full tits, using them as an extension of me so I could pay attention to every single part of her. With my hands, I worked my way up her thighs, gently nudging her legs further apart to make room for me.

Her pussy was a mess of cum and lube, her swollen nether lips slick and bright red with arousal. I ran a gentle finger along her center, halting when she winced.

"Sore, baby doll?"

"I'm okay. Don't stop." The words came out tight and forced.

"No, don't do that. Don't set aside your own needs just because it's my turn." I examined my finger as I sat back. There was more than a mixture of cum and her arousal. A faint tinge of blood streaked the fluid. "Tor, do me a favor and get me a warm washcloth, will ya?"

The Viking was on his feet so fast the chair groaned in protest.

He was at our side seconds later, the square of terry cloth held out in offering. "Want me to do it?"

"I got it, thanks," I said, hardly bothering to spare him a glance as I accepted the cloth and began to clean her up.

"Hades, what are you doing?" she asked me, propping up on her elbows now that my shadows had retracted into me. I wasn't going to restrain her while I was taking care of her.

"They made a mess of you. It's my job to put you back together."

"But . . . aren't you just going to make a mess too?"

"No harm in getting clean before we get dirty." I smirked as I ran the cloth over her entrance. "I don't do sloppy seconds."

"You don't know what you're missing out on. It's great." Caspian had his hand around his dick as he watched us.

"Technically it's thirds," Dahlia said with a laugh.

I lightly slapped the top of her cunt and grumbled, "Quiet, you."

"You know the only surefire way to get me to shut up, Daddy."

I cocked a brow at her. "You asking for a dick in your mouth, baby doll?"

"I volunteer!" Cas said, jumping to his feet.

I shoved him down with my shadows, binding his legs against the wood. "Be a good puppy and stay."

"What if I don't want you in my mouth?"

The thought of hurting her by fucking her after she'd had so much already didn't sit right with me. I wasn't as long as Tor or as thick or monstrous as Kai, but I could still do some damage when she was already clearly battered.

"Baby, you've been loved so well already. I don't want to take things from sore to unbearable. The last thing I want is for you to be in pain when I'm inside you."

"I won't be, I promise."

"You can't know that."

"Please, Daddy. I need you."

Cas snickered with unconcealed glee. "I called it! Figures he'd like to be called Daddy. The bossy ones always do."

I had to bite back a growl of annoyance because the fucker had actually called it way back in that first group session before he knew a damn thing about me.

"She can call me whatever she wants. I wouldn't complain," Kai said.

"Puff?"

"Stop."

"Falcor?"

"Caspian."

"Smaug."

I used a shadow to muffle his mouth before the pirate ended up on the wrong side of Kai's dragon fire.

"Thanks," Kai said.

"It was kinder than what I was about to do," Tor added.

"Me too," Kai agreed.

I rolled my eyes, refocusing on my Dahlia. "Are you sure you want them to stay? They're distracting, and not in a sexy way."

"Oh, I dunno," she murmured, eyes moving over the men behind me. "I find them pretty sexy."

Leaning down, I let my lips hover right over her freshly cleaned cunt. "I find this pretty sexy," I murmured before kissing the top, just above her clit. "And definitely distracting."

"Mmm, me too."

"Feel good, baby doll?"

"Yes, so good. Don't stop."

"Wouldn't dream of it."

I took my time, worshipping her like the goddess she was. She whimpered in pure pleasure when my tongue slid over her swollen nub. I wasn't going anywhere near entering her. She needed more from me; that much was clear by the way her hips writhed, but I wanted to be sure before I sank inside her.

I looked up her body, taking in her flushed skin and hooded eyes with pride. "You ready for more, baby?"

"Yes. Please. I need you inside me."

I pushed one finger slowly inside her, teasing her with shallow thrusts.

"More," she begged.

"Shhh, trust me to know what you need."

Her hands found my hair, fingers burying themselves in the thick strands as she tugged and then pushed my face down into her in search of more. Fuck, I loved it when my little brat showed me how impatient she was.

When her pussy was dripping only for me, walls clenching around my finger, trying to suck me deeper inside her, I pulled back.

"Cain," she whined.

I growled against her clit. "My name is Hades."

She came around my finger, screaming my name, my true name, and I rutted into the mattress like a fucking teenager. I couldn't take it any longer. I had to be inside her right the hell now.

Removing my hand, I took her by the hips and pulled her down until she was impaled on my cock. The bark of pleasure I let out would've been shameful if I hadn't been so pent up. Gods, she felt like a dream. Like everything I'd been missing in my long life. Because she was.

"Hades," she moaned, reaching for me and scoring her nails down my back as my pelvis ground against her needy clit.

I rocked into her, giving her the friction she needed even though I knew every thrust brought me closer to the release I had been edging closer to since this started.

"Come with me, please. I want to feel you spilling inside me."

"Fuck, baby doll. Fuuuck." I turned into a grunting, spasming demon atop her, thrusting hard and fast as my orgasm hit me.

She pulsed around me, milking me for all I was worth as I gave her every last drop of my seed. She could have it all whenever she fucking wanted it. I was hers. Body and soul.

I brushed some sweaty hair off her forehead so I could press my lips against her damp skin.

"Love you," she breathed into my chest, filling me up with joy I hadn't felt in . . . centuries.

"I love you too," I admitted, my voice tight.

"What? That's it?" Caspian asked, my shadows having disappeared while I'd been distracted by my release. "Was he trying to set a land speed record or something? Are we supposed to be impressed? Oof, I think you broke my sternum," he wheezed.

I turned my head in time to see Tor pulling his elbow back. "You're lucky you still have your tongue."

"What now?" Dahlia asked, eyes already drooping with sleep.

"Now you rest up and get ready for round two," I answered.

"Round twenty-two, you mean," she said with a sleepy smile.

Tor approached the bed first, his hand pressed to the headboard, and as I watched, the entire thing increased in size, becoming something all of us could fit on.

"Now we sleep. All of us together," he said.

"As it should be," Kai added.

Dahlia snuggled in as her other three men joined us. Tor on her left, me on her right, Kai with his arms wrapped around her hips and his head resting on her lower belly. And then Cas, at her feet, where bad dogs belonged.

SESSION TRANSCRIPT: DECEMBER 21ST

Dr. Masterson: This is Dr. Elizabeth Masterson. It is December 21st, and the time is 9:07 a.m. This is a recorded session with Malakai Nash.

<<chair squeaks>>

Kai: *Exhausted sigh* Do we really have to do this so ungodly early?

Dr. Masterson: I'm afraid so, Kai. We're already . . . seven minutes behind schedule, and my diary is full for the day. Last-minute appointments before the gala. Everyone is cramming them in prior to the festivities.

Kai: Very well, let's get this over with so I can get back tae my mate.

Dr. Masterson: Tell me how things are going with Dahlia.

<<clothes rustling>>

Kai: Fine.

Dr. Masterson: Just fine?

<<dragonesque growl>>

Kai: I don't want to talk about her. She's mine.

<<furious typing>>

Dr. Masterson: *musing hum*

Kai: Why are you sitting behind your desk at your bloody computer? You're always across from me, scribbling on your wee notepad.

Dr. Masterson: Because there's less time and more to take note of. Clearly your dragon is more present. I can see the dragon fire in your eyes. How are you feeling about that?

Kai: Fine.

<<furious typing>>

Dr. Masterson: Mmm-hmm. It's a bit of a one-eighty from your feelings when you arrived at Blackwood. Why the change of heart when you used to be so against the idea?

Kai: I'm working on balance, as you always say I should. That means giving him more agency.

Dr. Masterson: And is that the only reason for this new symbiotic relationship?

Kai: *snarl* Why ask questions when ye already ken the answer?

Dr. Masterson: Kai? What's happened? He's never been this vocal before.

<<unzipping sound>>

<<wings unfurling>>

<<items falling to floor>>

Kai: This. This happened.

Dr. Masterson: W-w-wings? Oh my stars. I've never seen dragon wings in the flesh.

<<chair pushing back>>

<<footsteps>>

Kai: Don't fucking touch them.

Dr. Masterson: *startled gasp* I-I'm sorry. I didn't mean to overstep. *clears throat*

<<footsteps>>

<<chair squeak>>

Dr. Masterson: When did this occur?

Kai: You don't want to know the answer to that question.

Dr. Masterson: You don't seem to understand the meaning of therapy. I am a safe space. You can share anything with me. There's no limit to what I'm willing to hear.

<<wings retracting>>

Kai: That may be true, but there's a limit on what I'm willing tae share. Especially when it concerns my mate.

Dr. Masterson: *defeated sigh* Fine. But it would seem you and your dragon have found a . . . balance, as you say?

Kai: I am no longer fighting against our bond, if that's what you're inquiring.

<<furious typing>>

Dr. Masterson: I'd say that's excellent progress. And have you found your previous fears unfounded?

Kai: Aye. It would seem the two of us can coexist without razing the village.

Dr. Masterson: Do you think you'll ever allow him to fully manifest?

Kai: Not unless it's the only option.

Dr. Masterson: All right. I can confidently say that you don't pose a risk to Blackwood, so you are cleared to attend the gala tomorrow. I hope you have something dapper to wear.

Kai: *chuckle* Dinnae fash yerself. Of course I have something to wear. I'm a Scotsman and fae besides.

Dr. Masterson: Are ye planning on wearing a kilt then?

Kai: Is that even a question? My dragon was right. You have a tendency to ask questions you already ken the answer tae.

<<knock on the door>>

<<door opening>>

Dr. Masterson: *sighs* I don't even know why I bother closing the door.

Joffrey: Ma'am, the duke and his entourage have arrived earlier than scheduled. Where should I put them?

Dr. Masterson: *quiet groan* I'll handle it. We were just about finished here anyway. Malakai, you're free to go. Joffrey, cancel the rest of my appointments for the day.

Joffrey: As you wish, ma'am.

<<static>>

End of transcript.

CHAPTER THIRTY-FOUR

DAHLIA

"Kiki was right. This dress is still fuck-hot," I said, running my palms down the fabric as I looked myself over in the mirror.

This time, I wasn't going to let the guys do any unhooking of anything until the gala was over. We'd never leave the room if I did. And while getting dressed up and spending some quality time with my guys with our clothes *on* sounded like a nice change of pace, the undercurrent of anxiety couldn't be denied. Especially as the minutes ticked by and the event grew closer. What if I freaked out? What if I saw the malevolent spirit again, and I killed everyone? What if . . .

I closed my eyes and breathed through my nose, counting backward from ten as I worked to get myself under control. I couldn't have a panic attack right now. I'd made so much progress, and dammit, I wouldn't be stopped by my past.

As if they could sense the imminent spiral, a knock sounded on the door.

"Coming," I called, moving as fast as I could to the door, not an easy feat in the hip-hugging gown. I wasn't sure which of my mates was on the other side. They'd drawn straws to decide who got to formally escort me downstairs where the other three would be waiting. As far as fair went, I was pretty impressed with their plan.

Was I expecting them to actually follow through with it?

Of course not. Have you met Caspian? Or Tor? I'd bet my last Twinkie all four of them were waiting on the other side, crowding around so they could all have a prime viewing spot.

And I was right, mostly. Tor stood at my door, a swoon-worthy smile on his face as he leaned against the doorframe in that way he had.

"Hi," I murmured, taking him in. A suit on a Viking would've been hot, but the traditional garb with the fur and leather breeches was catastrophic to the panties I wasn't wearing.

"Kærasta," he whispered. "You're beautiful."

"So are you." I ran my fingers through the soft fur at his shoulders. "Wow."

The other three weren't at the bottom of the stairs but standing a few feet behind him, looking more dapper than I'd ever seen.

"Is that a kilt?" I asked, eyeing Kai. Traditional highland dress might be a thing for me now that I'd seen him in it. Jesus. The jacket and vest might've covered his dragon, but I saw the sneaky head poking out of his collar on the side of his neck. And my Scot spared no detail when it came to his ensemble. He wore every piece with pride. From the kilt to the sporran, he looked like he'd walked right out of a romance novel.

He smirked under my appraisal. "I told you she'd like it."

"Yes, yes, good for you. But what do you think about me, love?" Caspian asked, running his hands down what could only be described as pirate formal wear. He had on a fancy maroon coat that fell to his calves with gold embroidery and big buttons. There was a waistcoat beneath it and a pristine white ruffled shirt beneath that. And his legs were molded in tight black leather and knee-high boots.

"Impressive," I said, intentionally understating my reaction so as not to stroke his ego. His head was big enough. "Where's your hat?"

He narrowed his eyes. “Don’t ask. It’s a sore spot.”

I giggled but gave him an approving look. “You are . . . mmm, let’s just say my pirate fantasies have nothing on this.”

That made him perk up, his shoulders a little straighter as he puffed out his chest. “Course they don’t. Fantasies are never as good as the real thing, darling.”

Hades was silent as usual, his eyes blue embers as he took me in. There was something wickedly sexy about his patience. As if he knew he was the biggest baddie in the room and had no reason to shove his way to the front of the line. He was simply waiting for me to go to him, as if it was inevitable. Because of course it was.

Dressed in black from head to toe, Hades looked every inch the god of the underworld. He was the most delicious bad boy with that black suit and flaming stare. My mouth ran dry until I pulled myself together.

“Like what you see, baby doll?”

“Nope. Not even a little,” I shamelessly lied.

“Brat,” he said, but it was so tenderly uttered there was no mistaking it as anything but an endearment. “You’ll pay for that later.”

“Promises, promises.”

His lips hitched up in a smile that told me I was in for a world of trouble. The fun kind.

“Well, shall we get this over with?” I asked, more than ready to say fuck the whole thing and invite them in.

“Not just yet, gem. I have something for ye.”

My gaze flicked up to meet his, excitement bubbling in my chest. “What is it?”

He pulled the most beautiful jewel-encrusted hair comb from his pocket, the emeralds matching my gown perfectly.

“Kai,” I whispered, noting that his dragon tattoo had shifted so that he could watch my reaction as well. That, more than anything, clued me in that this was no ordinary gift. “Is this from your hoard?”

“Aye.” He cleared his throat, pink dusting his cheeks. “It’s customary for a dragon to gift his mate items from his trove. We spend our lives trying to find the most perfect treasures so that we can give them to the one who is *our* most perfect treasure. Her acceptance of our offering is akin to her acceptance of us."

"I love it." I trailed my fingers over the delicate design. "Put it in for me?"

Pride shone on his face, and he waited for me to indicate where I wanted it. After he slid the teeth of the comb in place, I gave myself one more inspection in the mirror. The emeralds caught the light from the side of my hair and glimmered, just a tease of sparkle.

"Perfect," I murmured.

"Yes, Kærasta, you are. Now, I won the right to have you on my arm as we walk in, so allow me to escort you, my beauty. Please?" Tor crooked his arm and God save me, my heart fluttered.

"It would be my honor," I said, doing my best to live up to the moment.

"No, beauty. The honor is mine."

Fucker. Over here one-upping me. Fuck it, he could have it.

I wove my arm through the crook of his elbow, and he swept me down the hall. The other three followed close behind us. Close enough I was sure that was Caspian's hand brushing against my ass, and Kai's fingers sweeping over my spine. Hades was biding his time, which meant when he finally did touch me, it was going to be more than worth it.

Strangely, all my nervous energy seemed to have melted away now that they were with me. I felt strong. Confident. Powerful. Not something I was used to.

"You know, you look quite like a queen right now," Tor said.

"What does that make you?"

"Your consorts." He dipped his head and pressed a kiss to my hair before inhaling my scent.

"Mmm, I don't hate the sound of that."

The walk to the ballroom was over before I was ready, a crowd already gathered before the closed doors.

"I guess they want to have a dramatic reveal," I muttered, clocking the servers with their trays of champagne and giving Tor's arm a light tug so he'd head us in that direction.

Caspian snaked his way through the people and returned with an entire tray he'd pilfered, one flute for each of us balanced on top. "There you are, love. No need to seek them out. Your captain will always provide."

I rolled my eyes but took a glass. He was delightfully campy today. Definitely feeling himself. If the alternative was him talking to people we couldn't see, I'd take campy all day long.

"There she is. And of course you're the belle of the fucking ball." Oz's voice was light and jovial as he came toward me, his smile broad. He was basically a human disco ball in a glittering blazer and matching loafers. My friend was accompanied by Bru, who looked so damn handsome I had a hard time tearing my eyes from him. I'd always seen Tor's burly guard dressed in his work clothes, but this skinny black suit and white button-down look took him to another level.

Oz reached out and pulled me in for an embrace, black leather gloves on his hands surprising me.

"Gloves?"

He shrugged. "A precaution. Can't risk an accidental mind violation, you know? Lots of people I'm not used to being around, alcohol, lowered inhibitions . . ."

"If it was that easy to prevent, why send you here?" I asked, perhaps naively.

"Because it's not about prevention, sweets. This is punishment, remember?"

"His control is much better than it used to be, as well. If you recall, you were wearing gloves when you did what you did to get sent here. However much a punishment this is, you've also grown." Bru snagged two glasses of champagne from a passing waiter and handed one to Oz. "To you. The strongest man I know."

"Aw, now I feel like a shit for shipping that creep Brian."

Bruno rolled his eyes good-naturedly. "He never stood a chance. I wasn't threatened."

"Well, now that you've made an honest woman out of me, there's no reason for my eyes to stray," Oz gloated.

I clapped my hands. "You two are official? Like going steady? Oh my God, Bru, did you give him your ID bracelet?"

"What year do you think this is, 1957? Get out of here with your ID bracelets." Oz was teasing, but I could tell how happy he was. How happy both of them were. "He gave me his signet ring, of course."

Hades slipped his arm around my waist and tugged me out of Tor's hold. My Viking only growled a little in response. "I'll give you a ring if that's what you want, baby doll. Just say the word."

"Oh my God, it's like she bathed in pheromones and they're all going feral." Sorcha's voice from behind me had me both on edge and laughing. It was a strange dichotomy of emotions. She was just this side of too scary for me to get close to.

We turned to face her, my eyes widening slightly at how stunning she looked. Her dress was a long-sleeved, floor-length black velvet number, but it was far from demure. The skintight gown revealed as much as it concealed. She'd give Morticia Addams a run for her money with the deep cut of the neckline and the matching slit that ran to the top of her thigh. One wrong twitch of her shoulder, and it would be Tits Out for Christmas, for sure. Although Sorcha struck me as the kind of woman who could make even fabric cower in submission, so I wasn't betting on any wardrobe malfunctions tonight.

"Wow, Sorcha. Way to leave some to the imagination," Oz teased.

"She doesn't need to do that. I know exactly what she looks like naked, and I prefer to see as much as possible." Kit slid up behind her, weaving himself around her like a snake.

Sorcha bared her teeth in what was probably supposed to be a smile. "I'm here. You're welcome."

"Yes, we're so blessed to be in your presence," Kai said, sarcasm thick in his tone.

"Glad we are all on the same page."

A server brought her a special tray carrying a solitary champagne flute filled with a bubbling crimson liquid. She daintily took the offered glass and brought it to her nose for a delicate sniff.

"This donor was a fine vintage. I do love champagne."

I cocked my head, a question on my lips, but she smiled and answered before I could ask.

"Mmm, it's only champagne if it comes from that region in France, you know. Of course Blackwood's blend would come from a Frenchman."

Still a little unsure, I started to ask for clarification, but Hades leaned close and whispered, "They've mixed champagne and a Frenchman's blood for her specifically. Spoiled brat that she is, she probably wouldn't have accepted it if he wasn't from the region."

"Just because I have taste, you heathen, that doesn't make me—" She stopped midsentence, her shoulders stiffening as she sniffed the air. "Blackthornes."

"What?" I asked.

"There are Blackthornes here. I can smell them."

She was as tense as a bloodhound, which was appropriate in a creepy way, her eyes narrowed and scanning the room. I knew the instant she spotted them, though I might have missed it if I hadn't been staring at her so intently. Her expression didn't change, except for the subtlest flare of her nostrils.

Following her gaze, I found a group of newcomers standing together in the hall, nine of them all together. But there were two in particular she had to be talking about. There was no way they weren't related to her based on the color of their eyes alone. That, and they were staring at her with no small amount of shock.

"Oh shiiiit," Oz breathed.

There was a blur of color accompanied by a slight gust of wind as the two Blackthornes suddenly appeared directly in front of us. I'm sure to the non-humans in the room, it didn't seem sudden, but my eyes couldn't track the speed with which they'd traveled, so for all intents and purposes, they fucking teleported.

"Auntie Sorcha," the female Blackthorne breathed. "Is that really you?"

"Bloody hell, it is her, Rosie. We thought you were dead," the man said, shaking his head in pure shock.

Sorcha flinched away when the woman tried to touch her. "Which one of my degenerate brothers sired you two?"

"Cashel," the man answered. "My name is Noah, and this is Roslyn."

"You can call me Rosie. Everyone does."

"Not everyone," a new voice interrupted. "I still prefer Roslyn, or wife," he added, pressing his face into her neck.

"And you are?" Sorcha drawled.

"This is Gavin, my husband."

"Gavin Donoghue, Duke of Canterbury." He held out a hand, and Sorcha turned up her nose at it.

"I don't associate with Donoghues."

"Times have changed, Auntie. The feud is over." Rosie threaded her fingers with her husband's. "You've missed a great deal."

Hades cleared his throat, pulling focus from the family reunion. "Are we fighting or getting along? I need to know so I can prepare. These clothes are too restrictive for a good old-fashioned brawl."

"No one is fighting," Noah said. "I'm Noah Blackthorne. Pleasure to meet you . . ."

"Cain. And this is my Dahlia."

"Your Dahlia?" Caspian piped up. "Did you forget already? She belongs to all of us."

"I am not a toy, Caspian. I don't belong to anybody."

Rosie's voice was whisper soft, her head tilted toward her husband. "That sounds like a familiar conversation."

Gavin chuckled, his expression tender. "We know how that ends, don't we, petal?"

"In the sexy dungeon," she quipped, firmly cementing my interest in their whispered conversation.

I should be taking notes.

"Tor?" Noah said on a gasp, his gaze fixated on my Viking, who had slipped into the shadowy alcove behind us. "Bleeding hell, Tor, is that you?" Noah glanced over his shoulder and called, "Sunday. Moira. Come here."

All my protective instincts came to life as soon as I realized Tor was uncomfortable. I put myself in front of him, blocking the vampire's path, useless as that might be.

"Leave him alone."

"Dahlia, I don't mean him any harm. I swear to you."

"It doesn't matter what you want. My mate doesn't want to see you, so do yourself a favor, and fuck right off."

Tor's hand wrapped around my hip, his fingers digging in as he tugged me back against him.

Two women came skidding up to Noah's side, one a voluptuous brunette and the other a petite goth girl with white hair tipped with pitch black.

"Oh my god, Tor. Alek and I have been so worried. What are you doing here?" the brunette blurted, hands reaching out for my beast.

"What happened to keeping in touch, Viking? You need a reminder on how to spell your name?" the goth girl sniped. "It's pretty easy. T-O-R. I can spell mine for you too. Moira. M-O—"

"Tor, do you know them?" I asked.

"I'm his sister-in-law, Sunday," the brunette said.

"And we're basically besties." Moira flipped her hair over her shoulder.

He heaved a sigh and stepped into the light, his big body tense. "In another life."

Sunday gasped as he came into full view, her hands shooting to her mouth. "What happened to you?"

CHAPTER THIRTY-FIVE

TOR

Sunday's heartbroken expression was exactly what I'd hoped to avoid. This was why I hadn't reached out to Alek. Why none of them knew about my plight. I didn't want to see the pity in their eyes. This was never supposed to be their burden. I'd taken it so they could be free and bask in their hard-won happy ending.

"Sunday, I can ex—"

"G-get away f-from my mate!" Bentley Mercer snarled, charging over to our ever-swelling group.

Wonderful, just what we needed to add to this shit show—more fuel. I'd nearly killed him in an underground fight before I'd been shipped off to Blackwood. That's not to say he wasn't dangerous. The Mercer twins were formidable opponents. Deadly, even. Ben was an alpha wolf who had never lost a fight—until he had to face off against me. That had to have been a bruise to his ego.

"I thought Sunday was married to your brother," Dahlia asked, confusion painting her beautiful face. "Is this one of her other mates?"

"No," Rosie said with a sigh. "That one's mine." Rosie stepped between us, stopping him in his tracks with a gentle palm to his chest. "It's fine, Ben. He isn't going to hurt me."

"So you aren't mated to a shifter?" Dahlia asked, turning her attention to Sunday.

"Oh, she is. And she loves it, don't you, Sunshine?" Kingston joined us, all swagger and hair. He'd started growing it out, but it wasn't quite long enough to tie back yet. I didn't have the heart to tell him he looked like a shaggy surfer. "Hey buddy, that's a new look for you. Horns, huh? Bold choice. Get tired of the identical thing? Or is this some kind of marketing ploy? You gonna take The Novasgardian Nuisance on the road?"

"It's the B-Beast of N-Novasgard," Ben said, his body still trembling with the urge to protect what was his.

I understood the feeling. My hand wrapped around the nape of Dahlia's neck in a possessive hold, and my beast was snarling at me to get her as far away from these other men as possible.

"Stars and stones, you assholes can't go for five minutes without trying to start a pissing contest. We get it, you all have big dicks. Jesus." Moira groused as Father Caleb Gallagher approached us, looking broody and stoic as ever.

"Tor," he said, nodding. "You look . . ."

"Beastly, padre. He's going for the whole primal thing. Sunday likes it from time to time, right, baby?"

I shook my head, the chaos of the last few minutes giving me whiplash. My beast was unsettled, not sure if we were going to battle or if it was safe. Sensing my unease, Dahlia curled herself into my side.

"It's okay, big guy. I'm right here. We're safe. But if you need to make a speedy getaway, just say the word, and I'll get us out."

"What word?" I whispered back, loving that she was once again attempting to take care of me when it was supposed to be the other way around.

Her teeth bit down into her bottom lip as she considered my question. "Hmm . . . codswallop? Whippersnapper? Skedaddle? Honestly, just a growly 'come on' will probably be enough."

"A growl I can do."

"Are you going to introduce me to the white-haired beauty at your side, Tor? Something we need to know about her, maybe?" Moira asked pointedly.

I pulled Dahlia closer, letting out a huff that was almost a growl as every one of the newcomers trained their gazes on her. "This is Dahlia. My mate. Dahlia, this is Sunday, her mates Caleb, Kingston, and you've already met Noah. Rosie and Gavin I'm just meeting tonight. And as you probably inferred, Ben and I have a past."

"That's one w-way to describe r-ripping m-me apart," Ben muttered.

"Wait, what?" Rosie asked.

"It's a long story," I sighed.

"There seem to be a lot of those going around," Sunday muttered.

I scanned the room, my heart lurching with a mixture of panic and hope. "Where's Alek?"

"At home, taking care of Eden," Caleb answered.

"We drew straws. He lost. We got to get dressed up and come to the fancy party. And then escort the good father over to his new post," Kingston said with a grin.

"New post?" I asked, struggling to keep up.

"He's the new headmaster at Ravenscroft," Noah explained. "He's taking over after the winter holiday."

That felt appropriate. It also explained why so many of them made the journey across the pond.

"I couldn't just leave the place in shambles. Ravenscroft has a long and storied past, and until War nearly destroyed it, the hallowed halls were revered for a reason. I intend to restore it to its former glory," Caleb offered.

"Amen," Caspian added, his brows waggling. "Do I smell incense? Holy oil? Which one of you is a priest?"

"He is," almost all of us said, pointing at Caleb.

"I was. I haven't been a priest for a very long time. You'd do well to remember that, Mrs. Gallagher," he said, shooting a sly grin at Sunday.

DAHLIA WATCHED all of this with rapt attention. "I wish Kiki was here. She'd absolutely die."

"And who are you?" Moira asked pointedly, staring intently at Caspian. "I have to assume you're relevant. Or do you just go around inserting yourself into other people's conversations? Follow-up question. Why are you dressed like a pirate?"

"Oh sweet Jesus, here he goes," Hades mumbled.

"One, two, three," Kai counted with feigned patience.

Caspian swooped into a deep bow. "Captain Caspian J.—"

"Hook! I thought that was you." Rosie threw herself at him, wrapping the pirate in her arms.

"Careful there, barmaid. Your mate isn't as tolerant as his twin. Something tells me Bentley here doesn't play like Remi."

She released him and then quickly took Ben's hand by way of apology. "Your crew is lost without you in Aurora Springs. Why didn't you say goodbye before you left?"

"I wasn't really given much of a choice," the pirate said, clearly sulking at having his big moment stolen.

"Oh, so you're one of the patients here," Moira said as though speaking to a child. "Let me guess, you're a lost fae prince? Went too hard on pixie dust?"

Caspian blinked at her. "How did you know?"

"Glinda knows everything," Kingston said.

"Who the fuck is Glinda?" Kai asked, his frustration evident.

"Who is this chucklehead?" Kingston pointed at Kai. "He doesn't even know *Wicked*? Tor, "Defying Gravity" is our go-to karaoke song."

"You karaoke?" Dahlia asked with a sputtered laugh.

"Once. When I was drunk."

"No-o," Moira corrected, holding up a finger in the air. "You were the karaoke champion, my friend. Your Bon Jovi medley was legendary."

"Oh, this I have to see," Kai said.

"Me too. I just can't picture it."

Caleb let out a snort. "It was burned into my brain for all eternity. You won't soon forget the sight of a drunken pair of Vikings singing on a stage so tiny it bowed beneath their weight."

"You, me, and a bottle of whiskey. We're recreating this, big guy," Dahlia said, her lips twisted in laughter. "And there will be a recording for posterity."

"Do you think The Hag's Tooth has a karaoke machine?" Caspian asked. "I do a smashing rendition of "It's Raining Men"."

"Of course you do," Hades said.

"What's your song? "The Devil Went Down to Georgia"?" Kai asked, giving him a good-natured ribbing.

Hades stared him dead in the eye. ""The Sound of Silence." *Your* silence."

"I'm sorry, who are these two?" Moira asked, pointing to Hades and Kai.

Dahlia stepped forward. "These are my mates. You've already met Cas. This is Kai and H—Cain."

"So there are three of us with multiple mates?" Rosie asked, rejoining the conversation. "And we all seem to have a connection to each other. Interesting."

"Concerning." Caleb wrapped his arm around Sunday's waist.

"I agree," Gavin said, frowning as he slipped his hand into his pocket. "If you'll excuse me, I need to make a call."

"Asher?" Rosie guessed.

Gavin nodded distractedly as he moved away.

"So, how many mates do you have?" Dahlia asked. "Four as well?"

"Five, actually. Ben and Gavin you met. Pan is around here somewhere, talking to Lilith, I'd wager, and Asher and Remi stayed home."

It was a strange coincidence. Why did it feel like destiny was in the air? That same unsettling tickle ran down the back of my neck. The one that preceded Finbar's appearance the night everything changed. But what did it mean?

Sunday turned her attention on me, hurt and concern shining in her eyes. "I guess all this explains why you haven't been in contact."

"I didn't know how to tell you—" I began, but Moira interrupted.

"Oh, I don't know, maybe a call to your favorite Belladonna witch to tell me you got yourself in a pickle would've been a good place to start, Viking. God, it's just like a man to completely discount a woman's power. You didn't even give me a chance to try and fix whatever this is." She gestured to my horns, frustration in her eyes. "Instead you get thrown in Blackwood? Alek has been worried sick about you. And, you know, so have the rest of us. I need you to explain what happened."

"I'm not going to stand here and rehash my curse with you. What's done is done."

Moira scoffed. "Typical. You made a bad decision and don't want to deal with the emotional fallout."

Dahlia stepped forward again, and for a moment I worried she'd jump to my defense without all the facts. I almost stopped her, but she said, "You're the Belladonna witch? You're here to strengthen the spell."

"What spell?" Kingston asked. "I thought you were just doing some witchy yule ritual?"

"The one that keeps us all prisoner," Dahlia said, arms crossing under her breasts.

"You didn't tell me it was a Belladonna witch," I said, connecting the dots Dahlia had already put together.

"I didn't know it was relevant."

"Wait just a second. I'm not keeping anyone prisoner. I'm just upholding a centuries-long tradition my coven has been part of. Once a decade, the head of the Belladonna coven is charged with returning to Blackwood to perform a ritual that will strengthen the protective wards that keep the humans from stumbling past the gates. We're keeping people out, not locking them in."

"Are you sure about that?" Dahlia asked, one brow raised.

"Of course! Why would we do anything different?"

"I think you and Sorcha need to have a little chat."

"Ugh, don't bring me into this," Sorcha groused. "The facts speak for themselves. I already did my part."

I could tell my mate wanted to press the issue, but before she could, the doors to the ballroom swung open and Joffrey announced, "Enter."

"Excellent. I call dibs on the first dance," Caspian crooned, snatching Dahlia before I could and ushering her into the ballroom.

A soft snarl of frustration left me at their retreat, but if I was being honest, my Berserker was focused on other things.

"It's all right," Kai said, patting my shoulder as the others followed behind them. "You'll get your turn with her."

"We'll make sure of it," Hades said.

I shook my head, muttering softly, "That's not what I'm worried about."

CHAPTER THIRTY-SIX

HOOK

"Bad form," I growled, eyes locked across the room where the god of the underworld had stolen my dance partner. "Did no one ever educate you on the meaning of the word dibs? Allow me to illuminate you. Dibs. Noun. The right to share or choose something." I stamped my foot in absolute consternation, my ire swelling by the second, along with the ever-present madness. "Vis-à-vis, I chose *her* and that's my dance you stole, you absolute rotting wanker."

"You know, once upon a time, we could've made quite the bargain to ensure he suffered a drawn-out, painful death." The voice came from my left. A tall man with long purple locks and a tumbler of whiskey in his hand stood leaning against the wall next to me.

"Why not now? Go on. Strike him down."

"No. Shan't."

"Well, why the bloody hell bring it up then? Who are you anyway?"

The man laughed, then stopped as suddenly as he'd started when I didn't join in. "Oh, you really don't know. I'm Pan."

I blinked at him. "Is that supposed to mean something to me, mate? I didn't shag you once upon a time, did I?"

Giving an indignant huff, he pushed off the wall and stood to his full height. "You would be so lucky." Then, under his breath, he muttered, "Honestly, I get no respect. Give up your horns and sacrifice it all to save the world, but no one remembers your name."

"Everyone knows my name. I've been immortalized."

"In a children's story. It doesn't count."

"Ah, but you have heard of me. Point made, Captain Hook wins the day." Then, standing at attention as if struck by a bolt of lightning, I gasped. "Wait a bloody second. I'm Hook and you're Pan." Reaching for the cutlass that wasn't there, I unsheathed my weapon. "En garde, you scallywag! Thought you'd catch me with my pants down, did you? Well, not today."

"Are you well?" Pan asked, brow cocked in concern.

"Come on, boy, let's dance." I got into position, ready to jab at him with my invisible sword.

"I'm confused. Are we dancing or fighting? Either way, I'll wipe the floor with you."

Lunging forward, I slapped the side of his face, imagining that I was slicing him with the tip of my blade. "Coward!"

Pan gaped at me, his shock swiftly bleeding into fury. "You dare lay hands on me? Me?"

"Annd I th-think that's a-about enough of th-that," Bentley said, taking Pan by the wrist before he could return my strike with one of his own.

"I could've crushed that ridiculous pirate with one blow if I were still in my demon form. You know that, right? You remember the destruction I wrought?"

"Yeah, s-sure I d-do. Rosie's a-asking for y-you. Go spin h-her around on th-the dancefloor."

He smoothed out his shirt. "Good idea." Pan gave me a final withering look. "Let's never do this again."

"That's right, run away! Ha! Never would be too soon." Then I chuckled, giving Ben a nudge with my shoulder. "The day was won by Captain Hook. You're my witness."

"G-great."

Ben left me there, watching forlornly once again as Hades held my darling close.

The tidal wave of energy that I'd gotten swept up in at the thought of facing off with my nemesis began to ebb as the reality of my situation crept back in.

"You're never leaving this place."

"You're going to die here."

"And so is she."

There was no reprieve, for on the heels of the whispers came the cursed beat of the dreaded clock.

Tick

Tick

Tick

"Stop it," I hissed, plugging a finger in each of my ears to drown out the sound. I knew it was useless, but I couldn't help the reflex any more than I could cease loving my Dahlia.

Out of the corner of my eye, I caught sight of the distinctive flick of a heavy, scaled tail as it slithered along the floor, weaving between feet.

"Crocodile," I whispered.

Tick

Tick

Tick

I blinked a few times, shaking my head to clear my vision. The croc was gone, but the tick, tick, bloody fucking ticking continued.

"Cas?" My name in that most beloved voice didn't register before the gentle touch at my shoulder.

I flinched so hard you'd think I'd just been shot. "Jesus, darling, don't sneak up on me like that. I'm a pirate. I'm liable to stab first, ask questions later."

"I said your name four times. Are you okay?"

Clarity was a bittersweet blessing. Realizing the madness had pulled me under like a riptide, swift and merciless, I could only offer her a chagrined smile. I needed more of her. She was my port in the storm. It took the span of a heartbeat for me to grab her by the hand and tug her bodily against me. Ah, that was better. She wasn't my port. She was my anchor.

"Let's dance, love. And next time, remind them what dibs means, will you?"

Dahlia's giggle wrapped around me like a lover's caress, protecting me and brushing away all lingering insanity. "Aye, aye, Cap'n."

"Don't talk dirty to me in public, love, unless you're prepared for me to act on it."

My fingers trailed over her bare arm, sliding down until I found her wrist, my bracelet plain as day. Her heated gaze caught and held mine as I gave the braided leather a gentle tug. Her sharp intake of breath had me feeling the echoes of that tug all the way to my balls.

"This doesn't match your dress."

"Didn't you hear? Leather goes with everything."

"I'll take that under advisement."

"I have it on good authority it goes even better with my dress on the floor."

"Fuck me, sweet girl. These breeches don't leave anything to the imagination. You can't keep teasing me."

She smirked. "Who said anything about teasing? I wore it for you."

All the blood in my body had officially taken up residence in my cock. Leaning close, I took her earlobe between my teeth and nipped her just hard enough to make her squeak. "I guess I'll have to find out for myself later."

"Promise?"

I opened my mouth to give her a solemn vow, but the music cut off, and Dr. Masterson stepped onto the stage in front of the band.

The doctor tapped on the microphone a few times, sending feedback screeching through the room. We all winced collectively in response, Dahlia stepping out of my hold and covering her ears.

The second her skin left mine, I was assaulted by the never-ending countdown to my demise.

Tick

Tick

Tick

"Bloody fucking hell, will this torture never cease?" I grumbled.

Apparently not, because Masterson decided to grace us with a speech, which was arguably a step above the tick, tick, ticking, but not by much. And we weren't going to talk about the fact that the ticking was still there, faint but audible. My eye was about to start twitching in time with the clock.

"Ladies and gentlemen, thank you for joining us for this year's annual donor benefit gala. We're pleased to have in attendance our new benefactor and his mate. His Grace, the most noble Duke of Canterbury, and his wife, the Duchess of Canterbury." A soft smattering of applause came from the crowd.

"Ugh, not again with these ridiculous titles." Pan's voice filtered to my ears from somewhere to my right.

Masterson shot a withering glare in his direction before clearing her throat and continuing. "Tonight we also have the added benefit of bearing witness to the revival of our wards, the rite being performed by the Belladonna coven's new high leader, Moira Belladonna."

The applause was more golf clap than standing ovation, and it was clearly forced.

Tick

Tick

Tick

"As per tradition, the rite will commence at midnight. Until then please eat, drink, and enjoy yourselves and this most sacred night. Happy Yule!"

She gave a small smile and bobbed a curtsy as the quartet

resumed their playing. I, on the other hand, had lost my partner. A-fucking-gain. That dragon-tattooed motherfucker had swooped in and spun her away from me. Oh, he'd pay for that one. Maybe I could enlist the help of the Viking to restrain him so I could show him exactly why she wears my bracelet and not his.

Speaking of, where the devil was that behorned monster man? A glance around the room showed him ducking out with that little witchy menace on his arm. Ho, ho, ho, what's all this about? A covert mission? A secret dalliance? How very bold. And right beneath the nose of his lady love.

All right, scratch that plan, then. Hades and his shadows could do just as well. And once Dahlia was in my arms, I could tell her all about her Viking's betrayal and catch her tears with my tongue. While I sank my dick so deep inside her, she didn't miss him for very long. Our dance would take place between the sheets, and really, that was the best kind of dance after all.

"You'll never get her back."

"She's not yours to keep."

"She was never meant for you."

Tick

Tick

Tick

The heavy slithering sound of a crocodile's belly dragging on the floor had my heart in my throat. I had to get the fuck out of here. He wouldn't catch me.

Tick

Tick

Tick

Tink's pendulous titties, I wasn't made to be croc food, especially not in front of an audience.

"You must flee."

"If you stay, they will win."

"Go. Now!"

Right. Retreat it was. No dishonor in living to fight another day.

Eyeing the exit, I beelined toward it, weaving my way through the dancing crowd. I took an elbow to the shoulder hard enough to make me stumble.

"Oof. Do you mind? I'm walking here."

I shoved the elfin prince until *he* stumbled and his stupid crown fell off.

"Take that, you festering turd."

"Watch your tone. I am elfin royalty." He picked up his crown and replaced it, sniffing as he looked down his aquiline nose at me.

"I beg your pardon. *Royal* festering turd."

I ducked away before he could reply, making it only a few steps before a hand caught me 'round the elbow.

I turned, fist ready to swing, when I saw it was Hades rather than my disgruntled elf.

"Oh. It's you." I dropped my arm. "I'm in a bit of a hurry."

"Yes, I can see that. Where are you running off to?" Hades asked.

Tick

Tick

Tick

I cast a frantic glance over my shoulder, spotting the slithering tail only a few couples away.

Tick

Tick

Tick

It was coming. I had to leave.

Tick

Tick

Tick

"Anywhere but here, mate."

"You can't leave Dahlia. You're here with her. We all are."

"Tell that to the Viking. He fucked off with that little snack of a witch."

"He what?" Hades asked, sparks shooting out of his fingers.

"Take it up with him. I've got to go." I shook my head, frustrated as hell that this useless god couldn't understand I needed to leave. "It's almost here."

"What are you talking about? Where are you going?"

"Danger. It's coming." Shaking him off, I resumed my hasty retreat.

"What danger? Hook! Get back here, damn you. Hook!"

But I was done wasting time with this blithering idiot. I had to leave. It was a matter of life and death.

Tick

Tick

Tick

Shoving through the doors, I raced for the safety of my room, not looking back once, even as the ticking followed hot on my heels.

CHAPTER THIRTY-SEVEN

HADES

I watched Hook flee like the hounds of hell were nipping at his heels. What danger was he so afraid of? I swept my gaze over the room, finding nothing out of order. My eyes instantly went to Dahlia, like a magnet drawn to its mate. Gods, my heart fucking fluttered as she flashed me a smile while Kai spun her around on the dance floor.

If Asshole was here, he'd tell me to go get my girl. Fuck, I missed him. Not that I'd ever admit it, even upon pain of death. I was taking that one to the grave.

I took a step in that direction, thinking perhaps I'd do just that, but then Hook's expression and his frantic admission had me rooted in place.

He'd looked genuinely terrified. But was the danger he sensed real, or was it a symptom of his madness? It was so hard to tell with him these days. And every passing hour only made it worse. It was obvious to all of us.

But could you live with yourself if he's right and you didn't take it seriously?

The short answer was no. That niggling worm in my stomach

wouldn't let me discount his claim offhand. If it was just in his mind, well, there was no harm in checking it out. And if it wasn't, perhaps I'd be able to stop something before it unfolded. I couldn't risk putting my mate in danger. Not when she finally seemed happy.

Watching my little flower from across the room, I knew keeping her just like this needed to be my priority. She'd changed for the better since we'd all come together. Even the set of her shoulders told me that. There was just something about her, a lightness that gave her an air of contentment. It reminded me of the first morning I woke with my wife in my arms after we finally accepted one another. I wouldn't be the one to take that peace from her.

With that thought in mind, I scanned the ballroom, looking for any obvious signs of discord. With this many people in attendance, strangers and residents alike, it was hard to immediately suss out shady behavior.

Fuck, I missed Asshole. He was the perfect tiny spy.

No one saw him unless he wanted them to.

My attention stalled on the woman with a head of gleaming dark hair curled into a style I knew was what inspired pin-up girls many years ago. She stood with a glass of champagne in her hand, pointy black fingernails promising scores along my back if only I gave her my essence in exchange. That woman was death in disguise. She'd bleed me dry, and I'd thank her for the experience . . . if I was stupid enough to fall for the ruse.

Lilith.

And there, at the end of her glittering gold chain, Crombie. Few knew the story of the reclusive fae prince. How he came to this realm. Why he'd shunned his birthright as heir to the Night Court. I'd done my fair share of digging, but all I'd come up with was that there was a price on his head, and if he were ever to return home, the Wild Hunt would claim him. Hiding under Lilith's skirts was probably one of the best options he had.

If anyone would know about nefarious deeds taking place this evening, it would be those two. Lilith couldn't keep herself out of trouble if she tried. Her finger was in every pie.

She caught my eye, and her crimson lips tilted up in a wicked smile as she began to glide toward me even as I moved in her direction. "Cain, darling. You look absolutely delicious this evening."

"Keep your hands to yourself, succubus. I'm a mated man."

"Are you? Well, well, the writer works fast. Must be those delectable curves. You always were a fan of the voluptuous vixens when you'd visit *Iniquity*." She winked. "That figure suits your goddess much better than her last form."

"You knew?"

Her laugh was the tinkle of a bell without any of the softness. "Oh, poppet. I know everything."

"Do you know what's going on here?"

"You're going to have to be a titch more specific. There are so many devious plots afoot."

"Lilypad, stop tormenting the poor boy."

"Never. I have so few pleasures in my life."

"You and I know that to be a bald-faced lie," Crombie said with a sensual smirk.

"You hope it is, at least."

"The way I had you writhing this morning and the bruises on your hips in the shape of my fingers says exactly that."

"Mmm, it must have slipped my mind. Maybe we should have a repeat performance to help jog my memory."

"I'll take you right here, Mistress. Just say the word."

I could feel the sexual tension rolling off them both. An aroused succubus was a dangerous thing. We'd witnessed that firsthand when sweet little Merri was reading a romance novel in the rec room. Thoughts of Lilith's ward had me scanning the room for her.

"Where's your little puppet?" I asked pointedly.

To my surprise, Lilith stiffened. "Puppet? I have no idea what you mean."

My eyes narrowed. "Hit a nerve, did I? What are you up to, Lilith?

Why is it you would willingly send your ward to a place like this? If you know everything, then surely you know Blackwood's more sordid secrets."

Her eyes shone like shards of glass, and I'd have sworn the temperature dropped several degrees. "Careful, Hades. Don't go digging where you don't belong."

"So you are up to something. And Merri is your pawn, isn't she?"

She trailed her finger up my chest. Sharp nails I could now see weren't solid black, but a dark red with black tips dug into my shirt as she stopped just over my heart. Against my will, my cock twitched awake.

"Lilypad, you promised you wouldn't touch," Crombie groused.

"Don't be jealous, poppet."

"Me? Jealous?" Crombie scoffed, but there was little doubt he was exactly that. "What reason do I have to be jealous? I'm the one wearing your chain."

As if to emphasize the point, he gave it a little tug.

"I think you forgot what this chain symbolizes, darling one," Lilith purred.

"It means I'm yours."

"No, sweetheart. It means I *own* you. Now be a good boy, and don't say one more word." The hand that was poking me in the chest moved so that it was none-too-gently cupping Crombie's crotch.

Holding her gaze, his lips hitched up. "One. More. Word."

Lilith's hand tightened around him, and he let out a strangled gasp that was all sensual approval and no pain.

"Worth it," he rasped.

"Mmm, such a petulant brat." Her gaze flicked to meet mine. "But you know quite a lot about that, don't you, Hades? Gods, I do love to see you in love. It's such a beautiful arrogance you exude."

I rolled my eyes. Lilith and her power plays were never-ending. Not to mention exhausting.

"Seriously, Lilith. Something is going on here."

"Besides the serial killer?"

"Yes. Besides the Ripper. Unless it's all related," I mused, mind wandering as it considered the possibility.

"There are no such things as coincidences, Hades. You and I both know that." She leaned in and whispered, "The Fates wouldn't allow it."

Her mention of the Fates had my blood running cold, but I focused on the first part of her statement. "So it can't be a coincidence that you're here. Trouble follows in your wake, or perhaps you're the one who finds it."

"Why, whatever do you mean?"

"The last time I saw you, you were in the middle of plotting with the angel Gabriel how to stop the apocalypse."

Her soft gasp of shock had me fighting the urge to smile. "There's no way you can know that. Did Gabriel blab to you? He's such a gossip."

I tutted and shook my head. "An angel and a demon, working together. What will they think of next?"

Crombie snorted. "Clearly you have never read Neil Gaiman and Terry Pratchett. Just because you're millennia old doesn't mean you have to stay ignorant of the world around you."

I ignored the fae prince and focused my attention on Lilith. "Gabriel had nothing to do with it. You should be thankful I didn't share any of the details of your clandestine meeting. What business of yours is the apocalypse, anyway?"

She narrowed her eyes. "You and your bloody shadows. You were spying on me."

"Guilty."

As the admission left my lips, an idea sparked in the back of my mind. I didn't need Asshole to do my spying. I could use my shadows.

Lilith held my stare, and Crombie let out a whine of impatience. "Come on, Lilypad. I'm bored. You promised we could play after we made an appearance."

She gave him another brutal squeeze. "Patience, pet. Not until I get what I came for."

"Which is?" I drawled, beyond curious what game she was up to.

"That's for me to know and you to never find out. Hopefully. Now, if you'll excuse me, I do have other matters to attend to this evening. Remember what I said, Hades. There's no such thing as coincidences. You're closer to the apocalypse than you think, but then what else would you expect when you're in bed with death?"

A shiver ran down my spine as she and her pet walked away, his hand resting possessively on her ass. Closer to the apocalypse than I thought? In bed with death?

What in the name of my realm was she talking about? I wasn't afraid of death; I ruled over it. It was my kingdom. I'm Hades, the god of motherfucking death. Of course it's in bed with me. It's my birthright. My blood.

"Fucking succubus."

THE THING about shadows was they were really just a trick of the light. No one noticed a shadow, not until it grabbed hold of you and pulled you under. Mine spread across the ballroom, basically invisible, innocuous, but acting like a microphone transmitting hundreds of conversations in real time. The noise would've been overwhelming, save my ability to sift through it like I was panning for gold. All relevant conversations would float to the top while the rest would drift away on the wind. Or if you needed a more modern equivalent, it was like a radio. All the frequencies transmitted at the same time, but I chose which station to tune into.

For my part, I positioned myself at a table, legs spread, posture relaxed, finger toying with the rim of my rocks glass filled with untouched bourbon. No one would bother me. They never did. I exuded enough fuck off energy to ensure it. My only job was to sit back and let my shadows work the room.

"Why isn't he talking to me? I was good enough to take to his bed last night, and now he's busy with that fucking mermaid?"

Not quite what I was looking for.

"Ugh, this tie is so tight. How much longer do I have to endure this farce?"

Thank you, next.

"Look at her. She's so fucking hot. Why is she with that dragon when she could be with me?"

My eyes narrowed on Logan, that asshole shifter, and my fingers tightened on my glass. While not the sort of conversation I was interested in, I couldn't let his words go unpunished. Giving my shadows a bit more substance, I tripped the stupid fuck, biting back a grin when he fell into a passing server and knocked over the entire tray of drinks.

"She seems to be doing quite well. No one has died thus far, at least."

Ah, this one should be interesting. What did the good doctors have to say?

"Lizzie, you know as well as I that's only because nothing has triggered her yet."

"And it won't."

"You can't be sure."

"Calm down, Nate. There's no need for you to worry. We've taken every precaution. If Dahlia screams tonight, we have people in position to neutralize her before she can do serious damage."

"Ma'am, your presence is required. Something about the ritual needs your attention."

"Guess that dance will have to wait. An administrator's work is never done."

I'd been hoping for something a bit more illuminating after Lilith's parting shot, but it was good to know that my little flower had more than just her men looking out for her. Speaking of . . .

"Are you doing all right, gem?"

"I am, actually. I was pretty anxious before we got down here, and again when I saw all the people, but knowing all of you are here watching

out for me has gone a long way to calm me down. Mostly I'm just worried about Tor. Did you see his face when he thought his twin might be here?"

"He'll be okay."

"I know he will. We'll make sure of it. I just hate the thought of him, or any of you, in pain. I think he's worried his brother won't accept him."

"It wouldn't make sense if he wasn't worried about that. But you accepted him without question. We can only assume it will be the same with his family. And if it's not—"

"We are his family. He will always have a place with us."

Pride and love washed through me at her words. Dahlia's concept of family was so different from what I was used to. Hell, it was different from what she was used to. I had the kinds of relatives that would stab you in the back at the first opportunity. But what she was talking about was something different. Something built on trust and support. What a novel concept. I didn't hate it.

Leaving the two of them be, my shadows continued transmitting as I focused on more of the conversations around me.

"You can't perform this ritual, Moira. You'll condemn us all to a lifetime of purgatory."

"What do you suggest I do, Tor? I have to do it. This is what I was invited here for. I can't just say, 'Peace out guys, those runes aren't the runes I'm looking for.'"

"Can you undo it?"

"Undo what? The wards? No. Well, I mean, yeah, I could if I had enough time and knew exactly what I was working with, but I have less than an hour. This isn't the sort of spell you want to wing. I could blow the whole place up. Create a giant sinkhole. Open a gaping, angry vagina in the middle of the Highlands."

"What?"

Yeah, what?

"Never mind. The point is, this isn't something to fuck around with. That spell is old and powerful. I'll need the full force of my coven to get it handled."

"So what are you going to do? Go through with it?"

"At least you'll be safe here?"

"For eternity."

"But you have your mate, that's something, right?"

"I'm disappointed in you, Belladonna. Where's the fiery little witch I met when I first came to Ravenscroft? That woman would never allow this to happen. She'd move heaven and hell for the people she considers part of her family."

"I'm gonna need you to trust me."

Enough of that. The Belladonna witch didn't owe us anything. If we wanted out of here, we'd find a way. I'd take them all to the underworld if need be. Well, I would if it was possible.

"Puffed-up stuffed shirts think they're better than me. Can hardly wipe their own arses without my help."

Nope.

"If everything goes to plan, my next guest will be arriving soon."

Interesting, but not helpful.

"S-something feels off about this p-place, sugar."

"I know. I feel it too."

That's more like it.

"W-we should get out of h-here. I d-don't care h-how important Gavin is."

"I wish we could. Is it just me, or do you feel like she's *going to pop out of some dark corner and try to end it all over again?"*

"N-no, sugar. It's n-not you. But w-we kicked h-her ass. Sh-she can't be b-back."

"Are you sure about that?"

"As s-sure as Gabriel is."

"We should try and contact him. He said it wasn't over. What if he knows more now?"

"N-not a b-bad idea."

Gabriel. Not the angel? Surely not. But Lilith mentioned him as well.

"What are you up to, Messenger of God?"

Part of me expected him to pop up in a flurry of wings and

leather, but he remained suspiciously absent. Suspicious only because he was clearly connected to what was happening here. Especially with Lilith's warning about coincidences.

"Blimey, Oz, for someone dancing with the man of his dreams, you look frightfully miserable."

"I'm sorry, Bru. It's not you. It's just so . . . loud tonight."

"Loud?"

"The thoughts. Even with my walls up, they're pressing against me. There's this undercurrent of ominous anticipation. Something big is coming."

"Want to get out of here? We can go to my room. It's quiet there."

"God, yes, please."

"Come on. I have to earn that man of your dreams title."

That made yet another pair sensing the promise of something dark hovering on the horizon. But what kind of storm was coming? And when would it hit? I despised not knowing the answers.

"Hey Thorne, you think Caleb has an extra large stick up his ass or something? His face is more constipated than usual."

"Jesus, Kingston. Do you ever give it a rest? Just one night to be grown-ups. That's all we want."

"I'm a grown-up. I'm a dad. That's the most grown-up of grown-ups."

"If you have to call yourself a grown-up grown-up, you are not, in fact, grown up."

"He doesn't ever look constipated. Caleb is broody, yes, I'm actually sure that's part of his DNA, but you're right, Kingston. Something is wrong."

"See, my Sunshine understands me."

"Sunday might be the only one of us who consistently can."

"Thorne, you're such a liar. You know you love me. Wankmates, remember?"

"It was one time, Kingston. One time."

"You say once, I say at least thrice."

"Does it count when you do it when I'm in the room? Because if so, it's way more than thrice. The two of you are always wanking off on me."

"If we weren't in the middle of a room full of strangers, Dove, I'd show you exactly how much it counts."

"Ha! See! More than thrice. Wankmates for life!"

"I hate you."

"Love you too, buddy. But seriously, look at the priest over there. He's all storm clouds and doom and gloom. He's been weird since the moment we met up with his royal dukeness."

"You're right. It happened right after we realized there were three groups of us. Thorne, Kingston, you don't think Dahlia is . . ."

"Are you serious? Another one? How many times is this going to happen? I just want to raise my wolf pups in peace."

Think Dahlia is what? Spit it out, dammit. That fucking wolf shifter Kingston wouldn't let her finish her observation. I needed to know.

"If it is, do you really think we should be talking about this in the open where anyone can hear us, Kingston?"

"Good point. Maybe we dance with our girl and revisit this once Caleb is done talking with the count."

Well, it looked like I knew exactly who to focus on next.

"Something's not right here, Gavin. Can't you smell it?"

"I sensed it the moment I walked through the door. This place has been touched by death."

"We already knew that. The Ripper has been in the news for weeks."

"No. Not literal death."

"You feel her?*"*

"I do. Lingering in the shadows."

I couldn't help but wonder if he was talking about me. But no, he said *her*.

"Caleb, do you think it's happening again? Is she taking her turn?"

"Gabriel warned us it wasn't over. There are four of them. I've seen them with my own eyes. Just because we've had our turns and played our parts doesn't mean that there aren't other pawns being put into place."

"Do you think they'll succeed? Are they even prepared?"

"You can't prepare for something like this. We didn't."

"You're right. We just had to face the trials as they came and hope it was enough."

"Hope. What an interesting choice of words, Mr. Donoghue. Not something I'd have expected from you."

"My Duchess gave me a lot of things. Hope is one of them."

"Aye. Sunday and Eden did that for me as well."

"So what are we supposed to do? We can't just sit back and do nothing, but we don't even know who the players are."

"I don't think there's anything we can do, save watch and wait. But if it comes down to the apocalypse, I'll fight with everything I have to save my family."

"From the stories Rosie has shared, you already have."

"Aye, and I'll do it again if need be."

Well, shit. This was the second time tonight the word apocalypse has been bandied about. I guess Lilith was right. There are no coincidences.

Wait.

Apocalypse.

Four of them.

Her.

The Horsewomen were up to something again. Fuck.

That didn't bode well. Especially if Blackwood was at the heart of it.

As I pulled my shadows back into myself, I caught one final but intensely distressing conversation. Just a whisper from Oz and Bru, who'd gotten held up by the exit, but it was still loud enough for me to catch it.

"I heard his mind. He's here."

"What did you hear?"

"He's going to use the ritual as a distraction. He's going to strike. Tonight."

CHAPTER THIRTY-EIGHT

DAHLIA

Staring into the mirror, I did my best to tame my hair and get all the flyaways to behave. It was a lost cause. I was sweaty from dancing, but my hair looked like a cross between Magenta from Rocky Horror and the Bride of Frankenstein. It was sticking up all over. As I ran my palm over it a final time, the white-blonde strands tried to follow my hand, lifting as if pulled by invisible strings. It reminded me of that time my cult-school teacher taught me about static electricity by using a balloon and rubbing it on my head.

"This is wild," I muttered.

The long waves were as smooth as they were going to get. Honestly, after all that dancing, I looked more like a mermaid than a screen starlet. That was fine by me. Cas liked mermaids, right? All I needed were a couple of willing jumbo starfish, and we could have ourselves a roleplay.

Giving myself a last cursory once-over, I had to admit, crazy hair aside, I was pleased with what I saw. My eyes were bright, my cheeks flushed, and there was no hiding my smile. I was happy. Go figure. I was stuck at an asylum during a black-tie event, surrounded by at least a hundred people I didn't know. It had all the makings of a disaster. My very own trigger buffet. And yet . . . I didn't feel any of the usual anxiety weighing down on me.

Was this personal growth? Was I getting better? Had Blackwood and all those sessions with Masterson actually been good for me? Or did it have more to do with the four hot guys railing me nightly—okay, and daily?

Guess the why didn't matter, given the results.

Hands resting on the counter, I stared at myself in the mirror, really allowing time to take in the woman reflected in the glass. She looked back at me, big gray eyes set in a kind face, and for the first time, I saw her for who she had become. This was the adult I needed when I was a child. The person I would've felt the safest with. Trustworthy. Loyal. Loving. Gentle. I grew into her, and it made sense.

Eyes prickling with tears, my reflection beamed at me. "Way to go. I'm really proud of you. Doing the things. Not chickening out. Hanging out with real live people and some dead ones too. Falling in love with four hot men. Hell, letting them even get close enough for that to happen. You are a badass bitch. You're on your way to becoming a productive member of society or something."

Technically I was already productive, but I don't think anyone could argue that I was a member of society with a straight face. I avoided that bitch like she wanted money. Or at least I had, before the choice had been taken away from me. And damn if I wasn't thriving. Guess they—they being the doctors and Kiki—showed me.

Pulling a tube of lipstick from my cleavage, I leaned close to the mirror as I reapplied, but ice bloomed in my chest as a familiar and unwelcome buzzing began in my head.

"No. Nope. Not today," I muttered, closing my eyes and taking a deep breath.

I did not have evil bitch ghost on my bingo card for this evening.

Opening my eyes, I focused on my reflection as the mirror filled with frost, the icy coating fanning out from the corners like the fronds of a fern.

"Leave me alone. I'm too busy for your brand of bullshit."

The harder I tried to keep my eyes on myself in the mirror, the harder it was. My attention was drawn to the black writhing mass manifesting just over my right shoulder.

"Shit. Shit. Shit."

The bitch was back. And here I was without Hades or Asshole to help send her packing.

"Guess I'm just going to have to do it myself."

Later, I would reflect on this moment as another tick in the 'personal growth' column. I wasn't screaming, crying, or running. I was taking control. But in the moment, all I cared about was establishing dominance. She was not the boss of me. Kiki was. And also Hades. And sometimes me.

Spinning around, I faced the spirit that haunted my nightmares. My heart beat so hard I worried it would break through my chest, but I held fast to my strength. I'd had her in my grasp once before. I could do it again, but dammit, I didn't know what to do with her after that.

She looked more human tonight, her eyes strangely familiar, hair still a bedraggled mess in front of her face, mouth open on a soundless scream. Until the most bone-chilling rasp escaped her.

"Dahlia."

Jesus in the manger with the donkey, isn't that what Kiki always said?

Goosebumps scattered down my neck and arms. It took everything in me not to bolt. I kept an arm raised in front of me, like it would somehow fend her off. "Listen, Linda. I don't know why you are up my ass, but maybe let's not tonight, okay? It's kind of a big night and in case you haven't noticed, I'm in formal wear."

"Dahlia."

Ooookay, so we weren't going to listen. Cool. "What do you want from me? I'm not too inclined to help you when you keep leaving bruises on me and fucking terrorizing me."

Her skeletal hand reached out for me slowly, like it was moving through freezing water, but just before she touched my skin, the loud roar of applause caused me to flick my gaze toward the door on instinct.

The ritual. It must have started.

The ghost must not have liked that she'd lost my attention—let's just add narcissist to the list of red flags this bitch was carrying, shall we?—because an ear-splitting scream filled the room. On reflex, I covered my ears, but not before I heard glass shattering behind me. Projectile pieces of the mirror fell to the floor, a few shards slicing my bare arms.

"Ouch," I hissed. The little nicks in my skin stung like a motherfucker. "What the hell was that for?" I snapped, but the ghost was gone.

Heart still racing, I straightened, looking around and up in each corner like she might still be lurking in the little powder room. Thankfully, she was not perched on the ceiling like a gigantic spider queen. Small mercies, I guess.

"So . . . that happened."

I was going to have to go up to my room to take care of the bleeding. The last thing I needed was the attention of the vampires in attendance tonight.

Huffing a breath, I flicked open the lock and opened the door. The swarm of voices filled my ears as I stepped into the warm light of the empty hallway. Just as the doors closed behind me, the lights went out, leaving me in a sea of inky darkness.

"Oh, come on."

Not sure if the power outage was due to the ghost's return or something more innocuous like a winter storm, I took a second to get my bearings.

Big. Fucking. Mistake.

A rough, warm palm encircled my throat as a powerful arm wrapped tightly around my waist. Fear laced my blood first, followed by excitement and arousal.

Cas.

He'd noticed I was wearing the bracelet for him tonight. He'd come for me. Waited until I was alone to strike. He did love his elaborate plots. Cutting the lights was absolutely something he'd do, seeing as how he'd drugged me last time.

Excitement coursed through me for one potent second, weakening my knees and making my heart race. But then a little voice in the back of my head chimed up. Something was off. It took me another heartbeat to register what it was.

The scent of the sea was missing.

This wasn't Cas.

I opened my mouth to scream, but a cloth gag filled it instead.

"I've got you now," a deep, distorted voice growled in my ear.

CHAPTER THIRTY-NINE

DAHLIA

A dull throb between my eyes woke me from a dreamless sleep. I couldn't remember going to bed, or much of anything after my ghost encounter in the powder room. Shit. Had she affected me so strongly I lost consciousness?

I blinked groggy eyes, the swimming shapes around me not making any sense. This wasn't my room.

God, my head hurt.

Instinctively, I went to check my head, but I couldn't move my arm. It was stuck.

No, not stuck. Bound.

I gave a jerk, my whole body moving in an attempt to break free. That's when I realized it wasn't just my arms that were bound. My legs were too.

Panic clawed up my throat as I tried again and failed, the cold air making me shiver.

The crunch of footsteps to my left had me turning my head in search of the source. I caught sight of a dark, shadowy figure. The bright flare of a match being struck illuminated him, but not enough for me to place the man.

He moved in a slow circle, and with each candle he lit, my surroundings came into sharper relief. The candles had been placed on headstones. I was in a graveyard—technically a kirkyard, since this was Scotland. Jesus.

The little flames guttered in the wind, but they didn't go out. It was almost as if they were eager to bear witness to whatever the fuck this was.

Your murder, dummy. This is where the Ripper took you to murderate you.

When he'd lit the final candle, he stood with his back to me, but still I strained to search for some identifier on him. Slim build, tall but not excessively so, hair cut neatly. Nothing exceptional about him.

I cried out around the gag still in my mouth, angry, frustrated, and scared.

The man turned around, the glint of a blade in his hand making me struggle harder as he came closer. Once his face was fully bathed in the warm light of the candles, though, I lost all focus on the weapon. I knew this face. I knew him.

He smiled down at me and removed the gag.

"Doctor Temperance. Oh my God, it's you. Cut me loose. We have to get out of here."

Rational thought hit me like a sledgehammer as soon as the words left my lips.

He wasn't here to save me. He'd have come straight over, not wasted time setting the mood with some candles.

"It's a miracle you've survived this long, stupid girl."

I blinked, worried that I'd hit my head harder than I thought, because I didn't recognize that voice. Not only did it lack a British accent, but it was rougher around the edges, lacking all of Dr. Temperance's polish. But also, it wasn't the voice I'd heard when I'd been taken. Were there two of them?

"W-wait. I . . . but you . . . you're British."

He laughed. "I have to admit, the accent was harder than I'd expected." Then he leaned in and whispered in his British accent, "Have you never seen a scary movie, love?"

A chill ran down my spine.

"You're the Ripper?"

He pulled out a small device from his pocket and raised it to his lips. "In the flesh," he said with a grin that was fully psychotic. I knew that voice. It had been the last thing I heard before he took me. "And you will be my final victim. My crowning glory. Sacrificed on an altar made of all my previous victims."

Bile charged up my throat as I heaved. I couldn't even process the words. The thought that I was bound on an altar of the dead, that *pieces* of people I knew were touching me, it was too much.

Still looming over me, he reached out, brushing my hair off my forehead and making me jerk away from the repulsive feel of his skin on mine.

"Now you have a scar to match the one you gave me," he said, showing me the faint pink scar that disappeared into his hairline.

"What the hell are you talking about? I never gave you a scar."

He laughed, a cold, menacing chuckle that had me ready to piss myself.

"Oh, Dahlia. You pathetic sheltered child. Time in the real world didn't do anything for you, did it?" He ran a hand down my body, calling attention to the rough-hewn fabric of the shift he must've changed me into. "This would've been so much more beautiful if you hadn't ruined everything the first time."

"What do you mean?"

"With your scream, of course. In fact . . ." He replaced the gag, and his glittering gaze locked on mine.

That was the moment I knew.

His name wasn't Nate. He probably wasn't even a real doctor.

This was Samuel, or Brother Sam, as he'd been back when I'd known him.

The boy my father had promised me to. The one who was

supposed to help him sacrifice me. But I killed him, didn't I? So how was he alive?

"I can see the questions swirling around in your mind. You always had the most expressive eyes. It's all coming to you now, isn't it? Who I am? Our destiny? The part you are about to play?" He let out a maniacal laugh.

I let out a garbled string of words behind my gag.

That only made him laugh harder.

"Sorry, sweetheart. You can't be trusted. But don't worry, you don't need to say a thing. I already know what you're thinking. Don't believe me? Here, I'll demonstrate. I'll play all the parts. As you know by now, I'm quite the convincing actor. First you say, *'But you're supposed to be dead!'* To which I respond, *'Sorry to burst your bubble. Our goddess had other plans for me. Plans you're going to help me realize'*."

He leaned close, grinning down at me. "You did me a kindness when you gave me this scar. Your kick not only saved my life, it marked me with your favor. And as Death's chosen sacrifice, that meant I must be the one to carry on your father's great work. Just think, if you hadn't lashed out, I'd be dead right now."

I struggled in my bonds, hating his words even as they burrowed their way beneath my skin.

"Ah yes, I can see how much you hate me, but the two of us are more alike than you realize. In fact, you're a bigger monster than I am. Don't believe me? Well, just think of it this way. If I'd died that night so long ago, how many people would still be alive today?" He laughed, adopting his playful mimicry of our imaginary conversation once more. "*'But you killed all those people,'* you'd say. To which I'd point out that while I may have been holding the knife, their blood is on your hands because you're the one who left me alive to kill them. And if you'd simply died like you were supposed to, none of these other deaths would have happened. So really, you're the Ripper, and I'm just your weapon."

As if orchestrated by death itself, the clouds parted and the moonlight spilled down onto the altar. Brother Sam looked up, a beatific, psychotic smile splitting his face.

"Ah, showtime. Let's finish what your father started, shall we?"

I wriggled hard enough that the gag slipped free, and I spat, "What do you think you're going to accomplish with this stupid ritual? My father was a crazy cult leader. He had no power."

Face twisting into a sneer, he picked up the gag and forcibly shoved it back into my mouth. "Nah-ah-ah, not a peep from you, please. Women are supposed to be seen and not heard, remember? Not that I suppose it matters, since you won't be alive much longer. Pity you won't be around to witness my accession to greatness. You have grown into quite the beauty. You would have made a lovely bride. I would have preferred your virgin blood, as was originally planned, but alas, that ship has already sailed, and I am nothing if not adaptive. How else would I have gone so long without detection?"

In stereotypical serial killer fashion—stereotypes have to come from somewhere—he continued with his monologue. This guy had clearly been waiting a long time for this, and he wanted me to appreciate every single detail of his genius plan.

Icy acceptance coiled in my gut. With every new word he spewed, my fate was becoming more clear. I wasn't getting out of this. No one was coming to save me. I couldn't use my scream. I was going to die here.

At least if I died tonight, I knew I would see Hades in his realm. He'd make sure the others knew I loved them. And Asshole would keep me company. That was a nice silver lining. Surely ghosts could still pet Cerberus.

Kiki's voice hit me in the conscience, hard and judgmental as fuck. *What the hell is this? We don't just roll over and let Ted Bundy kill us. Would you write a heroine that just lay there and died? Fuck no, I'd send that shit straight to the recycle bin. You are better than this. Fight, damn you.*

I wanted to argue, but she was right. I still had one card up my sleeve. Better yet, I was in a fucking graveyard. Where there was a graveyard, there were ghosts.

"This might hurt, but this ritual requires copious amounts of your blood."

That was enough to pull my focus back to him. The dagger glinted silver in the moonlight as he dug the tip of the blade into my arm, starting at my shoulder and dragging it all the way down to my wrist.

Burning pain radiated through me with every tortuous inch. I wanted to jerk my arm away, but that would only do more damage.

"Nearly there. You're doing remarkably well. Your father must have prepared you for your fate better than I thought." Moving around to my other side, he placed the blade at the top of my other arm. "One down, one to go. If you're lucky, you'll pass out from the pain before we get to your legs."

Inside my head, I was screaming, the sound bouncing around inside my skull as I trembled from fear and pain. I had to stop this, somehow. He couldn't win, not after everything I've been through.

While he may have been familiar with the supernatural world, he was still just a human man. Maybe I could scare him away with the only power I had that didn't require my voice.

I'd only tried to summon a spirit once, so I had absolutely no way of knowing that this would work, but I had to try. It was my only chance.

Squeezing my eyes shut, I pictured my vengeful spirit. She was the strongest ghost I'd encountered and clearly connected to me. Maybe this was why.

"Please. Come to my aid. If you help me now, I promise I will help you. Please. Please, come."

It wasn't my best work, but it was honest and I was desperate, and that was all I had to go off of. I didn't know exactly what it was I said or did that summoned Nautica's spirit, but it had to be tied to my need. And there'd never been a moment in my life when I'd been more in need than this one. That had to count for something.

Agony ripped down my arm as he dragged the dagger with deliberate slowness, my limbs already feeling heavy and cold from blood loss. My heart sank as the familiar buzz of a spirit's presence never arrived, but I kept trying. Kept calling out.

"Raise them, Dahlia. Raise your army." The sweet voice whispered across my skin, in my ear, causing my eyes to pop open.

Turning my head slowly, I came face to face with the lovely blonde I'd seen so long ago during this very same ritual. She hadn't aged a day. And once again, here she was, trying to save me.

Was she my guardian angel?

My eyes shifted to where Sam was gleefully running his fingers through the blood pooling beneath me. He hadn't noticed her, which meant he probably couldn't see her since she was less than a yard away from him. She had to be some kind of ghost.

"Raise your army, Dahlia. Now, before it's too late."

My army? Oh shit, my *army*. I didn't need ghosts to stop him. I had bodies at my disposal. I could raise the undead. I'd proven it by making Nautica into a zombie. With every ounce of strength and power remaining, I called to them, no longer begging, but commanding.

The ground began to shake as I sent my intention into the earth.

"Yes! She's coming. She hears me! Hel, I am your faithful servant." Sam cried, head thrown back, dagger raised and dripping with my blood.

No the fuck she doesn't, asshole.

"Don't stop. You're nearly there," the woman whispered in my ear, spurring me on.

"Rise."

As one, skeletal hands shot through the graves circling Sam's altar. The hands were followed by heads and shoulders as mostly rotted corpses clawed their way out of their final resting places. Ten reanimated bodies stood waiting for my orders. The psycho holding me captive didn't notice a thing. Yet.

"Stop him."

The sound of snapping bones filled the air as my zombies turned their attention to my would-be murderer.

It didn't take long for him to see we had company. His eyes widened, and as the nearest zombie reached for him, Sam screamed and narrowly escaped the snapping jaws.

"What is this? Leave me. I command you. I am Death's consort!" But they didn't. Instead the small horde shambled toward him, one zombie's teeth finding purchase on his neck, tearing flesh and making him scream.

He ran into the night, leaving me still bound, but alive.

CHAPTER FORTY

KAI

The Belladonna witch moved through her ritual with practiced ease, selecting items from her altar and lifting them for the goddess's blessing while murmuring the incantation softly beneath her breath. There was a grace to it akin to a ballet dancer's a pas seul. Most everyone around me watched her with rapt attention, but I couldn't. Even knowing she was personally sealing our fate and perpetuating our captivity, my focus was elsewhere.

Dahlia should be back by now.

"Where are you, gem?" I muttered, stalking through the crowd as my gaze raked the faces in search of her.

She'd told me she wanted to chat to Sunday, presumably to discuss the finer points of wrangling a group of dominant males just like hers, but I couldn't find her in the room, and that bothered me.

"Find her."

My dragon's order was sent with unrestrained annoyance. He couldn't understand that I was respecting Dahlia's space. She'd made it clear that she didn't love having the four of us breathing down her neck every second of the day. I strongly doubted she'd react favorably to me barging in on her girl talk.

Gaze sweeping over the crowd once more, I stopped when I came upon Sunday standing near a cocktail table surrounded by Caleb, Noah, and Kingston. My heart lurched when I didn't find Dahlia amongst them. Something wasn't right. My dragon agreed, his anxiety spiking and sending the magical ink that decorated my body slithering around until his eyes peeked out over the collar of my shirt.

"Now look what ye did."

Relax. The rest of her men are near. I'm sure she's fine.

But I wasn't. Sure, that is. Too many terrible things had happened of late, and anxiety was a bitter pool in my gut.

I hadn't taken more than two steps toward Sunday and her group before the room went black, all the lights cutting in unison. Fuck. It reminded me of the last time we were all gathered in the rec room, when Dahlia's ghost had attacked.

A few cries of shock filled the air, followed by a wave of hushed murmurs. In a matter of seconds, witches and mages were sending balls of witch light and fire into the air to re-illuminate the space.

"That wasn't part of the ritual, was it?" a bookish witch whose name I couldn't remember asked, holding up a wand with a ball of light on the end. Despite her youthful appearance, I recalled that she'd been sent to Blackwood for stealing an elixir that gave her eternal youth. When she'd gotten caught, she drank it and was sent here to live out the rest of her immortal days.

"I don't think so," I said, snagging her wand and striding through the crowd with my newly acquired torch.

"Hey! That's mine, Kai!"

"You'll live."

As soon as I reached Sunday, all three of her men put themselves in front of her, clearly sensing my agitation.

"Where is she?" I snarled.

"I'm gonna need you to take several seats, dragon," Kingston said, his voice more wolf than man as he defended his mate.

"I need to talk to Sunday."

"Not with those eyes, dragon boy. You're at about a twelve, and you're going to need to drop to something below seven before we let you anywhere near our mate."

"He needs to be at a zero," Caleb muttered.

"Agreed," Noah said.

Sunday, to her credit, wasn't going to be contained by her protective mates. "You guys, I'm fine. Kai won't hurt me."

"How do you know that, a stor? He burned down a whole village without a second thought." Caleb glanced at her over his shoulder. "I won't put you at risk."

"Then you shouldnae have brought her here, vampire. Blackwood isn't exactly known for its occupants' good behavior."

"Why do you think the three of us accompanied her?" Noah countered.

"I dinnae have time for this. I'm looking for Dahlia. She said she was going to come talk with you. Have ye seen her?"

Sunday's eyes went wide and she shook her head. "Not since we got here."

"I saw her," Kingston offered. "She made a beeline for those doors." He pointed to the side exit.

Where in the name of the goddess had she been going? The hallway beyond led to a powder room, the kitchens, and . . . oh, bloody hell, she wouldn't have gone out into the gardens alone, would she? Perhaps Cas had found her and swept her off her feet? Or Tor?

"Where is Dahlia?" Hades asked from behind me, his voice catching me off guard and causing my dragon to flare with defensive instinct.

Turning to face him, I snarled on reflex. "That's what I'm trying to figure out."

"You mean you lost her? She was with you. We can't let her wander off, not with the Ripper."

"You think I don't know that?"

"He's here. On the grounds. Oz overheard him plotting."

"What?"

"That little power outage? It wasn't a coincidence. There are no coincidences. Oz heard his thoughts when he was planning to strike."

Caleb cleared his throat. "How exactly do you know this?"

"It's easy to learn things if you simply listen, Father."

Kingston piped up, an eager puppy looking for attention. "We call him Daddy G now."

"No, we don't," Caleb snapped.

"Do too."

"So help me, Kingston, do not start that shit right now," Noah groaned.

"I'm just sayin' . . ."

"We'll help you find her. Where could she have gone?" Sunday offered, stepping around a stormy-faced Caleb.

"Out for a midnight stroll in the garden?" Hades asked. "It's not implausible. She might've gotten overwhelmed with all the people and energy in this ballroom. Or Hook might have stolen her away. He's been known to do that."

I found it interesting he only listed Hook and not Tor.

"Tor was with Moira until she began the ritual," Hades added, as if answering my unspoken question.

"Why would Dahlia wander off alone?" Sunday asked.

"She wouldn't," I said, feeling the certainty of it in my gut. "Not now with all that's happened. She always tells us where she's planning to be, and usually it's her room. When she wanders the grounds, one of us is almost always with her. Especially recently."

Hades's eyes caught and held mine. He nodded his agreement. We'd both considered the possibility but had to dismiss it. She might be impulsive, but she just wasn't that irresponsible.

As I stared intently at the doors, a large form moved into my peripheral vision. Tor strode through the sea of people, at least a head taller than most of them and impossible to miss. What was equally impossible not to notice was the absence of Dahlia at his side. My heart sank.

He spotted us and barreled his way through the crowd. "Where is she? Why isn't she with you?"

At least we were all predictable.

"We thought she might be with you," I admitted. "She told me she was going to speak with Sunday."

"And I saw her leave," Kingston said, gesturing to the doors again. "She went that-a-way."

"Then what the fuck are we still doing standing here?" he growled, the beast pushing to the forefront.

"We were trying to get to the bottom of it without ripping innocent bystanders to pieces," I snapped.

"I like my way better," Tor said, pushing past me and heading toward the exit Kingston had indicated.

I followed, Hades hot on my heels. From behind me, I heard a small scuffle and realized it was Sunday, insisting on coming with us.

"A stor, no. Stay here with Thorne and Kingston. They'll keep you safe."

"When has telling me to stay put ever worked for you?"

Caleb sighed. "If you won't do it for me, do it for Eden."

"You don't play fair."

"No, love. But I learned with you one sometimes has to cheat to get the upper hand."

"Isn't cheating a sin?"

"I'll beg for forgiveness later."

She must've agreed, because when we reached the hallway, only Caleb followed.

"Which way would she go?" Tor asked, glancing first right, then left.

"I'll check the garden. You go the other way. We can meet back here." Hades began striding toward the glass door that led outside but stopped short when Caleb's grave voice rang out, "There's blood here."

Something within me went cold and scarily still. It took a second for me to register what I was feeling.

Fear.

Blood-chilling fear.

"Where?" I demanded, although when I spoke, my voice was that of my dragon.

Beside me, Tor vibrated with fury. He was barely holding on to his control. I didn't blame him; I was faring little better.

Caleb's head was slow to turn, but then he blurred and was standing a little ways down the corridor, right outside the powder room.

"Here," he said, pointing to the ground. Then his nostrils flared and his head snapped toward the open door. "There's more inside."

"No," I whispered, rushing to his side and crouching to the floor. Sure enough, there was a drop of crimson liquid on the hardwood. I ran my finger through it and brought the blood to my nose, praying it didn't smell like her.

My prayers weren't answered.

Tor burst through the bathroom door and let out a bellow of rage at whatever it was he found inside.

Hades followed him, his voice hard when he announced, "A ghost was here. I'd bet everything it was the one that's been fucking with her. If she hurt my goddess, she'd better prepare for eternity wrapped in a prison of my fire."

"Would a ghost be able to kidnap her?" Caleb asked. "I've heard of many powerful spirits being able to manifest, but not for long enough to steal a person away."

"It's the Ripper. It has to be him." Tor gripped the sink basin with both hands so tightly the porcelain cracked as he hung his head and breathed deeply. "The ghost being here is a coincidence."

"There's no such thing as coincidences," Hades intoned.

"What's all this?" Hook's voice came from down the hall. He looked worse for wear, his hair sticking out every which way as though he'd been tugging on it, and his clothes rumpled. For one fleeting second, hope set my veins on fire, but when my mate's form didn't appear beside him, I knew it was a fool's hope.

"Dahlia's missing," I answered.

His expression morphed so quickly I felt like I'd imagined his cocksure grin. "What?"

"You heard me. Unless you took her and are hiding her somewhere. But if you did, prepare yourself to be in a world of hurt because you spilled her blood."

"No, mate. You've got it wrong. I never touched her. I'd own up to it if I were able to kidnap her right under your noses again. That's not easy to do." Hook's eye twitched, and he glanced to the side, muttering to himself rapidly. "Whispers. Whispers. Tick. Tick. Tick."

"Has he gone mad, then?" Caleb asked.

"Almost certainly," Hades confirmed.

Tor's roar was so loud my ears rang. "What are we waiting for? Find her!"

"How do you suggest we do that? A few drops of blood and virtually no trail." Hades raked a hand through his hair. "There's not even a trail of spirit residue to help track her."

Caleb stood and walked seemingly aimlessly down the corridor. The way he went didn't lead anywhere, save a window overlooking the grounds. But instead of inspecting the window, he turned and crouched beside the wall.

"There's another drop of blood here."

Before any of us could speak, Hook crowed. "The passageway. Of course!"

"What passageway?" I asked.

"This one." Hook bounded to where Caleb was now standing. "Move aside, padre. Allow me." Then he shoved the wall hard, a crack opening up at the pressure before a doorway opened to him.

"There's more blood here."

Hook moved past Caleb and into the secret corridor, all the while murmuring, "Tick. Tick. Tick. Tickety-tock. Don't get eaten by the croc."

We followed, rushing forward until all at once we crashed into each other because the pirate had come to a dead stop.

"What the fuck?" Hades shouted.

"Sabotage. Mutiny! Someone will walk the plank for this."

If I couldn't see it with my own eyes, I'd think Hook was hallucinating. But he was right. A pile of rubble blocked the path from floor to ceiling. Tor and I could clear it, but that would take time we likely didn't have.

Reaching out, I grabbed Hook by the ruffles of his fancy shirt and tugged him until we were nose to nose. "Pull it together, pirate. She's counting on us. Now, where does this passage lead?"

"A tomb."

A shiver of foreboding danced down my spine.

"Which. Tomb," Tor growled, his words bitten off and filled with fury.

The light of Hades's fire filled the darkened passageway. "It doesn't fucking matter which tomb. The only place it could be is the kirkyard. Come on, fellas, let's go get our girl."

THE PRIEST STAYED BEHIND, claiming he needed to return to his wife, while the rest of us took the long way to the kirkyard. We were unusually quiet as we raced across the grounds, our fear of what awaited us stealing our words and fueling our feet. Even Hook remained silent as every step took us closer to finding her.

"I can feel her. She's terrified." Tor's words hung over us all, ramping up the urgency to get to our destination.

"Why dinnae ye mention that before?"

He looked at me, his eyes a sea of endless black. "Because up until now, I couldn't feel anything at all."

Shit. That couldn't be a good sign.

My dragon was right there, on the surface, begging for control. *"If ye let me, I can get us there faster. Free me so we can save her."*

"Nae, I cannae," I whispered.

"You can't do what?" Hades asked.

Shaking my head, I said, "We're nearly there. I can see the mausoleum on the hill."

"You can. You must. Free me. Let me stretch my wings. We will find her far faster if I'm in control."

"Why isn't she using her scream?" Hook asked through heavy breaths as we ran.

"Maybe she can't." The despair in Hades's voice cut right through me.

My dragon continued his campaign for freedom, his urgency a burning in my veins. *"We do not know what awaits us when we get there. You were born to protect her. To slay her enemies and neutralize all threats. This is your purpose, Malakai. Our purpose. Let us save her. Let us finally be what we were destined to be."*

"She's there!" Tor shouted, his form trembling as he grew fully into his beast and picked up speed. "Dahlia!"

"Is that blood?" Hook's horrified question tested my thin control.

"Yes, and he will burn for this," Hades said.

Their words registered, gasoline on an already raging flame.

"Yes," I agreed, my dragon's voice slipping out of my mouth. "He will."

Only Hook seemed to catch the emphasis in my response. Tor and Hades rushed forward, sprinting toward our brutalized mate.

As I surveyed the scene, scales erupted over my skin. Dahlia was bound and bleeding, her waxy pallor dangerously close to that of a corpse. But she was moving, slowly, her eyes tracking us, relief painted across her face.

Hook removed her gag, and the first thing she said was, "He got away. He ran. We'll never catch him."

"Now," my dragon ordered.

Now, I agreed, not needing any further convincing. My mate was dying, bleeding out right before my eyes. It was time for a reckoning.

Time ceased to have meaning as everything simultaneously slowed and seemed to happen in an instant. A flood of power I'd only felt once before tore through me, ripping me apart and remaking me. My consciousness stretched until it felt like I existed outside my body. My vantage point changed drastically as I grew. Trees no longer towered over me, people now so small they seemed like nothing more than playthings. I morphed into the form handed down to me by my father, by my destiny and duty to the Shadow Court. I was no longer Kai Nash. I was Malakai, dragon protector of my realm and, more importantly, my mate.

As I settled into my new body, I shook out my wings, arched my neck, and let out a roar that put Tor's beast to shame. The earth quaked, and birds took to the sky, fleeing the vow of vengeance I'd just unleashed. Everything felt right for the first time in my existence. My dragon and I were one, my mate and I hadn't been parted, and I'd accepted myself with no hesitation.

Glancing down at Dahlia as Tor held her in his arms, I pleaded silently with her to give me what I needed. I would not let the Ripper go free.

She swallowed hard, her eyes trained on me before she pointed a shaking finger into the trees and rasped, "He went that way, Kai. Don't let him get away."

There'd never been an order I'd been more eager to follow.

I took to the sky, leaving Dahlia in the care of her other mates. They would see to her, but this? This was *mine.*

My gift to her.

My purpose.

My destiny.

I skimmed across the treetops, not needing to go far at all before I spotted the pathetic excuse for a being bolting through the forest. He was nothing compared to me. Less than a worm writhing on a hook. He was insignificant.

And he was about to be dead.

It would be easy to burn him to ashes here and now, but by the looks of my gem, he'd tortured her. Taken his time. Made it hurt. That's exactly what I would do.

Swooping down fast, I knocked him to the rocky ground, watching with glee as he rolled down the hill and hit stone after stone, blood blossoming on his cheek and lip.

"D-dragon. Stop!" he cried as he got to his feet.

I reared back and shot fire at his feet, making him dance to avoid the flames.

Part of me wanted to play with him, but then the arsehole made the mistake of pulling his weapon. He grinned a savage, unrepentant smile as he brandished a blade covered in what could only be Dahlia's blood.

"She bled so prettily for me," he sneered.

They were the last words he ever uttered. Without hesitation, I drew my fire from deep in my belly and lit up the night sky as I let it pour out in a jet of merciless death. He never even had a chance to scream. By the time I stopped, all that was left of him was an oily scorch mark and a melted dagger. And unfortunately, a few smoldering tree stumps.

Alas, a dragon's vengeance was rarely without casualties. But this time I carried none of the guilt. He deserved to be sent straight to the underworld. I only hoped Hades would get the chance to greet him at the gates and spend eternity punishing him for every vile thing he did.

One death was far too few after all the lives he took.

Hell, one death was too few after he dared touch what was mine.

Taking to the sky, I let out another furious cry. Although this time, instead of vengeance, it was one of victory. The Ripper was gone. Dahlia was safe. And I?

I was whole.

CHAPTER FORTY-ONE

DEATH

They're not even making this a challenge. I stretched and rolled my neck as my astral projection returned to my physical form. Poor sweet Dahlia. She was quite battered this time. Those marks would scar, most certainly, but I was confident that the reminder of how close she came to the end would help her stay the course when it mattered most.

This was twice now I'd saved her from that asinine ritual—which wouldn't even work, BTW. I was like her Phantom of the Opera—minus the mask and the singing. Her Angel of Music. I saved her and watched over her. Soon, she'd be calling for me and begging for my help. Just like I'd planned.

Master plans really were glorious. Like a cascade of dominos.

"You look like day-old shit."

"I know you are, but what am I?" I shot back at Grim. Gods, he was the most frustrating creature. Word to the wise: never plan world domination using your ex as a means to an end. Not unless you're a masochist.

"You've really let yourself go. Where's that biting wit?"

My head hurt, and I couldn't tell if it was because of the astral projection or the annoyance Grim caused me.

"You won't be so eager to tease me when our next guest arrives." I inhaled deeply and smiled as I felt the energy in the room charge. "He's on his way. Mmm, it's so delicious, the power I have contained in this tiny space."

"You can't possibly think you're going to get away with this."

"I don't think, Chaos, I *know*. But it's cute that you believe your threats hold any weight. I'm glad to see that ego of yours hasn't been impeded by your latest change of address."

Tingles built in my fingertips, and I could all but see the dragon hurtling through the sky as Malakai gave himself over to his nature.

"It's happening," I squealed, clapping my hands gleefully. "Get ready to give your newest roommate a warm welcome."

"What are you doing with us all, Hel?" Chaos asked, his tone gruff and filled with impotent rage.

"That's my little secret, handsome. But I'll tell you this much: I can't wait to play with you."

"The last time you played with me, you ended up heartbroken and cut all your hair off. Are you sure you'd like to try that again?" One silver brow arched as Grim sat in the corner of his cell, one knee bent and his other leg splayed in front of him. Casually cool, as always.

I hated him.

No, I *loathed* him. Hate was too close to love. But sadly, I needed him.

Chaos grinned at his brother. Seeing any of the horsemen smile was a bit like feeling the edge of a dagger run along your skin. There was no kindness in the gesture. No actual joy. Though even I had to admit the effect was staggering. He really was a pretty male. They all were.

The fuckers.

Before I could go down that particular rabbit hole, the cell across from Grim shimmered as reality warped and my next prisoner materialized.

"You've gotta be fucking kidding me," Sinclair groaned as he pressed his palms against the cell's wall and took in his surroundings. "I was in the middle of something."

"Oh, great. Stop the presses. Fucking Famine is here. He's going to suck the life out of every single being in the room because he just can't help himself." Chaos frowned as his eyes remained focused on the newest horseman to join us.

"People will be looking for me," Sin said, his gaze cutting to mine. "The Apocalyptic Unicorns' frontman can't just go missing."

Grim snorted. "They're not even relevant anymore. When was the last time you toured?"

Sin shot him a dirty look. "They care. My fans are still rabid. They'll wonder where I am."

I couldn't help but laugh. You had to love the narcissist's confidence and self-importance. It was the only way they could get ahead. "They'll write you off as dead and mourn you. You'll become immortalized in their pathetic little hearts. Either way, not my problem. And it's not like anyone is going to find you. You'll be nothing but a husk when I'm through with you."

That parting shot caught all of their attention. They may not like each other very much, but nothing brought them together like a threat. In that, they were very much like me and my sisters. While not tied by blood, we were united in purpose, our ties forged by the centuries we roamed this realm. We could bicker and pick at each other all we wanted, but the second someone else interfered . . . well, it was the last mistake they ever made.

Let me tell you, being the sole recipient of three of the horsemen's undivided attention was truly something. I think I might have been a little afraid. Or I would have been if I wasn't the one so clearly in control.

"One left. One final piece to collect. That's all I need to win this game." Grinning, I strolled around the space, stopping in front of

Chaos's cell first. I touched the magically reinforced glass and felt his power. "The heart of a beast." I walked to Grim's cell next and trailed my fingers over the clear barrier. "The will of a god." Then I stopped in front of Sin's and sighed happily. "The soul of a dragon." Tapping my chin, I flicked my gaze to the last remaining cell. Empty, but not for long. "Now all we need is the whisper of a devil. That's when the fun really begins," I said with a conspiratorial wink.

Grim snarled and got to his feet as I laughed.

"Now you get it, don't you, Grim?"

"You don't actually think you can harvest our power," he sneered.

"I can and I will. I'm going to start this apocalypse, and there's nothing anyone can do to stop me." Feeling like an absolute badass, I spun toward the door and gave the three fuming men behind me a cheery wave. "Toodles."

CHAPTER FORTY-TWO

MOIRA

About an hour earlier

This fucking place gave me the creeps. You'd think after attending Ravenscroft Academy and then doing my post-grad work at Ravenscroft University, I'd be used to the Gothic spires and gargoyles and, you know, looming air of doom. I sure thought I was, but something about Blackwood made my skin crawl.

It's what my grandmother would have referred to as 'restless' and my wife would have referred to as 'haunted.'

Both would have been correct.

I was going to call it 'stained.' There was a stain on this house that couldn't be erased. If it wasn't such an auspicious occasion, I would have broken out into my rendition of WAP by my girl Cardi B, but with new and, dare I say, slightly improved lyrics. *There's a stain on this house. There's a stain on this house. There's a stain on this house.*

Anyway, moving on.

"Why did you drag me away from Dahlia, häxa? I promised her a dance, and I haven't had the pleasure." Tor, all 6'4" of him, now with fun accessories like horns and scales, frowned down at me.

"Don't you go all Viking on me . . . Viking." The way I had to crane my neck to meet his eyes would've intimidated a weaker woman. I was not that woman. I could turn him into a toad if I really wanted to.

Or maybe something cute and cuddly. Like a ferret.

Annnd now I was thinking about Arnold Schwarzenegger. Wow. Talk about random throwbacks. Didn't expect to be standing here thinking about Kindergarten Cop, but some things are just core memories and cannot be helped.

It's not a tumor.

Listen, when I'm stressed, I go off on tangents. It's a coping skill, okay?

"I just don't understand why we're standing here staring at the wood panels surrounding this doorway. Do you need me to smash it? I can do that. Otherwise, let me return to my mate so I can make good on my promise to her."

"I need you for two reasons. One, you're the one who got mad at me for this ritual I have to perform. Two, I need you to lift me up because I am a short, and you, sir, are a very tall. I want to inspect the runes I'm refreshing. If you're right about the spell, the last thing I want to do is contribute to it."

He squinted at the wall. "What runes?"

I sighed. Men were so predictable. Rarely did they believe in things they couldn't see. "These runes," I said, drawing on my power and waving a hand so that the magically hidden symbols came into shimmering view. They pulsed a soft, dull pink. Once they were renewed by tonight's ritual, they'd be a vibrant red. "Wait . . . that's not . . . lift me up, Tor. Lift me up right now."

Tor's big hands went around my waist, and he hoisted me into the air. A little pang of disappointment stabbed me. This was the closest I would ever get to my very own Dirty Dancing moment, and I couldn't even enjoy it.

"Your girl was fucking right. These aren't wards. Oh shit. This is the strongest compulsion spell I've ever seen. Anyone bound to it is unable to resist the urge to return to Blackwood once they've been gone for more than five hours. It's like a timer starts as soon as the gates are breached. This thing is so intricate, I doubt anyone even realizes the need to return isn't their own."

I ran my fingers over the pink runes and winced when, even in their weakened state, a faint electric current ran through my arm. "I've never seen anything like this. It's beautiful."

Tor growled in response. A warning reminding me that while it was a thing of beauty, this spell was a violation of the High Council's code. Or at the very least, what started off as a way of ensuring those sent here couldn't escape had been horribly corrupted.

I couldn't imagine any Belladonna witch agreeing to help create this spell. Not without knowing there was a rip cord of some kind. Something to free a person from it once they were deemed safe enough to be released back into society. As far as I could tell, that ripcord didn't exist. Runes existed as a sort of alphabet. When read together, they created a story, or intention, for the spell. They gave it shape. The way these runes were shaped made this compulsion indefinite. Unending. i.e., Blackwood had become a prison, and everyone here had been given a life sentence. Maybe that's what it was intended to be all along, but it flew under the radar with the High Council's help—because there's no way this could have been going on this long otherwise.

Had my grandmother known what she was doing when she renewed the spell? Had she even thought to check? I wouldn't have, not without Tor and Dahlia giving me the heads-up. How many other witches blindly followed orders without ever realizing what they'd done?

Our coven had been the High Council's unwitting pawns all

these years. Oh, that really burned my biscuits. No one played with me without my consent.

"What a fucking can of worms. Of course I get pulled in. I don't even go looking for the drama, the drama finds me," I grumbled before tapping Tor on the horn and indicating I needed to be put down.

"Well?" he asked.

"Well, I'm definitely not recharging this thing. Sure, there might be some baddies in here who shouldn't ever return to society, but most of you don't fit that bill. You, Dahlia, even Sorcha. This is a dark fucking secret, Tor. We could get in a lot of trouble for figuring it out."

"How are you going to explain the ritual is off?"

Opening my velvet bag that was tied to the waistband of my most excellent dress, I rifled through the contents. A witch was always prepared, after all.

"Oh, the ritual is going ahead as planned, just with a few . . . tweaks."

"Tweaks?"

"Give me your hand," I said once I found my trusty dagger.

Tor gave me a healthy dose of side-eye.

"Tor Nordson, I've never given you a reason not to trust me. After everything we've been through together."

"The last time you wielded a blade around me, you shaved off my beard."

I patted his cheek. Yes, I had to reach as high as I could to do so, but still. "And you never looked better. Beards are gross and unhygienic. I did you a favor."

He raised a pointed brow.

"Present look excluded, obviously. Horns really work with your bone structure."

Rolling his eyes, he held out one large, meaty palm. "Tread carefully. I'm not as . . . stable as my brother. The beast is prone to act first and apologize never."

"You won't hurt me. Your freedom depends on it." I brought the blade to his open palm and locked gazes with him. "The ritual requires my blood to successfully strengthen the spell. I'll still perform it, but without the necessary ingredient, nothing will happen. Your blood will be my decoy. No one has to know."

"And when they figure it out?"

"Hopefully by then, my coven and I will have figured out how to break the spell for good. The Council already has a prison. It doesn't need another. Blackwood is supposed to help rehabilitate people, not act like a dirty little secret. This cannot be allowed to continue. I won't let it. You have my word, Tor. So will you help me?"

He clenched his jaw and nodded before I dragged the steel point across his palm. His harsh breaths and deep growls would've frightened me if I hadn't known him so well. It took all of a few minutes to collect his blood in the small vial I always carried with me. As long as I was careful and performed some solid sleight of hand, I'd be able to pass his blood off as mine.

Once I finished collecting his donation to the cause, I corked the vial and placed it in my bag.

"What now?" he asked, licking his palm clean.

"Gross," I said, wrinkling my nose. "You're an animal."

"Yes. Haven't you been paying attention? I'm a beast."

I rolled my eyes. "So you say. You still seem like the Tor I know and tolerate."

A serious cloud hovered over us as we half-heartedly played with one another like we used to.

"To answer your question, the spell will still be in place, but it will continue to weaken now. Just like with any weak barrier, the more you test it, the easier it will become to get past it. Be careful though. There are always eyes watching, and someone will catch on if you aren't on your guard."

"I'm always on guard."

"Yeah, yeah, I get it. You Tor. You big, strong man. Super impressed, I promise."

"Miss Belladonna," the ginger troll intoned from the doorway leading to the ballroom. The man could not have sounded grumpier if he tried. He certainly gave Caleb a run for his money. "They're ready to begin the ritual."

"Coming," I chirped before giving Tor an intense stare, hoping everything I couldn't say out loud was conveyed in my eyes.

Stay safe.

Be careful.

Don't do anything stupid.

"I'll be in touch," I promised.

He nodded. "Looking forward to it."

Soooo...who wants to know what's going on with Asshole? Us too. Check out this special bonus scene from his point of view. You can download your copy at www.themategames.com/PrinceBonus or you can download it on audio and listen to it at www.themategames.com/PrinceAudioBonus

THE MATE GAMES UNIVERSE

BY K. LORAINE & MEG ANNE

War

Obsession

Rejection

Possession

Temptation

Pestilence

Promised to the Night (Prequel Novella)

Deal with the Demon

Claimed by the Shifters

Captive of the Night

Lost to the Moon

Death

Haunting Beauty

Hunted Beast

Hateful Prince

Heartless Villain

MORE BY MEG & KIM

<u>Twisted Cross Ranch</u>

A dark contemporary cowboy reverse harem

Sinner's Secret

Corruptor's Claim

Deadly Debt

Also by Meg Anne

Brotherhood of the Guardians/Novasgard Vikings

Undercover Magic *(Nord & Lina)*

A Sexy & Suspenseful Fated Mates PNR

Hint of Danger

Face of Danger

World of Danger

Promise of Danger

Call of Danger

Bound by Danger (Quinn & Finley)

The Chosen Universe

The Chosen

A Fated Mates High Fantasy Romance

Mother Of Shadows

Reign Of Ash

Crown Of Embers

Queen Of Light

The Chosen Boxset #1

The Chosen Boxset #2

The Keepers

A Guardian/Ward High Fantasy Romance

The Dreamer (A Keeper's Prequel)

The Keepers Legacy

The Keepers Retribution

The Keepers Vow

The Keepers Boxset

The Forsaken

A Rejected Mates/Enemies-To-Lovers Romantasy

Prisoner of Steel & Shadow

Queen of Whispers & Mist

Court of Death & Dreams

Gypsy's Curse

A Psychic/Detective Star-Crossed Lovers UF Romance

Visions Of Death

Visions Of Vengeance

Visions Of Triumph

The Gypsy's Curse: The Complete Collection

Standalones

My Soul To Take: A Forbidden Love Meets Fated Mates PNR

ALSO BY K. LORAINE

THE BLACKTHORNE VAMPIRES

THE BLOOD TRILOGY

(CASHEL & OLIVIA)

BLOOD CAPTIVE

BLOOD TRAITOR

BLOOD HEIR

BLACKTHORNE BLOODLINES

(LUCAS & BRIAR)

MIDNIGHT PRINCE

MIDNIGHT HUNGER

THE WATCHER SERIES

WAKING THE WATCHER

DENYING THE WATCHER

RELEASING THE WATCHER

THE SIREN COVEN

ETERNAL DESIRE (SHIFTER RELUCTANT MATES)

CURSED HEART (HATE TO LOVERS)

BROKEN SWORD (MMF MENAGE ARTHURIAN)

~

STANDALONES

Cursed (MFM Sleeping Beauty Retelling)

~

REVERSE HAREM STANDALONES

Their Vampire Princess (A Reverse Harem Romance)

All the Queen's Men (A Fae Reverse Harem Romance)

About Meg Anne

USA Today and international bestselling paranormal and fantasy romance author Meg Anne has always had stories running on a loop in her head. They started off as daydreams about how the evil queen (aka Mom) had her slaving away doing chores, and more recently shifted into creating backgrounds about the people stuck beside her during rush hour. The stories have always been there; they were just waiting for her to tell them.

Like any true SoCal native, Meg enjoys staying inside curled up with a good book and her fur babies . . . or maybe that's just her. You can convince Meg to buy just about anything if it's covered in glitter or rhinestones, or make her laugh by sharing your favorite bad joke. She also accepts bribes in the form of baked goods and Mexican food.

Meg is best known for her leading men #MenbyMeg, her inevitable cliffhangers, and making her readers laugh out loud, all of which started with the bestselling Chosen series.

ABOUT K. LORAINE

USA Today Bestselling author Kim Loraine writes steamy contemporary and sexy paranormal romance. **You'll find her paranormal romances written under the name K. Loraine and her contemporaries as Kim Loraine.** Don't worry, you'll get the same level of swoon-worthy heroes, sassy heroines, and an eventual HEA.

When not writing, she's busy herding cats (raising kids), trying to keep her house sort of clean, and dreaming up ways for fictional couples to meet.

www.ingramcontent.com/pod-product-compliance
Lightning Source LLC
Chambersburg PA
CBHW020307030826
48979CB00029B/2281/J

* 9 7 8 1 9 6 1 7 4 2 3 4 5 *